Legacy
of
Fire and Wind

Legacy of Fire and Wind

Book I: Fires Within

Pei Kang

iUniverse, Inc.
New York Lincoln Shanghai

Legacy of Fire and Wind
Book I: Fires Within

Copyright © 2006 by Pei Kang

All rights reserved. No part of this book may be used or reproduced by any means, graphic, electronic, or mechanical, including photocopying, recording, taping or by any information storage retrieval system without the written permission of the publisher except in the case of brief quotations embodied in critical articles and reviews.

iUniverse books may be ordered through booksellers or by contacting:

iUniverse
2021 Pine Lake Road, Suite 100
Lincoln, NE 68512
www.iuniverse.com
1-800-Authors (1-800-288-4677)

This is a work of fiction. All of the characters, names, incidents, organizations and dialogue in this novel are either the products of the author's imagination or are used fictitiously.

ISBN-13: 978-0-595-37563-9 (pbk)
ISBN-13: 978-0-595-67530-2 (cloth)
ISBN-13: 978-0-595-81956-0 (ebk)
ISBN-10: 0-595-37563-4 (pbk)
ISBN-10: 0-595-67530-1 (cloth)
ISBN-10: 0-595-81956-7 (ebk)

Printed in the United States of America

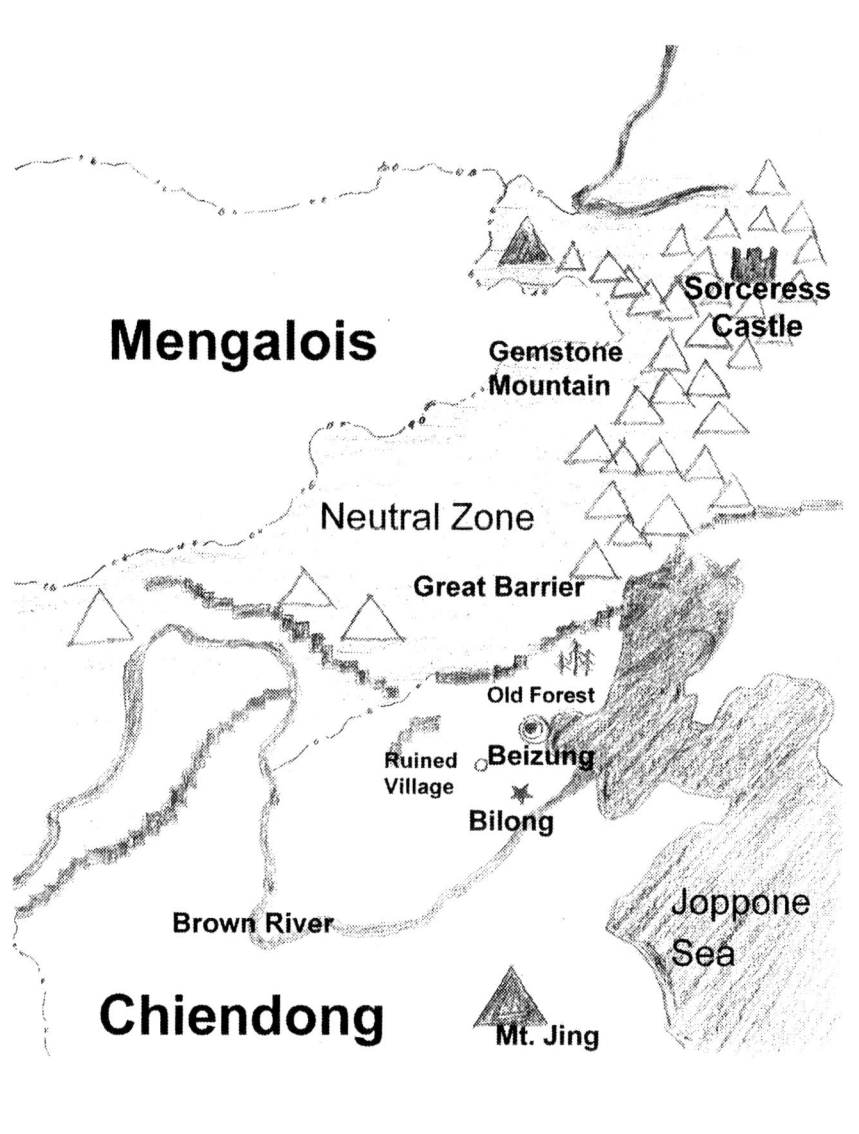

DEDICATION

Mom, Dad, and Bro, my real Heroes of Legacy, thank you for years of unconditional support and love. Without you, I would not have been able to achieve my dreams. You are my strength. To Ingshong my late Akita, thank you for being my emotional crutch!

For my family Kang: Jing, Dong, Kai, Summie, Tian, Victor, David, Bob. Julie; to my Grandma Kang, Grandpa Tsou, to my late Grandpa Kang and Grandma Tsoua; to all my aunts and uncles, thank you for rooting and being there for me and being my childhood memories!

For my Tsou family, An-Chi, An-Ning, Lashon, An-Li, Jennifer, Jeff, Chris, and Brian and all the aunts and uncles; to my first and only nanny, Mrs. Cheng, your true support helped me through a lot, more than you'll ever know.

For my friends, Brindisi Chan (for trying to make me more than who I am), Norman Wong (my very first reader, other than Dad, and book advisor), Vanessa Liu, Harold, Margaret Chang, Jason Liu (for being like an extended family), Ali Ahmed, Scott Underberg, Zack Hample, Dave Geist, Yeshe, Dan "Huckleberry," Shimp, Dan Martin, Laurette Hakar, Pamela Wilson (for inspiring me), Tina Chen, Annjoe Wong-Foy(for reading through the early stuff), Cynthia Chiu, Wes Padfield, Stephanie Garibaldi, Josephine and Joanne Fan and Nina Zheng, Uncle Lamont, Aunt Adele Epstein, Mrs. Margaret Duchovany (for teaching me to hang on to my dreams) and Mrs. Sally Henry.

The wonderful people at Special Olympics.

Last, but not least, authors Marjorie M. Liu, Andrew Fox and Mitchell Graham (for taking the time out to review this monster!)

And everyone else I may have forgotten—please forgive this Forgetful Writer.

Thank you for all your support and love; this book would not have been possible without you guys.

This book and series and, ultimately, person would not have been possible.

You ROCK!

My editors and all the people at iUniverse.com, and all those who helped get this book out; And to Mike Altman.
Thank you so much for this—the Impossible Dream can come true!!

To the True A-Team: Dr. Mary Ellen Engle, Dr. Allen P. Demayo, Dr. John Tsou, Dr. Patrick Flynn and Dr. Harold Chin.

To fellow authors who have influenced me over the years: J.R.R. Tolkien, R.A.Salvatore, Raymond E. Feist, Margaret Weis and Tracy Hickman, Orson Scott Card.

To the creators of *Iron Chef* (original).

To the makers of the *Quest for Glory* series; and TSR for Advanced Dungeon and Dragons; Mindi Abair, thank you for your smooth jazz that helped get me through all those years and months of writing and editing.

Finally, to those who have dreams and pursuits: yes, it IS possible to reach the impossible dream. Just keep at it and you may get there one day.

CONTENTS

PART I

Prologue: CHAOS 3
1   VISITOR 7
2   FESLEN 14
3   PROPHECY 18
4   OUTCAST 25
5   INAUSPICIOUS MEETING 36
6   AMBUSH 49
7   GUILT 62
8   MEMORIES AT MASTER CHAI'S 75
9   MASTER AND STUDENT 78
10 TRAINING: KNOWING YOUR PLACE 84
11 FRIENDS 92
12 FESLEN'S STRUGGLES 103
13 KA-WEI'S REPORT 115
14 A PRINCESS APPEARS 122
15 PRINCESS AND THE BEAST 124
16 SCHOOL AND LIFE 129
17 EMPEROR'S DECREE 137
18 THE CHOICINGS 145

19	FESLEN'S FIRST SPELL	158
20	REVELATION	168
21	DEATH	175
22	NEW MASTER	185
23	DISCOVERY	199
24	TO THE RESCUE!	222
25	CLASH OF TITANS	230

PART II

26	REVERSED ROLES	241
27	TEMPLE DISTRICT	248
28	CONFRONTATION	253
29	BUBBLING BROOK	265
30	NADINE'S TOUCH	274
31	TEST OF THE FOREST PROTECTORS	292
32	PEOPLE'S COUNCIL	306
33	PREDICTION CARDS	317
34	SHOWING SIGNS	331
35	WINTER'S CELEBRATION	343
36	SHRIEK OF THE DAMNED	350
37	THE NECROMANCER	363
38	GEMSTONE MOUNTAINS	371
39	THREE BE ONE	383
40	THE GIANTS' TEMPER	391
41	ROAD TO SORCERESS' CASTLE	403
42	JERENKO-I'S CASTLE	411

43	FACE-OFF	423
44	MAGE vs. CHEF	430
45	BROKEN ROYALTY	433
46	ESCAPE!	438
47	FESLEN FAILS	444
48	FESLEN BIDS FAREWELL	454
49	BROTHERS AWAKENING	464
50	WINTER'S END?	474
51	ACCEPTANCE	481

CAST OF CHARACTERS

Black Robe, Immersing: one of four mages sent by Master Drak to find Feslen.

Blleunist, Lioin; aka Gui-Pan Wu: a young local thief who befriended Feslen and his friends.

Celeste: a spy sent to test the Raster brothers.

Chai, Master: the premier Martial Artist in all of Chiendong, physical trainer and spiritual teacher for Feslen and Ka-Wei.

Chai, Mei Xue: a childhood friend of Feslen's and only child of Master Chai.

Eve: a mystical immortal that Feslen meets.

Fu, Gong, Kil: an expert archer in the Prince's personal battalion.

Fu, Dou Poa Ma: the High Forest Protector and unofficial leader of the free people.

Fyo, Wang, Hei-Tai: the Pink Robe Mage of the Great School of Magic Stuff.

Gai, Ohr-Hu: the leader of the legendary and mysterious Floating Isle of magic and mystic, the Emperor's right-hand man.

Hu, Kuan: Another disabled student of Master Chai's.

Jang Jyung-Sae: a rich merchant mage, former archrival of Feslen's.

Jungoo, Jeizen: a gypsy's daughter, master of the mysterious Prediction Cards.

Miaynuemo, Chef Master: the main chef for Master Chai's school and home.

Nadine aka Nai-Hua, Princess: a mysterious princess from Nu who knows about the wielders of the Ancient Truth and the Prophecy.

Quoi, Rhoi: an odd Water Spirit that Feslen befriended.

Rabbit, Little: a spy for Princess Nadine who died trying to protect Feslen.

Raster, Feslen: a disabled fourteen-year-old sought by those who believe in the Prophecies.

Raster, Duxan: Feslen's real, older brother by four years.

Robe, Red: one of the four magicians sent by Master Drak to seek Feslen.

Scallion, Garland Captain: an old mentor and friend to Prince Ka-Wei.

Monk, Protector: the nameless Thai-Thurian monk who watched the Ethereal Discs and sought help from Feslen.

Seng-Fu: the Blue Yellow Robe magician sent to watch Feslen by the Great School of Magic Stuff.

Shang, Ka-Wei Prince, aka Kalman the Red: the Prince and WuSha of Chiendong and the only child (acknowledged) of his late parents.

Shang, Jerenko-I: a powerful Sorceress and Ka-Wei's aunt.

Shang, Tsu Jien King: the acknowledged current King of Chiendong, uncle to Ka-Wei, younger brother of Ka-Wei's father.

Swuai, Tang: aka Kai-Lornu: a student of Master Chai's who tried to protect Feslen.

Tojoh: a rival classmate.

Tan-Bey: a girl competitor in the Choicings.

Tsai, Buhkahta, Emperor: the Emperor of Chiendong (East and West).

Wien, Elhong: the leader of the somewhat secret New Priest organization, actual head of the Elhong Wong School.

Wien, Ge-Moi, Master: the older brother of the New Priest, head of the Emperor's Martial Arts program.

Wong, Father and Mother: he is the silent wage earner of the family; she is the strength behind the Wong Empire.

Wong, Ai-Yen: the only true Wong son and "oldest" child, fourth oldest by birth in the Wong family.

Wong, Mei-Whuay: the oldest girl in the Wong family, oldest child by birth.

Wong, Trisha: the second oldest girl in the Wong family, second oldest by birth.

Wong, Ghong-Hung: the fourth oldest girl in the Wong family, third oldest child.

Wong, Li-Pei: the youngest of the Wong children.

Zhou, Officer: one of Ka-Wei's Blue Soldiers, the first commoner to befriend Feslen.

NAME PRONOUNCIATIONS

Alternative name (both Chiendonese and Western), meaning, and pronunciation.

Blleunist Lioin/Wu, Pan-Gui: Louan Bel unist "Lion Heart/Guu-i Pahn Woo "Ghost River Waif"

Chai, Xue Mei: May Suu Chai: "Pretty Song" or "Pretty Snow"

Fu, Dou Poa Ma: Ma Pu ou duo Fu: "Spicy Tofu"

Fyo, Wang, Tai-Hei: Fiio, Waang, Tie-Hey: "Flying King Tigress"

Gai, Ohr-Hu: Wuu-huur Guy: "Lightened Shadows"

Jang, Sae-Jyung: Say-Gee Ung: "Lightened Clouds"

Jungoo, Jeizen: Jun-oo Jay-shen: "Wandering Spirit"

Nai-Hua/Nadine: 'ni'-huu-ah: "Grandmother Flower"

Raster, Feslen: Fe-slen Ra-ster or Huo-San: "Fiery Mountain"

Raster, Duxan: Dou-Shan: "Earth Mountain"

Rhoi-Que: Roa-Ku: "Healthy Spirit"

Shang, Jerenko-I: Jeren-ko 'ee': "Wind Beauty"

Shang, Ka-Wei/Kalman The Red Warrior: Kaa-Way Shang, Kal-man

Seng-Fu: Sua ahng-Foo

Tang Swuai/Kai-Lornu: Tan-g Su ai: "Sweet Water"/Kai-Lorr-Nnu

Tsai, Buhkahta, Emperor: Tz_ai, Buu kat ata

Wong, Mei-Whuay: Wo-ong, Who-ahn-May: "Pretty Flower"

Wong, Ai-Yen: aa Yen: "Oldest Son"
Wong, Li-Pei: Lei-Pah ei: "Light Nurture"
Wien, Elhong: Wean, hung-El: "The Sting"

PART I

Prologue

CHAOS 混沌

Archmage Feslen Raster watched the destruction and chaos with grim satisfaction. Fires from the depths of blackness burned the world around him. A brief ash storm blew his cloak away from his face. The sun danced in and out of the darkening clouds. The sun's light revealed the young Archmage's new symbol on the back of his gray cloak: an open gate with flames billowing through it. It replaced the standard mage's Yin Yang symbol he had worn earlier in the year.

Pillars of ash plumed upward into the skies again, blocking out the sun. Choking winds spread across the land. But the storm's cruel, merciless pounding elicited no feeling from the Archmage; no sign of emotion was revealed in his eerie walnut-shaped silvery eyes. Wind blew his long, thick copper hair back and forth; his neatly tied ponytail was disheveled, but he didn't show any signs of caring. Fist-sized hail struck his bronze-tanned skin. Years of inhabiting the North Regions had inured him to odd, inconsistent weather. Feslen's once pale yellow skin had hardened to an almost-scale-like texture. It glittered in the brief moments of light.

Even though he was once a citizen of this world that was being destroyed, the Archmage thought, "It serves those fools right". The gray, nearly lifeless lands below him mirrored Feslen's ashen soul.

Thunder clouds rolled in along with the ash storms. Lightning accompanied them, followed by swirls of new-born tornadoes. Down below, hordes of the undead feasted upon the few who had been hardy enough to survive. Two-headed winged snakes, with demonic human faces, arms, and hands, sprouted from the clouds. Shadows of humans reflected against the ground as the sun struck the serpents' gray scales. These shadows sent waves of terror to the people below.

Feslen watched all this, leaning upon his silver inlaid staff as he climbed to the peak of Chiendong's Mount Jing. Feslen's staff was carved in the shape of the mouth of a monkey, its ruby eyes glittering at each of Mount Jing's awakened volcanic bursts. Bored by the scene, Feslen looked down momentarily at the vibrating object hooked on a belt loop on his thigh: it was a magic container holding five glowing lights. The lights rushed out, making a dash for freedom, when the cover suddenly bounced open. He closed the container tightly.

Laughter rose in the air. It was laughter from the spirits invading the human soldiers below, and it stirred Feslen to laugh as well. But a moment later Feslen gasped in astonishment: the ashes of the dead below had begun to stir. Out of the ashes walked a bald-headed boy, completely untouched by the destruction all around him. A sense of serenity and purity emanated from him. Feslen watched as bloody tears streaked the boy's face. The show of emotion from the boy stirred the Archmage's stone-cold heart, but all he could do was to laugh once again. The boy gave him a nod and began to walk towards him. Torn between duty and curiosity, Feslen stood waiting for the boy.

Heat and fire spouted from Mount Jing, reddening the skies above. Knowing he had time, Feslen planted his staff. When he reached the Archmage, the boy just stared at him. Flashes of fire and waves of shock raced through Feslen's soul as he locked stares with the boy. "Why are you here? Who are you?" Feslen asked, after a few minutes of awkward silence. The boy's calm but steady eyes had unnerved the Archmage, causing him to speak first, which was a rare occurrence for him.

Clashes of the remnants of a world war went unheard by the two of them. A total hush followed. Then the boy replied in a soft but strong voice, "You don't understand?" He detected a hint of sadness in the boy's voice. The boy's voice became stronger next, "You never will. Before you can offer help, you must accept the Truth and you must accept yourself."

"Those who accompanied me have gone. Those who allied with me have died. My enemies perished. What is it that I don't understand? I am the only one left who could save this pathetic world. What am I missing?" Feslen asked with a half-twisted smile and a grand sweeping gesture.

The boy coughed slightly as the ferocious winds rushed all around them. The Archmage knelt and unfastened his robes and placed them around the boy for protection. But the boy refused to wear the robes and dropped them to the ground. Anger arose in Feslen and he readied a destructive spell, pointing a finger at the boy.

"Open up to the world before you understand and seek," said the boy.

The whispering, hissing sound of fire alerted the two of them to the presence of a serpent who was an enemy spirit. But Feslen and the boy remained unmoved. The winged serpent's red lantern eyes burned bright as it neared. The beast reared and struck Feslen, but he felt nothing. Flames billowed out from Feslen's body, destroying the serpent spirit.

"As I was saying…" Feslen grinned, pleased to have shown the boy his powers so easily.

"Power is only fleeting. True power comes not from destruction," the boy replied with a steady tone.

Feslen snarled and pointed his finger at the boy once more. He hated this cryptic game. Then the boy licked his cracked and blistered lips. Again, pity took Feslen. The Archmage clapped, and music flowed from his supple hands to stop the chaos for a moment. A celebration feast of food and wine and water materialized at their feet. The boy made no moves to take the presented food.

"Well? What is it that you want?" Feslen snarled.

"I am what you wish to be and what you seek. But only when you want it, will you realize," said the boy. He bowed and turned down the mountain towards the ashes.

Infinite wisdom had radiated from the boy, something which the Archmage himself lacked. So Feslen ran after him and tried to stop him. Panic and confusion splinterted Feslen's ego when he reached out to touch the boy. But the boy had started to return to the dreamy ash world from whence he came. Feslen was gripped by a sudden need to know the true meaning behind his actions, his life itself, and the Powers At Hand. "Wait, who am I?" Feslen blurted out.

No answer came, but at last the boy whispered softly, "You already are; you just need to find peace."

City of Beizung

New Priest First Temple

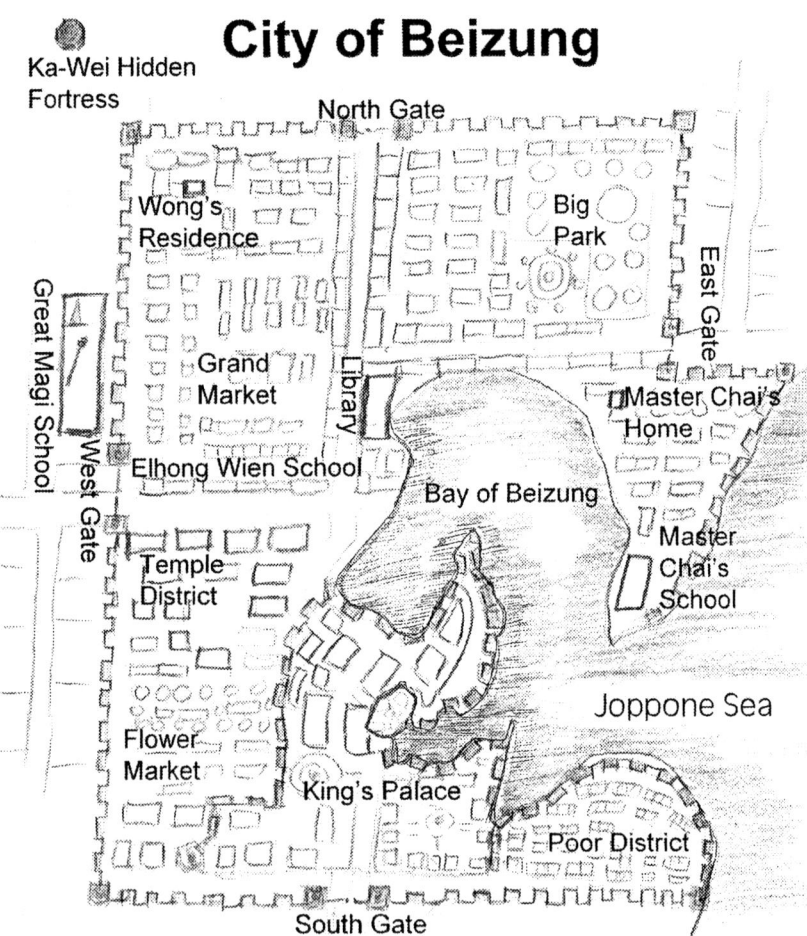

Cave of Silence

Ka-Wei Hidden Fortress

North Gate

Wong's Residence

Big Park

East Gate

Great Magi School

Grand Market

Library

Master Chai's Home

West Gate

Elhong Wien School

Bay of Beizung

Master Chai's School

Temple District

Joppone Sea

Flower Market

King's Palace

Poor District

South Gate

1

VISITOR 訪客

The soft tapping noise awoke Feslen. He groaned a bit and blinked. The moonlight from the second moon lit the bedroom with the brightness of sunlight. Feslen thought that it must be past midnight. Good thing I'm a light sleeper, unlike Duxan. He never had been. Feslen grinned as he looked at his older brother, who slept soundly. Then he yawned and rolled back under the covers, trying to return to sleep. But the tapping noise was loud enough to awaken Feslen for good this time. He looked around for the source of the sound. About that time, the first moon rose, in accordance with the usual cycle of the two moons, revealing a cloudless night. The tapping increased in pitch. Feslen followed the sound to a door marked with the Chiendong character "Passage of One." "What does that mean?" Feslen wondered. He recalled something he read in a book once about how a dream used random things to represent real-life experiences. It said that languages would occur in the dreams of people who read a lot. He remembered that this was called "dream speech". Then Feslen chuckled to himself, surprised to realize that his imagination was that wonderful and powerful.

    He opened the door. When he entered, he was enveloped in a peaceful but almost blindingly bright light. For one instance, Feslen saw himself in two different places at once! "How could this be?" he wondered, distracted for a moment from the search for the tapping noise. He saw his own body, in a meditative posture, standing at the bedroom door. Yet, he was also here in this brightly lit place at the same time. Wherever here was…Feslen thought. But there was little time to ponder the matter, for he suddenly spotted a figure dressed in maroon robes heading directly towards him. Feslen dashed behind a pillar to observe.

Then Feslen noticed an almost invisible silver cord hanging down his body from his back spine. Am I still standing in the bedroom in a meditative state? Or have I somehow changed into an ethereal form without trying? He stopped and waited a bit and then heard the sound of sandals across the floors of this ancient Chiendonese monestary and turned his attention toward it. Feslen followed a familiar-looking, maroon-robed monk when he ran by him. The monk inhaled and paused at an oak door, fingering the Ancient Chiendonese characters, "Life and Death," which were engraved in the wood. Feslen watched the monk shake in fear, and, in a sympathetic reaction, he shook with some unknown fear himself.

When the monk opened the door, Feslen followed him in. He watched the monk scan the poor lit room. Feslen felt a sudden gust of warm wind and looked for its source, as he observed the monk do the same thing. From a distance, the monk studied some statues standing against the wall of the room. Feslen approached them with caution. Nine giant statues with Ancient Chiendonese characters inscribed upon them lined the wall. Even though the hands of the statues appeared to be empty, Feslen's instincts told him otherwise. Feslen walked up close to the statues and saw that they held strange-looking objects: "Ethereal Discs." Feslen touched them lightly, feeling their power. He knew that no mortal—with or without magic—could even bear to be near these powers without going insane; nevertheless, Feslen stood there unharmed. His instinct told him the Ethereal Discs held great power and that they were the keys to unlocking a world mystery.

From a distance, the monk nodded to himself and readied to leave. This was when Feslen notice that one of the statues was broken. This was the source of the warm wind. Feslen watched the monk as he gripped his prayer beads tighter. Feslen heard the monk mumbling as he counted the statues: only eight solid statues remained, with one broken. He watched the monk make a cautious approach to the statues, repeating a special mantra that allowed him to do so.

Two blood-covered objects lay beneath the broken statue. Feslen recognized them. One was the symbol of the New Priests: a hawk's talon adjacent to a broken sword. The other object was a small, sharp, golden hammer with an edge. The monk moved nearer to the hammer and began to gnash his teeth. "No, you fool!" Feslen shouted. But the monk continued, unaware of Feslen's presence. The hammer's evil aura had forced the monk to move towards it. Both Feslen and the monk then began to shake with terror stemming from the hammer's evil presence. When the monk picked up the hammer, vivid and frightening images flashed through Feslen's mind and he heard the feverish chants of the New Priests. The hammer glowed brightly. The monk dropped the hammer, his hand scalded.

Feslen shifted his sudden attention to the doorway. "Help me!" the monk cried and reached to the tall, cloaked figure that made a sudden appearance at the entrance. An ominous chill entered the room from the shrouded figure. Feslen knew the monk suffered from the hammer's evil auras, but in his ethereal form he was helpless to give him aid.

"Help you? You mean fix the statue or help you with your pain?" The black-cloaked figure responded with his arms folded inside his cloak.

"Help me!" the monk repeated.

Feslen shuddered as he felt the cloaked man's evil magical powers. With a slight sneering smile on his face, the figure entered the room. A look of depressive madness, deep scars, and thick facial hair marked his otherwise young face. His gray-black beard and mustache covered his thick lips. His deep-set, reddened eyes arrested Feslen's attention; the young monk shivered at the sight of them. From this man there arose a sharp smell of the graveyard and the herbal stuffing used for dead bodies.

Something else seemed out of place about him. His body convulsed, and he turned his back a moment. A Yin Yang symbol shone on his cloak. He chanted something under his breath and then seemed to relax. His large hands held a part of a statue. At that moment, he emitted a distinctive smell of onion.

"You…are magi!" the monk stated, gasping for breath.

Feslen's eyes widened when he saw a silver cord dangling down from the mage's spine! But, unlike his own, this silver cord seemed less solid. Feslen had heard tales and theories about Spiritual Travel, Out of Body Experience, and Ethereal Form, but, in all the excitement, they flew out of his brain. He tried to pull himself together and listen to what the mage and the monk were saying.

The tall mage sneered slightly as he asked the monk, "Will you give me what I desire?"

"No."

"Very well," the mage sighed softly and then made motions with his fingers, chanting all the while. When he concluded his chant, he pointed his finger at the already suffering monk. The monk began to scream as hideous boils erupted suddenly on his body.

"It will get worse and worse…until you want to pick out your very eyes."

The monk clawed the air in his terror. Feslen now knew what a chicken must feel like just before it got its head cut off.

"Give me what I need," the tall man said, "and the pain will be reduced, I promise."

The monk struggled for a long while. Feslen felt an odd gnawing hunger for power flow into his own body when he felt the energy of the mage's dreadful magic. Feslen struggled between wanting desperately to help the monk and admiring the raw power of the evil mage.

"My my, how stubborn. You do your people's reputation good, monk. But I can make anyone talk," hissed the mage. He raised a hand and snapped his fingers, from which a needle sprouted. He chanted once more. The monk's screams shook the entire chamber as his skin crumpled, dried up, and turned a sickly shade of green.

"This mage is a Necromancer!" Feslen realized.

The monk struggled to get up and even made an attempt to fight the mage. But all he could do was stand on one leg and stare hopefully at the door.

"No help will be coming your way, I assure you," the tall Necromancer said as he grinned, his lips caked in blood. Then he leaned toward the monk and opened his mouth as if to bite him. A nauseating green smoke erupted around them. Even though he was in ethereal form, Feslen staggered back as though he was physically threatened by the foul vapors. He felt the young monk's energy being sucked up by the Necromancer and he tried in desperation to help. A dark aura enveloped the Necromancer as his red eyes glittered. Although he didn't truly understand what was happening, Feslen saw and felt the Necromancer attempt a mind-soul connection with the monk. The Necromancer chanted again and then drew a beaker from his robes, opened it, and slowly poured out onto the ground a foul-smelling liquid. He chanted and hissed, "Let me in, stubborn monk!"

Feslen felt the monk's pain as he writhed and screamed at the negative energies assaulting him. Feslen's compassion for the monk rose sharply and he said aloud, "I can help! I will help!"

He raised his hands and started to chant, even though he did not know how or why he did this. "After all, this whole thing is a dream, isn't it?" Feslen asked himself in part of his mind. An invisible spurt of pure energy shot out from Feslen's hands and flowed in between the monk and Necromancer. Feslen's power temporarily shattered the connection between the monk and Necromancer. The monk fell back. The Necromancer's eyes widened, and he chanted again.

This time, a dark hand shot from the ground to grip the monk. The monk scrabbled and tried to fight, but his body shuddered in response to the Necromancer's spells. Finally, looking haggard and drained, the monk croaked, "What do you need?"

Feslen couldn't blame the monk for giving up after such a struggle. The Necromancer's eyes widened in surprise at his victory, and he replied, "I want locations…Bane Sword, Ethereal Eternal Flow…"

The monk gasped and offered up some answers, but the tall mage grabbed up the monk with one hand and growled, "Do you take me a fool? I want real answers, dung eater." He flung the monk aside with force and began another chant.

The monk crashed to the floor and gasped, "Wait…I'll tell."

The Necromancer laughed, "I knew you'd see it my way."

Then the monk crawled to the Necromancer and gripped the hem of his cloak. No! Don't do it! Feslen thought. The Necromancer tried to shake off the grip of the monk. The Necromancer released another spell with an annoyed grunt. Strange dark lightning struck one of the statues and it cracked and shattered. In the light from the Necromancer's black lightning spell, Felsen saw that the man's silver cord became more solid as his energy increased.

"I'll tell you what," the Necromancer said, with his booted foot on the whimpering monk's stomach, "I will even fix the broken Second Statue. The Ethereal Discs will break in time." Chanting all the while, the Necromancer pointed at the shattered statue and its cracks disappeared.

With his own energy depleted and the monk's final barriers broken, Feslen watched helplessly as the dark mage advanced upon the monk once more. This time the Necromancer devoured the monk's information just by locking eyes with him. Finally, he let go of the unconscious monk and faded away into the darkness.

Feslen blinked to clear his head. Was the Necromancer in Ethereal Form like he was? Did he then somehow turn solid when he entered this monastery? Feslen wondered about these things and shook his head once more. No matter, he was gone now. Feeling a bit safer, Feslen went to check on the monk. Then he suddenly felt the evil mage's presence again. For a brief moment, the boy and the older mage stared at one another in shock. Feslen prepared his best defenses. The Necromancer thundered at him, "You!" Intense energies built up, from the dark mage and from Feslen as well. Feslen watched in mute horror. He felt negative energy from the mage hit him like a tornado. It almost wiped him out, but Feslen managed to hang on. He even sent back a bright globe of energy that slammed the dark mage, burning him.

The Necromancer sneered, "Your battle is not with me yet, young one. I already got what I came for anyway." The dark mage, with his cloak burning, gestured twice, once at Feslen and once to begin another spell. He vanished on the wing of a magic spell, hurling dark energy at Feslen as he disappeared. By instinct, Feslen tossed up his own energy barriers to protect himself and then he woke up the monk. After a moment of obvious disorientation, the monk stared at the broken statue.

Feslen tried to offer the monk some reassurance but he was too weak to even lift his head. He blinked, staring straight into the monk's ageless eyes. It was almost as if they saw each other even though Feslen was in ethereal form. But to his relief and shock, the monk did not see him. While the monk ran out and called, "Master!" Feslen closed his eyes to rest.

2

FESLEN 火山

Fourteen-year-old Feslen threw off his bed covers; his sweat soaked him. He awoke from what seemed like an intense dream of battles against the Necromancer. It was nearly the end of winter, the twenty-first month of the year, but the winter's odd heat still crippled Feslen, so he opened a window and took off his pajama top.

"Go back to bed, Huo-Shan Wong," his older brother Duxan murmured in his sleep.

"I am in need of thought, big brother," Feslen replied calmly. He didn't even get mad at Duxan for using his Chiendonese name. Really, he didn't know why he bothered to answer his brother when he knew Duxan was just talking in his sleep. Feslen chuckled to himself, figuring that it was an automated sibling response. He shook his head and sighed, closed the window, and then went back to bed to try to go back to sleep. He tossed a few moments, but he couldn't shake off his earlier dream vision.

"I need a snack," he suddenly realized, hopping out of bed. The lights of the twin full moons caught his attention. He opened the window again and it creaked loudly. Feslen inhaled deeply and stood frozen a moment in front of the open window. He waited for some family members, like Duxan, to come scold him for opening the window. He could hear them telling him, "You're disabled, and yet you want to expose yourself to the cold winter? You know how our parents disapprove when you wear too little, even if it's a warm winter." It was winter, but the weather was too warm. Feslen checked his anger and internally thanked his brother for his reproves, which were often gentler than Mother's and Father's. Feslen chuckled again when he heard Duxan's snore. His brother could sleep through an elephant stampede. Feslen sighed and, out of habit, put on a warm silk shirt and buttoned it.

This temperature did not bother Feslen too much yet, but he knew his brother and family were right. Any amount of exposure to odd weather or extreme changes in temperature made him sick. The odd thing about his congenital blood disorder was how healthy he appeared to be compared with many other disabled people. None of the New Priest physicians or the normal scholar physiciasn of Chiendong understood his unique condition. The unnamed and apparently unknown blood disorder from which Feslen suffered often made him feel dizzy, out of breath, and weak in the joints. It often made him so weak that he couldn't stand on his own. When he ran out of oxygen, his yellow skin would pale to an odd, bleached white.

The only thing that branded him as disabled was his perpetually bent frame. He was always a head shorter than everyone, even girls. The strange red pockmarks were only on his chest, nowhere else. They covered up his sugar cane-shaped birthmark as well. He had these pockmarks since he was a baby, or so his adoptive parents had told him.

Since Chiendong's winter weather was as hot as summer, Feslen often wore his shirts open, exposing his chest. During the true summers, he would go bare-chested, like other true Chiendonese. The thing that irritated him most was that he did not resemble most Chiendonese people. Yet his birth certifactes and official documents indicated that he was one of them. Classmates often and local peasants often derided him because of his walnut-shaped eyes, round nose, hawkish face, and large eyebrows. To make matters worse, his full head of strawberry-brown hair stood out like a jewel on a gypsy's navel. Most of Chiendong's population had brown or black hair. The color varied little, mostly from tan or light brown to shades of black. His gait was different too. The way he walked made him resemble a frog, so his nickname became "Little Toad" or "Froggie."

Staring out the window, he studied the neighbor's houses where Red Lantern decorations sparkled. They reminded Feslen of the tall mage's eyes.

What happened? It was no dream, Feslen thought as he studied the hilltops. The night's warm breeze stuck to Feslen's skin a bit, but he enjoyed the brief relief of fresh air that blew in from the East off Beizung Bay. He listened for any sound at all from the outside. A few wild dogs yipped and their noises mingled with a few sounds of drunken politicians, but there was nothing more. Every now and then, Feslen heard the pounding of the surf. His eyes scanned the wondrous night beyond his home. He saw the capital city of Beizung's bright lights a ways away and the tall ships that patrolled her harbor.

Suddenly, in the distance a robed man caught his eye. The person hid behind a large pile of rocks on the far hilltops. Feslen thought to investigate and put one leg out the window. The person, dressed in deep, shining black robes, gave him a nod and beckoned him forward. "Am I dreaming again? Or are my dreams coming back to haunt me?" Feslen wondered, shuddering. He looked down and, seeing the forty-foot drop to the ground, and thought better of leaping out of the window. If I was skilled in the Martial Arts, like Prince Ka-Wei, I might be able to do it, he thought with a grin as he ran downstairs, hoping to get a better glimpse of the robed man. Feslen passed by the windows on each floor, watching the robed man as he moved further away. On the second floor, Feslen stumbled as dizziness and shortness of breath overcame him. He clutched at himself in pain, grabbed the stair rail, and cursed his disability. The weakness passed, but it seemed to take hours. Finally Feslen managed pull himself up and drag himself downstairs.

By the time he succeeded in catching his breath and struggled to the front door, the robed man was gone. Feslen sighed and grumbled. His energy waned and his stomach complained. He dragged himself over to the food storage box and opened it to retrieve a snack.

"If I was like everyone else, I would've caught up to the man in robes by now," Feslen grunted aloud, his body trembling with weakness as he poured some soymilk into a teacup, splashing most of it.

"If my health were normal…if I weren't a *cripple*…"

Feslen coughed up blood and phlegm. He knew he shouldn't get angry, as his New Priest physician had advised him, but anger overcame him anyway. Feslen raged for another twenty minutes and then sighed and growled, "One day, I will be more than normal. One day, they will all see." He gripped the nearly empty cup and brought it to his parched lips to drink, laughing when he realized how little liquid had made it into the cup. He forced himself to get up and walk back to the storage box to get some more soymilk. Then something to his left caught his attention: the Lunar Calendar. His mother circled on the calendar the eighth day of the eighteenth month and of the twenty-third month. Two important Chiendonese events approached on these dates: the Choicings and Winter's Festival.

Outside, the first moon brightened the night more than the second. He grabbed a mooncake from the storage box and nibbled. A thought struck him: he realized that the man in the robes outside his window differed from the one in the dream vision. The robed man in the street did not have reddish eyes. He hoped the vision he saw would never occur in reality.

The year of the Monkey had begun like any other year for Feslen and his country. Soon their lives would change forever, beyond dreams and nightmares.

3

PROPHECY 預言

The next night, Feslen tossed and turned in his sleep. He heard tapping noises again and the murmuring of voices. This time, when he got up to investigate, he saw his silver cord following him. Oh no, not again! He thought as he followed the noises once more to the same door marked "Passage of One." But, this time, he could not open it. As he stared, the Chiendonese words changed before his eyes and read "Passage of Three Becomes One." What does this mean? Feslen thought, as he tried to fiddle with the door knob. Nothing worked.

Without warning, the familiar presences of Duxan and the broad-shouldered Prince Ka-Wei appeared besides him in spiritual form. They stared at one another in shock.

"What are we doing? Is this a dream?" Feslen asked Duxan and Ka-Wei at the same time. They all laughed. "Wait, weren't you on a mission?" Feslen asked Ka-Wei.

The Prince shrugged and responded, "I am. But maybe I'm also here to help you in a dream."

"If this is a dream, I don't think I could sneeze, but I need to. Curse the Sun Goddess for the freezing cold!" Duxan complained as he sneezed.

Feslen and Prince Ka-Wei stared at him in shock.

"What?" Duxan asked. "Can't a guy sneeze in a dream? I know I do that, every…"

"It's not that you sneezed," Ka-Wei began in his baritone voice.

"It's that you cursed," Feslen finished with a grin. "You kidder, I thought you never cursed."

Duxan smiled and winked and said, "Hey, in a dream, you never know what's real. Besides, it's not like I never curse in my mind anyway."

The three laughed and then stared at each other some more when the laughter subsided. A warm, peaceful sense of calm entered Feslen whenever he was near his best and only friend, Prince Ka-Wei. He observed him in silence. Feslen noticed how their spirit forms looked very much like their physical selves did in reality. At more than six feet, Ka-Wei's spirit form stood nearly two feet taller than Feslen. He had the same broad shoulders, the same muscular legs. As usual, he wasn't wearing a helmet. His handsome, shaven square face showed no new scars. His bright, almond-shaped eyes revealed the same bitter sadness and stubborn honor. His long, dark black hair looked a little unkempt.

Feslen noticed a silver cord connected to Ka-Wei's back. At the sight of it, he frowned with concern as a theory popped in his head. Then he turned to see if a silver cord dangled from his brother. His brother gave him a warm smile, and Feslen's frown disappeared. Duxan, his true brother, stood at the height of Ka-Wei's chest, and, at a solid four foot five, Feslen stood at Ka-Wei's waist. Duxan's thin but angular frame showed a hint of strength, sturdiness, and hidden agility. His spirit form wore the same thick glasses. Strawberry red highlights were apparent in his clean-cut, light brown hair. Duxan had attempted to grow a mustache and beard, despite Feslen's numerous taunts. Feslen had seen Duxan once with a mustache and beard and claimed that it made him look like a scared rabbit. Duxan's relaxed, good-natured face won many people over. His lively and full eyes did not show the same intensity, desire, and arrogance as Feslen's did, but Feslen knew they hid something deeper.

"So, little bro, why are we here?" Duxan asked in his usual calm manner.

"I don't know. Help me open this door, guys," Feslen pleaded. "I really need to go there, and I don't know why."

He knew it was really Duxan and Ka-Wei, because Duxan never wrinkled his pajamas and Ka-Wei wasn't wearing his engagement ring. The

Prince once told the Raster brothers in confidence that he hated the idea of an arranged marriage to a princess he didn't even like. He agreed to the future marriage in the name of duty and for the sake of his country and his unlawful uncle, the current King, but the Prince always took off his engagement ring in private.

Duxan's eyes opened wide as he asked, "Are you sure we're not under a curse or a spell?"

"I thought you didn't believe in those things, Dux," Ka-Wei snickered. "Sure, Fes, I'll help you. What do I need to do?"

"I don't know. Perhaps your strength can open this door, Ka-Wei."

Ka-Wei and Feslen both tried to turn the knob. Nothing happened. Ka-Wei then tried to chop through the door with his ancient sword. The sword made the sound of metal against metal and didn't go through. Ka-Wei backed up and tried to break through the door. His plan did not work. Then an idea struck Feslen. "Let's try to open it all together at the same time," Feslen said. The companions placed their hands on the knob and it turned…not like a normal doorknob, but sinking in, shifting like a secret panel.

Feslen entered and found himself alone again. "How could this be?" he wondered. He was distracted from his thoughts by the sound of footsteps approaching. Feslen hid behind one of the monastery's supporting columns when the person passed. When people travel in ethereal form, little harm can befall them, and they can communicate with other ethereal travelers like normal people do. He followed the Thai-Thurian monk down the long hallway and through a twisty passage up to a door with the Chiendonese character "Master."

The younger monk flung open the door of the Elder Monk. The thin-haired Elder Monk, dressed in traditional Thai-Thurian maroon robes, remained meditating, sitting cross-legged on a silk pillow embroidered with the images of elephants and elephant-like humans. There were four incense candles sitting next to the Elder Monk, two black and two red. The black candles smelled of cilantro and the red smelled of whey. Hanging on the wall in a glass case behind the Elder Monk was an ancient scroll written in their language. In some strange way, Feslen understood it even those he did not know any of the words. Under the scroll was a table with a small open coffer and some official documents beside it.

The Elder Monk spoke, "I know the winds of change."

"You already know?"

The younger monk kept his eyes downcast as it was proper for one of his rank. Feslen watched the Elder Monk's skill in Martial Arts in silent appreciation. Although the Elder Monk's physical form did not twist itself into any unusual Martial Arts aspects, his color of his body lightened as it floated an inch off the pillow. The incense candles went out as the Elder Monk's body relaxed. The aroma of sweet berries was injected into the air. Feslen understood these signs and felt the Elder Monk's dying spirit and so he chanted in respect. Suddenly, the candles relit once more, one at a time.

"You must depart and begin your search."

"If I find one, will the others appear, Elder?" The monk's voice rose sharply at the end, almost like a prayer. Feslen knew that the younger monk now felt his Master's departing energy. He saw him grip the Elder Monk's sleeve as he lowered his head. He repeated his Master's name, but since there was no response, the young monk bowed deeply and left.

The monastery faded quickly from Feslen's view. He heard monks' voices mingling in his mind:

"*Inattentiveness, weariness, granted thorough happiness, change is coming:*
Three children of the Ancient Truth must unite with a fourth,
One twice borne,
One delivered from the Lost Ones,
One who dwells in the Ancient Past.
These not found, the gentle caress turns to stinging burns from that which
We take for granted as ever-blowing softness.
The First of these begin and your doom is sealed."

These visions kept Feslen awake for three nights in a row and then they began to appear to him in the daytime as well. Feslen yawned, trying to stay awake. He understood little of what had transpired over the last few days. Worse yet, the dream haunted him while he was at the Red School, the place where he least wanted any trouble.

"Feslen! Feslen Raster! What is the answer?" the astronomy professor, Teacher Lai, shouted.

"From the Book of Lost Proverbs, Volume I," Feslen answered.

The other students laughed.

"No! This is an astronomy class; you know well that is a history question."

Teacher Lai gripped him by the ears and said, "Mocking me, are you?"

Feslen held back a glib remark.

Teacher Lai snarled, "Have you forgotten the New Priest's Red Book Rules?" The old man waved a thick copy of the Red Book with golden letters: "New Commandments by New Priests."

Feslen walked out without his usual remark, his footsteps echoing in the Red School's hallways just like in the monastery. He walked to the waiting area in the Head Office. He ignored the other students who were waiting there. Some jabbered with one another; others twiddled their thumbs. The well-lit room stank of thick smoke. Feslen held back his cough, determined not to show any weakness to the Principal or these other students. He studied the drab walls. Looking up on the opposite wall, Feslen saw a huge painting of the New Priest leader, Elhong Wien, with his infamous wicked grin. The New Priest's raven eyes stared back at him as though he were in the room with Feslen right then.

Tired of the glare of the New Priest, Feslen turned to face the other wall. The portrait of Emperor Tsai stared back with cold arrogance. He wore heavy jewelry, much of it jade and faux diamonds. Feslen frowned and turned away to stare at the gritty floor.

The Head Principal's secretary opened the door and called to him. Feslen walked in with his head bowed. The boy glanced about, ignoring the pudgy, red-faced man who sat in a plush chair. On the walls of this room too, more portraits of the new leaders, Elhong Wien and Emperor Tsai, seemed to mock Feslen. A banana leaf scroll of the Rules and Regulations hung on the wall. *Is everything meant to mock me?* Feslen thought. He ignored the first line of the Rules: "Disabled people ought to be killed or exiled unless they are sons." Then he turned to see the pudgy Principal waving his hands in the middle of an emotional tirade; he stared in disgust at a copy of the Red Book next to a still-litcigar and cigarette holder on the desk. He did not stop to ask himself which was more disgusting, the Red Book, or the lit cigar. The fumes caused him to cough. He ignored the Principal's deep scolding voice telling him, "You're lucky you aren't in more trouble. Your family's reputation keeps you in good respect, even with me, Feslen."

The old man prattled on, and Feslen sneered at him as he said to himself, "Yes, my adoptive family's money helped give you your job. I doubt that you could have gotten it on your own."

"What do you say to a load of more homework, Feslen? Or a day of Notification?" The Principal's thick, disgusting hands waved a yellow disqualifying marker. One mark meant a temporary suspension from school, two marks meant explusion.

"Would you really do that, Principal? My family wouldn't like it," Feslen said, staring the old man down. The man's paper-thin graying hair exuded sweat. His body trembled, whether out of fear or because of bad health Feslen did not venture a guess. The man's putrid alcoholic breath forced Feslen to turn his face aside.

"You should be more careful with that tongue, young friend. You are a trouble maker. Yes, you are," the fifty-year-old man leaned in and reached to grab Feslen by his vest. Feslen glared at him. The Principal muttered and sat back in his chair. The room filled with smoke. "What am I to do with you, Feslen?"

"Kick me out; we'll see how much my parents like it."

"You trouble teachers for no reason, get into fights. Do you find yourself superior?" The Principal sneered. "You are nothing but a disabled street urchin."

"Don't forget my family's station. Perhaps I am nothing, but you were nothing before my parents helped you into this position. Do what you will with me, Head Principal. I have more important things on mind,"

Feslen replied with a very slight bow. Feslen had regained his sense of patience by thinking about the return of his friend, Prince Ka-Wei.

The Principle went on to say, "You should know your place, act correctly, and wear appropriate clothing to your class. Why do you come in wearing the same shabby clothes? Don't you know there's a Clothing Standard, or do you wish to look like a cripple?"

Despite the rage he felt, Feslen kowtowed to the Principal and was let go without punishment.

4

OUTCAST 棄兒

Winter heat forced Feslen to stay home from school for a few weeks. Even for Chiendong, this year's winter weather was odd. It was at least ten to twenty degrees hotter than average. What made matters worse was the weather produced no snow or rain for much of the winter. The peasants prayed to Ao Chu'Yien, the Dragon King of weather and thunder, in hopes of good weather. Even the merchants and the nobles started to believe in the god. Few in Chiendong ever witnessed such oddity in weather, even the oldest people in every town.

Three snowcapped mountains surrounded Chiendong. The large Bay of Beizung lay to the East and opened onto the Sea of Joppone, the site of much of Chiendong's foreign trade. The weather conditions were ripe for snow and rain, but none had fallen. The farmers and even some nobles started to pay more tributes to the New Priests for so-called "miracle" help since they were in desperate need. Feslen paid little attention since rain in spring and summer didn't add much relief from the suffocating humidity. On some occasions, like today, the heat became so oppressive that it forced even the healthier Chiendonese to slow down their rapid everyday pace. The warmth this winter's rivaled the burning summer days of Chiendong.

Feslen had been reading some weather records in Beizung's First Library just yesterday. No one understood what was going on, not even the magicians of the Great School of Magic Stuff. The Thai-Thurian monks and the Forest Protectors of the Old Forest were the only weather recorders; few people bothered these isolated Forest Protectors and forgotten monks.

In the Wong household, family members busied themselves because the sons were setting out on a business shipment. Father Wong had already left at three in the morning to handle other business matters. Mother Wong prepared breakfast at five and called out to her children and reminded Duxan, "Don't forget to set up the monthly prayers!"

"Yes Mother," Duxan replied and went about his important tasks. He relished the opportunity to pray to the gods of the world, Hahn-Hah and the Four Dragon Kings. He knew no other sibling bothered with such a traditional task, but the older Raster did not mind.

In the family dining room, Duxan set up incense candles and prayer beads to the idols of GenCom, Goddess of Healing and Well-Being, and T'Shian Sheng, God of Fortune and Wealth. He lit the candles and, in an instant, cilantro and sweet-smelling oil made from almonds wafted in the air. He knelt and performed a traditional waist-length bow in front of each statue three times and murmured the ritualistic prayers for each god. The slim female form of GenCom, the Goddess of Health, seemed to dance when Duxan prayed to her. He knew it was the sweet-smelling incense that affected him a bit. Unlike most god statues, GenCom always squatted on a cloud in the lotus position, which created the illusion of her dancing for health. He offered a sacrifice of fruits and fresh flowers to GenCom and thought about Feslen's health. Then Duxan turned to T'Shian Sheng, God of Fortune and Wealth. His rotund belly protruded and his empty right hand seemed to beckon to Duxan. The god's left hand held a money sack. Duxan placed his first month's wages within the money sack of the God of Fortune in symbolic offering. Duxan then placed a jade amulet about GenCom's neck and prayed once more, still thinking of wellbeing for Feslen.

Duxan heard Feslen chuckle, "You done with the ritual, brother? I hope to meet Ka-Wei in time."

Duxan smiled and said, "Ka-Wei knows I'm always a little bit late. He will wait."

Feslen said in a somewhat serious tone, "Do you think the gods are listening?"

"They did when they helped you to survive," Duxan said with strong conviction in his voice.

"Perhaps," Feslen said and did a mock bow to the statues.

Duxan shook his head and said, "Try not to show your irreverence, little brother."

"Sorry. I just don't believe it helps," Feslen said.

Duxan sighed and replied, "I know, I know. Let's get a move on before Mother yells at us."

"Duxan, Feslen, Ai-Yen! It's almost time to meet up with the Prince for the shipment delivery!" Mother's voice sailed from clear across the house.

Duxan and Feslen chuckled and replied in a loud shout, "Yes Mother! We're out the door!"

With their adoptive brother, Ai-Yen, they left the house in relatively good spirits.

Today's cloudy weather made Feslen want to stay home and read, but Father had forced him to accompany his brothers, Ai-Yen and Duxan, on a delivery to Master Chai. Instead of wearing the usual winter clothes, Feslen wore a light flannel shirt; Duxan was a little more dressed up, and Ai-Yen was the most dressed up.

Feslen studied his adoptive brother Ai-Yen and shook his head. Ai-Yen wore some makeup to hide the moles and acne on his face. He also pulled back his long black hair into a girl's ponytail style, which glistened due to the large amounts of gel in his hair. His tall, somewhat muscular frame betrayed his actual personality. His large, uncalloused hands showed off his perfectly groomed nails. Despite his somewhat chubby stomach, jutted chin, and the fact that his round black eyes showed little intelligence or imagination, many women found Ai-Yen attractive. Feslen could not fathom why.

Feslen sat in the back of the wagon with the goods. Today, the Wong family wagon carried certain supplies that Feslen found fascinating: rare surgical supplies; spices from the South and East; fresh bamboo and dried bamboo husks; new swords, daggers, crossbows, and other items of war; two strange scrolls with ancient Joppone characters inscribed on them; several new maps of the world, Hahn-Hah, and some old maps of Chiendong. These maps Feslen found most interesting: one of the highlighted areas on a map showed the recently abandoned lands around the Three Mountain's Gorge. That was where the first mages of Hahn-Hah had battled it out in the Breaking Wars, or at least so say the legends he had read. The other spots marked on the map included the sole forest of Chiendong, a huge place called the Old Forest, which contained the legendary Forest Protectors. The last place marked on one of the maps was a new but lesser-known political hot spot at which Feslen took a quick, forbidden look. This place used to be the home of one of Prince Ka-Wei's aunts, Jerenko-I. Along with these other places, the Wong's home and those of known business associates and businesses were marked. Why these places were marked Feslen did not know. But he did know why Master Chai requested the Wongs to bring him these goods because he understood their importance. Another few items intrigued Feslen: a book which contained legends about the Gem Mountain, Mount Jing, and the Thai-Thurian monks. This book contained bits and pieces of information on the Prophecy and the Yin Yang Swords. Other items in the wagon included silk, fresh produce, rare pearls from the Shinjoudou peoples, and thick furs of certain rare animals.

Ai-Yen drove the wagon, and Duxan walked behind. Ai-Yen's shadow overlapped Feslen's smaller one as the sun made an appearance at high noon. The group paused and Ai-Yen wiped his brow with a handkerchief. Feslen turned and studied his adoptive brother and chuckled. That's why I wear the same light shirt everyday, he thought. Sure, I may look like a common street performer, but I'm so much more comfortable.

His brother took out an extravagant fan and fanned himself. Sweat dripped from Ai-Yen's fat face and large eyebrows, making him look like a legendary ogre. They came in from the North Gate at a slow pace. Prince Ka-Wei planned to meet them there.

"Ai-Yen, I told you not to wear so much in this weather," Duxan said, "It's hot. Sure, it's good to dress nicely, but at least I don't try to dress like a king."

Feslen heard the sarcasm in his true brother's voice and said, "Yeah, right, aren't you supposed to wear down-filled clothes in hot weather?"

"We're rich. We're supposed to wear this," Ai-Yen responded with a growl.

Yeah, sure. You've got on three pairs of heavy silk cloth vestments, you idiot, Feslen thought.

"Even rich people sometimes wear less, see?" Feslen said, pointing to a couple the brothers knew. They wore only one layer of silk vestments rather than three.

Duxan and Feslen chuckled.

"Father should've let you stay home," Ai-Yen grumbled. But then some public notice signs humbled Feslen in an instant. He tried to ignore the Province Regulations written on them and turned to eye Duxan. Duxan nodded in understanding. Father Wong ignored Province Regulations and the Empire Rules by letting Duxan and Feslen Raster, his adopted children, accompany shipment missions across Chiendong. Rule number twenty of the Hundred Rules from the New Priest's Red Book stated that non-Chiendonese cannot travel within city borders without proper identification or guardianship.

His father's attitude puzzled Feslen, although Duxan knew why their father did it and admired him for that. When they approached the city border, Feslen and Duxan ignored the huge signs that said "Foreigners will be stripped of valuables and humiliated." Another sign read "Disabled people, if seen, will be imprisoned without freedom or shipped out of the country."

They approached and stopped at the border. Red-armored guards asked for their papers.

"You know, Father is taking an awful chance for having you with us, you dog," Ai-Yen muttered to Feslen. "Disabled people belong in homes. Do you see them walking around out here?" Ai-Yen, who knew well that he was the only Wong son by birth, continued in an endless tirade.

"I don't look disabled, so stop bringing that up, okay?" Feslen said in his own defense.

"Your disability comes out, toad. Then there are your non-Chiendonese eyes. I don't know what's worse, your blue lips and pale skin or your broad face with those non-slanted eyes."

The brothers knew that to be true. One of the New Priest's new rules banned any people with disabilities to roam Chiendong streets. Feslen held his anger in check and sighed. When his rare congenital blood disorder flares up, a bright blue color appears on his lips and fingernails, as it was doing now. As Ai-Yen shuffled through the papers and mumbled something with the guards, his occasional glares back at Feslen made the boy scrunch down even further. Feslen scratched his neck and wished he was not undersized or underweight for his age. He heard the comments the guards made about him, "Hey, maybe you should let the ugly toad go back home. Or perhaps you could marry him to an ugly witch." Ai-Yen laughed and waved as they moved on.

Prince Ka-Wei's crown seal on an official royal document helped them bypass the guards. Feslen heard the admiring coos of the women and the compliments given from passersby to Ai-Yen. He patted his own reed-thin, unkempt reddish-brown hair. *I don't mind the way I look except when others comment on it*, thought Feslen and he sighed.

"I don't know why Father wanted you along anyway. You don't have a business mind," Ai-Yen continued.

They passed familiar customers who shouted insults at Feslen but greeted Ai-Yen with warmth. "Hello there, Mr. Tiger Wong, with the fair hair," said a healthy, male family friend with some status. "Oh, you brought them along…. even the dishonored one."

"Yes, I had to. Father made me do it," Ai-Yen replied. "If it were up to me, he'd be thrown out or executed." The man laughed and tipped his hat to Duxan, who walked in silent rage. Other passersby and people who followed Chiendong's Hundred Rules ignored the Raster brothers. They believed that outsiders without family and land holdings deserved no better treatment. Some people greeted Duxan, but no one greeted Feslen, not even the servants of each Merchant House. The servants and the bodyguards who accompanied the servants of the House of Elhong Wien gave the Rasters an especially cold shoulder. The sunlight peeked out a moment or two and glistened off the rings of the servants from the House of Wien when they paused in front of the Wong wagons. Feslen and Duxan shared a silent, intense look. Each thought of the rivalry Master Chai shared with the Wiens. This was a time when few could tell the brothers apart.

Most of the passersby did not shout insults at Duxan because last summer he saved the life of a young child prince in the King's extended family. He also held the nation's highest mark on the Entrance Exam for the second time. Chiendonese of all walks of life respected test results and degrees. The first time Duxan Raster achieved the highest mark on the Entrance Exam was at the age of twelve. Three years ago, he turned down an entrance offer from Beizung University of Medicines because he wanted to help take care of Feslen's health instead. Feslen should have taken the Entrance Exam by now, but his inherited blood disorder overcame him. He sighed inwardly but remained as emotionless as possible. He turned away from Duxan. He sat, legs dangling over the edge of the wagon. He patted the empty bamboo sticks bundled together. Master Chai's bamboo specialists would turn the bamboo into Bo and Jo sticks, crossbows, chopsticks, blowguns, and housing materials. Feslen imagined Prince Ka-Wei practicing with the weapons.

Someone passing by them gave Feslen a very intense look, almost like an interrogator studying a prisoner. He shivered, and the young woman disappeared as they rounded a bend. Feslen caught the inscription on the woman's robe, the arcane Yin Yang symbol. Why did she watch me? What do the mages want? Feslen thought. He started to mention this to his brothers, but they were intent on arguing.

"You know full well why Feslen has to come," Duxan said, his voice soft but firm with intent.

"Keep an eye on the road, Ai-Yen. I hope you won't tip the wagon like last time," Feslen said.

Ai-Yen said nothing, but his face reddened. The wagon jerked over a big piece of rock, reflecting its driver's mood. Duxan caught Feslen before he tipped over. Duxan readjusted his thick glasses.

"I thank you again, my brother," Feslen said with an exaggerated bow.

"Don't thank me, little brother. Thank Ai-Yen for his clumsy driving skills," Duxan said.

"What was that?" Ai-Yen asked and turned to glare at them.

Beizung's Grand Market in the Rich District was crawling with people. Today the Wongs carted in all their important goods. After watching the scenery for a moment, Feslen became bored and let his mind wander. This has to be the hottest winter in Chiendong history, Feslen thought. People are excited about the Winter's Festival Celebration, even though it doesn't feel much like winter, Feslen thought with a wry grin.

"The market, guys, we're supposed to meet up with old man Chai, right?" Duxan said.

"I know. We're here," Ai-Yen replied and continued, "But who the heck is Chai? Why does he want all this sugarcane for goodness sake? Sugar is good for facial makeup and sweet drinks, but for not Martial Arts. There are other more important business men that we could be dealing with."

"First, dear brother," Feslen grimaced, "Mei-Whuay, our lovely sister, doesn't even use sugar from sugarcane. The juice is part of her products; she told me that herself. Second, these are bamboo; any idiot can see that, even the village drunk."

The younger Raster saw his adoptive brother, Ai-Yen Wong, tense up and felt Duxan's warning hand upon his shoulder. Feslen continued anyway; he reveled in this type of moment.

"Master Chai is our country's most talented Martial Arts master and teacher, dear brother," Feslen finished, sticking out his tongue at his brother's back.

"Martial Arts is not important. Like you, it should be ignored," Ai-Yen growled.

"The importance of Martial Arts staggers the mind. A true man would understand that; even the new King does. You, however, would certainly have little clue about it."

"You should be the one talking, dog-boy, you have little grace. You're clumsier than any foreigner," Ai-Yen replied as he continued to clean his long nails.

Feslen knew he should not allow anger to reach him, since his adoptive brother and siblings berated him all the time. Yet anger billowed like fire from a blacksmith's fireplace in his belly. Even after Duxan coughed to warn him and stared at him, Feslen yelled, "At least Duxan and I are like real men. My brother does more than his share of work. I am what I am."

Feslen slid off the wagon when Ai-Yen stopped it. The two turned to face each other. Feslen and Ai-Yen stood face to face. Despite Ai-Yen's physical strength, Duxan would bet three months' wages on Feslen to win. "You two, come on now, there's a more important task at hand," Duxan pleaded as he tried to intervene.

"Oh, shut up!" Both brothers turned to Duxan. "It was *you* who said one wagon was enough for an entire shipment!" They glared at one another, gaining attention from the crowd. Passersby shouted exclusive support for Ai-Yen, none for Feslen. Soon, Feslen sagged to his knees. His illness was acting up again.

"Feslen, are you all right?" Duxan asked. If Feslen could make a response, he would have, except he ran out of breath. Ten years ago, he started going to Master Chai because of this condition. Master Chai, as a famous Martial Arts Master for the disabled and unhealthy, practiced healthy cures like *reflexology*, acupuncture, Tai-Chi and the like on Feslen. He thought of his friend, Mei Xue and Prince Ka-Wei to calm down.

"We need to make the shipment," Ai-Yen said. "Let dogs lie where they are."

"Feslen is our brother," Duxan's face turned an ugly red.

"He is your brother, not mine."

Duxan realized that Ai-Yen would never come to terms with the situation. More commoners walked by, hurling various insults at Feslen: "mutant," "parasite," "bug." Duxan glared at the commoners. How dare they? He thought. "Listen, Master Chai is also different from you, yet you treat him with respect," Duxan retorted through clenched teeth.

Feslen needed something to hold onto. He wanted his brother to calm down and stop defending him. Somebody hurled a rock at Feslen. Feslen flinched more from the insults. The ground shook from the Red Guards' metal boots. Duxan relaxed some.

"What's going on?" an officer asked.

"Nothing, officer," Ai-Yen said. "We're on our way to a delivery." Duxan glared at Ai-Yen.

"All mutants must be out of sight," a guard repeated as he held open his Red Book. Duxan held in his anger. The people in the crowd laughed along with the guards.

"Leave him alone," Duxan lifted his voice. A guard pushed Feslen back down. "Is this really necessary? Do you have to do this? What has he done to you?" Duxan said in a whisper.

"He lives. He takes up space," someone from the crowd replied. It might have been a guard, a commoner, or even Ai-Yen; neither Raster brother could tell.

Duxan held his anger. "Why do you say that? My difference is as apparent as Feslen's. He and I may not be true Chiendonese, but we do our jobs for country and King," he said.

"You do. You work, Duxan," someone said.

"True. And he does what he can. What did your elderly parents teach you? Didn't ConSuFu teach you to respect your elders and those who are different from you?" The brothers watched them as their faces changed from anger to shame. This strategy started to work. The crowd began to break apart.

"He is still a parasite," hissed a cloaked man. Several men gathered again to jeer at Feslen.

"If you love your Prince, who is our friend, please leave us be. I know all of you are good, law-abiding citizens," Duxan murmured. The crowd broke then, and Duxan sighed with relief.

Feslen rose, dusted himself off, and glowered. All he could see was evil and ugliness. "One day, you will regret this," Feslen said. Feslen took out a pretend spell scroll that he always carried. Feslen imagined casting spells at all his foes, including Ai-Yen. No one heard what he had said except for Duxan. The brothers continued arguing. Feslen thought people attacked him out of pure hatred of outsiders and out of their own stupidity. Ai-Yen disagreed, claiming it was a matter of Chiendonese perfection. Duxan tried to calm both of them down by saying that they were both right.

At the appointed spot, they waited for their long overdue friend and country hero, Prince Ka-Wei. When they settled the wagon, Duxan split the brothers apart to talk to them. Duxan mollified Feslen by whispering, "You're smarter and more talented than Ai-Yen, so don't lower yourself to his standards." Duxan appeased Ai-Yen, "Girls clamor for you, you have many friends. Why do you need to fight with Fes?"

Feslen nursed his anger by remembering how they met the Prince. Duxan hated the angry silence steaming between Fes and Ai-Yen and shook his head. Then Duxan chuckled, realizing that he would rather have this moment of quiet than continued fighting. He predicted that the arguing would soon recommence.

5

INAUSPICIOUS MEETING
倒霉的相遇

Prince Ka-Wei took his time to return home; his troops did not object. Light talk among some of his men spurred Ka-Wei to remark, "It's good that you can joke, Jokata." He did not turn to address one of the youngest members of his team.

"I try to be lighthearted in general, Red Warrior," replied the soldier.

Ka-Wei nodded and started to speak again when Fay Fong, one of the few women he had in his army, asked, "How would Lady Mei Xue Chai react if she found out her friend Rei-Rei was missing?"

Ka-Wei shrugged his shoulders in discomfort and said, "I am sure Mei Xue would understand. Her friend chose her career." It doesn't make Rei-Rei's disappearance any easier, Ka-Wei thought, half-turning to face the North. "Explaining things to Mei Xue will not be easy. But fortunately, unlike Feslen, she's mature enough to understand special situations." He tried not to let his feelings show. Showing emotions to his troops revealed weakness and dishonor. He grinned a bit, knowing Feslen would disagree with this assessment. If I show emotions to my comrades in arms it reveals my weakness, at least in my own opinion, he corrected himself in thought.

"I bet that Lady Unimaysha and Lady Sho would love seeing you again, sir," said Ichi Ken, jumping to his rescue. Ka-Wei chuckled.

"Don't forget, I can't go make my rounds any more. I'm about to be married," Ka-Wei said. His men chuckled and Fay Fong grunted.

Ka-Wei couldn't help but sigh, recalling his group's failure. It was bad enough his Honor was lost when the recent defeats decimated his personal retinue; but having his uncle and the Emperor sending him to put down 'rebel' countries…weighed heavy on the young Prince's mind. But then he and his group approached the center of town, and he grinned when he saw his best friends, the Raster brothers, and Ai-Yen Wong arguing. He could guess what they argued about. A jingle of horse reins got the attention of the arguing brothers. "It is good to see my friends, even if they are arguing over semantics," Prince Ka-Wei's voice boomed.

"Ka-Wei!" Feslen shouted enthusiastically. Those who had attacked Feslen now bowed, scraped, and tried to touch the Prince. Blue Soldiers kept the crowd away. Blue Soldiers represented the Prince's royal bodyguards. The Raster brothers and Ka-Wei studied one another for a moment. Heroes and celebrities never took the time to visit commoners, even important ones such as the Wong family. But Prince Ka-Wei, hero of Chiendong; never failed to visit the Raster brothers.

Feslen admired Ka-Wei, and he deliberately avoided making notice of the man's obvious new scars and dried bloody scabs. This latest mission roughed him up good, Feslen thought. Feslen counted ten men left from the Prince's original twenty-eight, but he knew better than to bring that subject up. Unlike his brother Duxan, Feslen's emotions would seep through if he brought it up. The hand of the broad-shouldered Prince never strayed to the ancient silver-edged pommel in the shape of a dragon—Xsi-Arak, *Kei-Trui-Nahohie*—strapped on his right hip.

Chiendong blacksmiths created three known Xsi-Arak blades. Those with birthright, true honor, owned these swords, and the right to them was passed down to each subsequent generation. Rumors floated down throughout Chiendong history that immortals had passed the secrets of making the Xsi-Arak to the first blacksmiths. Ka-Wei earned the right for the sword from his father. The brothers and the Prince shared a story about how he earned that sword. A few years back, when the Prince was still in training, a whole village was forced to relocate due to a devastating flood. A group of known bandits attacked the village's caravan and Ka-Wei came to the rescue with his Black Rock Turtle Squad, routing the enemy. In that battle, Ka-Wei's troops experienced no fatalities and he received his father's sword.

The sunlight gleamed off the Prince's armor and all his weapons. On Ka-Wei's left hip, a short sword and black mace hung on a belt loop. He was an imposing figure, who stood at least two heads taller than the average Chiendonese. The wind whipped his long, sandy hair around his dark onyx eyes. His youth shone despite some rugged lines on his concave cheeks. Already Ka-Wei's presence had helped Feslen forget about the populace's attack. The Prince continued to wear his parents' Stork Crest and green armor. His Blue Soldiers wore the King's falcon symbol and blue armor.

Look at the worry and stress in and under his eyes, Feslen thought, studying his friend. I wonder if his mission to the North lies heavy on his consciousness?

Ka-Wei studied Duxan and Feslen. Duxan looked about the same; his noodle-thin strawberry-black hair had weathered some. His strength was deceptive for his average height. The thick glasses seem to weigh him down; his sharp, oval eyes gleamed. "Well met, Duxan. You're keeping well," Ka-Wei said.

Duxan bowed formally and replied, "You too, my friend."

"You're looking like a member of the King's retinue, Ai-Yen," Ka-Wei said.

Ai-Yen bowed, beaming.

"Do the ladies love your scars more?" Feslen grinned.

"And my, you've muscled up," Ka-Wei returned. The young Prince smiled at his young friend's transformation. Feslen had added muscle to his frame although he still was somewhat hunched over out of habit. His skin and strawberry-brown hair glowed, and his doe eyes showed even more clarity, intensity, and yearning. Feslen fumbled an awkward bow when Duxan ribbed him. Ka-Wei laughed at that, and the brothers joined in.

Ka-Wei's men accompanied them up to the point where they started on their delivery run to Master Chai again. Ka-Wei bid his most of his men farewell when they reached the split fork in the road. Officer Zhou, however, stayed on with five men.

"How goes the mission, my friend? Where did the King send you this time?" Duxan asked Ka-Wei.

The Prince did not reply for a while. "He is not my King," Ka-Wei said, his voice bitter. "He is my uncle, nothing more. Remember that, Duxan." The Prince's men gasped at the Prince's outward defiance of the King, but otherwise said nothing.

"Yes, my mistake," Duxan, he arched his eyebrows at his friend's open display of anger. He knew about some of the Prince's anger, but not all of it.

"As for the mission…" Ka-Wei's voice trailed off… "Let's just say I doubt that my uncle has control of what he does anyway. Most of the King's men and Chiendong's nobles fear the Emperor. As for the New Priests, even though they are supposedly neutral, they all report to the Emperor in some fashion."

Duxan nodded and said, "Do you think the people will stand for much more of this outside interference?"

Ka-Wei glanced at his friend a moment and then said, "Let's not talk about it where ears and eyes can hear and see us. Master Chai's would be a much more convenient place to talk."

Duxan nodded again. They fell into deep conversation about small things after that until Ka-Wei looked up, realizing that Feslen lagged behind. "Stop a moment. Let Feslen catch up," he stated.

"Ah, the little abnormality can wait," Ai-Yen complained, but then he quieted down after a stern gaze from the Prince.

Duxan cursed himself for letting his little brother fall so far behind, and during the worst season of weather in Beizung too! How could he have been so thoughtless? He started to move towards Feslen. Feslen fell to his knees, his face turning pale blue. A strong hand stopped Duxan from helping Feslen. He recognized Ka-Wei's steady grip and relaxed some. Feslen saw the reaction and smiled. "Look, at him, Duxan! Give him a chance to get up on his own!" Ka-Wei demanded. Duxan waited, all tensed up. Feslen staggered, breathing hard. He had closed his eyes when the dizziness struck. One…two…he concentrated and tried recalling the Breathing Technique taught to him by Master Chai. "Relax deeply," Feslen could almost hear the old Master's laconic voice enter him. Pain seared his lungs, then his chest, and toes. Fire seemed to rip apart his innards.

But once they reached a shadier path, Feslen recovered. He leaned against a squat single-tiled building. He considered the strangeness of why people were willing to give him space when his disorder attacked him. Usually people milled about, minding their own business, ignoring him or even bumping into him. Suddenly he spotted a young woman in green robes. She gave him a nod and then vanished before he could say anything. Feslen inhaled and coughed.

A small form snuck up and brushed against the conversing friends. Ka-Wei roared and he and his Blue Soldiers jumped into action. A small, brown figure sped away. He or she had bumped into Feslen on the way. "Hey!" Feslen said; his scroll had been pilfered. The others ran after the thief and he turned back and tripped, falling against Feslen. They tumbled to the ground together.

"I sorry," the thief apologized. Still out of breath, Feslen tried to respond. But the thief bolted away the instant the Ka-Wei fell upon them.

Ka-Wei paused for a second to help Feslen up, but the boy waved him away and mouthed, "Go ahead without me."

Ka-Wei's big easy strides parted the crowd and soon brought him just a step behind the panicked thief. Duxan pulled Feslen up and they chased after the thief together. Ai-Yen wore such a confused look that Feslen attempted to laugh, but thick phlegm invaded his lungs. He paused to breathe. By the time the Raster brothers caught up with Ka-Wei, he and his men already incarcerated the thief. Ka-Wei shook the young man until his nose bled. "Where is it?" Ka-Wei demanded.

"Please don't kill me," the thief pleaded. It was Pan-Gui Wu, the infamous local thief boy. Feslen's eyebrows arched.

"Tell me, or by Kuan-Ti, God of Justice, I will rip your lungs out," Ka-Wei threatened.

Feslen and Duxan exchanged alarmed glances. This sort of anger from Ka-Wei seemed unreasonable and new to the Raster brothers. The Prince drew his serrated curved Xsi-Arak sword level with the boy's neck. "Ka-Wei!" Feslen and Duxan shouted together.

"Stay out of this," snarled Ka-Wei. "This trouble maker has been a thorn in my side for months now."

Out of breath again, Feslen studied Pan-Gui Wu. The young man trembled. Thinner and shorter than one of the rice-paddy women, the thief looked no older than fifteen. Dust and grime covered his entire body. His brown-gray eyes glittered. He resembles one of the River Ghosts, Feslen thought. "Ka-Wei, wait." Feslen pleaded. "Killing innocents loses one's Honor more than disobeying an Order,'" Feslen quoted from the Book of Rules.

Ka-Wei lowered his Xsi-Arak. Pan-Gui Wu sighed in relief. "I sorry for bothering your Grace," he spoke even though Ka-Wei still held him by the collar. "I willing to serve your just sentence."

The thief's response helped crack a grin on both Ka-Wei and Duxan. "Well, young thief," Ka-Wei said. "It seems to be your lucky day. Return the items you have stolen to their proper owners, and you shall be released."

Feslen sighed in approval. Feslen noted a frown on the thief's face and signaled to him for compliance. The young thief muttered under his breath and handed back the rightful belongings. Ka-Wei turned to his Blue Soldiers. "Keep an eye on this one," Ka-Wei commanded as he fished out three copper coins. "Take this, Pan-Gui. This should feed you for the rest of the week."

"Make sure he feeds himself," the Prince said to his remaining Blue Soldiers. The thief gave a sarcastic bow. The Blue Soldiers bowed deep at the waist to Ka-Wei and left.

Ka-Wei sighed and said, "I will not need any protection, Officer Zhou. You can help attend to our friend over there, make sure he gets into less trouble than usual." The Blue Soldiers bowed in return, the officer convincing Ka-Wei to keep some guards with him.

"Hurry up now, don't bother the Prince and the most important family!" they told the thief. Pan-Gui Wu had stopped to study Feslen. He stumbled a little but caught himself and took the rough treatment from the Prince's guards with pride and quiet dignity. Feslen respected this proud thief.

Ka-Wei, Duxan, and Feslen returned to the Wong wagon only to find Ai-Yen gone. One of Ka-Wei's men told him that Ai-Yen had left during the thief's appearance. Because Feslen's health problem struck yet again, Ka-Wei decided to send the wagon ahead with two of his best men and then dismissed the rest of them.

They neared Master Chai's famous Golden Dragon School. Two giant golden dragons greeted visitors on the stone path. Feslen smiled with warmth as he saw the statues and bowed in honor to them. Ka-Wei kowtowed in front of the dragon statues as well, and Duxan prayed before they moved on.

Excitement mounted in Feslen at the prospect of meeting up with Master Chai and his teenage daughter, Mei Xue. They walked at a brisk pace, listening to the sounds of nature greeting them. Soon, two more grand dragons standing guard along with two lion statues at the entrance came into view. The three friends gazed at the famous Martial Arts School with which they had become so familiar over the past ten years. Several animal statues looked down on people from the blue granite rooftops. Zodiac symbols and portraits of famous Martial Arts masters were etched in the rooftop façade.

"Can't wait to see Mei Xue, eh, little bro?" Duxan asked with a grin.

Feslen blushed and stammered to respond, but Ka-Wei saved him and asked, "Shouldn't she be out to greet you by now?"

Feslen thought about it and said, "You're right, Ka-Wei, what on Hahn-Hah is going on?"

The Prince did not give an immediate response. Instead his body tensed as he noted that no students, servants, or guards came to greet them. Peasants and common workers without permits cannot enter within two hundred feet of Master Chai's school grounds. They continued on down the beaten dirt path. The wave of towering bamboo trees soon came into view, and for some reason Feslen felt uneasy.

"What's wrong, little brother?" Duxan whispered to his nervous brother.

The Prince's face was stretched tight with worry, and his hands twitched, moving toward his ancient sword. Feslen glanced at the Prince and frowned. Feslen took some time to respond to Duxan. He studied him and realized a completely truthful response right now would trigger a knee-jerk reaction of concern from Duxan. A brief but knowledgeable response from Feslen now might cause a complicated response from Duxan. "It's just the weather bothering me again," Feslen told Duxan.

Feslen studied the Prince. The Prince's eyes flicked about and narrowed; he kept his hand upon his sword, whose slow, melodious ring echoed with every step the trio took down the twisted stone path to the Master's school.

"Don't worry. When we get to the school, they'll have tea to cool us down," Duxan said.

"Duxan, there's trouble," Feslen began, but Ka-Wei cut him off.

"Hsst," Ka-Wei warned.

"Danger?" Duxan asked both Feslen and Prince Ka-Wei. He stepped closer to Feslen and felt him stiffen in response. He realized how defensive his brother was about someone coming closer to him just then and he sighed. Feslen realized this too and relaxed as much as he could. He also saw Duxan lifting his arms up in a questioning gesture. Feslen thought again for the right words, but Ka-Wei had already swung his sword in warning. The brothers had spent enough time around the Prince Warrior to recognize his signals. They quieted down as soon as he signaled them. Feslen nodded in response to his brother, his back arched and his body shivered, his inner alarm was set.

"Warrior's Instincts," Ka-Wei mouthed to his companions. He used hand signals and Feslen and Duxan nodded. Although the brothers never fought in an army or underwent serious training, they had observed the Prince often enough in practice. They had also trained privately with him on occasions and had some private lessons with his mentor, Captain Garland.

Ka-Wei called for his men. They waited a few minutes. No response. The brothers exchanged glances at each other and then at the Prince. "You two wait here," Ka-Wei ordered the brothers. "I'm going to check on ahead. Don't come to help me if I'm in trouble."

Feslen said nothing to Duxan, but he felt unsafe without the Prince around. Duxan nodded and motioned for them to walk ahead. "Kid," Duxan spoke in his no-nonsense Big Brother voice. Feslen turned to give him a knowing nod. "If there is danger beyond what Ka-Wei and I could handle, will you run and get help, please?"

Feslen gave a tight-lipped nod. Duxan relaxed a bit and gripped his brother tightly on the shoulder.

Half an hour passed, and still no Ka-Wei. Then Feslen cocked his head and signaled to his brother. The two nodded and approached. At the school's entrance, Ka-Wei stood rigid. There they found two of Ka-Wei's four soldiers brutally murder. Servants, students, and guards of the school had also been slaughtered. Feslen gagged and vomited. Although Duxan had seen a dead body a long time before, he too averted his eyes. Duxan patted Feslen on the arm to comfort him.

In the branches of the trees, they saw remnants of the characteristic weapons, the throwing stars with the snake character inscribed upon them. "*Ninkattas*," Prince Ka-Wei said through clenched teeth. "But this doesn't seem like their style; it's too straightforward. Why now? Why these two? Damn it, Dux." Duxan stood by the Prince. Anger and grief were etched on the Prince's face, and his hands had turned red from his clenched fists. Duxan heard the Prince murmur a vow of revenge.

Then Duxan heard his brother call out to him from a few feet away to the West, in the more wooded area. Duxan excused himself from the Prince for a second and sprinted towards where his brother stood in shock. Feslen had found their family cart looted and overturned. He slumped against the cart and closed his eyes and bit back the need to cry out. This really isn't good, Feslen thought. My parents will be very angry about this.

More blood and destruction surrounded their family wagon. Master Chai's servants and several students had been slaughtered here. Duxan came over to his brother and patted him on the arm again. They watched Ka-Wei examine the area with methodical movements. They heard him muttering to himself, "Too many different cuts in different places…students scattered in death at odd distances…this could only mean…more than one attacker."

I can't even image what this ambush is doing to Ka-Wei, Feslen thought. He exchanged a meaningful look with Duxan. Honor means everything to a WuSha warrior. Since Prince Ka-Wei, or Kalman the Red as he was known in the other countries of the world of Hahn-Hah, was indeed a WuSha warrior, the deaths of the innocent students and servants of Master Chai and the deaths of his own soldiers would stain his Honor. The WuShas live and die by the Code of the Warrior and the Sword. Every misstep and action taken against the WuSha could mean something against his or her Honor. An Honor stain such as this equals is as serious as a brutal rape would be to a virtuous woman. Ka-Wei would have to take an Oath of Vengeance or an Honor Pledge in order to "balance the lives lost in his line of duty."

Duxan watched his friend's stiff actions and thought, Poor Ka-Wei. It's things like this that make me glad that I am not a WuSha warrior. I wouldn't want this sort of responsibility. It's hard enough to watch over Feslen as it is.

Duxan kept a close eye on his younger brother, making sure Feslen was all right. He placed a sturdy hand on his brother's shoulder, but Feslen shrugged it off and moved a few steps away from him. Duxan sighed and thought, Okay, sorry, Kid. Just trying to make sure you're okay.

Feslen shook his head and growled. He pointed to Ka-Wei and said, "I'm more worried for him." Duxan nodded. They returned to the Prince when he called them over. Ka-Wei prayed over his men. Then he took out his ancient sword and knelt to the East, facing the sun.

"To my men's departed souls: you fought well, you have given your lives for the innocent, you have taken a few of the evil murderers down. You have given Honor to your Family Name. Your Ancient Forefathers' pride will be obvious to you when they greet you at the Haven Gates. May the Sun Goddess and her Emperor God welcome you with safe and open arms. You will be dined, greeted, and treated like the heroes you are. You will guide fallen innocents to the rightful path. May your karma lead you to happiness. I will Honor your memories and swear upon your ancestor's graves, Ko-Ler and Tai-Poa, that I will avenge those who killed you in cold blood. Know that your efforts have not been in vain. I, Prince Ka-Wei, swear as your leader, your friend, and your brother, that this shall be done. If I do not manage to achieve vengeance, may I sacrifice something great and dear to me."

The Prince concluded by moving his sword once straight out to the left and then to the right. He then kowtowed to the departed ones and cut his left hand with his sword. He let his blood drip on each of the departed soldiers' faces. He then gathered their identification sashes and Black Rock Turtle Daggers. Ka-Wei cried for each of the fallen victims and even took the time to honor the *nirhakos* who had attacked them. These nirhakos, the secondary fighting minions of the *Ninkattas*, had provided the Prince with all the necessary clues of their enemies. He turned to his friends and said, "Run, go get help."

Feslen shook his head even before Duxan replied, "No, Ka-Wei. These men died for our family. Our Honor is stained along with yours. Besides, the attackers wanted something from our wagon, though I'm not sure what it was."

"Nothing is missing other than the obvious, my brother," Feslen pointed out. He noted that the maps and the book about the Gem Stone Mountains were missing. "Also, Ka-Wei, remember that we're in this together. Your men got in the way when the ambushers attacked the school. The attackers wanted Master Chai out of the way. I don't think I even need to point that out to you."

Ka-Wei sighed. He could not argue with their logic and so he turned to face the brothers and said, "I guess I taught you both too well about the meaning and responsibility of Honor." Duxan and Feslen shared a light-hearted chuckle even as Ka-Wei continued, "Here, take this mace with you. Duxan, the ambushers may be inside. Let's make sure Master Chai and his daughter, Mei Xue, are all right," Ka-Wei said.

Duxan frowned at the mace and said, "Ka-Wei, you know I don't like violence."

Ka-Wei nodded and sighed, "I know, my friend. I know. But you may need it. How else will you protect yourself or Feslen?"

Duxan scratched his arm in hesitance and cleared his throat, "I don't think I will need it, my friend. You are with us. Wouldn't it be better if my brother and I were not here?"

Ka-Wei nodded and smiled, "Perhaps. But I don't wish to risk you two any more than has already happened. The enemy watches us even as we speak. If you turn back without me, who knows what trouble you might encounter? Besides, I believe in your abilities—both of you."

Duxan and Feslen exchanged glances at the last comment but said nothing as Duxan warily accepted the mace. He had gripped the sharp end by mistake, and that drew a chuckle from both Feslen and Ka-Wei.

"This is how you do it, Duxan. Most of the mace is sharp for a good reason. Unfortunately, you may find out why too soon. Here, grip the less obvious handle like a staff," the Prince instructed Duxan with infinite patience. Duxan held the tip of the mace with unease and looked over at Feslen and Ka-Wei for approval. "Swing it a few times to get a good feel," Ka-Wei recommended. "It'll be like using a plowshare. You look like a natural."

Duxan did as he was told, and the surprisingly heavy mace started to feel more natural to him. "You should go home and warn your family, Feslen," Ka-Wei turned to Feslen.

"If this murderer intends to strike at my friends and family, I need to know who he is and how to defeat him," Feslen gulped. *Don't treat me like a child, Ka-Wei.* He thought to himself, *I already get enough of that from my family,* but he did not voice this opinion.

"Be prepared to run. Don't try to save us if we are in trouble," Ka-Wei said.

"The three of us standing together are stronger than one of us alone," Feslen replied. Ka-Wei smiled at Feslen's remark.

Blood had spattered on the school's sign with the golden dragon engraved on it. The huge sign in front of the school swung back and forth, creaking eerily. The golden characters carved into the ancient wood seemed to be marked up with something other than the *Ninkattas'* blades and special weapons.

The three nodded to each other, formed a triangle, and entered with steady purpose. Ka-Wei led the way. Ka-Wei stopped at the entrance one more time and said, "If we are dealing with real *Ninkattas*, then we must be wary."

"What are *Ninkattas*?" Duxan asked.

"Warriors who hide in the shadows," answered the Prince. "They are trained in the dark and use the shadows as their ally. They often attack with weapons called throwing stars to wound their enemies and confuse them. They are deadly in the Martial Arts as well. Most *Ninkattas* are tough to deal with, even in single combat, like the Emperor's Sabers."

Duxan nodded and Feslen gulped. Both brothers nodded again. Feslen's inner voice screamed even louder, and his body shuddered. But Feslen ignored all this as they pushed the creaking doors open.

6

AMBUSH 埋伏

The bitter **smell of** death hung in the air. The well-lit and comfortable room did little to cheer the companions. Feslen tried to hold tears back but they flowed free. The sight of the dead bodies would haunt Feslen forever. "Why, Ka-Wei?" Feslen murmured, doing his best to dry his face.

Ka-Wei did not answer immediately and knelt and prayed over the bodies. They had found *Shurikens,* the small, handheld Martial Arts weapons used by *Ninkattas,* embedded in some of the bodies. He moved on and found four more victims near the bodies of their attackers. Next to one of Master Chai's departed students, the Prince discovered a servant's ring from the House Wien. He examined some other bodies that turned out to be those of servants from the House Wien. The bodies of servants of the Houses of Wien and of Chai lay side by side. Ka-Wei frowned and considered this latest evidence.

Duxan's eyes darted into the gloom, and he gripped the mace tighter. Shattered furniture, smeared blood, scattered weapons, everything lay disturbed, but nothing had been taken. Master Chai's school, like his home, housed rare valuables. The Shakien Blades on the northern wall remained in place. An original third-century Shang Vase on the oak desk was undisturbed. No obvious scratches showed on the rare paintings of the First Dragon Kings by Kushiko, the fifteenth-century Joppone artist.

Even the second Xsi-Arak blade in its display case in the middle of the school's entrance hall was there. "So, this is not a robbery," Feslen said.

"Indeed," Ka-Wei said. "Yet they took your family goods."

The brothers frowned at that. "*Ninkattas?*" Feslen grimaced.

Ka-Wei nodded. As soon as he had discovered the murders, he should have raised an alarm to his King, but Ka-Wei's first loyalty lay with Master Chai. Ka-Wei wanted answers. Someone had killed his men without mercy and thus sullied his Honor. "These men will forever have a place of Honor," he murmured.

The three continued on and entered the hallway that led to Master Chai's room. They found more bodies of Master Chai's servants, apprentices, and even several teachers. All had been slain except for one, the disabled student from the East whose name escaped Feslen at the moment. The poor wretch groaned at the sound of approaching feet.

"Kuan Hu," Ka-Wei said, kneeling in front of the broken man. He leaned against the wall, his body cut open and bleeding. The wound was open from the back. His skin looked pale and bleak, as if poisoned; his shallow breath rattled; his hand twitched violently. A peculiar odor of decayed flowers came from the man along with some other unidentifiable scent.

"My Prince!" whispered the dying man. "You must leave now! They took us from behind; they have spies in the House!"

"Try not to talk," Ka-Wei murmured. He placed his Xsi-Arak blade down on the ground and fell into meditation. He moved his hands and feet in the Tenth Dragon Technique of Healing. Feslen watched, entranced, while Duxan kept his eyes open for the approach of enemies.

Ka-Wei's energy expanded outwards from the wounded man, washing over the group. Kuan Hu's groaning stopped. The Prince then reached into his pouches and took out a silver needle for acupuncture. He mouthed a healing prayer and continued to perform the Tenth Dragon Technique of Healing, followed by the Third Dragon Step of "Calm the Body of Pain." He recalled his lessons of anatomy and medical sciences and found Kuan Hu's meridian points. The Prince wove the silver needle in a triangular pattern in the air, chanting at the same time and then pointed the needle and moved in nearer as if to puncture the skin. He said a healing prayer three times and removed the needle from the meridian points, returning it to his pouch. Black blood spurted from Kuan Hu's wounds, but his skin color and breathing returned to normal. Before he passed out, he said "Be careful, my Prince, and thank you."

Feslen watched with awe. He had heard of the Healing Steps and the acupuncture cures but had never witnessed them. He saw Duxan's eyes moisten with tears. I can't believe Ka-Wei managed to hide those skills from me even though I've known him all my life! Feslen thought, greatly impressed with the Prince.

Ka-Wei's body relaxed a moment and he said, "I know I shouldn't have used that energy, but he was poisoned and dying quickly. I couldn't leave a man to die like that."

"What do you mean when you say that you shouldn't have used that energy?" Feslen asked.

"Just remember not to exert too much energy, especially if you expect combat up ahead," Ka-Wei answered. Then he gave Feslen a sideways glance and wondered if the boy had absorbed the training lessons he had just given to him. Feslen's eyes sparkled in eager understanding. The Prince broke into a quick, secret smile. We weren't wrong about Feslen's quick mind, Master Chai. There's more here than meets the eye with this boy, Ka-Wei thought.

"How do you know the wounded man isn't a spy?" Duxan asked.

"Kuan Hu was one of the first students Master Chai recruited," Ka-Wei replied. "Besides, a gaping wound from the back like that could only have been the work of a *Ninkatta*." The Prince rose and picked his sword back up.

Okay, but that doesn't necessarily mean he's not a spy, Feslen thought, and he shared a look of agreement with his brother.

"Where's Master Chai?" Duxan asked.

Ka-Wei fell into the Twelfth Dragon Step called "Way of Shadow and Light"; he crouched like a tiger, stork, dragon, and then snake in positions he performed in less than a minute. The young Prince felt all sorts of presences, most of which came in the form of the dead. Although he had mastered the execution of the Twelve Dragon Steps, he did not fully comprehend their deeper meaning. He searched for his former mentor, Master Chai.

How odd that he doesn't seem to be present, Ka-Wei thought. Distorted energies attacked the Prince's stable mind and he groaned a bit. He shook himself and came out of his meditative state even as his friends asked him if he was all right.

"Yes, Master Chai warned me not to do that Step too often," Ka-Wei chuckled. "I'm not a true master of his Steps. It's strange, I couldn't sense his presence."

"Let's look in his room at least," Feslen said. The three checked his darkened room. The candle stand had been knocked over, and the lanterns on the walls were unlit. The furniture seemed undisturbed. A lone window allowed little light in the room. The three left, frowning with puzzlement.

"I feel like we're being watched. We should leave right now," Feslen whispered, feeling queasy.

"I agree with the Kid. Shouldn't we warn someone?" Duxan asked in nervous tones. Feslen glanced at him in astonishment. Duxan burned with shame and anger. As the older brother, he had wanted to hide his feelings to protect Feslen from further discomfort. It seemed as though Feslen already recovered from his earlier stages of disgust. Then they noticed that Ka-Wei's Xsi-Arak glowed for a brief instant when he gripped it above his chest. He looked at the two brothers and at Feslen in particular for answers. Duxan blinked in shock.

"Magical?" Ka-Wei asked.

Feslen started to answer when he heard another groan. "Ka-Wei, I feel Mei Xue's spirit beating, although she has been weakened!"

Ka-Wei said nothing, but his face showed disbelief. Having spent so much time alone, Feslen had long relied on his heightened senses and instincts. "Trust me," he said, pushing his way past the two for a moment.

"Hold on a minute, little brother! It may be a trap or worse. You aren't armed," Duxan said. Feslen paused, surprised. "Please, little brother." Feslen nodded. They edged forward with caution.

Feslen sensed wrongness. "Mei Xue's in trouble," Feslen said.

"How do you know?" Duxan asked as Ka-Wei gave him a skeptical look.

"I just do," Feslen said and flushed.

Without warning, Duxan pushed Feslen to the ground. Three figures clothed in black seemed to materialize from the darkness itself. Feslen remained calm and stayed out of harm's way by flattening himself against the wall. He saw his brother attempting a clumsy parry and then, within seconds, one of them penetrated his defense and dealt him a blow on the left shoulder with a *ninkaa-to*, a short black blade.

"Honorless *Ninkatta*," Ka-Wei spat and drew his silver-edged Xsi-Arak. "Prepare to feel the mete of justice."

"I think not, Prince of Chiendong. My family has long waited the opportunity to stain your Honor," whispered the lead *Ninkatta*.

"Prepare to die!" The rather tall man in black leapt, drawing a glowing, black *Ninkatta* sword with a serrated blade.

Feslen was as surprised as the attacker who felled Duxan when he saw Duxan start to move again. The first attack would have downed most ordinary citizens for the entire remainder of the battle. Nevertheless, shaking himself out of his reverie, Duxan managed to dodge the next blow. He tried to defend himself, but he slackened and dropped his mace. One of the *nirahkos* who was beating him suddenly stopped, under orders from the leader who attacked Ka-Wei with savagery.

Ka-Wei leapt aside from the first attack with eased grace and then deflected the second, third, and fourth attacks quicker than the brothers could follow the action. The Prince ducked and rolled as the fifth attack whirled over him. He estimated his distance from the brothers and the other two *nirahko* and sprung from his roll to land right in between them. The *Ninkatta* and his minions grunted in surprise.

"This is for Ko-ler!" Ka-Wei said when the attacker lost his footing. Ka-Wei slashed one of them before he managed a parry. The *nirahkos* fell without a sound.

"Ka-Wei!" Feslen shouted in warning, but his tongue fell lame.

Ka-Wei felt the rush of the second *nirahkos'* movement well before he had even started his thrust and dodged to the right. With a one-handed slash to the left, the Prince gutted the *nirahkos*, who fell without a sound. "And that is for Lo-Na and his family," Ka-Wei growled.

Duxan yelled his warning, "Ka-Wei! Look out!"

Feslen watched agape as the movements of the *Ninkatta* and the Prince blurred. The *Ninkatta* leapt towards Ka-Wei, his blade in both hands. The younger Raster caught subtle movement from the *Ninkatta* and shouted a warning to Ka-Wei. The dark-clothed man raised his sword to waist height and started to bring out a secondary weapon. But Ka-Wei was ready. Performing the Seventh Dragon Step and the Third Dragon Technique in one action, his body collapsed like a spring, and the attacker's sword missed him completely. Then, Ka-Wei kicked out with one leg at the man's stomach and whirled his sword to deflect the man's secondary weapon, a metal hand claw. The *Ninkatta* crashed against the wall, struggled to stand, and said, "Cursed Prince, you should think of the welfare of others." Before the companions reacted, the *Ninkatta* sprang from the wall and grabbed Duxan in a choke hold.

"Murderous dog! There will be no justice for you today!" the Prince yelled, taking a starting run at the *Ninkatta*.

Duxan choked, "Ka-Wei! Help!"

The Prince looked at his young friend, torn between what to do. A throaty female spoke, "Don't you dare take the Honor away from me, Keizao."

"Don't use my real name, you fool!" the *Ninkatta* hissed.

A sound of female chanting and then a smell of burnt banana leaf signaled someone casting a spell. Light flashed and the friends shouted in surprise. The spell blinded both Ka-Wei and Duxan but Feslen was able to withstand it.

So that's the light spell, Feslen thought as he studied the spell caster. A sorceress! he thought. Feslen saw a slender silhouette of a woman in her late thirties or early forties wearing an embroidered white gown with wind symbols on it. Her dark hair was tucked up in a bun secured with chopsticks. Her amber eyes showed the years of endured pain or suffering. Her angular nose resembled Ka-Wei's. For a moment, Feslen felt sympathy for her. She wore an amulet of the Emperor, and a ring signified her married status. But her left hand showed her own symbol, an amber ring with the Wind Elemental carved in it. Several pouches hung around her thin waist.

Duxan whispered to the *Ninkatta*, "Let me go! If you kill me, your Honor will go down." He felt the *Ninkatta*'s grip loosen, so he continued to speak, "Listen, you are a real warrior. Real warriors fight people who know how to use weapons, not unarmed boys like me." Duxan nodded to the Prince, and he turned to face the Sorceress. Duxan sighed with inward relief when he felt the *Ninkatta*'s grip relinquish all together.

The Prince had reacted sluggishly, almost as though he were afraid. Feslen only surmised what went through his friend's mind. Although Chiendong's government allowed the practice of magic, mages cast their spells less often than the common populace believed. Feslen realized through Ka-Wei's stumbling action that in this battle he fought a magician in close quarters for the first time.

"No, Jerenko-I, he is mine. You are wrong to take him from me," said the *Ninkatta*.

"You are wrong," cried the Sorceress, even as she reached into her pouches and pulled out yet another banana leaf scroll. She chanted and tossed the scroll at the companions. The scroll burned underneath their feet, and, all of a sudden, the cries of a thousand sorceresses invaded them from all directions. Ka-Wei groaned and slumped, and Duxan covered his ears and closed his eyes. Somehow, Feslen had escaped the effects of the spell. Ka-Wei shook off his initial daze and advanced towards her, locating her by voice.

"Why have you attacked us?" Feslen asked.

"This doesn't concern you, little one, not yet. I don't know why he ordered me to look at you," said the Sorceress, her eyes focused on the Prince. She turned her gaze on Feslen for the first time, and as she studied him her face paled. "Can it be true then? Are you the One? You radiate the Mark of Chu Jung!" She exclaimed. Her body and jaw trembled as she continued to murmur to herself, at first out loud, and then, finally, her voice faded all together: "His *Chi*, his energy, I've never felt anything like it. Could the Emperor be right?"

Understanding nothing, Feslen blinked in blankness at the Sorceress and mumbled, "Come again?"

"She's right. We are here to discuss the Prince's future," the *Ninkatta* interrupted him.

"You can discuss this with my sword!" Ka-Wei shouted and leapt in complete blindness as he attacked the Sorceress. Feslen winced in anticipation, knowing full well that the Sorceress would have a magical protective barrier around her. Ka-Wei yelped as his sword banged against a hard invisible shield. The Sorceress laughed.

"Not even a parley? Why your fool uncle chose you to be the next heir is beyond me!" The Sorceress scorned.

"What does this have to do with my uncle?" Ka-Wei said, as he blinked and shook his head.

Feslen understood that the spell's effects had started to wear off, and he tried not to smile openly in relief. The battlefield would soon be even again.

"This is not your affair. You and your friends are as good as dead, once I am done with you and her, that is," promised the *Ninkatta*. Ka-Wei turned from the Sorceress and stalked the *Ninkatta*.

"I can aid you with more than this, Ka-Wei, nephew. I offer you my allegiance after you return my Honor," the Sorceress said.

"I don't ally myself with terrorists and murderers," Ka-Wei spat. "Why do I need allies? What have I done?"

"You'll see soon enough."

"And you, *Ninkatta*? What have you to offer me?" Ka-Wei asked.

"Don't listen to her lies, Prince. I fight with true Honor, unlike magicians."

"You are a fool, *Ninkatta*," the Sorceress said.

Feslen knew Ka-Wei was bidding for time and recognized that Ka-Wei must have also felt an intense throbbing of the heart. Feslen felt it too, a faint stirring of life within this terribly blood-stained school. Ka-Wei leapt after the Sorceress, and again his sword banged against her invisible shield.

"Jerenko!" a new voice rang out. Master Chai! Feslen thought with relief and almost fainted. Everyone turned at the new arrival. A sharp-featured sixty-year-old man with glistening black hair, dressed in a simple yellow cloth, appeared out of nowhere and immediately hurled a handful of yellow dust at the Sorceress and *Ninkatta* before they could react. Master Chai sported unusual sword scars and minor wounds on his well-muscled chest. Most of his clothes had been torn from him. His neat, long hair was disheveled, and his sharp, oval-shaped black eyes burned with fire. Feslen cheered the Master's appearance on the scene.

Out of control, the Sorceress coughed repeatedly as the *Ninkatta* attempted a parry with his *ninkaa-to* against a roundhouse kick from Master Chai. The Master's kick cracked the *Ninkatta*'s primary weapon and slammed the invading warrior against the wall. "You will pay for this, old man!" the Sorceress declared, still gasping for breath. The enemies turned to flee.

A trail of poisoned smoke followed the witch. The poison also surrounded the companions. Master Chai, Feslen, Duxan, Ka-Wei, and the *Ninkatta* all caught the brunt of it. Ka-Wei coughed once, sputtered briefly, and fell to his knees like his friends, but his body did not twitch. He sprung back quicker than a tiger to his feet. Even though Feslen felt like his throat had constricted and his head had split open, he saw the shock on Ka-Wei's face. Ka-Wei had remained almost completely unaffected by the poison even though his companions were still coughing wretchedly. The *Ninkatta* fumbled to put on a gas mask. During this time, Master Chai closed his eyes to meditate for a brief second. Duxan squatted on the ground gasping for air.

In a flurry, gowns flowing about her, the Sorceress turned towards the room of Master Chai's daughter, Mei Xue. Ka-Wei paused to check on his friends, but Feslen waved him on. The Prince nodded and ran after the Sorceress. Feslen checked his brother. Master Chai finished meditating and went after the *Ninkatta*.

"There shall be another time for you both, Prince, old man!" The *Ninkatta* shouted and threw down an object and escaped as smoke filled the room.

Together, Duxan and Feslen raced towards Mei Xue's room. Ka-Wei entered first. The dark-eyed Prince gasped for fresh air as the sudden smoke curled around him. He spotted Mei Xue struggling against the Sorceress who was casting a spell on her. Mei Xue did not seem to see him, even as Ka-Wei struggled to reach her. When Feslen and Duxan appeared, Mei Xue screamed, "Feslen! Help me!"

"Mei Xue!" Feslen shouted. Then she fell limp and the Sorceress picked her up.

"Let her go, witch!" Ka-Wei shouted.

The Sorceress turned, her eyes wide, "You are still alive! I thank you for coming, Prince. Come to my homeland, or this girl will die." She waved her hands, chanted, and pointed at Mei Xue's precious antique fans, which exploded into flames. She waved her fingers and fires expanded from her fingertips. She directed the fires with the power of the wind! The fires leapt and danced, burning any and all perishable goods.

"I will never come to your homeland! You will surrender and face the King's justice," Ka-Wei spat. He lashed out with his Xsi-Arak.

The Sorceress laughed and dodged. She chanted and reached into her pouches again and sprinkled metal particles around her. A bolt of lightning rushed from her hands and struck Ka-Wei, singeing him. He shook it off and strode forward. "My, you're stubborn," she hissed.

The Sorceress chanted again, reached into her pockets, and brought forth one of Mei Xue's pillows. She shook out the pillow, and feathers flew every where and animated into living bats! The bats danced around Ka-Wei and exploded into dancing fiery lights. The lights seared the Prince, but he ignored the burning sensation. Ka-Wei calculated his next attack and made a thrust with his sword, but she dodged and he missed. She had avoided his three calculated blows with skill, making him angrier and angrier. She laughed, "You're Master Chai's best student and the kingdom's hero?"

To Ka-Wei, it felt as though his blows did indeed touch her, but her wind magic had prevented his sword from actually hitting her. She chanted, taking a small paper puppet of a wind spirit from the secret folds of her dress.

"Ka-Wei! Look out! She's summoning a Wind Elemental!" Feslen shouted. Ka-Wei nodded, but he lost his footing and tripped when the huge Wind Elemental emerged from a small vortex of wind. This creature stood ten feet high, ripping apart the ceiling of the school. Flaming beams came crashing down. Its opaque body was composed of air, water, and minerals. Ka-Wei slashed at it, but his sword went right through it. "She's run out of tricks, Ka-Wei! She's using her top spell!" Feslen said, trying to reach his friend.

But rage entered Feslen when he saw Mei Xue handled roughly by the Sorceress. The astonishing fight continued. The Wind Elemental pounded away at Ka-Wei. The Prince parried every other blow. Due to the creature's magical nature, he was the most imposing opponent Ka-Wei had ever fought. Feslen cried out incoherently when he saw Ka-Wei in peril and the Sorceress chanting for yet another spell.

"Ka-Wei! She's getting away!" Duxan shouted as he stood on the periphery of the action, overcome by the flames' intensity. Ka-Wei nodded, choking as the Wind Elemental pushed him down and tried to suck his breath out. In a desperate act, Ka-Wei heaved his sword right through the Wind Elemental, aiming it at the fleeing sorceress! She cried out in alarm. The sword's flight had interrupted her spell.

Feslen raced through the fires, a burning beam almost crushing him as he reached Ka-Wei. Feslen shouted at the Wind Elemental, "Leave my friend alone!" Suddenly, an idea struck him and he reached deep within the air. He saw the glowing particles of air molecules and grabbed hold of the Wind Elemental's hand. The giant creature roared as if in pain and shock. Feslen corralled the flames and shaped them into a hammer. The hammer smashed into the Wind Elemental. "Go home!" he commanded it. The Wind Elemental roared with what seemed like keen pleasure and abruptly vanished.

Ka-Wei, Duxan, and the Sorceress looked at Feslen, totally stunned. The flames raged unchecked, and Feslen gasped for air, his energy spent. Ka-Wei reached for his sword and tried to wrestle it away from the Sorceress as she chanted again. The Prince managed to retrieve his sword, but the Sorceress had vanished, taking Mei Xue with her. The school's roof collapsed around them…

"Mei Xue gone, my Honor, my men," Ka-Wei moaned. He fell to his knees, ready to plunge his heart with his own sword. But he urged his friend to get out of the room. His ability to speak and think blurred as the smoke filled his lungs. Ka-Wei's intense, dead-eyed look stopped Feslen. The Prince growled at him again, "Go! Get out of here!"

"No!" Feslen shouted. "What's more important, your life or your Honor?"

Before either one of them could react, a sudden wind pushed the friends apart. "It is my Honor that was unavenged today, Prince. You will have to come someday," laughed the Sorceress. In a gaseous form, the Sorceress bent down and picked up the Prince's sword. She carried an unconscious Mei Xue in her vaporous arms. The two friends had no time to take action. The magical wind had pressed them against the wall. The Sorceress vanished, leaving the friends to struggle against her spell.

With effort, Feslen reached the rigid Ka-Wei, who screamed, "I have no Honor! I want to die!"

"No! I will not let you die," Feslen stated. "Mei Xue's been taken from me. I won't lose another friend to the Sorceress."

The roar of the flames thundered around them, drowning out Duxan's cries. Duxan saw his brother and best friend surrounded by the fire and the burning pieces of falling beams. Master Chai and his remaining servants and students came to put out the fire.

"There's no way they can make it," one of the students murmured.

Nevertheless, Feslen, unscathed, half-dragged and half-carried Prince Ka-Wei out of the angry flames. The Prince lapsed into a slight coma and bled from various wounds. Duxan, overjoyed, embraced Feslen. His eyes widened as he found his brother's skin was actually cool to the touch. Feslen grinned and, before he too collapsed into a coma, said simply, "I did it. I did it."

7

GUILT 內疚

Feslen shut his eyes; it pained him to think about the ambush. A few days had passed and Ka-Wei remained in a semi-unconscious state. The Prince was being cared for in the New Priests' House of Healing. This House of Healing was in the King's Palace of Judgment. Sick patients, soldiers wounded in battle, and victims of crime came here to heal. Higher ranked New Priests came to attend Prince Ka-Wei while he rested in a private room. The Raster brothers were allowed a visit, but instead they were shown the door. Some of Ka-Wei's other family members came to visit, but they did not acknowledge the Raster brothers. A parade of politicians, nobles, and royalty came by to greet Ka-Wei. A stream of soldiers, including retired or disabled soldiers, visited the Hero Prince. The peasants who heard about the incident were not invited, however. But Feslen and Duxan knew Ka-Wei would not have minded if they came to see him. Ka-Wei fancied himself as a "people's Hero." The King, who was also Ka-Wei's uncle, did not come by. The New Priest physicians continued their frantic work of trying to revive the Prince. The brothers sat by the door on two wooden chairs, Feslen nearer to the entrance. He kept peeking in.

    The New Priests kept taking the Prince's blood with empty vials and dirty needles. They chanted in an odd language and shook the vials. Then one of the New Priest physicians took out a large cylindrical object and placed it above Ka-Wei's heart, in between his eyes and above his stomach. Each time the New Priest chanted, the object glowed in a different color. When it was above the heart, it glowed gold, and a fluid mixed with blood and something else entered the object. When they placed it above the stomach, it glowed silver, and above the forehead it glowed blue. The blue was most intense. Feslen pondered this even as the New Priest phyisican placed *Shi-Pang Jyang*, a type of cooling herb, onto each spot. Heat escaped from the Prince's body each time this procedure was done, but it was repeated despite the protests of Beizung's top physicians. Feslen wanted to stop them, but Duxan shook his head. He said, "They did that to you too, Kid."

Feslen frowned and started to speak, but the brothers heard loud footsteps and looked down the hall and saw Captain Garland enter with half a dozen soldiers. He thanked the Raster brothers for their heroic actions. He posted guards at the entrance and by the Prince's bedside. "By the way," Captain Garland said as he paused to speak to the brothers, "I owe you a great deal of debt and gratitude, as does the rest of the country, especially to you, Feslen."

Feslen thanked him and returned to his hangdog expression and hunched over posture. He kept looking back into the room at the comatose Prince and the busy New Priests. Tears formed in Feslen's eyes. He was startled when he felt a hand upon his shoulder and turned to face Captain Garland. His sea-worn skin is more shriveled than wet scallion, Feslen thought, studying the old man.

"You did a fine job, Raster. You've grown much since I last saw you and your brother," Captain Garland said smiling. "Don't worry about Ka-Wei. The Prince is tough. He will pull through." Feslen nodded and swallowed some of his tears. "Don't worry about him, Raster," Captain Garland continued. "Don't blame yourself. The Prince knew the odds. In fact, you are quite the Hero."

Feslen nodded.

"Should we really draw more attention to the Prince?" Duxan asked Captain Garland, pointing to the guards. "After all, the Prince did find evidence of…"

"Hush, don't speak of it here," Captain Garland said, lowering his voice and gesturing in the direction of the New Priest Healer and his apprentices. Duxan nodded.

The older man's wizened face wrinkled into more worry. He wasn't wearing any armor, but he displayed his sword to the Healing House. Captain Garland commented, "If necessary, I think you two should be guarded every hour on the hour. I know my boy wouldn't want his best friends to be assassinated on my watch."

Duxan smiled and said, "We'll be fine. Besides, your guards will be enough."

"Are you two boys, er, I mean young men," Captain Garland corrected himself, "doing well? If there's anything you need, just ask me." Duxan and Feslen nodded.

Then Captain Garland, the Captain of the King's army and former mentor of Ka-Wei, stood by the young Prince's bedside a moment and watched him in silence. He turned to the Raster brothers and studied them. "You know, young Feslen," Captain Garland began, his voice choked up in sadness, "it pains me to see young people in such situations as this. I remember when my boy Kai-Wei came to see you when you were ill. I am glad he has such loyal friends."

"Thank you, Captain," Duxan answered since Feslen was too embarrassed to answer. He glanced at his younger brother and sighed, guessing what went on in him. Feslen disliked it when people brought up his illness and the fact that he owed people for help. One of Feslen's private dreams and goals was to become independent and healthy. To him, having to be dependent on people hurt, even if he truly needed their help. To Feslen, being a burden to everyone and having help from the people he met was a dishonor to his soul.

"I'm sure you have duties to attend to, Captain. We will report to you of any changes in the Prince," Duxan said as he stood and bowed. The three of them and the four soldiers who guarded Ka-Wei all glanced at the still form on the bed.

"Very well, good day, gentlemen," Captain Garland said and bowed. Duxan bowed back. The Captain left with his remaining entourage.

"It's my fault he's in there. I should be there, not him," Feslen said under his breath.

Duxan patted his brother and said, "No, it's not, Kid. Ka-Wei made his decision to enter that room. Don't blame yourself; you did more than your share of heroic actions." Duxan continued, "With the help of the New Priests' top physician and Beizung's top physician, he should be fine."

"You really believe in those educated types, don't you, big brother?" Feslen asked with a sneer, his sarcasm dripping on the word "educated."

Duxan sighed, 'I know, I know. You don't think much of their years of study. But they do know about the human anatomy. Their herbal remedies and Far Western medicines have saved countless lives."

"And have killed countless others," Feslen snorted, his eyes on Ka-Wei's still form.

"True, but you need to make mistakes and learn to find a cure for everyone," Duxan conceded and then added, "Magic is like that too."

Feslen said nothing but glared at Duxan a moment. Then he said with such quietness that his brother was forced to lean close to him to hear his next words, "If you hadn't been there, Dr. Li would have killed me with his random experiments and herbs."

"True, but he did ultimately save your life from the infection," Duxan said.

Feslen shrugged and returned to his worried study of Kai-Wei. A silence fell over the brothers as they sat outside the Healing House's entrance and waited for Ka-Wei to recover. Duxan read a religious book about Ja-Dao and prayed for Ka-Wei's recovery. Feslen looked this way and that and stared at his brother. He poked Duxan a bit, who seemed intent on studying the book and praying. Then he fished a jade ring from the pocket of his breeches. This ring was carved in the shape of a phoenix. Feslen gripped it and sighed. "Why her? Why Mei Xue of all people? She didn't deserve it," Feslen said, and he bit down on his tongue, hard. He did not cry out in pain, only in shame. "It's my fault she's been abducted. My fault. If I were only stronger in magic," Feslen growled.

"I'm sorry, Mei Xue. So sorry!" Then memories flooded Feslen, and he cried out again, "Mei Xue!"

"*Mei Xue!*" *A six-year-old Feslen cried.*

"*Help me, Feslen!*" *Mei Xue cried. She had twisted her leg when she lost her footing on the slippery crags while running from a pack of hungry wolves. These wolves, however, were not like normal wolves. Magic had changed and mutated these wolves into giant wolves, three times the size of their wild cousins. The two kids explored and played around some old ruins near Master Chai's home. These, of course, were the ruins which Master Chai forbade them to go near. Like all children, they did not pay attention. Now they wished they had listened to Master Chai. For his part, Feslen was coughing a lot because of the rain. He felt the water seep into his skin and bones, sapping his strength. He was the one hiding in their game of hide-and-seek. He had bolted out of his spot when he heard her cry out. In normal circumstance, he knew she could take care of herself, since her father had trained her in the Martial Arts. But as soon as Feslen heard the wolf cries, he knew they were more dangerous than ordinary wolves. Somehow he could feel their twisted energies.*

Feslen's face contorted in worry and agony, for he was in pain himself. His blood disorder had acted up again and he did not know what to do. The odds weren't good: four mutated wolves against two children. The wolves surrounded Mei Xue and she screamed as one leapt towards her. Feslen picked up the nearest tree branch and heaved it at the wolves with all his might. It managed to hit the lead wolf, who then turned his attention to Feslen. Feslen shouted at him, "Yes, come on! Chase me instead!" Then he tripped and fell flat on his face, almost knocking himself out. The wolves sprung.

"*Oh no you don't!*" *Mei Xue shouted and grabbed the lunging wolf by its tail. The wolf yelped and dropped Feslen. It turned and snapped at Mei Xue, who shrieked and scrambled to get away. One more wolf followed its leader as the last two stayed to attack Feslen. Fear overwhelmed Feslen and he covered his eyes with his arms in a fruitless defensive gesture. Then he heard Mei Xue's scream. He saw the wolf clamp down on her delicate arm!*

"No! You leave her alone!" Feslen screamed and lifted an arm. Energy swirled around him; the ground shook. And then Feslen blanked out.

"Feslen? Hey, Kid?" Duxan asked softly, shaking his brother, who seemed to have fallen asleep. Feslen's arms cradled his head as he hunched over. Something glittery at Feslen's feet caught Duxan's eyes and he picked it up, a jade ring carved into a phoenix. Duxan sighed and whispered, "I'm sorry, Kid."

"Duxan, Mei Xue's gone and Ka-Wei's hurt, because of me," Feslen blubbered. "Why? It's not fair. These things should happen to people like Sae-Jyung or Ai-Yen instead."

Duxan was surprised at his brother's wishing it had happened to other people. He sighed and patted Feslen and said, "I don't know. Think of it as an experience. We'll get her back. Just wait and see. Ka-Wei's tough. He'll be back on his feet today. Then he'll go after Mei Xue, I promise."

Feslen lifted his head, his eyes swollen and his nose dripping, and said in a small voice, "I feel so helpless! I hope Mei Xue can hold out."

Duxan nodded and replied, "Me too, bro, me too."

"She's always believed in me, Duxan. Why don't I believe in myself?"

"It takes times to build confidence, Kid. You did an exceptional job in your first combat situation."

Feslen gave Duxan a sick smile and looked about for the jade ring he had dropped. Duxan grinned and handed it back to him. Feslen sighed and studied the ring some more. *"I give this ring to you, Fessy,"* eight-year-old Mei Xue had told him the next day. *She gave him a long kiss on the cheek, making him blush. "You saved my life. You're my hero. You were so brave. Remember, I will always have faith in you." Then she handed him a jade ring with a phoenix carved on it. Feslen gasped and said, "B-but, your mother gave you this, you shouldn't…"*

"Then you know how much this means to me," Mei Xue whispered and hugged him tight.

The scent of aromatic herbs hit the air, mixing with the strange medicinal smells of the New Priests and the Healing House. Duxan nudged his little brother, who hung his head. Tears filled Feslen's eyes. "Mages," Duxan whispered. Feslen's head snapped up in attention almost instantly.

They noticed a tall, thin mage in a green and white striped robe enter the hallway along with a short, plump mage in a pink robe. The pink robed mage, a middle-aged woman with a pasty yellow face and short brown hair, turned to the brothers and asked in a somewhat husky tone, "Is the Prince in there?" Feslen nodded. Except for her robes, she showed no outward appearance of being a mage, unlike her companion, the green and white robed mage, who turned, thanking them. Hanging on her thin waist were several pouches filled with aromatic herbs.

She smiled gently and said, "Your friend will be all right. Especially now that we have arrived." Yin Yang symbols glittered on their backs as they turned. A pleasant aroma of herbs and the sharp smell of the root of the Jungai plant hit the brothers' noses.

Duxan went back to his book and Feslen, though intrigued by the appearance of the two magicians, sat in a dull state. His mind was too full of guilt, his heart empty. Hours went by. The brothers peeked in and, to their great relief, heard Ka-Wei's deep inhalations of breath.

The two mages left without a word, just a slight nod. A New Priest acolyte ushered the brothers into the room at Ka-Wei's request. "You've been crying, Feslen," Ka-Wei murmured, his voice sounding sleepy. Feslen nodded and ran over to hug the Prince, but the guards stopped him.

"It's all right, Lei Ohm, let him," Ka-Wei ordered the guard in a tired voice.

Feslen embraced his friend. "I'm sorry for letting you down, Ka-Wei…I…"

"Nonsense, Feslen. You did well, better than me," Ka-Wei chuckled. "Don't worry. I will report it to the King, in detail. We will go after Mei Xue." "But how are you holding up, Feslen?" the Prince asked after the boy finally released his embrace.

"Better, thanks. Better than you, at least."

"Don't worry. I'll do the worrying about Feslen for the both of us," Duxan said with a chuckle. Feslen gave his brother a quick grimace and then ignored him for a second.

"How are you doing, Ka-Wei?" Feslen asked. "I hope you aren't still thinking of suicide or taking the Oath to an extreme…"

Ka-Wei frowned and took his time to choose his words. He looked at Duxan, who nodded with understanding. At least someone was mature enough to understand, he thought to himself. "You are an amazing young man, Feslen. How you managed to carry me out, I don't know. I think you understand enough about Honor that I am indebted to you. So, once my debt to you is taken care of and balanced out, I'll worry about my other aspects of Honor."

Feslen held a sigh in check. He knew which "other aspects" of Honor the Prince meant. In terms of Honor, the possibility of a clean slate for a warrior or even a commoner only happens when all matter of dishonor in any form has been negated. Debt, for instance, takes first and foremost importance for a WuSha, especially debt referred to tax collectors or favors owed to friends, family, or Ancestral Spirits. Feslen suspected that he understood Ka-Wei's thoughts about his Honor: the slaughter of his men was a huge stain, of course; Mei Xue had been abducted; his former mentor's school had been attacked and defaced; and the innocent lives of the servants had been taken, not to mention the Prince's family heirloom being taken by an enemy. Feslen sighed and Ka-Wei understood his friend's sigh.

Ka-Wei shooed out everyone who was not one of his friends. When the guards left, they discussed the situation. "Do you think the ambush was intended for all of us?" Feslen asked. No doubt that it was, Feslen thought.

"I'm not sure," Ka-Wei responded and continued, "But I can guarantee that there's more to this than just petty revenge by my aunt. The *Ninkatta* only hire themselves out to the richest people in all of Hahn-Hah. I found one of the *Ninkatta*'s men carrying a symbol that you two would not be happy to see." The Prince motioned to the drawer next to the bed. Feslen opened the top drawer and gasped at what he saw:

the less well-known symbol of the New Priests' Dragon Organization, a dragon holding a serrated sword.

"What does this mean?" Duxan asked, picking up the black-colored disc. It was the size of a thumb and smoother than polished glass. He gave it back to Ka-Wei when the Prince asked for it.

The Prince made a fist and gripped the object in his palm with such intensity that it left a red impression when he opened his hand again. "It means the Emperor plans to betray us. Or someone who worked or is working for the Emperor plans to break away from the Emperor. It could be your old friend, Elhong Wien. He is, after all, the Head of the Dragons and New Priests organizations. But I need more proof before accusing such a powerful man."

"Why would the Emperor want to strike Master Chai down? Master Chai advise him every now and then, right?" Feslen asked almost at the same time Duxan did.

Ka-Wei would have nodded if his neck hadn't hurt him so much. He replied with a dry cough, "I'm not sure. I hope you'll ask Master Chai, Feslen. He trusts you, you know. Do an investigation."

"Why should I investigate? All I want is for Mei Xue to be returned home safely, and I know your aunt abducted her. She's our enemy."

"True, for now. I think you should come with me to save her, Feslen. You know her best, and she will be grateful," Ka-Wei began, but Duxan interrupted him. The older Raster brother's face was screwed up in anger.

"Absolutely not, Ka-Wei! I forbid my little brother to go on such a dangerous journey with you. It's hard enough for him doing everyday things," Duxan huffed. "Besides, you forget, our family will strongly object."

"Duxan..." Ka-Wei began, but Feslen interrupted him.

"My brother, this is not about you. Nor is it about me. It's about Mei Xue being kidnapped. It's also my fault and responsibility that she is in the hands of the enemy," Feslen said, his tone bordering on anger.

"How does Mei Xue's abduction become your responsibility or your fault?" Duxan asked. "Have either of you given thought to how Feslen will accomplish a journey such as the one you're proposing, my Prince?"

"I made a promise to Mei Xue once," Feslen said, holding up her gift of the jade ring. "She is my best friend and one of the few women who has ever accepted me for who I am. I can't let her down. As for going on the journey, I don't know. I haven't planned that far. I'll let karma take its course."

"I think Feslen should complete his training with Master Chai first. Duxan, my friend, listen, it's not up to you to decide Feslen's future! Remember when you came to me years ago to ask for help with your brother's health? This is the right time to do it," Ka-Wei said in steady, calm voice.

"You're wrong, my friend. It is up to me and my family to decide whether Feslen goes or not. He's not capable of going, regardless of what he may think," Duxan said, raising his voice in anger.

Feslen growled and kicked aside a chair in his rage. He turned to face Duxan and yelled, "No! You are wrong! You are just as bad as our sister, Mei-Whuay, and our brother, Ai-Yen! Or worse than Mother! They don't think I'm an individual! I don't want you to start thinking that too! If it weren't for me, our friend Ka-Wei would be in a grave right now or at least in the critical burn ward! Mei Xue's important to me! I will go!"

"Feslen, calm down!" Ka-Wei and Duxan said at the same time. Duxan raised his hand in defense and started to speak, but Ka-Wei jumped in first. "Listen, Feslen. Your brother has a point, but so do I. I understand how important Honor is to you and how much Mei Xue means to you. I've seen the two of you play together. Think about the situation this way, Duxan, if it was your best friend in dire straights, wouldn't you risk everything to go find her?"

Duxan sighed and said, "Of course, but the situation isn't the same, Ka-Wei."

"No," Ka-Wei relented a bit, "it isn't. But in a way it is the same. Besides, I want both of you to think of and remember two things. Duxan, your brother believes in himself and so should you. Treat him as a person, not according to what you might think is best for him. That's your parents' job, and you're not his parents. I will talk to them soon. Secondly, do you wish more guilt for your brother? I can't say what Feslen's entire motivation is, but I do know that he feels guilt."

Duxan grew quiet and studied his brother's anguished face. Feslen sat down and buried his face in his hands.

"The last thing I'll mention is that I think Master Chai will actually want him to go. I don't believe my uncle and Emperor will want me to be the one, alone, to look for her, at least, not in an ordinary way," Ka-Wei added.

"Why do you say that?" Duxan murmured, patting Feslen on the back. His brother kept crying and muttering to himself, "Mei Xue! I will come. I promise. I have to!" Feslen sounded like a trapped animal.

Ka-Wei answered, "Let's just say that I think Master Chai holds the key to this entire thing. The Emperor strikes only when forced to it; something has spooked him. I'd guess that the Emperor wants something to do with the materials your family intended to send to Master Chai."

Feslen and Duxan exchanged concerned looks. Duxan even went over to feel his friend's forehead. The Prince chuckled and said, "I'm not feverish, mother hen. Listen, I want your family warned. The Emperor doesn't like dissenters. I believe he thinks that the Wongs don't support him. I don't think your father has ever given outward signs of impertinence, but you can't ever be too sure with what goes on these days."

"You think the attack was planned? By whom? My father doesn't have any enemies," Duxan said, giving Feslen a startled look.

"True, your father's reputation is a good one. He does honest business," Ka-Wei conceded, "but you two don't spend much time with him in business. You don't know who you might anger at the wrong time."

"Why do you think they were after us as well?" Feslen asked.

"Remember the two Joppone scrolls and the map with the places marked? The books on the Prophecy and legends of Gem Stone mountains were also taken," Ka-Wei said.

"They are related? How do you know all this?" Feslen asked, his face screwed up in confusion. "Aren't you spending more time in the North and South than at home of late?"

"Of late," Ka-Wei agreed and tried to laugh, but the pain in his ribs stopped him. "Listen, I don't like being away from home all this time. You two know it. But I purposely leave the country so I can gather information on my own terms."

"Illegally," Feslen mouthed, and Duxan hid his laughter.

Ka-Wei grinned and said, "What, you don't think the last true Shang heir has ears, eyes, and mouthpieces in the castle in addition to other royal players in the country?"

"Yeah, but surely not the Emperor himself," Feslen began with a shake of his head. He knew his friend's political savvy was considered to be unrivaled, but he did not realize how far it went.

The Prince smiled and said, "You never know. Listen, just be prepared."

"Do you think the *Ninkatta* and the Sorceress work for Elhong Wien or even...?" Feslen asked, letting his voice trail off purposely.

"I don't know. I think they all work for the New Priests and the Emperor to some degree, whether they're in league with each other or not remains to be seen," Duxan surmised.

Ka-Wei agreed.

"What about the magic she has? And what did she mean by 'the Mark of Chu Jung'?" Feslen asked.

"I don't know. I wasn't paying much attention while I was getting hammered to pieces by her magic," Ka-Wei laughed. "Listen, she's an important piece of the puzzle, but she's only a piece. The bigger puzzle will become clearer when we set off."

They went on to discuss a few more tactical matters and what they should do to plan for the future. The Prince reassured his friends that everything would work out. They promised to meet in three weeks' time again at Master Chai's. Ka-Wei watched his friends leave. He doubted if they really wanted to know the truth of what was happening in the royal world anyway. He closed his eyes and tried to rest, but his rest was troubled.

8

MEMORIES AT MASTER CHAI'S
回憶蔡大師

Master Chai invited Feslen to return to the school the next week. Feslen dreaded the return so much that he hid in the basement and attic most of the week. Then, when the day came, Duxan forced him out and said, "Just see what the old man wants. Humor him, all right?"

The bright sunny day and birdsong were in stark contrast with Feslen's depressed mood. With great reluctance, Feslen's father allowed him to return to Master Chai's alone at the Master's special request. When Feslen stood on the outskirts of the school grounds, his memories assaulted him once again.

"Let's play a game, Fessy," Mei Xue giggled.

"Dollies?" Feslen asked with a grin. Mei Xue poked him.

"Aww, you know Rei-Rei was the one who wanted to play dolly. This is my grandmother's treasure, not mine," Mei Xue pretended to protest.

Feslen laughed. "Ok, you know what would be cool? I bet I can make your doll come alive," Feslen replied, pointing to one of Mei Xue's dolls.

"Uh-uh, they do make great imaginary friends, Fessy," Mei Xue giggled.

"No, no. I don't mean it that way. Yes, you and Rei-Rei pretend they're alive. Remember Master Yu's magic show?"

"Yes," Mei Xue began.

"Watch," Feslen instructed as he began to chant the words: "I bring myself to the dolls, make earth, wind, and fire be part of their life, or else I would create strife!"

Mei Xue giggled at his chant, even though Feslen recited word for word one of the chants of Master Yu, the Puppeteer. He tried it again and nothing happened.

"You can do it, Feslen! I felt something," she encouraged him, and she stopped giggling even as Feslen growled in frustration.

He smiled as she placed a hand on him and squeezed. He repeated the chant one more time. One of Mei Xue's dolls rose and twirled to Feslen's command! Mei Xue's high pitched scream of delight sent Duxan, Prince Ka-Wei, and Master Chai all running from the Golden Dragon School.

"Unbelievable," Duxan whispered. Feslen had replicated word for word and move for move the Puppeteer's performance.

"Master Chai, can he be trained?" Ka-Wei asked in a voice too deep for a twelve-year-old.

Before the fifty-year-old master replied, the doll wiggled and wrapped itself around Mei Xue in a hug. The two children laughed, but then they started to cry for help when the doll suddenly caught on fire. Ka-Wei and Duxan struggled to wrench the doll away from Mei Xue's leg, but, in a matter of seconds, Master Chai had freed the children with a simple kick.

"No, my Prince. He is too young and undisciplined. But, unlike what I've seen in most young apprentices, Feslen has the ambition and drive to live and succeed. Perhaps in the future he can be trained in magic, but not now."

"Sorry to have wasted your time, Raster brothers," Ka-Wei sighed. Duxan sighed, but Feslen shrugged. Mei Xue gave him a wink and glance. He thought to himself, looking at Master Chai, *I will prove you wrong. I need this.*

For some reason, Mei Xue said to her father, "I've never seen anyone perform a trick at that age. He will be a great mage one day." The brothers could hear what she said even as they parted. Master Chai responded with a grunt.

Feslen sighed, "Mei Xue's faith in me is unwavering for some reason, and I have failed her now. I need training now more than ever, and I will make Master Chai train me. Well, here goes." So he turned up the path to the school. Feeling both guilt and powerful negative energies wash over him, Feslen almost fainted at the school's entrance. But he placed his hand on the knob, opened the door, and entered.

9

MASTER AND STUDENT 师徒

"Master Chai?" Feslen called. Nerves still on edge, he entered the Martial Arts school. He slipped off his sandals and walked down the dim hall. The chill of the remembered attack overwhelmed him. His heart rate increased too rapidly for him to control, his breathing became labored, and his vision blurred. Feslen knew this was not an effect of his chronic blood disease which didn't usually affect his vision this way. "Get a grip on yourself, Feslen!" he scolded himself. Soon his panic attack subsided and he reflected on the sadness and shame he felt about Mei Xue's abduction. He sighed and continued.

Feslen spotted Master Chai at the center of Mei Xue's garden. The old man squatted; it looked like he was doing something with some flowers and gold-speckled pots. When he came nearer, to Feslen's shock he saw that the old man's shoulders were quaking. Was he crying? Master Chai almost never expressed his emotions, other than the delight he took in raising Mei Xue.

"M-master Chai?" Feslen hesitated. It seemed too private a scene for Feslen to interfere.

"I am glad that you could come here and that you came on your own, Feslen. You did not have a hard time, I hope?" Master Chai asked.

Feslen shook his head, stunned by Master Chai's addressing him in such an open manner. Master Chai walked in silence around Mei Xue's garden, and Feslen followed. Soon, the aroma of breakfast wafted in the crisp air, and the two went to the dining room and waited to be served. The mid-morning meal consisted of sea shrimp braised in mayonnaise and hot spices, pigs ears spiced with Southern red coriander and anise spices, and long-life stir-fried noodles and hot egg drop soup. Hot ginger beer and tea were served.

"My compliments," Feslen burped and called an older servant over by her first name. This female servant, known for her steady hands, frowned at Feslen and started to pour him some hot tea, but she missed and instead soaked his breeches. Feslen started to protest, but a sudden insight hit him. The servant then poured tea into Master Chai's cup with practiced ease and walked away. He sniffed the chrysanthemum tea with a hint of pepper and rose, and the memory nearly knocked him off his feet. This was Mei Xue's favorite tea.

The master chef stood in the doorway and glared at him. These dishes happened to be Mei Xue's favorites! Everyone missed Mei Xue's buoyancy. Intense, chill energy from where the abduction took place drew Feslen's attention. The energy did not come from an old Xsi-Arak or from the carpets that hung on the wall. Feslen did not linger. The strange energy puzzled him. Unexpected, faint red energy outlined everything he saw surrounding him: the servants, cooks, houseplants, and even the kittens. This sense of energy overwhelmed him, and he gripped the edge of the table. The energy he felt was being emitted from the Master himself, but, instead of red outlining, a blinding blue energy surrounded Master Chai. Feslen tried to understand. He caught sight of Master Chai's slight nod just before he blacked out.

Feslen awoke sitting on a bench; Master Chai sat next to him. "Master, what was that?"

"Shall we walk to my garden, young Feslen?"

Feslen groaned and struggled to stand up. Once he managed to get up, he followed Master Chai easily. He burned with the thought of learning new information. Faint blue energy still ran alongside the Master's body. They entered Mei Xue's favorite garden. The different aroma of a hundred flowers entwined in their noses. Feslen felt at peace here.

"What do you see?" Master Chai said nothing more and then inhaled again.

"Flowers, squirrels, birds. Why do you ask?" Feslen answered as he looked around Mei Xue's garden. The garden glistened with life. Mei Xue took careful loving care of her garden. Every plant was pruned and tidy and the pond was bright and clean. But when he looked again, Feslen spotted outlines of red pulsing energy throughout the entire garden! However, within each red pulse was an occasional streak of yellow and blue. The energy raced through the garden. Myriad particles of pulsing energy forced Feslen to close his eyes. When he opened his eyes again, the colors had disappeared. He arched his eyebrows in a question. "Whatever are you showing me, Master?" Feslen asked. "Am I going crazy?" he wondered. He had seen rainbow arches and the true colors of life!

"Tell me again, Master Feslen. What do you feel? What are these energies? Very few individuals can even see what you see. I shall explain to you once you understand," said Master Chai, as he balanced on one knee and bent it backward, interlocking both his arms. Feslen wondered how this particular exercise could help, but he had witnessed the Master perform close combat positions and so he watched in admiration.

It took Feslen a while more to study each particular pattern of color. The ancient bamboo, the only thing ancient in the garden, gave off a strong, beating energy that sounded similar to a frog's mating call. The Master's blue energy had expanded to cover most of the energy patterns around him. Feslen recognized that the exercise Master Chai performed had helped increase the strength of the blue energy! Suddenly, a nearby servant killed a mosquito. Feslen jumped up and cried out when the servant squashed the small light pulse. Then he understood. "I can see the life force!" he whispered in awe. The universe was suddenly all beautiful and new to him.

"Indeed you can. I noticed your aura when you first showed up at my doorstep with Ka-Wei and Duxan long ago. I do not know what you are exactly, Feslen Raster, but I can tell you this much: you have a rare Flair that no one else has ever had or will have. I want to train you as much as I can to help you become even healthier."

"What do you mean by Flair?" Feslen asked Master Chai. The boy had encountered the word before in some of his research books, but these texts never went into much detail.

"You know how magicians use only the Yang or Yin side of energies, right?" Master Chai began. Feslen nodded, the answer beginning to dawn on him. "Flair is the ability for a person affiliated with magic to be able to draw on either the Yang energies or Yin energies at the same time," Master Chai replied.

Feslen stared at him with some suspicion and a grunt of disbelief. I have Flair? How can you be so sure? I'm special? He thought.

"You are doubting, young one. That is wise."

"How do you know this?" Feslen began to ask Master Chai, but he interrupted.

"Shall I show you your touch, what it can do? Call Old Grey," Master Chai asked.

Feslen half smiled. "How do you know all this? Were you ever a mage?" Feslen asked, his voice filled with both respect and incredulity.

"I once associated with them, yes," Master Chai said, with such a light tone that Feslen did not stop to guess at the potential hidden meaning to the words.

"Besides, once you master Martial Arts to the level that is called "enlightenment" by Faosists and Dhai-Hahnists, you can attain a certain understanding of all aspects of energy." Master Chai paused in his lecture and trained a keen eye on Feslen. The fascinated boy hung on every word.

"Besides, magic is the use of energy. But wait, it's better to show you than to tell you," Master Chai mused.

"What do you mean? Am I a mage?" Feslen studied Master Chai's response and thought he saw a slight grin from the older man.

Master Chai said, "Call the dog. Call Old Grey."

Feslen stopped in his tracks and felt an odd feeling of wrongness. He knew it did not come from Master Chai. "How do I call Old Grey?" he shrugged, wondering what all this had to do with rescuing Mei Xue. "What could Master be hinting at?" He tried to read the Master's thoughts. He pushed the edge of his inner feelings and instinct just a bit, and a sense of intoxication ran through his blood. But then a hint of sorrow hit him suddenly. He yelped when an incredible iron wall seem to loom up in front of him, and he fell to the ground, groaning.

"Don't try that again, young Feslen, not until you have been trained in it. You do have the potential to use your *SAI* in that mode or any form you so choose, but not yet. Try again."

"*SAI*? Does he mean Soul Energy?" Feslen grimaced.

As clear as holes in a moth-eaten sweater, small circles of sudden insight opened up in Feslen and he called out to the mutt, "*Old Grey, come here.*" He called out again, without using either physical words or even words within his mind. He used the energy he saw as the connection to all life. At first Feslen felt nothing yet. He waited. His mind blurred with the enormity of feeling he perceived in the world. His own heart squeezed when his body tensed to the sense of all other hearts beating. Feslen fought the urge to run from fear. His spirit moved deep inside of him and he laughed. His brain froze in terror, and his limbs were unable to move. He cowered until a thrilling chill went up his spine. He had sensed a kiss! He had experienced someone else's first kiss! Startled, he stopped and refocused on Old Grey. "*Hey old friend, it's me, your pal Feslen.*" He then saw a tiny beating yellow light. He saw the tail wag from afar. The dog ran up to him and licked him. Then Feslen laughed and reality set in as the Other World broke away. The scenes shifted as Feslen readjusted to reality. Old grey was wagging his tail furiously and looking up at him expectantly.

"Careful, Feslen, you haven't stopped…" He didn't hear all of his Master's words. Someone screamed a choking scream followed by a dog's howl. By instinct, Feslen created an energy globe to protect Old Grey. Old Grey stopped howling when the energy encircled him.

Feslen blinked and saw nothing but dark shade mixed with rainbow colors. The rainbow colors blinded him to the Master's frantic movements. His dreams blurred into reality: dark-robed figures were chanting. The hawk's talon adjacent to the broken sword gleamed in his mind's eye. Feslen began to scream like the poor monk. A hammering red force seemed to explode in the distance and Feslen scrambled and started to run. A blue glow eased itself into the red force next to Feslen, defending him against the red hammer, but the red force still prevented him from moving. He felt heavier than a bear. The darkness sought to overtake him. He felt two unfamiliar presences: a terrible but not so dark entity and a pleasant, calm light with the pleasing aroma of honeydew and Forever Rose perfume. He saw Master Chai thank the two presences and they bowed in return.

There were chants and more chants in the distance, sounding terrible and frightening to Feslen. A tall, black-cloaked man interceded on the behalf of the exhausted and sweating Master Chai. He raised a hand holding a staff and pointed to the blue force coming from the New Priests.

Through flickering and wavering energies, Feslen saw the silhouette of a woman with a green aura supported the blue aura of the Master. Then a green light intersected with the Master's blue nodes and disappeared into the tall magi's dark lightning bolts. The chants ceased in Feslen's mind and soul, leaving only wails of anger.

After a long rest, and before Feslen left, Master Chai walked out to greet him. A female student accompanied Master Chai, her name escaped Feslen. "What?" Feslen asked, reacting to Master Chai's smile. Feslen shouldered his pack and thought it odd; Master Chai smiled at him for the first time! Did I do something right? Feslen wondered. Master Chai said, almot as if to the female student; but really to a more powerful presence the young Feslen suddenly felt, "I told you I was right about him. He is the Chosen One, he will succeed where I have failed."

The female presence nodded and left on a whisper of magic words.

Feslen smiled and he began to understand what transpired here and left, ready to tackle his brave new world.

10

TRAINING: KNOWING YOUR PLACE
鍛鍊：知道自己的身分

Three weeks passed and Feslen's training sessions had intensified. He spent the majority of his time at Master Chai's. He even roomed and boarded there. They practiced in the Main Private Training Room at the school, where two statues dedicated to the Gods resided in the front of the room and where Master Chai sat in front of the bronze set of mirrors. Kuan-Ti, the God of War, Martial Arts mastery, and Righteous Justice watched over them. The other idol belonged to Long Shi, the Goddess of Mercy and Protection. Despite his hardened look and his huge sword, Kuan-Ti's human-looking face eased the students' minds. Feslen and a fellow girl student named Kai-Lornu completed the monthly sacrifices. Kai-Lornu wore her hair down. She outfitted herself in the school's color with a silver vest, white pants, and silver slippers on her small, delicate feet and a gold sash around her thin waist. A mask of cold indifference was on her face whenever he approached her. He did not give much thought to her, nor did he study her. He did not like or generally appreciate most women all that much. Why should he? After all, he was just a boy!

"You're looking nice in that outfit," Feslen remarked nevertheless. He did not really care much about appearances, but he hoped to be friends with her at least. She did not respond. He felt that she gave him the cold shoulder. He just shrugged, and they continued their monthly prayer ceremony. They placed a tiny dagger at the feet of Kuan-Ti and used a child's blanket as a sacrifice before the Goddess of Mercy. The agility jungle bar made from bamboo, the rock-lifting platforms, the stuffed dummy opponents for Martial Arts, and the racks of training weapons had remained untouched so far.

A surprisingly calm and sunny day had greeted Feslen every day for the past few weeks. The weather was so nice that he did not need to change out of his favorite light weight clothes.

"To be a Hare, one must begin as a Turtle," the Master began. Feslen trained with two other expert students: Kai-Lornu and Kuan Hu, the disabled man whom Prince Ka-Wei had saved in the ambush. Feslen sighed and attempted to emulate Master Chai. They practiced *Tai-Thri-Ki* in the Lotus Position. Their legs were clamped over their backs, with their feet dangling. Their arms lengthened as they breathed deeply.

These positions are not easy to maintain, Feslen said. The simple breathing exercises the Master taught him paled in comparison. A ring of "hi-yah" rang out all over the Martial Arts school. The *Tai-Thri-Ki*, a form of Martial Arts developed by Master Chi for disabled people, could be practiced by normal people too. For normal people, the forms only enhanced their Martial Arts skills; for disabled people, this training gave them courage. The brilliance of Master Chai might be understated by Feslen's fellow countrymen, but the *Tai-Thri-Ki* branched into the Twelve Dragon Steps.

The Steps, a more advanced version of the Martial Arts, not only helped students become masters at Martial Arts, but somehow also brought them towards the desired enlightenment faster. At the moment, Feslen did not believe enlightenment to be all that useful. The Twelve Dragon Steps eventually extended to the Sixty Dragon Fists, but the Master never showed anything beyond twelve moves, nor taught anyone else the Sixty Fists. It was rumored in the Martial Arts world that few if any living today knew the Sixty Dragon Fists. "True Martial Artists never show their power," Master Chai always said.

In slow motion, the Master bent one knee, lifted a leg, and formed the Crab Stance. Inhaling twice and exhaling twice, Master Chai moved his hands in front of his neck. The Full Crab Stance and the Second Breath

Move caused Feslen to get tangled up in his own feet and he fell over in a heap. "I give up," Feslen huffed. Then he sprung up too quickly, hurting a back muscle that he never knew existed.

The girl, Kai-Lornu, sniffed, crossed her arms, and glared at Feslen. What did I do to deserve her anger? Feslen thought. He started to shrink from her gaze, which made him feel like a bug. She gazed at him in the way his old schoolmates at Red School and the commoners of Chiendong often did. Yet he also detected a sense of sadness within her gaze. He sighed and tried to ignore her. Kuan Hu, the man with one real leg, said nothing. His skin was paler than most Chiendonese; it almost matched Feslen's own complexion or that of a Mengalois or even a pasty white Far Westerner. The man said nothing, but he gave young Feslen a distinct nod, and the young Raster felt a sense of camaraderie even though he did not know why. Then the man got up and struggled to perform a difficult part of the Balance Self or the Seventh Dragon Step.

The young girl, however, continued to scowl at Feslen. Feslen felt her scorn and left, scowling. Feslen went and skulked around in Mei Xue's favorite garden. The fragrance from a small patch of blooming lavender intoxicated him and reminded of Mei Xue. He moaned in his depression. Then he saw her happy smile in the flower buds. *"What? Don't tell me you're giving up already?"* the flower voices teased him.

"You know how hard it is for me..." he started to answer the voices, half-jumping off the log.

"Oh come now, that doesn't sound like the Feslen I know," responded the flowers, whose soft breathy sounds were much like Mei Xue's giggles. *"Come now, remember how you said that we shouldn't give up when the monkey took our ball? Remember?"* she continued.

Feslen smiled and nodded. Her scared voice remained deep within him. *"Come Feslen, I need your help! Help me!"* Feslen trembled and wiped sweat off his brow. The evil smell of briar smoke had filled the air. He turned his head a bit and gave Master Chai a long look. The Master stood on the balcony of his Dragon School with Kai-Lornu. She still stared at Feslen with skepticism and scorn. Feslen sighed and gathered thoughts of Mei Xue to fill his empty and aching heart.

"I just don't know what the Master sees in you," the young girl said the next time they crossed paths. Two weeks more had passed and Feslen had almost completed the Second Dragon Technique. Feslen did not respond to her; he took a sip from his waterskin. "You think you're ready for this, Raster?" Kai-Lornu rolled her eyes and took out a Bo stick from the training weapons rack.

Again Feslen did not reply. He kicked the lighter Jo stick and flipped it up in one motion. Then, feeling energy running high, Feslen tapped into the natural resources of his ancient birthright. The Jo stick felt light in his hands and he spun it in a circle four times over his head, as he had seen the expert students do. He jabbed it forward and knocked the Bo stick out of Kai-Lornu's hands. Feslen smacked the Bo stick, which flew up in the air. He caught it and balanced it on its edge using the Jo stick. He twirled the sticks and they hit against each other with high-pitched sounds, like cicadas singing.

Feslen wielded the two sticks with incredible strength and speed. Kai-Lornu's eyes widened. The newer students flooded in when they heard the noise. Feslen slanted the two bamboo staves together and made a triangular sixty-degree step. He grinned and bowed. Feslen flipped the Bo stick to Kai-Lornu and was about to place the Jo stick back when he saw his Master frown. He sighed and let the energies release. "Can't a guy ever have fun?" he wondered.

"Don't show off your prowess," Master Chai said later.

"Mei Xue would've appreciated it," Feslen muttered.

"What was that?"

"Nothing, nothing. I'm sorry for mocking you, Master. But my energies just come and go and when I have them I want to use them."

"Real masters don't show others up or bruise their egos, Master Feslen."

"But…"

"You have Flair, yes. A rare kind you are. Discipline, practice, and patience lead to a better self, Feslen. You know why you can't do the simple breathing moves and the first six steps?"

"Yes, but I have feeling you're going to tell me anyway."

"It's because you're a foolish young boy. You have no right to throw away such talent. I am glad you haven't quit, Feslen, but you need to learn discipline and respect for the energies."

Feslen sat quiet, stunned; he never heard Master Chai be so blunt with him.

"Besides, if you are to go after Mei Xue and if a certain New Priest whom we all know is behind this…" the Master's voice trailed off. Feslen nodded in understanding, still shaking his head in disbelief at his mentor's strong words. "I asked Ka-Wei to investigate the ambush, and even the King has as well. Ka-Wei told me through a courier when he was up North that it seems a New Priest's hand was in it. It might even involve my rival school, Elhong, somehow." Feslen frowned at the mention of the name "Elhong." "You need to increase your powers, Feslen. You need to advance your skills before you can take them on and help everyone," the Master paused and became somber. "I was young and foolish like you once."

"Young and arrogant, you mean," Feslen said to himself. He knew what the Master meant.

Master Chai continued, "I was in an important caravan at a time before I knew enough about what I was doing. I lost important people thanks to my mistakes." Feslen's eyes widened and he stared at his older master. Here he heard regret and some bitterness in the old man's voice. All his young life, Feslen had never detected even a hint of those emotions from him until now. "Through lack of discipline and thoughts of foolishness I lost those people," Master Chai said and continued, "I don't want to see you end up on the wrong side, Feslen. Promise me you will try to be more serious, for the sake of your loved ones if not for yourself."

I will. I promise, Feslen said, as his throat stuffed up.

"Thank you, Feslen. I know it's hard, but, believe me, the rewards of getting to your goals are great. You can't imagine what it's like to gain the respect of the hardy people," he sighed.

"I can, but how can you?"

"Because I too live with a rare congenital blood disorder," Master Chai responded.

Feslen fell to the floor in surprise. He thought, "Perhaps there is a cure? Ahope for me after all?"

"Let's continue our training," Master Chai gave Feslen a rare smile.

Feslen nodded and his fondness for the old man swelled.

A week went by, with Feslen practicing hours and days on end. His favorite place to practice was in Mei Xue's garden. The other students began to accept him. He bent so close to the ground in the Full Crab Mode that cinnamon-and licorice-smelling flowers tempted Feslen to lick. He did not. The lunch bell rang. The boy ignored his growling stomach.

It took him four hours to learn this move. He bit his thick lip and held his hunger in check. He had eaten a light meal thirteen hours ago and nothing since. *"Discipline, young Raster, is the key to mastery of your life,"* he could hear Master Chai.

I have to hold on to the Full Crab Mode! he thought, his body trembling with pain and exhaustion. His hands crossed over through his legs and over his heart for two more hours. Soreness shot through his frail legs. But as he thought of poor Mei Xue, the pain melted away.

He closed his eyes, inhaled deeply, and completed the first three Dragon Techniques in a fluid, watery motion. He did this in under two hours, after he had practiced the moves for several days. He was concentrating so much that he did not notice Kai-Lornu's nod of appreciation or feel his Master's presence. The two of them left quietly.

Intense fiery pain shot through Feslen's body, numbing his legs and then the rest of his body. But he recalled one of Ka-Wei's harsher exercise routines, one that he had practiced when he was a trainee for the King's army.

Ka-Wei squatted as far down as his body allowed, holding his spine as erect as possible. He held over his head a solid boulder many times his weight! His legs were spread apart uncomfortably, and, worse yet, he could not move out of this position for six hours. He also had to do an exercise called "squats," during which he said, breathing hard, "Ten, eleven…you think this is difficult, Feslen? Wait until you see the Stone Stair Exercise!"

At the time, Feslen and Duxan exchanged grins. Feslen said, "You must have a strong heart, Ka-Wei. I don't know how any normal person could stand such a rigorous routine."

"I'm not supposed to be normal," Ka-Wei replied with a chuckle, and then he said, "Fifteen…"

"Nice try, Ka-Wei," Feslen said with a laugh, "That was fourteen."

"He's right," said Lieutenant Garland as he returned from observing another trainee. The repeated statements of the hundred trainees rang in the Raster brothers' ears, "Ten! Eleven!" The numbers were followed by grunts of defeat.

"Try not to skip, my boy. You'll set a bad example for the others. You are the Prince, after all. And, Feslen, perhaps you should stop distracting him. Next time you two talk, you will join him," with that said, Lieutenant Garland walked away to observe another trainee.

Feslen laughed and stuck out his tongue at the strict disciplinarian. Ka-Wei chuckled and continued his squats while counting, "Fourteen! Fifteen! Sixteen!"

Yes, even back then, Captain Garland Scallion was a tough teacher. Feslen smiled at the memory. If Ka-Wei did it, I can too, he thought. Feslen did not flinch. Someone tossed a rock near him. Feslen did not react. "Not bad, young Raster. You are much improved since we last met; soon you may even be a match for me," said the girl who also studied with Master Chai.

"Go bother someone else, Kai-Lornu. I don't work with women."

"Oh no? It looks like you will work for the sake of a woman, one named Mei Xue." Feslen's cheeks flushed. Kai-Lornu grinned and slipped away.

"I have work to do," Feslen snorted. He sighed and saw his Master coming toward him. Then Feslen shook his head to clear it and gave his Master a determined look. The Master gave him a rare smile.

When evening had set in, Duxan came to visit and found his brother running up and down the rocky pathway of the school's vast training grounds. "Come on," shouted a plain brown-haired girl as she raced up the next steep slope. Other students gathered to watch and urge them on.

Duxan bowed to Master Chai. Duxan watched. A servant poured tea, and Duxan accepted some although the weather was quite warm. Feslen, a step behind the young girl, halted abruptly because of a violent twitch. Duxan's plate shattered when he dropped it. He jumped up to help, but Master Chai stopped him. Feslen grabbed at his chest for a moment. He heard his heart thump louder than a drum and closed his eyes. Pain forced him to inhale. He felt Kai Lornu's concern when she placed her cold hands on his throat. He hadn't turned blue yet, which was a good sign.

Seconds later, Feslen smiled and the girl relaxed. "That won't stop me from racing to the top," Feslen declared and began again. He made it up the steep, twenty-foot hill, but at least ten minutes behind Kai-Lornu. Her eyes glittered with admiration. At the top, Feslen felt free—free from being away from his accursed life! Kai-Lornu congratulated him and skipped back down the stone steps. Feslen found himself watching her with admiring eyes. Then Duxan came to get him and the Raster brothers bade Master Chai farewell for the evening.

The brothers enjoyed the rare moment of temperate weather and stared at the stars for a few moments before they walked home. Duxan grinned and said, "I thought you didn't like women." At least half of the way home, Feslen was still blushing so much that his face matched a red-armored citizen's guard.

11

FRIENDS 朋友們

The next day, the Raster brothers witnessed a commotion they will never forget while walking through the Poor District and the Southern Gates. The constantly cloudy weather had done little to lift to their mood, despite Feslen's having changed into bright clothing. Duxan commented on the difference and Feslen gave a slight grin. "Well, Duxan, you always look like a businessman no matter what," Feslen poked fun at him. Duxan chuckled. Duxan's new red and orange business attire gleamed.

"Why? You can't do this. It isn't right," a fruit seller pleaded to red-armored Red Guards.

Feslen frowned and wondered what they were doing here.

"Come on Feslen; let's go home—this isn't our fight," said Duxan.

Feslen glanced darkly at his brother and they paused for a moment. They needed to stop for a breather anyway, because yet another one of Feslen's attacks occurred. *Breathe! Don't forget to breathe! I can't see or feel anything but this pain*, Feslen thought, taking deep breaths the best he could. His heart pounded too fast. But the boy realized that he was still standing, and then he started to relax some. This attack was mild. A more severe attack would force him to sit or squat. Feslen concentrated on the situation.

"You cannot prevent the Emperor from doing what it right. He is doing this to protect all of us from the barbarians," replied a Gold Soldier with a blue sash.

"Someone, please help! They're taking my stand and my right to make a living. First my sons were taken to war without my knowledge or their wanting to go and then…"

A mace smashed the limping middle-aged woman and she fell. The Emperor's Gold Soldiers moved in. Six Emperor's Gold Soldiers commanded the Beizung Red Guards to arrest the resisters.

"Resist the rule," a young woman student intervened. Students and other youths began to gather, alarming everyone present. Feslen looked at his brother, but Duxan only shook his head.

A man from another stall tried to intervene by offering bribery. The Red Guards of Beizung took the money, but the Emperor's men glared at the crowd.

"This is brutality. We have no rights," protested the gathering students. The Red Guards eyed the students. Finally, an arrow dispersed the crowd of protesters. Signs in the middle of the market read, "No demonstrations allowed." The crowd screamed. Feslen angled for a charge at the city guards. The Emperor's men made numerous official arrests. Rocks were hurled. Energy coursed through Feslen, and he hesitated no longer. Breaking free of his brother, he employed the First and Second Steps against the guards holding the injured woman. A fist smashed against Feslen's back. He dropped to the ground. Duxan shouted but felt a sudden presence. He looked to his right and saw a tall, dark-faced Chiendonese man with a black cloak.

"Let me help," said the tall man. He wore a hooded black cape that hid his face. Duxan gasped and saw the man's arcane symbol: a skull and crossbones in the middle of the Yin Yang icon! The man raised a hand and chanted. A flash of light and a bang of terrible noise erupted after he finished his chant. Even the well-trained Emperor's Red Soldiers covered their ears. Duxan nodded thanks and then raced over to drag the unconscious Feslen away. By the time the turmoil ended and the situation was under control, the brothers had left.

Feslen's parents grounded him after they heard about the fight. He felt like a prisoner because his sisters, Mei-Whuay and Ghong-Hung, guarded him in forced double-duty shifts. None of them enjoyed the situation, but, like dutiful daughters, the sisters did not argue with their parents. He was stuck in the attic room instead of his normal bedroom on the second floor. Fortunately, his parents had already grounded him so many times that he had stocked the attic room with whatever he needed. Rows of books, maps, and some experimental equipment were tucked along three shelves. He had even stocked some dried goods for snacking in the room. Feslen sat up on the uncomfortable bed and read a thick book called *Lioin the Remarkable Thief Hero*. Several other thick books lay across his bed. His bed sheets were messed up.

"You should shut up and be grateful that Mother didn't throw you out like Ai-Yen suggested," Mei-Whuay scorned. "And these bed sheets. Why do they always look like you tried to make a mess of them?"

Feslen said nothing. *At least I am not a woman,* he thought. *I get to have rights, not like you…or at least I should have rights!* Like most men in Chiendong, he viewed women with less than proper respect.

"Don't give me that look. It may work on our worthless brother, Duxan, and perhaps even on Father, but not on me! I had to cancel a meeting with a boy I wanted to see because of you," Mei-Whuay flipped her long, luxurious hair back away from her proud face and pointed her nose up. She strutted over to his window and closed it and then turned to scold Feslen, "You should keep the windows closed. You know how sick you can get during the winter."

"Yes, yes, you're right," Feslen muttered. "When did I open the window?" He wondered.

Feslen hid his feelings as best he could. He did not mean to show them. "You'll get plenty of chances for more proper meetings, Mei-Whuay. That boy you were going to see isn't worth more than a fish in…" He didn't get to finish his sentence before a brisk slap dazed him. She stomped downstairs.

Feslen sighed and returned to his reading. He put *Lioin the Remarkable Thief Hero* aside and picked up another book, *County Weather Records*. He was half way through when he stopped, alerted to something. He smiled and pretended to read again when he heard a familiar chuckle.

"Gui-Pan," he murmured.

The small thief emerged with a rakish bow. "How soon did you know I was here?" The boy thief asked.

"Soon enough," Feslen allowed. "But how did you get in? That window isn't even big enough for a swallow."

"It's my secret. By the way, you can call me Lioin. Gui is my nickname, and Pan is not exactly the name I want to carry for the rest of my life," Gui-Pan's eyes glittered. He was taller than Feslen but shorter than Duxan. His body was thin to the point of looking unhealthy. But Feslen had seen him in action several times and knew that you couldn't judge a person's strength by his or her appearance. Lioin's flimsy brown robes covered him from head to toe, hiding his thick head of brown hair. He sported several scars on his arms which Feslen could see because of his rolled-up sleeves. His eyes revealed intelligence, hardship, and sorrow. Feslen figured the young man's light-heartedness was just a front. His eyes also seemed to be desperate for something, but Feslen couldn't be sure of what.

Feslen said, "Lioin? You mean from the books? Like *Lioin the Remarkable Thief Hero*?"

Lioin laughed. Then Lioin and Feslen shouted at the same time "Lioin the Lionheart!" They both laughed. Already Feslen was cheered up by a few minutes spent with the young street urchin.

The story of a legendary thief named Lioin the Remarkable had become so popular in the early dynasties that people thought it to be true history. "Lioin the Remarkable" was later changed to "Lionheart" in the same series by a famous author of the Ghon Dynasty. The tales had fascinated generations of children. The author claimed Lioin's stories to be true, though no one ever verified them.

"Lioin it is then. You can call me Fes."

They grinned. "By the way…" Feslen said as he reached under one of his blankets and took out a silver dagger. This dagger was not ordinary, for it had an amber handle and a ruby-studded tip. Feslen wondered at the strange insignia in the middle of the amber handle. It had a stork crossed with a smiling deity. It seemed almost similar to the symbol used by Ka-Wei's parents. Feslen smiled, thinking of Ka-Wei's past happiness, and ran his hand over the sharp edge.

"My dagger!" Lioin cried enthusiastically. "I didn't think I'd ever see it again!" Feslen nodded and handed the thief his dagger. Lioin smiled, thanking him.

"No, thank you. You saved my skin that day with the street toughs. That was some amazing display of skills."

"Nah, it's just what happens when you live on the street forever," Lioin chuckled and waved his hand in a nonchalant manner as he put his special dagger inside his shirt. They shared a laugh and fell silent. Feslen thought about how they first met and when he thought of Lioin as a friend. During one of his trips to Master Chai's, Feslen had encountered a known street gang, not one of those led by Sae-Jyung. He did all right, scaring some of the toughs off, but the young thief had helped fend off six of the eight all by himself.

"So your parents have you trapped up here like a rat?" Lioin frowned.

"Yeah, I guess so. I've been doing some reading on what happened to me at Master Chai's."

"What did happen?"

"You mean, you didn't know? Everyone in this sector knows about the attacks by now," Feslen said, astonished.

Lioin chuckled and said with a shrug, "I don't pay much attention to rich people's news unless it has something to do with my guild. Why do you mention it to me? I am only a common street thief."

"Common? You're about as common as the legendary roc bird," Feslen replied. Lioin laughed. His high-pitched laughter reminded Feslen of the laughter of a ghost. "Since Gui-Pan meant 'Ghost River Waif,'" perhaps he was well nicknamed, Feslen thought. "Anyway, the books I looked up informed me little. Perhaps you can tell me some things I don't know?"

"Like what?" Lioin paused and took a step back; his eyes narrowed. "Wait a minute, what makes you think I can look these things up? It's not like I go visit the library every day."

Feslen chuckled and raised his hand in defense. He did not want to offend the boy who was apparently his new friend. "I didn't mean it like that, Lioin. It's just that a thief like you who strikes terror in the hearts of the law and even the Prince ought to have some contacts. You know, like perhaps someone in the East."

Lioin's eyes widened considerably. "The East? How do you know…?"

Feslen grinned, "Your face looks Eastern Chiendong. Anyway, please, look up some information, all right? I'll pay you well. Besides, I have a feeling that this ambush attack on Prince Ka-Wei, my brother, and myself may involve more than meets the eye."

Lioin smiled and shook his head, "I don't want payment. I don't take jobs like this to get paid. My jobs are arranged by special hiring. But for you, I can spare a yuan or two since you got me out of the Prince's holding cell. What do you need?"

Feslen heard his oldest sister's footsteps clink in tune with the bowl and chopsticks she carried and he said quickly to Lioin, "I would like to find out about the attacks and the weird weather, if you could."

Lioin smiled and merged back into the shadows. Feslen detected a small outline near his sister. She yelped when the hidden Lioin pinched her on the hips, almost causing her to drop the bowl of food she brought upstairs. "How kind of you, Mei-Whuay!" Feslen said at the same time as Lioin waved to him.

Feslen hid his grin as his sister whirled around. "Close the window, Feslen. Don't let the insects in!" she muttered. Feslen watched Lioin slip back out the window. "What?" Mei-Whuay asked him. She went over to the window Lioin reopened and slammed it shut again.

"Look at you, you ungrateful brat! I have cooked morning meals for you for the past two or three days, and I get no thanks!" His distracted expression must have triggered her remark.

"It's not that, sister. It's…"

"Oh, just finish your meal and be quick about getting healthy again," she said and left.

Feslen returned to health in a week.

The next weekend, Feslen's family began preparation for the Winter Festival. Idols and paintings of the Dragon King of Wind and Lightning were put up next to the Goddess of Weather. All over town, decorations of other gods and dedications to certain animal spirits were placed in front of every household. Memorials and rituals of good health for ancestors' spirits were performed for most of the people around Feslen's hometown of Bilong and the rest of Chiendong.

But Feslen's mind and heart wandered elsewhere. His heart was still heavy from missing his abducted friend, Mei Xue, and from his sense of personal failures. He wondered if he should do some research and investigation on his own and then remembered what he had asked Lioin to do.

His family had gone to town to buy items for the Winter Festival and to prepare Duxan for an important and necessary family religious ceremony. At this time, Feslen found that his health was weaker than before his training began. In town, they bumped into a young girl about his age, and her eyes opened wide with recognition. She carried five heavy looking sacks on her shoulders, slung over a ten-foot pole. "Raster?" She asked, her thin voice sounded familiar. He couldn't register her name, but her doe-eyes and sad face were etched in his memory. Her small frame looked deceptively weak, but Feslen knew better somehow. The smell of ginger and beer and smoked beef in her bags finally helped Feslen recall her name: Kai-Lornu.

She looked so different. "What are you doing here? I thought you couldn't come out on a day like this?" She asked him with concern and maybe a little scorn in her voice.

She wore a colorful low-cut gown, and her hair was pinned up in a bun. Despite a plain style, the dress was very feminine. Feslen stared at her without meaning to. She averted her eyes at his gaze. "Thank you for being concerned for me, Kai-Lornu. We're out to buy things for the Winter Festival, and Duxan here has to perform a religious ceremony."

"Oh," she said, biting her lip. They stared at each other a few moments. Kai-Lornu shifted her load a bit and looked down onto the ground. Feslen heard his sisters whispering and giggling. He coughed and said, "Would you like to come with us?"

"I..." Kai-Lornu started and then stopped speaking, seeing the look on Feslen's face. For some reason, Feslen had given her a hopeful gaze.

"I'm sorry, Raster. I must get these supplies back to Master Chai, but thank you for the invitation," she finished with a sigh.

"Oh, and who's this very becoming young lady, Feslen?" Father asked him.

Her thin cheeks flushed a bright pink, and she trembled so much that her bags tipped over and a few pieces of fruit rolled out. Duxan and Feslen helped pick them up and put them back into her bags. Feslen's hand brushed hers accidentally as they reached for the same fruit. They immediately withdrew their hands. They gazed at each other again for a moment.

Her bags look heavy, Feslen thought. How can such a thin girl carry such a load? Master Chai ought to be ashamed at making her work like that!

"Here, let me help with your bags, Kai-Lornu," Feslen said, and he started to lift the bamboo pole off her shoulder.

She gave him a flustered look and tried to shrug him off. "No, thank you. I've done this many times on my own," she replied, but she did a half-bow as she readjusted her load on her shoulders. Reluctantly, Feslen let go of the pole. She gave him a rather curious look and her eyes took in his entire family.

"How strange, did I imagine that interested look in her eyes?" Feslen asked himself. He saw it again when she continued to stare at him and then at his family. Then her doe-eyes crinkled into the sadness he remembered so well. Feslen stammered to speak, "Kai-Lornu…" But he didn't say any more, and she smiled a lukewarm smile.

"Feslen's got a girlfriend!" Ghong-Hung, Trisha, and Mei-Whuay chanted. To his great embarrassment, Feslen heard his sisters giggling. The bespectacled, scrunch-nosed Ghong-Hung laughed so much that she looked just like a pig, and her years of overeating didn't help hide the resemblance. As Trisha laughed unpleasantly, her slim good looks and kind attitude dissolved before his eyes. Trisha was the only older sister who showed a decent attitude to Feslen. He always expected abuse from Mei-Whuay and Ghong-Hung, but not from Trisha. Feslen didn't understand what had changed, but he didn't care and just let go with a low growl of disapproval.

Kai-Lornu blushed under the scrutiny and took a step forward as if she wanted to leave. She and Feslen stared at one another for a moment more before his Father stepped in.

"Young lady, our family would be honored to have you and your folks over. You're a friend of Feslen's, and it's not often we get to meet his friends."

Feslen shuffled his feet in some embarrassment. His blood condition was starting to upset him a bit. Kai-Lornu started to drop her bags of supplies and go to him, but then she stopped. Her sad look became a very concerned look, but she showed that only to Feslen. Feslen returned a grateful smile, for he understood what had just happened. She respected his disability! But just then he felt Duxan's strong arms around him. Feslen sighed and shook his head.

"Th-thank you," Kai-Lornu stuttered, turning her eyes down as Father Wong repeated his invitation to her. "But I must be on my way to the Chai's. I am glad to see you in good health, Raster. I am sure Master Chai will wish to hear the good news. It was good to meet all of you." She half-bowed again and shuffled off. She looked to be in a hurry.

Father and Mother looked as stunned as Duxan was by her reply. Father and Duxan tried to intercept her, but she ran off with great speed. "Kai-Lornu, wait!" Feslen shouted, but she was well out of hearing distance. Her body trembled, as if she were crying as she ran away. Feslen wondered why and then he saw Duxan, Father, and Mother exchange knowing looks.

Poor Kai-Lornu, Duxan thought, She's all alone. No wonder she stays with at Master Chai's school all the time!

"Oooh, she's cuuute!" Ai-Yen and Mei-Whuay taunted. "Feslen loves Kai-Lornu!"

"And Kai-Lornu loves Feslen!" Ghong-Hung shouted.

"Give Feslen a break, you guys," Duxan warned. The taunting died in an instance at the sound of his serious tone.

Feslen sighed and started to cough violently. His family slowed their pace and allowed him to leave. Feslen headed for home. Fortune had smiled on him though, for not only did he avoid going to the boring religious ceremony, but he got to come home alone. "It's a big step," Feslen thought with a smile. Usually, they always have one sibling with me. On his way home, he bowed his head down and covered his mouth with his hands to try to hold in the violent coughs.

He bumped into Lioin. A large grin immediately appeared on his face. Lioin said, "I have some information and a few extra interesting tidbits I picked up on my own. I'd rather talk about it in a private place."

"Say no more," Feslen, said. He struggled to breathe and his legs felt encased in rock. Lioin waited for him to pull himself together. Then Feslen said, "There's a small cave in that set of hills up ahead. You go ahead." Finally, Feslen caught up with him, sweat covering his face. Lioin reached out to help him, but he stopped when Feslen glared at him, wanting to preserve his independence.

"You'll never guess what I found!" Lioin bubbled. Feslen forced himself to stand when he wanted to sit.

"Okay. Just let me…catch…my breath," Feslen uttered in shame and anger at his own weakness. Lioin stopped to stare at his distress in amazement.

"Once I enter the cave, I will be cooler," Feslen growled. Lioin nodded and stood looking at the cave entrance intently as Feslen made his slow and tortured way up the path and inside the cave.

Feslen discovered this cave one time when he and his siblings went fishing. After boredom overcame him, he started wandering around the area and then stumbled upon this place. He called it "the Cave of Silence." It was really a deep animal burrow that had been abandoned. The cave resembled a yawning mouth, large enough to protect him from heat and sharp winds. Although it was situated in the Northeast, he could see the highest mountain in all of southern Chiendong, Mount Jing, the bustling liveliness of the city of Beizung, and the rolling green plains of the South. Feslen came here often to contemplate the mysteries of the universe and the habits of humanity. He kept several blankets in a corner, along with a tiny bookshelf, and some hidden food storage.

Lioin entered before Feslen and sat down. "This place could be a second home where you can come to have some solace," Lioin murmured.

"Yes, I call this my Cave of Silence." Lioin pulled out the *Book of Longevity* and waited.

After a moment of rest, Feslen asked, "Well? What did you find out?"

"The recent weather is so strange that even the Forest Protectors are confused by it. The information I received from my source said it was connected somehow to the Thai-Thurian monks."

"What else?" Feslen shook his head.

"Something to do with some odd Prophecies. I'm not really sure…"

"All right, go now. I need to think. I need to be alone," Feslen said a little testily.

When Feslen looked up, the young thief boy was gone. He had left the book and an odd scroll. Feslen picked up the scroll and read the fancy scripture. He chuckled. The young thief had tried to impress him. The message said, "When you need information or a hideout, let me know. Always watching your back, Lioin."

Feslen tapped the scroll against his leg and picked up the *Longevity Book*. He realized the sunlight was beginning to disappear beyond the horizon and left the cave to go back to his parents' house. Feslen grinned all the way home.

12

FESLEN'S STRUGGLES 奮鬥

Two weeks passed and Feslen pressed on with his training, disobeying his parents' request to remain at home. Urgency urged Feslen to complete his studies with Master Chai.

Master Chai said, "Let me see you complete the twelve steps today, Feslen." Master and student practiced the Twelve Dragon Steps together in the Old City. They stood at the beginning step on a particularly long set of stairs. He began the First Dragon Technique and the Fourth Dragon Step. It took Feslen almost two hours to reach the top, but he did so after Master Chai's fourth pass, and then he celebrated. He had never completed this step before! Master Chai ran past Feslen for the fifth time. All beginners needed to complete the Tenth Step three times in under twenty seconds. Feslen sighed, breathing hard, and studied the lion statues at the bottom of the steps.

"Why did you stop? The Eleventh Step is not yet started," the Master said.

"Why is exercise painful and shows me little gain while indulgence in food provides a quick gain?" Feslen huffed.

"Do you wish to attain greatness and prowess in eating or in the Martial Arts? One is more detrimental than the other," Master Chai responded.

"At least one is more fun than the other."

"Fun has nothing to do with becoming healthy."

"It should."

Feslen grimaced and started to speak again when he felt the wind sharp against his cheek. "The wind's getting harsher," Feslen murmured. However, this did not seem to affect Master Chai at all. The Master said nothing. Feslen studied Master Chai. Feslen got the impression that a bolt of lightning had hit him. Impressive energy engulfed the Master today.

"Look, even if the weather weren't hot, I couldn't continue just now," Feslen said. "I've already done more than I have in the past, I think."

"Want to quit?"

Feslen flinched but nodded in agreement.

"Very well, perhaps I could find someone with a greater sense of purpose and discipline, perhaps one of your brothers," Master Chai turned away.

"What do you know of me, old man? What can you know of my pains? What do you know of living with misfortunes? I am here not just because of Mei Xue, but for myself!" Feslen raged.

With a burst, Feslen began the Eleventh Step by jumping down and back up each step until he reached huge lion statues at the bottom of the steps. He pressed his hands against the one standing statue hard and pushed for all his worth. Crackles of energy coated his hands. What Feslen crushed to smithereens, four men could only move inches. Then Feslen crumpled with fatigue and didn't really look around him. In his mind's eye, the lion statues remained unmoved. The Eleventh Step was to push the statues a bit. He frowned bitterly for his weakness. Master Chai watched and nodded as he walked down to Feslen.

"I'm sorry, I did not pass your tests," Feslen's disappointed tone could not be hidden. I have truly failed, he thought. But little did he know, he had succeeded beyond his Master's wildest imagination and beyond his own ideas.

"The Twelve Steps are only to build your physical attributes, my young student. Physical health takes time to improve. It is time to move on to the next lessons," said Master Chai.

Feslen nodded, exhausted, and servants helped carry him into the house. He caught Master Chai's statement nonetheless. Master Chai went to his private study and penned a letter to an old friend about Feslen.

Later Feslen awoke and thought, Now that I have passed Master Chai's tests, I need to continue my regular schooling to please my parents. In half an hour, I'll be late to Red School. He hated to be late to Red School, especially to his first class with Teacher Lung. He hurried down the path as quickly as he could.

Red School was the typical school in Chiendong. Red School's reputation was that of very high quality; many of the workers in important positions had graduated from there. Many of the teachers were good, although a few liked to bend the rules. Red School's policies, as for all schools in Chiendong, were determined according to systems of age, social rank, and class rank. The Head Principal and his associates often enforced the prefecture's regulations, which differed considerably from the laws of the country. Sometimes Red School's teachers even taught girls separately from the boys. This school took tradition seriously: all students wore school uniforms, and girls and boys could not mingle until they were of age. Red School's subjects were standard: math, history, anthropology, science, calligraphy, New Priest religion and sometimes Dhai-Hahnism, and physical education. For a supposedly upscale school, Red School totally ignored the arts, ancient history, most other religions, geography, and the theory and art of magic and mysticism.

Red School was completely different from Master Chai's school, which was unique, not just as a Martial Arts school, but because Master Chai and his fellow teachers taught people of all cultures, backgrounds, including, more specifically, disabled people. The disabled people could come to the school at no extra charge. They came for free, though no one ever quite knew why. That part Master Chai kept secret; only Mei Xue may have known. Master Chai's school also taught the importance of free will and the need to keep the balance between physical health, spiritual, and mental health. Master Chai's school taught all of the other subjects that the Red School did not offer. Master Chai's Golden Dragon School also differed from most of the new fangled Martial Arts schools that had popped up in Chiendong over the last three centuries, including its rival, the Elhong School. Master Chai and his apprentices taught Honor and kept their intent on teaching the whole person, not just improving his or her physical might. Other Martial Arts schools just trained students in the practice of the Martial Arts.

Feslen struggled to stay awake in class. After he completed his training, his energies fluctuated wildly. Feslen sighed.

"Do you find something wrong with my lessons of the Heart Scroll, Master Feslen?" Teacher Lung chided. A soft whisper of giggles followed.

"No, not at all, teacher," Feslen sneered. His fellow students gasped at his tone. Someone sniggered. Feslen did not have to turn to know who it was: Sae-Jyung, a tall boy with long black hair. He looks impish, Feslen thought.

"Oh, you think you can teach better than I, Master Feslen?" Teacher Lung said.

"No, I just don't want to waste my time. I read and memorized the Heart Scroll when I was six," Feslen sniped back. The students oohed in the background. No one dared talk back to any teacher, let alone Teacher Lung!

With glee on his face, Teacher Lung took out a hard piece of wood. Feslen sighed and held out his hands. The students winced with each whack, ten whacks in all. Five whacks for talking back to the teacher and five more for disrupting the class. Although schools in the rest of the country had long ago discarded this sort of discipline, Teacher Lung and other teachers at Red School often employed such nasty traditions.

Once the blistering of his hands was finished, Feslen sat blowing on them. In the past, Feslen used to throw raging tantrums because his wounds healed slowly. Ever since he began training with Master Chai, however, he noticed that his wounds healed much more quickly. As extra punishment, Teacher Lung also confiscated his extracurricular books.

Of all the teachers Feslen despised, he wanted to make trouble for Lung the most. Feslen ran to the next class, history. He ran past some bullies and girls who watched and got tripped.

Sae-Jyung, captain of the Fast Ball Kick Team, caught up to him. Sae-Jyung's gang waited behind a water fountain. Sae-Jyung's raven eyes scared Feslen; their color shifted from amber to green. He had a fighter's build and a leathery face. His reedy black hair was usually clean and hung down to his waist. He looked athletic, but an almost undetectable aura of power also emanated from him. He smelled heavily of onion and wet dirt.

"Listen, I am not here to pick on you, at least not until science class, twisted one," Sae-Jyung spoke. Feslen tried not to listen. Sae-Jyung's tone of voice made him feel dirty. "I'm impressed, rat. You never showed any backbone before today. If you keep it up, maybe you can hang out with me," Sae-Jyung continued.

"I choose my own friends, Sae-Jyung," Feslen snorted.

"Suit yourself. See you later, lying on your face, flat as a pancake, rat."

Feslen endured the hard teasing. Sae-Jyung, his cohort Tojoh, and the rest of his gang moved on. It rather shocked him that Sae-Jyung talked to him at all. It was the first time they had exchanged more than a couple of insults at each other. Perhaps it was not a bad idea to hang out with Sae Jyung, Feslen thought. And after a shake of his head he thought, I am not like the others! He sat down, flipping one of his favorite books open and started laughing.

"Hey, look! The book worm is laughing!" a classmate said. "What's so funny? Are you the prince in the story?" he quipped. The other classmates laughed with him.

"Leave me be!" Feslen thought and sent darting looks to the kid who had spoken and to Tojoh and some of the others.

"Look at his clothes! It's so much like an urchin!" the same kid pointed to Feslen.

"I like the way I look," Feslen said, and his tone forced some classmates to back off. Some of the other students hurried to their desks as the bell rang. But even after that, this one boy would not let up. He knocked the book out of Feslen's hands. But instead of the stinging feeling, a sudden surge of happiness coursed through Feslen. Even though Tojoh had then smacked Feslen in the face with the book, the sense of pure happiness would not go away. It was as if someone continued to feed him his favorite foods.

Feslen's hands began to burn with a dark green color, causing his classmates to murmur. Strips of wood began to peel away from some of the nearby desks. "Stop bothering me, please," Feslen murmured. Then all of the students—except for Sae-Jyung—stiffened under a sleep spell.

The desks returned to normal as Sae-Jyung chanted. A bit of dried seaweed and some mirror shards sprinkled underneath Sae-Jyung's desk. Feslen narrowed his gaze when Sae-Jyung acknowledged him. "Is Sae-Jyung a mage?" Feslen wondered. he was so preoccupied with his thoughts that Feslen did not hear a horrified gasp from a shadowy corner. Feslen was totally astonished when he saw Sae-Jyung's silver aura appear to him.

In class, a round of "fast questions" had begun. The other students groaned, but, as an act of revenge, Feslen had decided to make the other students look bad. "What are the known materials behind the City of Steel's Backlash Sword? Can anyone tell me?" Teacher Fung asked. Feslen raised a hand. "Good. It looks like someone read his homework for today!"

"For three extra credit points and no homework, can anyone tell me why the Old Forest is called 'Ghost Forest' and what legends speak about remaining shrine like energies?"

"It's called Ghost Forest because no living things can be heard there."

"Excellently done, Feslen," said the teacher.

"Can anyone tell me what Emperor Whue Haen was doing in the Lands of Nu before the Breaking Wars began?"

"It is said that he searched for his…" Sae-Jyung began.

"Yes, Feslen?"

Feslen grinned, "He looked for a bride there to solidify his empire."

"Yes, correct."

Feslen heard Sae-Jyung growl, and his grin widened. He also heard the whispers of his other classmates. "Can anyone—besides Feslen—write the character symbols to the Lands of Nu and the Emperor's sign?"

"What does that have to do with us?" someone growled.

Sae-Jyung volunteered. "No, no. Sae-Jyung. Your penmanship is not right. The bottom half of the character is too scraggly, and it is too solid. Anyone else?" Sae-Jyung snorted and stalked back to his desk.

Tojoh volunteered. The young athlete's attempt resulted in some stifled laughing. The loudest laughs came from Feslen. He glanced and saw Tojoh's two looks: one at a girl classmate and one at him. One of the two girl classmates volunteered—the one in whom Tojoh had an obvious interest. "Not bad, Rui Lai."

"But definitely not hundred percent correct. The right way to do it is…"

"May I, Teacher?" Feslen coughed.

"Very well."

Feslen accepted the chalk and walked with swagger up to the board. "Air," he began, "is supposed to be fluid in motion, like dancing, or more importantly, like in the Martial Arts. Calligraphy isn't much different in its motion than those two."

Feslen first wrote in gentle waves the character for "light" and then wrote the character for "air" on top of the character for "light." "That," he said as he turned towards the class, "is the symbol for the Emperor of the Yu Dynasty." He bowed to the Teacher and walked back to his seat.

Everyone murmured at his handiwork. The Teacher blinked many times before he said anything. Then he turned. "Amazing. Simply amazing. Have you practiced calligraphy work before, Feslen?"

"No, but anyone can do it as well as I, since it is all part of the flow. I didn't know how to 'do' calligraphy before today; it just flowed," Feslen responded.

"Well, Feslen, you don't have to do homework for either calligraphy class or history for the next two days. For the rest of you, you will do double the amount. If you can come up with writing even half as good as Mr. Raster's, then I shall reconsider less work." The groans went up. Feslen felt a chill go through him as he considered the dark looks he got from Sae-Jyung and Tojoh. The Free Period bell rang.

Feslen sat in misery on a bench in the playground during Free Period. How many times had he wanted to talk to the others or play sports together for that matter? Feslen heaved a sigh. The other students knew about his health condition, so they avoided him.

"Hey look at him, sitting over there. Let's go see what he's up to," he heard a boy student say. The school rules separated boys and girls in the playground. Feslen kept looking at his shoes. "Look, the wormy boy misses his books!" Tojoh said. Feslen then smelled Sae-Jyung's awful odor of onion and wet dirt. "We've got something for you to do, squirt," Tojoh continued.

"I'm not interested in whatever you do, Tojoh."

"Oh? I saw you stare at us playing Kick the Ball. I know you're too wimpy to join us in that game, but why don't you play handball? Oops, I meant why don't you join the girls for kite flying?"

Calm yourself, Feslen thought, taking deep breaths as he heard the jeers. "No, thank you. I'm not interested in playing. Besides, the girls shouldn't be interested in bullies who pick on people with books just because they themselves don't know how to read." He bowed to them and started to turn away. A rough hand grabbed him and pushed him. He tripped and cursed as he landed on his face. Laughter surrounded him.

"Tough words for a worm," Tojoh countered. "Hey, look at what I have!" Tojoh heckled. He produced one of Feslen's favorite books, *How to Entertain Friends and Commoners with Tricks*. "How did you get that?" Feslen babbled. Teacher Lung had confiscated those! He growled.

"Too abnormal to play with the rest of us?"

"Remember to breathe!" Feslen told himself, feeling the heat of shame and anger.

"Why can't you crumbs leave me be? I leave you alone to do what you do!"

"Show him how we deal with show-offs, Tojoh," hissed Sae-Jyung.

"You got it," Tojoh shoved Feslen again.

Feslen shuddered and began to cry, even though, to his horror, he never meant for that to happen! "Now, you've done it, he's crying!" Someone else laughed.

"I'll do more than that," Feslen warned.

"What's going on here?" a teacher asked. Feslen fainted in relief. Where was his brother?

"They're picking on me, Teacher Sha!" Feslen said, scrabbling away.

"Just playing around, Teacher," Tojoh said.

"Well, make sure you're less rough," Teacher Sha said. Then he left. Feslen stared in disbelief.

"This will teach you to tattle, you rat," Tojoh said and ripped the book cover off Feslen's favorite book. Feslen screeched. Tojoh tossed the book back and forth to the rest of the playground boys. A large crowd gathered to watch Feslen jumping up and down, trying to catch it. Then, with a primal force of rage, Feslen feigned to leap for the book but instead used a combination of the Fourth Step and the Second Step on the offender. Tojoh cried out as Feslen gripped his exposed knees. Feslen then closed with surprisingly incredible strength and shoved him.

Odd energy throbbed through him. Feslen turned and smacked the nearest offender with a sound backhand. His habitual health exercises with Master Chai had activated when he stopped trying to get his book. It was as if he were working out again with Master Chai.

Someone rushed him. "Let's get at him!" As if by natural consequence, Feslen managed a parry of a clumsy haymaker. Feslen ignored the sting and ducked. He started creating his own routines. Feslen squatted down and punished a student with a blow to the abdomen. A fist whistled past his ear. He then gripped this other boy by the arm and swung him about, much to the amazement of the crowd. Tojoh rushed at him again, and Feslen cracked the boy's finger. A part of the young Raster enjoyed this as he saw Tojoh's blood hand and crying face. Feslen blinked and came out of his state in an instant. Out of pure instinct, Feslen grabbed Tojoh and flung him ten feet away. Before Feslen recovered from the shock of his own attack against Tojoh, another student bashed him on the head from behind. It was none other than the student he had used a spell on earlier. Sae-Jyung neither helped nor hindered Feslen and just stood watching the melee. Feslen returned Sae-Jyung's nod.

"Leave my brother alone," Duxan said. The fight ended As Duxan arrived with a teacher.

"Who started this?" the teacher, whom Feslen did not recognize, demanded.

"They did." Duxan began.

"We were having nothing more than a demonstration, Vice Principal," Feslen stated without hesitation. Sae-Jyung could teach me some tricks, Feslen thought.

"You are from an important family, Feslen. You must tell me the truth, and I will punish whoever did it," said the Vice Principal.

I am no Wong, Feslen thought with bitterness.

"Like I said," Feslen said with a smile. "Just a friendly game, nothing more."

The Vice Principal left Duxan and Sae-Jyung with a puzzled look. Feslen could see undisguised admiration from the girls and some of his classmates.

"Why?" Sae-Jyung asked when he approached after the crowd had dispersed.

"You owe me," Feslen said.

"Well," Sae-Jyung said as he handed over the torn book, "you'll get no trouble from me, I assure you."

"We'll see," Feslen stated. "We'll see."

Feslen waved when Duxan returned. "You did incredibly well, considering you just learned those moves last week," Duxan said. Feslen said nothing as they headed back towards class. Feslen mumbled to himself, "My parents should be glad I can defend myself now. I can't wait to tell Master Chai!"

Feslen shared an evening meal with Master Chai, who told him "You know, Martial Arts are not to be used for violence. You were lucky you didn't harm the boy more than you did."

"But he attacked me, Master!"

"No," Master Chai corrected. "You attacked him. On purpose, you used the boy's anger and momentum, just as you did with the student in the classroom. You may be happy now, but disciplined people do not do such things. Never strike out against others, even if they attack you, Feslen."

"What did you do back at school?"

"It is self-defense. I left no blood. I will not teach a student who thinks it is a good thing to harm others through violence, even if it is not of your own doing." Feslen growled. Master Chai took out his pipe and smoked. Feslen's face burned with rage and humiliation as he stalked out.

He walked to his Cave of Silence. Inside, his rage finally spent, he sat and tears formed in his eyes. He felt a familiar, friendly breath on him. He began to laugh as a tail brushed against him, and a wet tongue licked his cheek. "Hey, Old Grey," he hugged the dog. "How did you know I needed you?"

The old dog and Feslen played a little. When both became too tired, the old dog put his grey and fuzzy head on Feslen's thin lap. Feslen petted the dog, smiling peacefully.

"You know, Old Grey, I prefer your company to that of people."

Old Grey licked his face in response and Feslen looked deeply into his eyes.

"People can be crummy, can't they? I know animal companions are better."

Old Grey snuggled his head close to Feslen's stomach and barked once.

"Yeah. You said it, boy," Feslen laughed and patted his aging fur. He offered his friend the remaining bits of breakfast. He watched the dog eat the egg custard with fascination. Even without teeth, the old dog could manage the almond-filled egg custard. The dog slurped, and Feslen smiled. The tail thumped and swayed in happiness. Feslen caressed the old dog's furless head. It felt like a leather-bound book. He buried his head in the old dog's body and nuzzled him. The old greyhound returned a frantic nuzzle. "You are my one true friend, the only thing I will miss if I ever do leave," Feslen whispered, looking into the old dog's soulful eyes. The dog sniffed around his pockets. Then it licked him again and Feslen grinned. "You're a smart dog. People don't give you enough credit because you look like a blind elderly man. Here's to you, another of us Outcast Strays," Feslen said, gazing into the dog's eyes and tossing him a bit more of his breakfast, piece by piece, in the air.

He might have said, "Go get it boy," with a stupider dog, but not with Old Grey. The old stray dog cocked his head, looking at him. Feslen laughed, knowing the dog knew what to do. Old Grey waited until each piece fell next to his old grey nose. The dog ate quickly. Feslen grinned and opened his arms. The dog settled in his lap. The two friends gazed at each other and then up at the rising stars in happy silence.

13

KA-WEI'S REPORT 報告

Ka-Wei's eyes glistened with tears as he and his remaining Black Rock Turtle battalion studied their homeland. Two months had passed since he last saw his home. Everything seemed beautiful to him, even the ugly, false trees which the New Priests had planted. Even his beaten, sore, and very tired body felt relaxed and happy. "It's good to be home, right, Milord?" One of his men murmured. Ka-Wei turned a bit and his soldier paled in an instant. He stammered, "I…I…I am sorry for speaking out of term, Sire."

Ka-Wei laughed and said, "It's all right, Jokata. You may speak freely. And it is good to be home, even though home isn't as good as it was once." The Prince said that last bit under his breath. He dismounted for a moment and inhaled. The air surprised him with its unusual freshness. The birds greeted him with calls of happiness.

"Yes, Milord," Jokata said.

Ka-Wei grinned, not allowing his full range of emotions to show, and said, "Ichi Ken, gentlemen, I want to remind you, as long as we're outside the boundary of the country, don't address me as royalty. I'm just the Red Warrior."

"Yes Sire, I mean, yes, Red Warrior," replied Ichi Ken in a somber mood.

His soldiers asked all at once, "Are we mounting? Or walking?"

"I'll leave it up to you men," Ka-Wei said. He led his horse by the reins, as ten of his twelve men rode; the other two, Kil Gong Fu and Ichi Ken, walked behind their leader.

Behind him, Chiendong's highest mountain, Mount Jing's hawk-like peak, seemed to sing out in the early morning skies. Ahead of him and all around were Frog's Swallow Mountain and Gemstone Mountain. Even though the Prince disliked the landscape, he felt welcomed and comforted by the surrounding mountains and by Yellow Petal Lake. His black-haired archer, Gil Kong Fu, suggested that they hurry, and the Prince grunted in acknowledgement. Ka-Wei nevertheless lingered a little bit and took his time entering from the Northern Gate. His weary troops did not mind the slow trot.

The Prince even enjoyed the appearance of the first of the two moons. Only half of it appeared, and so he calculated that only three and a half months remained of winter. Only Ka-Wei took off his full armor when headed towards town. He hated armor. When they reached the stables, Ka-Wei dismissed his troupe. The Prince was already late for his appointment with his King. Ka-Wei had other plans in mind. He wanted to visit the Raster brothers. He walked to the central market through the various alleys and side streets. He stopped at the appointed place and waited, fingering a new scar on his cheek and the Promise Ring on his left pinky.

He caught a glimpse of a foreign wagon, decorated in red. The silk screen opened. The most angelic woman appeared in his vision. Her beauty overwhelmed his ideals of women and surpassed that of every woman he had known throughout his entire life. The silk screen closed again. Ka-Wei shook his head and thought with a laugh, *Even Feslen would want to touch her!*

Ka-Wei waited for Duxan to join him as he prepared to bring his report to Master Chai. He needed Feslen's help and knew that convincing Duxan and the family would not be easy. The Prince grinned and thought, *Live combat will seem easier once I've dealt with his family.*

He felt a rock solid hand on his shoulder. "You ready, my friend?"

Ka-Wei smiled a winning smile at his long time friend. Duxan returned a hearty glow. His oval-shaped eyes narrowed and he asked, "What have you got in mind, my Prince?"

"So formal, Duxan? We've been friends since what, we were seven?"

Duxan chuckled nervous and asked, "Are you all right, Ka-Wei? You seem a bit more bruised."

"We'll discuss it when we get to Master Chai's. How is Feslen?"

"He is good, just finishing the Twelve Steps again. He's really progressed."

"Good. Very good. I had no doubt he would progress," Ka-Wei said with a steady nod.

"Just what are you up to, my friend?" Duxan wondered as they walked in silent ease towards the Master's home.

Master Chai gave the Prince a laconic greeting, "Welcome back, Master Ka-Wei." Feslen completed the Twelfth Dragon Step in a whirl: he balanced on one leg on a large rock and he held two heavy rocks in his upright palms. He threw both rocks up into the air and jumped up and then kicked both rocks coming down. The rocks shattered, and then he clasped his hands in a Chi-Gong move and pulled the rock shards towards him. He whirled and twisted in mid-air as he touched the large rock below him every two seconds. After ten minutes of this spinning display, Feslen finally landed on the large, balancing rock below him and leapt away from it, spinning towards the Prince and Duxan. Both young men raised their hands in defense, but Feslen landed easily right in front of them at the last moment.

Ka-Wei started congratulating him, but the four of them heard soft hands clapping. Kai-Lornu clapped and gave him a half-wave. Feslen blushed at her retreating figure, carrying a full tray of empty teacups back into the school.

"Nice scars, Ka-Wei," Feslen grinned.

Ka-Wei chuckled and thought, *It's good to be back among friends.* They entered the cool interior of Chai's home to avoid the late afternoon heat.

"I fought the Sorceress, but she used powerful spells that we found hard to counter. When we entered, sudden blindness overtook us. Then we pushed against a wind so strong that it was hard to breathe. Also, I encountered someone with the ability to double himself…as an illusion…so many illusions," Ka-Wei sighed with a shake of his head. "Worse yet…the red eyes…the black cloak. It doesn't make sense why he would be working with the Sorceress."

"The Magic Art cannot be trifled with, Ka-Wei. I'm surprised she didn't do more to you," Feslen said. Feslen glanced at Duxan, who continued to eat, and asked, "Is that all she did?"

"I don't know." Ka-Wei said, hesitating. He mumbled a bit, almost dazed in his reply, "I can't remember anything that happened after the red eyes. I do believe she used some sort of wind spell, like the ones in the ambush."

"Are you all right, Ka-Wei?" Duxan asked, placing a concerned hand on his friend's arm. There was a feverish look in the Prince's eyes.

"Darkness so vast…the soldiers raising up from their s grave…my former comrades and friends…" Ka-Wei mumbled.

Duxan and Feslen exchanged looks and then gave Master Chai a questioning gaze. He shook his head.

"Hey, Ka-Wei?" Duxan asked again, as he shook his friend.

Ka-Wei closed his eyes a bit, feeling a strange frightened dizziness enter him. He shook himself out of the odd fright he felt and then opened his eyes. He smiled at his friends, but it was an empty smile.

Red eyes? Undead? Things from legend coming true? Feslen thought, frowning. How that could be connected with the Sorceress?

Silence fell upon the place as soon as the Prince spoke about the ambush. They sat around the dinner table along with Kai-Lornu. She sat next to Feslen and kept very silent. Feslen stole glances at her from time to time. She was wearing a purple dress and had kept her short hair down. The dress made her look very feminine. Feslen blushed and looked away. Master Chai said nothing as he ate delicately. He smoked his pipe even during the meal. Feslen coughed every few words.

"Yes, that's why I need your help, Feslen. That's why I demanded… asked you to improve your health and training."

"Wait, bringing him along on this adventure will surely be detrimental to him, Ka-Wei. You must not be serious. You know that he's only fourteen years old," Duxan pointed out.

"I am serious, Duxan. Your brother has proved himself against the Sorceress's magic and shown his veteran steadiness in combat. I could use his knowledge and abilities."

"Besides," Feslen intervened, his fists clenched, "the strike against Ka-Wei was also against both of us, Duxan. And Mei Xue's life is in danger. I owe her much."

"But she wouldn't want you to be in danger, Fes."

Kai-Wei cut off Duxan's pleas and said clearly, "Enough. My mind is made up, Duxan. I know you don't like it. I understand the family will be worried, but I need him. You know he can't stay here forever. You know how he is treated. It's time he learned how to be a man."

"Master Chai, what do you think?"

"Duxan, it is not my place to say. You sought my help to make Feslen a better person in health. I can only do so much. You know it to be right and true. My advice? Let him make mistakes. Let him explore and grow. Unfortunately, you and Feslen will soon have little choice in the matter."

"What do you mean?" Duxan and Feslen asked at the same time, with glances at each other.

The Master sighed, closed his eyes, and continued smoking his pipe. When it was clear the Master did not intend to give any answer, Feslen and Duxan peppered Ka-Wei with questions.

Kai-Wei concluded, "I've said my piece. We have to appease your family somehow, Duxan. Please, know that this decision is right."

Duxan sighed and chuckled, "All right. Let's go."

Feslen hugged his brother and beamed a smile at Ka-Wei. The Prince gave him a wink. *I hope this isn't my biggest mistake*, Ka-Wei thought. He looked at the happy boy and the reluctant older brother as they waited for him outside. Then he answered his own question, "No, it's not. My first biggest mistake was to listen to Uncle."

"By the way, Feslen and Duxan. Look out for the foreign princess I encountered on the road here, all right?" Ka-Wei mentioned with his hand covering his mouth. The young Prince waited for Feslen's reaction. He noticed Kai-Lornu fidget when he mentioned this foreign beauty.

Feslen and Duxan stopped before they left. Duxan turned and raised an eyebrow at his friend. He grinned and said, "a Princess? Anything special about her?"

Ka-Wei smiled and winked and said, as his eyes misted over in memory, "Let's just say, I've seen many women, glamorous and not. She's unlike anything I've ever seen. Her skin glistened in the sun. Her grace blossoms as if she is forever young. Her golden hair and golden acorn-shaped eyes…she walked with such purity, such serenity…even my worries ceased to matter."

Duxan grinned from ear to ear and nudged his brother. "Sounds like someone's in love," Duxan and Feslen laughed.

Ka-Wei chuckled, "Nah, I'm getting married in a year, remember? Besides, I sensed her sense of Honor and her youth. I know she's looking for someone just as pure. Maybe she's looking for Feslen."

Feslen harrumphed and said, "Why should I be interested?"

"She asked around in the first few villages close to our border until she saw me and my troupe. She said to me, 'I am looking for a boy nicknamed the Frog.' She asked me about you, Feslen."

Feslen coughed and sighed. I guess that nickname will never escape me, he thought. The name that Sae-Jyung had given him one day at Red School had stuck with him. Feslen exchanged a shocked look with Duxan and started to speak.

"I'm sorry to bring you pain, Feslen," Ka-Wei thought, as he knew full well of the bullying Feslen had received. Somehow the foreign princess from Nu knew of Feslen already! Ka-Wei interrupted, "Listen, Feslen, I'm not going to kid you about something like this. Besides, there's something about her that brings happiness, even to me. I believe her when she says she wants to find you."

"Do you know her?"

"No, I don't, Feslen. I've never seen her before, but she seemed familiar for some reason."

"All members of the royalty have their reasons, Prince Ka-Wei. You of all people are aware of that. Perhaps she may not be looking for Feslen," Master Chai interjected.

"Maybe. But I felt her truth when we locked eyes. By the way, Dux, you know more about fixing axles than I do. The wheels on her carrier kept falling off," Ka-Wei mentioned, changing the subject. He heard the door to the dining hall open and saw Kai-Lornu enter and shuffle in silence to stand by her Master. Ka-Wei nodded to Kai-Lornu and bowed to Master Chai and said to his friends, "I think we've kept the Master long enough from his meditations." He bowed again to the quiet Master Chai and exchanged knowing glances. The Raster brothers bowed to Master Chai and Ka-Wei and then left. Master Chai lit his pipe as Ka-Wei started to leave.

Ka-Wei coughed and shook his head and he reached into his belt pouches. "Ah, yes, I almost forgot, Master. Here are the papers you requested." The Prince then handed his Official Royal Papers to Master Chai. The Master did not make a move for them. Ka-Wei shrugged and placed the papers on the Master's desk. "Master, I believe there's some information you should read. It confirms our worst fears about the fate of the country."

Master Chai said nothing. Then Ka-Wei said, "I hope our plan works."

"If the conclusions we've drawn from all of our past experiences are right," Ka-Wei thought, "my beloved world, Hahn-Hah, might not be in as much trouble as we all think. Perhaps the potential I saw in Feslen when I first met him will be realized when we give him responsibilities."

"It should, my Prince. Feslen will save us all. Will you tell them, Ka-Wei?" Master Chai asked him, shaking him out of his deep thoughts. Prince Ka-Wei placed one foot out of the door and turned his head and said, "I hope you're right, Master. They will find out soon enough." He bowed at his waist to the Master and walked away. Kai-Lornu helped Master Chai retire for the evening.

14

A PRINCESS APPEARS 公主出現

A few weeks later when the month of Loe passed into the month of Jin, the hottest weeks of winter came to pass. The people of Chiendong placed minor statues of worship to the Goddess of Virtue, Ho Shien, and to the God of the Hearth, Mo Lai. These weeks were so hot that even the modest women of Chiendong wore little more than a under garment when they went outside to do their chores or went to school. Yet no one noticed for something remarkable and new occurred. Although many new things seemed to be happening all at once to the people of Chiendong, another new event did not phase them.

Old men played mahjong with each other as younger generations went about their bustling ways.

Thousands of bikes came to a halt, stopping everyday traffic. The bikes had only two wheels but were very sturdy despite their flimsy appearance. Peasants and even merchants used these bikes to get across the avenues of Beizung and over the rougher terrain of Chiendong. This new event, however, interrupted their routines. Men gawked, women fanned themselves, and even rough housing children stopped in wonder. People stared at the colorful stagecoach with decorative lamps. The driver shouted at the little old lady who dropped her food basket. The young woman inside the coach silenced people with her foreign beauty. Her long, vibrant hair, shining in the sunshine, streamed down to her perfect shoulders. Her hair, which seemed as lively as the woman herself, was of a color that flashed from golden to silver to brown, depending on the angle at which she moved her head as she watched her bodyguard step out. Her gray-brown eyes dripped like dew from a fresh rainstorm.

Those who were lucky enough to catch her look felt thunder and awe strike them. They forgot their troubles for months afterwards, and memories came in dribs and drabs for them. For those in business, it was a bane, of course. But for those who had experienced breakdowns in relationships and other hardships, the loss of memory was a boon.

Her light green kimono with its recognizable symbol—three entwined blue flowers and a pattern of golden Seng-Seng Birds—revealed to even the peasants where she was from. This same symbol also decorated her coach. She was from the mysterious land called Nu. Murmurs of her origins spread among the peasants, nobles, city guards, and the occasional New Priest acolytes that passed through the crowds.

A broken wheel had caused the accident. The bodyguard of the Princess called for help and city guards and the Emperor's guards alike rushed to her coach and ushered the crowd aside. The foreign princess with the golden-silver hair entranced all. Her amber eyes pierced everyone who met them with a sense of great kindness. Her beauty stilled the chaos of normal life.

Once her coach had been fixed, the Princess thanked the workers and headed towards the castle. The women were the first to come out of their reverie go back to their daily business. The men still gawked. When the Princess's entourage entered the castle, normal life finally returned to its busy bustle. After some time went by, and during the rest of the day, whisperings about the Maiden from the North and the Land of Nu were heard about town. People said the same things, "Was that the Goddess Ho Shien? If not, she's so beautiful that she resembles the Goddess in every way!"

15

PRINCESS AND THE BEAST
公主與禽獸

The next morning Feslen went to Beizung's First Library to do research on Jerenko-I, magic, and the ambush. His youngest sister, little Li-Pei, tagged along. It was only on rare occasions that he got to enjoy being himself and being by himself (or with just one relative). He took little or no notice of Li-Pei's constant talking to her imaginary friend. Feslen was the only Wong who could put up with her invisible friend, and Li-Pei was the only one who tolerated Feslen in the mood he called "the Thinker." A small, secret smile appeared on his face as he studied her dimpled cheeks. She tugged on her bun of brown hair, trying to pull it down to make it long. "So much for your attempts to make her into a little lady, Mother," Feslen thought with an appreciative chuckle, watching her. He had stayed up late last night, thinking about his problems. He was so preoccupied he almost didn't notice all the people that began to mill about in the crossroads.

"Li-Pei, can you be quiet when we're inside the Library? I can't study and keep an eye on you at the same time, you know," he said.

"I'm almost eight! I can take care of myself, thank you very much."

Feslen opened his mouth to speak, but he decided against it, because he hated lectures. He asked, "Why the increase of people?"

"Well, they are preparing for the Winter Festival," Li-Pei piped up.

Feslen pulled his sister close to him so she wouldn't be crushed by the throng. He ignored her small fists banging into his harder stomach as he studied the irregular flow of the commuters. Rage shook him from head to toe and he wanted to shout, "This is my only day without my family harassing me. Can't you all just leave me be?" But he controlled himself.

Despite the festival preparations that his sister had mentioned, this was an awful lot of traffic for the local roads. Then he turned north and west and the main roads were also in sight. To his continued agitation, overcrowded conditions jammed all the roads. Feslen did not like the movement of the city folk. He inched along with the rest of the sluggish pack. He sheltered Li-Pei the best he could; people pushed them. He cursed his small frame and his lack of physical strength. He even wished for some assistance from his family.

He wanted to get away from the crowd and onto the grounds of the Library. He liked what the Main Library of Archives offered. He especially enjoyed the vastly improved pathways. Walking in the main part of town on deep sloping hills with this many people around him was a burden for Feslen. Even with his improved heath, air did not come easy for him in this crowd.

"Are you all right, little sister?" he whispered.

"Yes," Li-Pei gasped. "But you're holding me too tight. You could let me breathe a little."

"Sorry."

Feslen knew a big incident had occurred. An attack of dizziness almost overpowered him. Feslen heard Li-Pei saying something in a concerned voice. But he felt nothing—no heat, no cold. Then he heard the sound ahead of him of a cart breaking apart, the cry of a family, and the whinny of horses.

"There's been an accident! Someone help my son!" The mother of the flipped caravan screeched. Feslen heard the commotion. He saw a draft horse's broken leg and a boy pinned underneath it.

"Don't kill the poor horse!" Li-Pei wailed. She tugged the dazed Feslen along. "My brother can help! He's a magus!" Li-Pei exclaimed to the family. A respectful hush settled among the crowd. They parted way for the siblings to get to the injured boy and horse. Some people in the crowd uttered derisive comments.

"The Raster boy, isn't it?" said some people in the watching crowd.

"Is your brother a healing magus?" the father asked, as he nodded sadly towards the injured boy and horse. He held a big hunting knife, ready to end the suffering horse's torment.

Feslen heard and saw everything but could not even move his lips to protest. Fear had paralyzed him. Then, all of a sudden, he saw energy lines, just as the Master had taught him to do. He saw himself reach for them. He saw himself heal the boy and horse. However, he did not yet move. He wept. He felt Li-Pei's tears as she buried her head in his stomach. A stone was hurled their way and hit the young Raster's head. The crowd spit on him. He felt their spittle but could do nothing.

Li-Pei ducked when another stone was aimed at them. "It's not his fault! He ran out of air! Look at him! He's all blue!" she defied the crowd.

The father of the injured boy sighed and nodded. He raised his knife. suddenly, a sense of peacefulness fell on the scene. "Halt. No need to kill today," a harmonious, soft voice filtered through the laughing crowd. Then Feslen's soul sang and felt free. The shock of the ability to move again made him act quickly to protect his sister. His eyes scanned the crowd for the person who spoke. The once unruly crowd became an ocean of peace. Remorse filled the crowd.

A respectful awe reverberated like an echo through the crowd. "It's her! It's the *waigouren* maiden! The Shining Maiden from the North!" the crowd whispered.

This must be her! Was the only thought that filtered through Feslen's chaotic mind. Ka-Wei's description of the mysterious maiden paled in comparison with this amazing reality. He wished he could catch a glimpse of her eyes, but she hid her face behind her long hair and hands.

Her graceful walk enhanced her svelte and athletic frame. Her waist-long strawberry-black hair glistened. She never looked up once at any man, not even the father of the boy she intended to help.

"But, Mistress, you'll get your beautiful kimono all dirty!" the stunned father stammered. Indeed, for the first time in his life, Feslen noted a woman's dress. Entwined blue flowers with golden Seng-Seng Birds patterned her silk kimono. The gown glittered like the lady who wore it.

A burst of shy laughter from the pure maiden awakened his soul. Feslen felt weak in the knees and a peaceful glow engulfed him as the Princess approached. A tremendous burst of joy and tantalizing ease surged through Feslen. "You shall rest now. Be at peace," she whispered. She lifted a dainty hand just above the injured boy's bleeding chest. A small burst of yellow dropped like dew from the maiden's fingers onto the boy. The wounds of the boy and of the horse mended instantly.

"My brother…" Li-Pei pleaded.

The maiden turned and smiled in gentle kindness. Feslen shut his eyes and started to cry. Her beauty was too great for someone like him to see. Thunder raced through his body, allowing him to move his arms as she lightly placed a finger on his face. He gasped at her touch. A thrill he had never before experienced sundered his entire being. Feslen's eyes flared opened. She said nothing, but she smiled. Better yet, he seemed completely at ease; his body's defenses had melted away. Feslen began laughing, and the laughter felt good. Tears of blood, pain, and sweat mixed with the laughter. He rolled around the ground, drawing the attention of everyone again. The maiden began laughing too. It was genuine laughter. Happiness flowed from her. Feslen laughed until his stomach hurt. The maiden locked her pool-deep amber eyes with his.

"My lady! Nai-Hua! You shouldn't be with this rabble!" shouted a stern-sounding man from somewhere within the crowd.

For a moment, the maiden named Nai-Hua showed her displeasure. A broad-shouldered man emerged from the parted crowd. Feslen sprung up and hugged the young woman. He ignored his little sister's astounded cry at his actions. The Princess returned his warm embrace.

"My lady!" the man shouted.

The Princess sighed and turned, but Feslen caught her wrist. Quicksilver ran through his blood as he touched her. Again, Feslen staggered back after staring into her ageless amber eyes. He shook as he tried to speak. *"We will meet again, I promise",* came her voice in his mind. *"You will never be alone again, Feslen."*

"Who are you?" Feslen asked silently in return, as the glow of love flowed through his eyes.

"Call me Nadine. My closest loved ones do."

"Alright, Na…"

However, before he could finish, the man, whom Feslen presumed was the bodyguard, growled as he tore Feslen away from her, "No rabble shall be touching the pure lady!"

"Then you, my friend, ought to do a better job of protecting such a valuable treasure!" he chuckled. The bodyguard glared at him. Feslen's eyes narrowed to regard the man.

The Princess spoke, "Don't argue with me. You are just my bodyguard. These young people are my friends here in Beizung. Come visit me when you're ready."

Li-Pei nudged Feslen in the ribs and he replied, "Th-thank you, Your Grace."

"Call me, Nai-Hua. You are my noble subject after all. What is your name?" She laughed again.

"F-F-…"

"His name is Feslen, Your Grace," Li-Pei said with an awkward bow. "His speech becomes afflicted sometimes. We would be honored to be your guests."

"I must go to the castle now. Please come when you can," Nai-Hua smiled. "I am lonely since I came all this way from Nu., I would like visitors."

Before young Feslen responded, the young lady left, as her bodyguard pulled her away from the silenced crowd. "Princess Nai-Hua! Did you hear? The Wongs got yet another favor!"

"Well, come on, let's go! We can't stay here all day, can we? Just look at these people!" Li-Pei tugged her speechless big brother along. Feslen's grip slackened and she tripped. The crowd parted and continued their daily routines and Li-Pei picked herself up. She looked at her older brother and sighed. She took his hand and they went back home.

16

SCHOOL AND LIFE 學校與生活

Feslen temporarily forgot Nadine, his love, and her invitation while he was preparing to impress people for the upcoming Choicings. The Choicings, an eight-thousand-year-old coming of age ceremony, had been brought back by the earliest missionaries from the Far West. Feslen spent his time trying to find the right spell or trick to improve his chances of becoming an Initiate for the magicians of the Great School of Magic Stuff and to impress everyone, especially Nadine. To him, magic was about creation and expressing himself like an artist. Feslen came across a spell called the *Show of Lights*, an expanded version of the ordinary spell called simply *Light*.

"Herein bright, outside dark. Make dogs bark, stars fly and fall. Release the brightness of it all!" Feslen uttered the words on the page loud enough to make all those in the Beizung Library look at him. He pointed at the empty lantern and watched with a trembling jaw. The crystal on the stand did not brighten as he expected. He growled, "What am I doing wrong?" Feslen muttered to himself, disturbing some students and other researchers.

Suddenly, a smell of onion and wet dirt hit Feslen in the nose. "Leave me be, Sae-Jyung Jang."

"Look, I came here to make peace. Tojoh was the one who…"

"Drop the dog dung, Jang. I'm not a fool, though I fell into your trap. Touch me again and I will burn you." A dark chuckle rippled through

Feslen as he looked up and curled his lip and glared at his tall rival. Sae-Jyung was wearing a black cloak and was accompanied by his henchman, Tojoh.

"I can show you some magic. I can show you the basics of what you're doing wrong," said Sae-Jyung as he raised his hands.

"Why? So you could hurt some innocent? What proof do I have that you can cast spells or do well? And what about him? Are you going to get rid of him?" Feslen's brooding look did not fade but deepened. Then the young Raster sensed the presence of Lioin nearby and felt comforted. He scanned the confines of the Beizung Library and saw the outline of the teenage thief in the shadows of two bookcases.

"Fair enough. Get out of here, Tojoh," Sae-Jyung told his brutish sidekick. Tojoh growled and bowed to Sae-Jyung. He walked out of the main room of the Library, but not far enough away to avoid overhearing the conversation between Feslen and Sae-Jyung. He gave a scathing stare of hatred at Feslen. Sae-Jyung and Feslen talked in low whispers.

"There, now. That nastiness is in our past," Sae-Jyung grinned and then said with a serious face, "A Prevention Spell surrounds the Library. Its energies are subtle but constant. You should be able to feel the energy cascading in here. That's why your spell didn't work."

"Fine. I can't forget how you treated me in the past though. But I am curious to see you cast spells. I don't trust you, but I have no choice," Feslen sighed and ran his hand through his hair.

They went out of the entrance and Tojoh followed them, but Sae-Jyung remained unconcerned. Then, as they neared the exit, Tojoh blocked their way. He showed his official magician's acceptance letter and gloated. "Look, I got in, Toadwort." Feslen swallowed hard and tried to leave. Tojoh blocked their way. Then, before either Feslen or Sae-Jyung could counter, the young apprentice lifted his fist. "Outsider!" Tojoh said and punched Feslen.

Feslen felt peculiar energy lines that were twisted, unsmooth. When Sae-Jyung cast his spell, it was steady and beautiful, almost like sheet music. The boy blinked and saw Tojoh's wand. "I felt something, instead of seeing it. Perhaps the life forces of living things differ from actual magic," Feslen thought. Could other things, such as magical elements, give off different forms of aura? I thought auras came only from *SAI* and living things?

"Why did you do that?" Sae-Jyung growled, lifting a hand and chanting.

"You told me to…" Tojoh started to accuse him but stopped as Sae-Jyung cast a spell on him. Dark sparks encircled Tojoh and the boy screamed. Beautiful auras came from the spell, entrancing Feslen.

"Can't advance much yourself, so you pick on the bright ones, huh, Tojoh?" Feslen goaded.

Tojoh gave a scathed glance at the two of them. Sae-Jyung had impressed Feslen.

"No spell casting in the Library, Sae-Jyung!" Teacher Lung warned.

"You saw what Tojoh did, Sir?" Sae-Jyung responded, his hand still glowing.

"I did, but retribution is not the way, nor is magic allowed here. You will be docked twelve points on the Year Merit if you continue."

Feslen did not know what to make of it, whether this had all been set up in advance or what. However, the anger in Sae-Jyung seemed genuine enough. "Don't do it, Sae-Jyung. Three strikes and you're out of school," Feslen remembered Master Chai's scolding.

Sae-Jyung looked at Feslen for a moment and relinquished his grip.

"What spell was that?" Feslen asked.

"The Illusionist's Trick. It's just a bunch of fancy fake lights."

"Impressive. How long have you been out of this magic school?" Feslen craned his neck to glare at Tojoh when they walked away from the Library.

They continued walking, out of the center of Beizung, and talking. "I am still in school, just a Third Year student. My magic is a hobby, like yours. I've been studying for longer than I can remember, though it's not Flair like yours." Sae-Jyung chuckled.

Feslen detected some jealousy under the controlled tones. They walked for hours through the Western Gates to a less populated road. But there were still many of the Jang's customers there who greeted Sae-Jyung.

Sae-Jyung took little notice of them. His magi's multicolored Yin Yang symbol was visible on his cloak. "By the way, I wanted to thank you for getting me out of a jam," Feslen and Sae-Jyung spoke at the same time.

The two exchanged stories of how they got into magic. Sae-Jyung mentioned that his aunt dabbled and his father used to be a physician and chemist with the New Priests. The road wore out. They walked for more than three hours to their destination. Lioin's presence reassured Feslen. There was a bit of truth to Sae-Jyung's words, but Feslen knew that the seventeen-year-old held back information. Feslen did not press it.

"How can you train with two different factions?"

"Money, power, influence, and a bit of cajoling," Sae-Jyung answered with a laugh.

The two arrived at an abandoned village with temple ruins on the outskirts near the Joppone Ocean. Sae-Jyung assured Feslen that no passersby would come this far out since no roads lead here. Although commoners across Hahn-Hah tend to be a little less frightened of magic, more so than the elite Chiendong were, the begrudging acceptance was just the same.

The day dwindled to a cooler evening. "Nice home," Feslen grinned and the merchant mage chuckled.

"Are you ready for instructions, Feslen?" Feslen nodded with childish eagerness. "You have to let your voice reflect what you feel and then let the spell flow like a river. Now watch me say the spell of *Light*." Feslen followed Sae-Jyung's instructions, enraptured as he watched his new teacher.

Sae-Jyung seemed to place difference emphasis on parts of the chanted words than Feslen had tried earlier in the Library. "Herein bright, outside dark. make dogs **bar**k, Stars FLY and fall, release the **brightnes**s of it all!" Sae-Jyung intoned, holding out his palms half-stretched. A chiming sound alerted Feslen to the start of the spell. The chiming increased when Sae-Jyung's fingertips began to glow. He pointed at the lantern. Then a little burst of light briefly showered the two of them before puttering out. Sae-Jyung sighed and mumbled something about "not being adequate with magic."

"Can you repeat that, Sae-Jyung?" Feslen tried to hold his excitement as he burst out. He wanted to know every inflection and change of motion!

"Of course!" Sae-Jyung nodded. He repeated the line more slowly. Feslen grabbed the light stand and readied himself. Shrugging, Feslen repeated the spell lines himself. A chime started. Nothing else happened. He repeated this many times; the chiming noises echoed many times. Then Feslen pointed at the light stand and it exploded—brighter than three lamps!

The brightness startled them both and they covered their eyes, but Sae-Jyung screamed, clearly in pain. Feslen saw Lioin's horrified and surprised look. "I can't see and I'm burning!" Sae-Jyung screamed as he flailed about. Feslen then ran to the young merchant mage, twisting his hands in misery. The young Raster waved Lioin away. The thief nodded, slipping away into the village.

"Wait! I can help myself!" Sae-Jyung growled a chant. Darkness extended from Sae-Jyung's hands and crawled over Feslen's light spell and countered it. The entire area felt a whole lot better once darkness covered it again. Sae-Jyung's entire body still smoked.

"Sae-Jyung, I…"

"I'm all right. You should try a lesser spell next time. You don't want anyone hurt, do you?"

His cynicism was not lost on Feslen, and he shook his head. "No, of course not, but I don't understand how…"

"You have Flair, remember? I've taught you all I know. Do no damage in the contest. Then you can get in the Great School of Magic Stuff."

Sae-Jyung bowed and walked to the village. Feslen watched him go and thought, If I have Flair, then why can't I cast even a simple spell that won't end up hurting people? He sighed and started to walk home. "Perhaps Master Chai lied to me so I could go rescue Mei Xue. After all, I don't even have the ability to cast spells, let alone use them at an enhanced level!"

Feslen searched for his pack and realized that, in his anxiety to learn magic, he had forgotten it back in the First Library. He managed the walk back with little trouble. Again he said a quick "thank you" in Honor of Master Chai and his many lessons. He got to back to the Library fairly soon. A few feet up the path, he saw Sae-Jyung talking furiously to a dark figure. This figure seemed to be enveloped in a cloud such that Feslen could make out only sketchy details. He wore a black cape, which was not unusual since a lot of people wore robes and cloaks. His Yin Yang symbol stood out in the darkness. His red eyes glowed in an eerie way that sent Feslen ducking behind three large trees. The man's aroma didn't reassure Feslen either: the smells of the graveyard and embalming materials. Feslen was sure that Sae-Jyung and his friend didn't notice him. He thought that the dark figure would do something horrible if he found out someone had eavesdropped on him!

Feslen heard snippets of their arguments. It was Sae-Jyung's deep voice, "The Princess is coming as I asked. I don't want to trick her again. I don't like this."

The dark figure laughed a chilling laugh, "You still lust after her like a schoolboy. Ah, those are the pitfalls of staying in the youthful mortal form. Why don't you stop fooling everyone and use your real form?"

"Why did you come to me tonight? You ought to stay away from me. My powers have grown. My Princess Nadine will see to your demise."

"Such faith you have in women," the dark figure scorned. "You know as well as I do that the Head Dragon New Priest seeks to conspire against us."

"Yes, well, he conspires against everyone. His own designs are not my problem and neither are yours," Sae-Jyung retorted and started to turn. The dark figure caught Sae-Jyung on the wrist. Sae-Jyung grimaced, and his face twisted in agony. A small roll of steam rose from where the dark figure had touched Sae-Jyung's arm.

"Listen," the dark figure continued, "my plans are rolling. I've met the Prince. I've convinced him to bring me the One. I know he's near. Do you know who he is?"

"No."

"If you double-cross me, you'll regret it, Sae-Jyung."

"I'm not afraid of you. You're not like the man who murdered my…" Sae-Jyung's voice trailed off as he moved further away and started to chant.

"I am not as weak as the mage who offended him. I offer you the chance you've dreamed about, Sae-Jyung. Let's work together. Our powers together are greater than those of the Prophecy Children! Even the Emperor will tremble with our combined might!" the dark figure said.

"No," Sae-Jyung said, but his voice sounded less confident. "The Princess will hate me forever for that."

"She already does. Wait and see," hissed the dark figure. "I will be waiting in the North. My plans are simple. You will come." The figure turned and disappeared.

Feslen blinked in shock and wondered if he even really saw the figure. He turned to see Sae-Jyung trembling so badly that he had to kneel down. It was as if he too were struck by a disabling congenital disorder. Several emotions ran through Feslen and confused him. One was so powerful that he placed one foot out of his hiding place. He wanted to help poor Sae-Jyung.

But then he heard Sae-Jyung talking to himself. He said other things that sounded dark and ominous: "I cannot fight him any longer on my own. I need Nadine's help. I hope she can help me. She did it before when she joined me in helping Master Chai." Sae-Jyung wiped sweat from his brow. He was bent over, with his back turned from Feslen's view. Other people entering the Library passed their gaze over Sae-Jyung for a moment. Then they entered as if he didn't exist. "Can she help my parents? Maybe she can see then? She's supposed to be one of the higher beings, after all," Sae-Jyung murmured to himself, his body shaking. Sae-Jyung's body hiccupped in what could almost be described as a chuckle and he shook his head, "No. She gave up her cause for me when *he* came into our lives. Feslen will be her new champion…" He paused and looked at the skies. He said, "I will have you back, Father, Mother. He's wrong. She'll come and help, wait and see." Sae-Jyung nodded his head and said, "She'll help, knowing that he's gotten stronger…She's going to come because of Feslen." His look of madness and misery pained Feslen. He chanted once more briefly and then vanished.

Feslen blinked and sat down, quite overcome. "What was that about? Whatever it was, doesn't sound good," He muttered. Before it got any later, he retrieved his backpack and left the Library.

17

EMPEROR'S DECREE 皇帝的命令

"To the people: the King has regrettably to inform you that taxes again need to be raised and longer working hours need to be enforced."

Feslen awoke to the loudness of the Crier shouting out the Emperor's Decree. He opened the window and staggered at the gust of winter's dust that blew in. The ordinary peasants and merchants knelt in front of the New Priest, his small group of bodyguards, and the Blue Soldiers who surrounded them. One of the merchants Feslen saw kneeling and kowtowing deeply to the New Priest was Merchant Li. Feslen saw the Emperor's Red Guards, even one Gold Guardsman, next to the fat New Priest, whom he did not recognize. Although this group looked intimidating, Feslen saw that they were outnumbered at least three to one. The Blue Soldiers who guarded the Emperor's men seemed reluctant at best. Feslen sighed when he saw the kowtowing of some of the higher officials of Bilong and Beizung who were there as well. He didn't understand the significance of the gathering but knew well enough that something had happened to get the Emperor and King all riled up. On a distant hill, Feslen spotted six Black Inquisitors. "What are they doing here?" he snarled to himself. His eyes narrowed, Feslen thought hard and scratched his head.

Easily noticeable in a splendid blue robe with star patches on it, the King's Crier went on, "Appearances of Princess Nai-Hua and the Sorceress. If any of the sons show signs of Primal Force, they must be handed over to the Emperor. If not, the good people of Chiendong must give up their firstborn sons or have their lands seized."

The crowd's anger grew, and Feslen saw a rock being tossed within the vicinity of the King's people. The King's Crier ducked and hid behind the New Priest, who nodded to the Blue Soldiers and then pointed in the direction of the peasant who threw the rock. Three Blue Soldiers went into the crowd and arrested the man. No one helped him or fought back.

Feslen clenched his teeth and raised a fist at the arrest. He did not know which made him seethe more, the fact that the New Priest had ordered the arrest or that the crowd did not resist. "The Emperor has gone too far this time. Some day the people will rise up against him. If any magic or strength remains in me…" Feslen grumbled to himself, letting his anger trail off. Then he stopped and listened to more of the meaningless babble coming from the New Priest's minion, the King's Crier.

"The Primal Force," the Crier continued. "For the non-educated, the Primal Force is magic in the crudest sense of the word. However, the mere practice of this energy smacks of religion, since it borders on faith. It is really a new religion, unregulated by the New Priests, and so the Emperor and the King cannot go unpunished! To identify it, all you need to know is that Primal Force casters do not need regular ingredients like normal mages. They do not act like ordinary mages. We, as the protective forces for you, cannot be everywhere at once. We ask you to keep your eyes open and to be vigilant at all times. We depend on you, the people, for the first line of defense against these barbarian magicians who act outside the Rules and Regulations. So the mages of the Great School of Magic Stuff beg you to watch out for those without the proper boundaries of magic."

Feslen thought, Hmm. Primal Force? What in Death's Basin did the Emperor mean by that? This was the first time that Feslen had heard that term.

The people in the crowd exchanged low murmurs of confusion. The New Priest sighed and handed the Crier a large sheaf of papers. "I shall have the Blue Soldiers post the ten most important characteristics for identifying users of the Primal Force!" the Crier said, as he began handing the papers to the Blue Soldiers. "And now, for some words from our Exalted Leader, through his helper, the New Priest: Ah Jak will now speak."

Feslen shook his head and said, "More persecutions of magicians? I wonder what the mages think of this. Didn't the Emperor and the King learn their lessons from history? The Mage Wars started because of actions like this." He slammed his left hand on the windowsill, getting a few splinters.

The Crier paused and gave way to the black-garbed New Priest. He looked like a mummy rather than a human. The people's anger and helplessness hit Feslen like a lightning bolt. He almost fell again as he saw their red haze of anger, but he managed to grip the windowsill. His body trembled even though he tried to keep still.

The New Priest, Ah Jak, read from a Decree: "This is a Decree from the Emperor. The Children of the Prophecy are coming. All parents must report to the Temple of Skies to see if their child has the Signs of being one of them. All normal children will receive blessings at the Temple. If we find one of the Prophecy Children from within this town, we will deal with it in our gentle way. Compensation will be given to the parents. That is all."

"The Prophecy is nothing but a legend. Even I don't believe in it! The Emperor Tsai is paranoid," Feslen sneered. He watched as the Emperor's men ordered the Blue Soldiers to seize any family with an older son or, in some cases, one son. The soldiers immediately reacted as a group when they saw a boy playing with a rope that seemed to float on its own. The soldiers moved in and grabbed him. The families did protest some, but they were threatened with severe punishment.

The Red Guards demonstrated their power to a family who protested too much. They first forced the husband to kneel down and then they punched him several times in the face, breaking bones. They then cut off his hand and forced him to watch them beat his wife. One of the Red Guards said in an unmoving voice, "See to it that you don't resist. Take this man away." Blue Soldiers dragged the bleeding peasant man away. They also took the wife away, leaving their remaining child, a daughter, with a confused look.

The New Priest, Ah Jak, looked on with laughter on his face. Feslen screamed in anger, but his tiny voice of reason merely blended into the sounds of the crowd. The New Priest announced one last thing in his squeaky voice, "There is one more announcement: you locals are not to interact in any form with the Princess Nai-Hua or her helpers. Doing so will be punishable by law. Rumors of the advancing Nomads is false. Prince Ka-Wei and his men have set them right. The King himself—our Lord of Light and Embracer of Good, may he forever reign—will personally make an appearance at the Wong's family home during the Winter Festival. Good cheer, and let us sing of the Nation's Pride:

"Cheer to our nation, so wide and pristine!
Clear and crisp, far and long, from the seas to the mountains,
Loyalty, diligence, always in good order to maintain!
Give your money, children, services, and life to the greater cause,
Always act without doubts upon our laws without pause!
Cheer to our Nation, so wide and pristine!
Long live the Emperor, King, and our Pride!"

Feslen snorted at the "National Song" and shook his head as everyone chimed in. Long before his brother approached, he felt his presence. "Over here, Duxan," he raised his voice above the outside noise.

Duxan chuckled, amazed at his brother's perceptive abilities. "Not liking the song, little bro?" Duxan asked.

"You know how I feel," Feslen grunted.

Even through the end of the song, harsh voices and loud knocking sounds had distracted Feslen.

"It's Black Inquisitors, go door to door," Duxan answered his unspoken thought.

Feslen frowned at his brother's cavalier attitude. The past month, this administration had sent its Inquisitors to the doors of innocent peasants all too frequently. Rumors flowed wildly about, saying that people had been dragged off in the night. If the Prince headed the Emperor's Four, he would put a stop to it. "Where's Ka-Wei?"

"I don't know. I haven't seen him since he accompanied us to the Master's place. There's going to be a family meeting in ten minutes. You have to be there, Fes. Hey! Gui-Pan, stop eavesdropping. You're not that good at it anyway." Lioin emerged from the shadows of sunset and frowned at Duxan's retreating back and then at Feslen's chuckle. Feslen could not help but laugh a little bit at the look on Lioin's puzzled face.

"I was rather good at it, until I started hanging around you folks, particularly you and your brother," Lioin said.

"Relax. My brother won't turn you over to the 'law.' What's going on? Are you keeping tabs on me?" Feslen grinned.

"I'm just making sure my only friend is all right. You don't buy that load of dog crap we just heard, do you?" the boy motioned to the King's men outside.

"What do you think? What news have you got for me this time?"

"What makes you think I have news? Can't I just come by and visit a friend?"

"Friends greet each other in the open, not that I don't count you as one. You come to me when you have interesting news, I've noticed," Feslen grinned without humor.

"Fair enough. It's about the Princess and this stuff," Lioin laughed.

"Feslen!" Father shouted from downstairs. Feslen fidgeted and sighed as his father called out a second time.

"I thought Duxan said the meeting was in ten minutes," Lioin remarked wryly.

"He's never been good with time," Feslen grinned. They both chuckled. Then Mother shouted as well.

"Your news will have to wait, my friend," Feslen said. Lioin nodded. Feslen slouched away and went down the stairs.

Feslen's entire family was waiting for him in the main dining room. Father held some official-looking documents. Feslen recognized the New Priest's health bills and tax forms. Feslen sighed and entered the room.

"Feslen, you need to hear this important news," Father spoke. Feslen nodded and sat unsteady. Feslen saw Father exchange a look with Mother. Father spoke, "Your health bills have cost us a lot over the last few years. The worst had been the past few weeks." Feslen blinked in shock at the frankness his parents showed towards him. Father continued, "You may have noticed that we've allowed you to go about in the absence of your siblings. We've let you run free like a wild animal."

Feslen had felt the difference but never questioned his recent good fortune of being free from family guards. His frown expressed his confusion. "What was the point? What does this have to do with me?" Feslen wondered.

"They're absent because they've taken on extra jobs with competing businessmen," Father said. His anger made the others jump.

"How? Why? Didn't I see more men coming to our farm and…"

"Quiet, dear," Mother said. Feslen clamped his mouth shut, his eyes saying much.

"Those men were tax collectors," Father said, without missing a beat. "The coffer's been opened wider than usual. There's been a bad karma in the air since the Sorceress came." Father shook his head.

Feslen's eyes flashed as he considered Father. His parents were traditionalists, people who do not like changes. They disliked magic, and they were orthodox religious people.

"Pay attention, Feslen!"

"Sorry," he grimaced and then grinned in embarrassment. "What were you saying, Father?"

"We are in worse financial straits than I originally estimated. Remember the cargo you and your brothers delivered earlier to Master Chai?" Feslen nodded. "We lost a lot of money that day," Father announced. "Do you realize that one shipment cost us an entire year's worth of salary? Not to mention the effect on all of the other people for whom we are responsible. They petitioned for the King to make us release some of our own savings for them."

Feslen wanted to speak, but Father held up a hand. Father's anger and sadness penetrated Feslen like an arrow. "I know, Father. But I thought that particular shipment was only for Master Chai."

"Wrong. Master Chai not only teaches the Martial Arts. He also ships out weapons and other items. He was our intermediary. Someone set us up, Son. Somehow, someone knew you were coming and tipped off your attackers," he roared, slamming his fists to the table.

"I will not go to the Red School any more or even to the Great School of Magic Stuff if I am selected, Father. I will be here for you if you need extra help," Feslen sighed, knowing that all of this was the lifeline of the family.

"That's not the answer," Father said with a slight smile. He looked at his wife who nodded. "We've decided to continue your schooling, Feslen. At least one of our children should get a good education. However, you will not waste your time on magic since it doesn't pay very well. We have appealed to Merchant Jun-li about a position for a boy with a mind like yours." Feslen could not help but moan in reply. But Father countered the moans by saying, "Now look, these health bills are expensive, Feslen. How will magic pay for them? Working as a street performer? No, no child of mine will have such a disreputable career! You know what Ai-Yen and Duxan will be giving up for your continued education. I heard that you talked back to your teacher today. Who was it, Teacher Lung? Yes, I know how you feel about him, but Mr. Lung is a respected man in this community. He deserves your respect. Also, he has direct connections with Merchant Jun-li. It's a good job, and I know you'll learn to love it," said Father. "Besides, your siblings love you."

Love? Hardly, Feslen thought. "But what noble sacrifices my brothers are willing to make!" Feslen narrowed his eyes and got up to leave. He felt Ai-Yen's hand upon his shoulder. He tried to shake it off. Anger boiled up inside Feslen hotter than soup on a stove. He slid out from under Ai-Yen and squirmed free from his grip using the Fourth Step. Ai-Yen looked totally flabbergasted. Feslen flicked his wrist away and energy passed from Feslen towards Ai-Yen. Ai-Yen let out a cry as the energy smothered him.

"Get back here! We are not done talking Feslen! Don't forget you're disabled, you shouldn't act like a normal person!" Mother said.

Feslen's heart shattered along with his mind when his adoptive mother said that. He cursed at them with the blackest thoughts he could muster up.

"Don't you dare use that outlaw magic on your own family or on anyone else! You're grounded!" Father's voice sounded like a lion's roar in Feslen's ears.

"I won't listen to meaningless orders from my non-parents," Feslen stated and stormed out of the house. The rapid heartbeats of the Wong family beat through the thick silence.

After his own shock wore off, Duxan tried to comfort and counsel his parents. At that very moment, Duxan's pride in his brother had increased because Feslen had stood up for himself for once. But there's no doubt about it. Feslen's diplomacy needs work, Duxan thought. Pride in his younger brother had overcome the anger that Duxan had felt towards Feslen for hurting their parents.

18

THE CHOICINGS 遴選大會

Feslen did not speak to his family since their decree and feigned excitement at the long traditional ceremony of the Choicings. Everyone watched the ceremony at the King's Judgment Palace in Rich District. Duxan had already placed more sacrifices to Kuan-Ti, God of War, and to GenCom, the Goddess of Health and Well Being. He placed new statues to several minor gods: the Goddess of Festivals, the God of the Townships, and a God of Music.

The Choicings had become a national ceremony back in the late Kong-Sui Dynasty. The Kong-Sui Dynasty discovered this ritual from the *waigouren*. Bands with musical instruments of all types waited with practiced patience on the marble steps of the Circumference Judgment Palace. Everyone who was coming of age stood in wait with scores of merchants, blacksmiths, sword masters, master-teacher magicians, martial artists, and others.

A troupe of Blue Soldiers protected the platform and the throne. Four different colored robed magicians were positioned near the throne. All three sects of the New Priests were gathered round the throne as well. Feslen scowled at them. His anger settled, in particular, on the middle-aged leader of the New Priests' entire organization and Head of the Black Dragon Sect, Elhong Wien. His nickname was also the Head Dragon. Elhong wore long, black, resplendent robes and liked looking more like a King. But he did not wear *glasssilk*, the traditional, silk-hardened armor worn only by the high-ranking royalty of Chiendong. Even with his fancy outfit, a powerful odor of aged garlic and scallions emitted from him. He turned his face towards Feslen for a moment, and the boy felt a moment of uncontrolled sickness. Elhong Wien's stare had no soul! Worse yet, Feslen's own image was reflected in the man's soulless beady eyes. A brief memory of the New Priest shivered through Feslen for a moment.

Then he saw the man talking to a nearly identical looking brother of his, dressed in the traditional yellow and beige uniform of the Elhong School's Martial Arts students. This other Elhong brother hurried over to the King's advisor and then to the King himself and pointed to some of Master Chai's students. After a few minutes of discussion, Master Chai's students were barred from entering. Two other New Priests from separate sects also presided: the Snake Organization and the Spitting Scorpion. The Snake New Priest head wore a purple and black robe with, of course, the snake symbol on the back of his robe. The Scorpion New Priest leader, a female, wore a deep red and black robe. Feslen's eyes narrowed in anger at all of this. But just as he began to think about it, he started to wheeze and then collapsed to his knees as a peaceful ray of energy flashed through him. Feslen turned his attention towards the mages. Pink, Blue, Yellow, Red, and Immersing Black colors represented their rank and experiences, not their politics. Maroon-robed Master Drak—Master Magician of all the mages in Hahn-Hah, Leader of the Great School of Magic Stuff—did not attend. Disappointed, Feslen had expected Master Drak to attend. The Choicings came once every five years. The last incidence of the Choicings, as Feslen heard, had ended in disastrous humiliation for the Great School of Magic Stuff. The chosen apprentice apparently had committed suicide. Perhaps that's why Master Drak is not here, Feslen speculated with a smirk. He chuckled at the thought of suicide.

"Finding something funny?" Ai-Yen whispered and poked him hard in the ribs.

"Yes, be serious!" Mei-Whuay chided. Feslen ignored them.

When mages became professionals, robe colors indicated the aspect of magic they chose to perform. Eager teens and children were dressed up in their Robes of Choice. Feslen shook his head and returned to studying each of the four magicians. I do not need a color, Feslen thought. Of course, to join their silly school, they'll force me to wear their colors. That's the rules. At least I know I will get what I want in the end, despite the stupidity.

"Beautiful, aren't they?" Mei-Whuay said him when she saw Feslen inhale sharply. She mistook his reaction for awe at the coming of the front guard, the first line of personal bodyguards for the King. The shining, silver-blue armor impressed most people. But Feslen had inhaled because of the rush of power he had felt from the four mages.

The woman in the pink robes had affected him the most. An imperceptible aura of smooth, bright orange surrounded the Pink Robe mage, and Feslen pondered its meaning. Her energies enveloped all of the people within a fifteen-foot radius from her. Her aura diminished and increased again. She controlled her magic without trouble; her companions took more effort to do so. She was short and stocky, pug-nosed and pock-faced, and had long, rather unkempt hair. One side of her face bore the scar of having been burned. Feslen gasped at that. He wondered why he didn't see it before and realized that she kept her long hair over the burnt side of her face. "Was it from a magical accident?" Feslen wondered. But before he could think any more, he saw her look at him! Feslen blinked again to make sure he wasn't seeing things! She tipped her head and seemed to nod at him in acknowledgement. It may have been the tears in his eyes, but he thought he saw the Pink Robe mage lean over to her colleagues and say something about him!

"What's the matter, little brother?" Duxan whispered. "Don't make our parents angrier than they already are."

"I think he's in love," Mei-Whuay taunted him. "He's looking at that female mage!"

Ai-Yen snickered, "I don't think Feslen could fall in love with anyone!"

"You take that back!" Little Li-Pei shouted. The Wong siblings fought each other.

Suddenly, a painful ringing noise shot through Feslen's head, and he gritted his teeth in pain. It must be the Sorceress, he thought. The crowd murmured as the guards stirred. She laughed in scorn. "Get me out of here," Feslen almost burst out.

Duxan looked on with concern and started to speak but was silenced by the trumpets acclaiming the opening welcome theme. "I've got to be strong and concentrate!" Feslen muttered through bleeding lips and gums, an effect, he assumed, of the Sorceress's powerful magic on him. To counter the effects, Feslen used the Third Technique taught to him by Master Chai: *"Deep breaths…focus your mind on the fourth breath."* Feslen fell into rhythm, ignoring everything around him, including his parents' chiding. Deep brass drumbeats highlighted the entrance of King's Rear Guard. Incense rose in the air and the reflections of candles shone brightly on the armor and robes of Elhong Wien. The Sorceress's powers radiated outward, even one hundred feet or more away from the ceremonial platform. She had a far greater reach than Pink Robe. Feslen's worry broke his concentration, and pain shot through his body.

"Are you okay, little brother?" Duxan asked, squeezing his brother's astonishingly muscled shoulders firmly.

"The Sorceress is here. Her presence alone makes me uneasy."

Duxan nodded and said, "Too bad Ka-Wei isn't here. He would deal with her." Feslen did not reply. He would have if he could speak. He was not so sure that even the Prince could deal with the Sorceress on his own. The King's entry music drowned out Duxan's comment. Feslen guessed at his brother's words and nodded in reply

The King's Crier announced, "Hail King Jien Tsu Shang, Most Holy of Heavenly Powers, second to the Great Emperor. May he live a thousand lives of ever so Prosperous Ways!"

The people repeated the statement, mostly in good cheer. Feslen managed to get his dizziness under control. The boy pondered what had just happened as the Crier's meaningless speeches continued. "Why did I feel the pain when I did not feel it before? What source did it come from?" Feslen wondered. Then he saw Sae-Jyung six rows down and tried to get his attention. When Sae-Jyung did not acknowledge him, Feslen's mind wandered. In the past, his blood disorder would act up and force Feslen to go home early. This time Feslen's improved health had allowed him to stay through the long ceremony. Someone or something had caused his dizziness and pain. He was sure of it. The chill of the day had forced everyone to huddle together.

The King acknowledged the Warrior Class first. The King's assistant held up an acknowledgment lantern. The National Song blared, and then the contests began with the master swordsmen, bowmen, and spear-jousters. The lantern's light flickered in acknowledgment for every accepted student. Each student showed his skill in wielding different types of swords and competed in duels against one another. The best ones would receive performance bonuses on stage with the masters of their professions. The lantern's fire seemed to engulf the lantern itself, but Feslen noticed that the fire was only an illusion. He glanced around at the other people in the crowd, who gasped every time the fire seemed to engulf the King's hand.

If a mere illusionist's trick amazes them, wait until they see my spells! Feslen thought with giddy joy. The New Priests chose their students in a typically boring chanting ceremony. After each Choicings Rite ended for the New Priests, each of the students and new acolytes bowed to them and trotted off the stage.

During the long intermission, the King's Crier took the time to shout out more good news. News? More like propaganda, Feslen thought with a sneer. Most of it informed the audience about how the Prince had jostled the "barbarians" in the North and the West of the Borders to convince them to agree to join the nation.

"Our nation's authority is strong. Isn't that great, Feslen? That means our family can continue without problems or threats and I can date whomever I want!" Mei-Whuay said to him.

The crowd erupted into a fanatical round of cheers. "Why can't you people see the King's tricks?" Feslen shouted at them in his mind and saw Sae-Jyung shake his head. Feslen ignored the crowd, for the most exciting part of the ceremonial Choicings had just come up for the boy: the Choicings of the magicians and the WuSha. Feslen crossed his fingers and hoped that the rumors about Ka-Wei he heard floating around the last few weeks would come true. Three young men bowed to Master Huang and performed on stage. A murmur stirred the crowd: the Prince was not there to present the beginning of the ceremony. The Sorceress's loud, halting laughter shattered the uncomfortable silence.

"Where is my nephew? Oraza, can you tell me?" the King began, his voice betraying an emotion only Feslen caught.

The Sorceress's magic had already forced all those near her to depart, and Feslen was immersed in it himself. She answered the King, "Why, I don't know. I have nothing to do with it, my dear brother. Apparently our nephew has more sense than you. Do not interfere with his future or mine."

"Just what do you plan to do?" Elhong Wien hissed. Feslen lurched and clutched his chest. I sense danger. But where and how? Feslen thought. He felt like throwing up, but he regained control and tried to pay attention to the royal clash. Feslen watched the King and the Sorceress with intense interest.

"My intentions cannot be stopped and neither can the Prophecies," the Sorceress said.

"Elhong Wien, I order you to…" the King began.

The Sorceress gave them all an icy stare and laughed. She chanted and pointed at them. For a moment, all seemed to be paralyzed by her spell. Feslen sucked in his breath; even Elhong Wien did the same. "Come after me brother, and consequences shall follow," her icy voice trailed in the air long after she had vanished in another spell.

A long moment of pause followed, halting the ceremony. Feslen cursed the interruption. The King and the New Priests retreated into the Judgment Palace to discuss matters. The King's Band played a meaningless tune. "What happened back there?" Duxan leaned over to ask Feslen, as the crowd broke into whispers.

"I don't know."

Duxan frowned, for this was the first time that Feslen didn't share his feelings with him. He started to point this out to him, but the Crier interrupted: "His Majesty would like to apologize to those waiting. The magicians may now choose their students."

Then Feslen felt the hands of Father, his adoptive father, on his shoulders. Feslen tried to move, but Father forced him to look at him. "You will not attend, Feslen. You are too young. Besides, Merchant Jun-Li awaits."

"No, I will not go to Merchant Jun-Li. I am a magician at heart and you know it. I will not allow my dreams to be crushed by the normal rule," Feslen frowned as he watched the forty students approach the platform.

"You will get your opportunities, Feslen. You must remember you are far too young to gain entrance to the Great School of Magic Stuff. You need the application form and…"

"Master Chai already gave me this application before we left him. He signed it without a parent's signature. I am ready for this. I have always been ready. Please, let me do it!"

"No."

Feslen ignored Father Wong's request and reached deep within himself. He felt the anger that had built up there since this morning and he unleashed it. Father Wong fell down, his eyes wide in shock. "Feslen, come back!" Mother shouted, even as Ai-Yen and Mei-Whuay reached to stop him. His brown eyes had begun to glow an eerie blue, and his siblings moved away from him a step or two. They backed off and helped Father up. Feslen walked down to the stage after the last of the students had left.

"You need official papers and signed documents from your parents," a Blue Solider officer named Officer Zhou said as he stopped Feslen. But Officer Zhou quickly backed off. Feslen's face must have shown his rage as his energies flared. He used Dragon Step Two, Mindless Form, to calm himself. The Blue Soldier lowered his weapon as Feslen handed him the official document from Master Chai and asked, "Will the consent of my legal guardian do?"

Feslen waited. He studied the faces of his competitors and the High Magicians. Seeing Tojoh startled Feslen. Clear anger reddened Tojoh's face; the rival boy's parents beamed with pride. Feslen sighed in envy and tuned down the level of his powers a bit. He studied the others. Shock ran through his system as he found that more than half of the competing mage students were female. Most of them were from sxiteen to twenty years old and they ranged from all castes and backgrounds. Again, the world of magic surprised young Feslen, for he now understood that the famous wizards of the past were sorceresses. Whether they had more power or had merely realized their Flair abilities far earlier than the males had, as rumor had it, Feslen did not venture to guess.

Clearly, women far outnumbered men in the magic field. Most of the spells Feslen researched were defensive ones that had been created by women.

"Okay, you're good to go, Raster," said Officer Zhou after looking over the document from Master Chai.

Although Feslen recognized him, he did not acknowledge Officer Zhou and went over to stand beside the students who lined up in inspection. If inner turmoil had not rankled Feslen's soul, he would have noted the debate going on between Elhong Wien and the magicians. Officer Zhou defended him. The Pink Robe mage's argument won out: "Elhong Wien, he's a merchant's boy. Why would you prevent any potential students for either side from entering tradition?"

For some reason, Feslen focused on his family just then. He saw the tears in their eyes, and he detected hidden pride within all of them. A sudden insight struck Feslen and he saw that his words and actions had hurt his family. He knew he should not have used his magic against his family or gone against their words. After all, one of the ancient sages, ConSuFu, and his Twelve Points read, "Respect your Elders, especially your Mother and Father." Master Chai also regulated his school by those words. Guilt rose in Feslen and he choked back tears.

He sighed and felt a nudge to his right. "What's wrong? You should be glad they accepted you. I barely got in, despite my references!" A fifteen-year-old girl next to him nudged him. Feslen felt perturbed that someone should bother him in his deep thoughts. But she continued, "Why did they argue for you and about you for so long? Who are you? My name is Bey-Tan. Which is your family?"

Feslen did his best to ignore her, but she would not stop talking. She was taller than he was, but then again everyone here was too. "Bey-Tan, what spell do you intend to do?" He asked her in a bored tone.

"Spells? I'm not going to cast spells. I thought people would just take a liking to me!" she giggled.

He ignored her; he failed to notice her pout. She held a wand in her hand but Feslen sneered at it. "You're going to impress people with that?" Feslen asked, indicating the wand with a finger.

"How many people do you know who can use a magic wand at fifteen? Can you, farm boy?" she looked hurt and replied with a toss of her head.

"I don't need toys to do my magic, girl. I've got a far greater spell on my mind than a simple light spell even," Feslen scoffed.

"*Light* is on the list of spells, or don't you know? What makes you think you're so great? What are your references, little boy?" she said as she huffed and puffed.

"I don't need to talk to you, but I intend to change the spell-casting world. I need no written words!"

"What an ass! I will kick your butt in class anyway, young turtle," Bey-Tan concluded and tried to move past him to stand next to another student. Feslen could not help but let out a laugh.

"Miss, where do you think you are going?" the Blue Yellow Robe mage inquired.

"That boy is bothering me, Sir. Can I move?" Feslen did nothing to acknowledge her and concentrated on thinking about his spell.

"No, you cannot move. To tolerate others is part of the learning experience of a young apprentice, Miss. Alright, light spells perform first!" the Blue Yellow Robe mage shouted. Feslen studied the Blue Yellow Robe mage a bit. The man might have been in his mid-thirties to early forties; it was hard to tell. His eyes showed the clarity of youth, and his face revealed no hardships. But his receding hair line hinted at what his true age could be. His large, strong frame did not resemble that of a typical user of magic. His kind face was relaxed and seemed to exude infinite patience. Feslen thought that he looked like a kind uncle.

"What order do we go in, Sir?" asked one student when she raised her hand.

"The qualifications are the following: you should be no younger than sixteen, you should be Chiendonese, you should have legal guardians, and you should have money and Flair," the Blue Yellow Robe mage replied.

"I can't meet all the requirements, but my parents sent a lot of money," the meek student said.

"Enough! No talking back," the Immersing Black Robe mage said. The man's amber eyes were like his black robes—they hypnotized the onlooker. The Immersing Black Robe mage's eyes distracted others from looking at his otherwise unimpressive frame. Feslen yawned.

"For those of you not familiar with our Rules of Competition, there are Four Steps in becoming a student based on spells alone. The rest are weeded out," the Blue Yellow Robe mage named Fu-Seng announced.

"The first is that each potential student and qualifier is sent a list of spells that can be good for society and performed without harming others. Some are above power level, training experience, and studying experience. They rank from easiest to hardest, but most dangerous spells are beyond your capabilities. During the qualifiers, those who don't pass—and most of you won't—will go home and try a different career."

Goosebumps rose on Feslen's skin as he felt familiarity of danger again. He honed in on it even as he pretended to listen to the Blue Yellow Robe mage. He was not aware that the Pink Robe mage was watching his every move. Feslen felt the same sense of danger now as he had when he entered Master Chai's school before the ambush. He had ignored it then, but now he decided to heed his internal warnings.

"The first spell will be *Light*, the simplest and easiest spell to cast. Everyone usually passes this one without difficulty. The *Light* spell, once properly learned, of course, can be beneficial to all," the mage continued with the instructions.

Meanwhile, the menacing feeling intensified in Feslen. *Someone uses a different source of magic!* he thought to himself. Feslen's eyes darted back and forth across the stage and audience as he traced color auras. "Where is this new energy? I know it's here!" Energy lines and auras were exploding in his vision in a scintillating fashion. The sensation tantalized him to the point of dizziness. Exotic and strange glows coming from the New Priests resembled the magician's magic. But none of the students performing on stage impressed Feslen and he focused his thoughts and emotions elsewhere. "I've felt this presence before…but where?" Feslen wondered, searching his inner feelings. The presence felt dark, with a terrible purpose.

Fu-Seng continued with the instructions for the young magicians: "Second, the spell will be *Danger Sense*. After all, most of you magicians might decide to go on adventures or you might be hired by mercenaries or have other dangerous jobs. We are the might behind the sword. Without our sense directions, how can we protect anyone, let alone ourselves?"

Danger Sense indeed, thought Feslen, breaking his concentration. All of a sudden a momentary flare of energy he saw in the crowd forced him to watch the stage closely. "What was that? A terrible thing will happen," Feslen said to himself. He knew that no one else noticed the flare, which flashed in and out of the crowd.

Then everyone let out a collective gasp as a blast of heat and wind ruptured the atmosphere around the platform. Heat made the people groan in pain. Feslen didn't drop his concentration, but the weather affected him as well. Sweat poured from his body; some people fanned themselves. The magician giving the instructions did not waver either and continued in his explanation: "The third spell will be *Locator*. After all, sometimes you need to find things and help parties find their way back home."

"Will all this be spoken or used with components?" asked a dark-haired boy.

The Blue Yellow Robe mage ignored the question and went on: "Finally, the last spell will not be anything dashing. You need to learn how to keep yourself tidy. This is a spell called *Neatness*, created by my fellow Dazzle-Razzle, Randazaian." He smirked and pointed to the Pink Robe mage, who grinned.

As the first student began his quest, Feslen was focused instead on determining the source of the negative energy he had felt so strongly. No! A *ninkatta*? Here? Feslen thought.

He kept a critical eye on the competition and noted with grim happiness that the first student had failed to create light and was sent off the stage. The students failed quicker than rain droplets fell from the skies. Most failed to make light; those that could do the first spell failed at *Danger Sense*. By the time the turn reached Feslen, heavy rain had begun falling despite cloudless skies. Feslen noted with amusement that four students had been chosen out of the forty and Bey-Tan almost did not qualify. Her best spell happened to be *Neatness*.

"Feslen Raster," the Blue Yellow Robe mage called out. Feslen was the last student to compete. There were others waiting, but the magicians hurried the clock. Soaked to the skin with sweat, Feslen grumbled and tried to ignore the chill he felt.

"Make light," the Blue Yellow Robe mage said to him. It rained harder. Feslen frowned.

The Immersing Black Robe mage shouted to Feslen, "Well, what's the hold up, young man?"

"He's trying to make a show of it!" Bey-Tan shouted.

Feslen tried to ignore the odd feeling of danger that would not go away. Chill seeped into his bones. He sneezed.

"Do you know the words or not? We don't have all day here," the Immersing Black Robe mage growled. Feslen sighed and reached deep within himself.

"Give him time," whispered the Pink Robe mage. The Immersing Black Robe mage just snorted and crossed his arms. Feslen looked at the short, squat, raven-haired man in reflective black clothes. He felt drawn to him, almost hypnotized. Feslen shook his head to clear it.

A coughing fit wracked his body and he lost energy, but he still kept the strong sense of danger. "How could these mages not be aware of it?" Feslen wondered. "I'm sorry. I can't," he whispered hopelessly. They all ignored Bey-Tan's mean laugh.

"You are too young anyway," the Blue Yellow Robe mage said. He gave Feslen a sympathetic look and took him aside, his face drawn with concern and some sadness. At this time, he felt like an uncle to Feslen. "I know the feeling," he said in a kindly voice, "It just takes time. You should try again soon. I can feel your energy tuning up even as we speak. You are just not ready yet."

Feslen felt that the Blue Yellow Robe mage might be right. A heavy depression set down upon him. Out of the corner of his eye, Feslen saw Elhong Wien holding a black bead in his hands, his lips moving in a chant. The New Priest had somehow forced Feslen's failure!

All bowed down to the King and repeated the National Song. The skies began to clear and Feslen sneezed. He felt a cold coming on. But he also still felt danger, and his body trembled when an odd energy zapped through his system. "Everyone down! Danger!" he bellowed. His Eternal Flow erupted and enhanced the strength of his outcry. suddenly, from the audience, three glowing arrows zipped towards the King. With his last ounce of strength, Feslen raced towards the streaming missiles. He reached deep into a powerful core of energy that was now coursing through his veins. He unleashed a vast energy beyond his own imagination. Feslen lapsed into unconsciousness.

19

FESLEN'S FIRST SPELL 初試咒語

The platform of Judgment Palace exploded. Blue Soldiers and New Priests tried to calm everyone. But Feslen's unleashed might had ripped apart any calm they attempted. Before he fainted, Feslen let out a huge gasp of surprise and fright at himself. His body trembled. Tremendous energies poured from him towards the King and the royal family. These fluctuating powers danced around them, frightening everyone until they stabilized. Then the energies bound themselves together into a blinding blue and orange energy barrier which streamed from the very ground itself and enveloped the King and his family.

Feslen lost consciousness after he expelled all that energy. *Ninkatta*-like warriors moved into the Palace and tried to attack the King and the royal family. They swung at the King but then encountered Feslen's energy barrier, which erupted into flames. Blood curdling screams shattered the air, shocking the scattering, screaming populace into a stunned silence. The flames of Feslen's energy engulfed the two attacking *Ninkatta*-style warriors and burned them to a unrecognizable crisp. The glowing arrows burst into flames as well when they hit Feslen's barrier.

"Who is that boy?" Elhong Wien asked, rubbing his mustache.

"That is Feslen Raster," the Pink Robe mage said with great dignity and respect.

Elhong Wien regarded Feslen with a contemplating gaze. He ordered his followers s to escort the King to safety.

"We can't get near the King, Head Dragon," complained the acolyte who had burned his hands trying to reach the King.

"What? You must get near him. We have to move His Majesty away from here!" Elhong Wien growled.

"The boy's barrier around His Majesty burns us, Head Dragon!"

Elhong Wien did not respond and the acolyte murmured. He studied the barrier the boy had erected and then spoke harshly to the group of mages, "Come, you magi! Dispel this barrier immediately!"

"I can try, but you know as well as I do that only the magician who erected such a defensive spell can remove it. How this young boy managed to create such a powerful spell without uttering any command words or using magical elements is beyond me. Our Master Drak was right. It looks like I lose the wager," the Pink Robe mage announced and then sat idle with a grin on her face.

"Excuse me? Could you explain that?" the Blue Yellow Robe mage asked his friend and mentor.

She grinned and replied, "It's nothing, Fu-Seng. Master Drak and I wagered, that's all, but it seems as though he has won."

Fu-Seng smiled and started to say something when the New Priest Elhong Wien strode up to them and snarled, "Forget your petty excuses! This rogue boy…" Elhong Wien's words died unfinished in the air when the *Ninkattas* abruptly got to their feet once again. The dead thing reached for its blade.

"Halt!" one of Elhong Wien's officers ordered the *Ninkatta*. A wave of energy erupted from the head of the New Priest's officer, aimed at the dead first *Ninkatta*. The *Ninkatta* wobbled a bit and its arm became detached, but the dead thing continued its advance—past the New Priests and straight for the King.

A very human voice sounded in its dead voice echoed, "Your betrayal ends, King. Your use ends here. Your minion, the New Priests, cannot stop me." The walking corpse of the *Ninkattas* reeked of hours of death, despite Feslen's magic killing them recently. The acolytes had formed a circle and were chanting, holding their holy symbols. A wave of darkness flooded the area after the acolytes had finished their chants. The *Ninkatta* laughed and continued its march, its arm raised, its sword in hand. "Your magic won't work against me. Only the One with the Eternal Flow can stop me. He sees me as I truly am."

The gathered New Priest acoloytes dealt with the second *Ninkatta*.

The magi all nodded their heads in understanding. "These New Priests are nothing more than magicians themselves," murmured the Pink Robe mage.

"What do you mean?" the Blue Yellow Robe mage asked her.

"Watch, my friend," she responded, and her hand touched his for a brief moment. A New Priest female acolyte had raised a finger in water movement. She took out a cube of ice and a ball of string. The others sang a melody not in the common Chiendonese tongue.

"If they enact another spell, it might disable Raster's barrier," the Blue Yellow Robe mage sputtered.

"Watch, Fu-seng, and learn. The boy has much potential, but his strength flows from within him, but their strength does not. His comes from the Ancient Truth, for his energies intertwine forever. Remember, he has elemental magic. Our magic and even that of the New Priests are as different from Feslen's power as the Ying is to the Yang. If we interfered, as Elhong Wien asked, when two magic spells collide…" the Pink Robe mage's voice trailed off and the Blue Yellow Robe mage nodded in understanding.

The *Ninkatta* jerked a little when the young acolyte had finished her spell. A block of ice now encased the dead *Ninkatta*. "High Dragon, that won't last long. What should I do next?" The young acolyte shivered when her master, Elhong Wien, glared in her direction. He then changed his gaze and stared at the still unconscious Feslen.

"Can he be revived? Can he remove the spell?" Elhong Wien, the Head Dragon demanded of the Pink Robe mage.

"He's not one of our own. You'll have to ask Feslen himself," the Pink Robe mage replied, still sitting in her seat. The Blue Yellow Robe mage half-rose when the High Dragon, Elhong Wien, reached down to touch Feslen. But the Pink Robe mage stopped him from interfering and shook her head again.

The High Priest reached down and screamed when his hands touched Feslen. Fire billowed up at him from Feslen's unconscious form.

"Lock him up! He endangers the King's life!" Elhong Wien demanded.

Feslen groaned and unclenched his jaw when he woke from the New Priest's touch. The New Priest's negative energies were enough to awaken him and arouse his defenses.

"Don't be foolish," the Pink Robe mage scolded. "He's done nothing to harm your King. In fact, he's saved the royal family twice now, I believe."

"If I can remove it..." Feslen said, as he struggled to stand. The Blue Soldiers blocked Feslen's family when they tried to reach him. But Duxan managed to break through their tight-banded ring without much trouble. Feslen waved his older brother away to protect him. He matched Elhong Wien's glower with his own stare and said, "I don't know if I have one more!" Feslen said. Feslen whirled while chanting in high-pitched tones and moved his hands in an odd circular pattern in the air. He pounded his right fist into his left palm three times.

The gathering mages and students of magic gasped. "What's he doing?" the Immersing Black Robe mage asked.

"Amazing! He's using a high level spell, but in his own image!" the Blue Yellow Robe mage responded, his mouth agape.

"Remember, Master Drak and Master Chai say that this boy has the Ancient Truth," the Pink Robe mage responded.

"Yes, but it's not possible...is there such a difference between his magic and ours?" the Blue Yellow Robe mage asked.

"No, I bet it's just some sort of trick," snarled the Immersing Black Robe mage.

"Not at all," the Pink Robe mage countered. "As you know, magic comes from within, and that's standard for all of us. However, for the carriers of Ancient Truth, their inner energies are supposed to come through a Higher Awareness that we don't have or fully understand. The relation of the Ancient Truth powers to ordinary magic is only partly understood, even by us and by those who are more in tune with the spiritual worlds."

"I thought we all could use that power?" the Blue Yellow Robe mage asked as he half-turned to his friend.

She shook her head and said, "We can detect it, since we all have Flair. Like Martial Arts, Flair is something all magic-using people can master to a point where it appears as though we have Ancient Truth. To be honest, only Master Chai, a true Martial Arts master, and our own Master Drak, the most accomplished magician in all the world of Hahn-Hah, can explain it better."

"You mean, you just don't get it either?" the Red Robe mage intervened with a half grin.

The Pink Robe mage chuckled and said, "We are master magicians, but that doesn't mean we don't keep learning something new about our profession."

"Granted," the Red Robe mage conceded.

Feslen heard her, but he did not break his concentration. Seven glowing spheres of different colors hovered around Feslen. Each sphere, the size of a human head, glowed at a different level of brightness at a different tempo. He closed his eyes and directed them about, with his lips murmuring soft sounds and sweat on his forehead.

"He detected those new missiles before I did," the Red Robe mage murmured. "He's making fools of us, a joke. Who is this child? Why haven't we spotted him before an ordinary man like Chai did?"

"Master Chai is not an ordinary man. As for this boy," the Pink Robe mage shook her head, "I feel his odd, clashing energies, don't you? Any of you? Look, even Elhong Wien feels them. He feels them. He fears them." She paused, holding her breath, and gestured to the frantically waving Head of the New Priests. She watched Feslen guide his spheres around Elhong Wien. The spheres expanded to protect the shocked King. Elhong Wien's face widened from shock to anger.

"The Master asked us to watch the boy," the Pink Robe mage continued in a hush.

The missiles dissipated without harm when they hit the spheres. The remaining onlookers murmured among themselves.

"One more assassin," Feslen panted. "One more, like him."

Then Feslen lost consciousness once more and slipped to the floor with a crash. With that, the energy barrier surrounding the King vanished, even as the spheres seemed to dance and enclose him. When Feslen's energy barrier dissipated, it's remaining fires engulfed the dead *Ninkatta* warriors, desotrying them at last. The Red Robe mage nodded to the Blue Yellow Robe mage, the Immersing Black Robe mage, and to the crowd. Then they transported themselves with a magic word. But before leaving, the Pink Robe mage spoke once more to Feslen, "No, you are not yet ready, young one, but far too soon for us, as Master Drak predicted, far too soon." She studied Feslen for one last moment.

Four weeks had gone by since the Choicings and the assassination attempt on the King. Feslen's actions had taken their toll on his health, so much so that his return to Master Chai's was delayed. He didn't even go back to practicing on his own. Instead, he just went through the drudgery of everyday routine life, even going back to the Red School. When the late afternoon moon rose, the Red School's classes officially ended. Feslen was already off school one day when he and his brother went shopping for family goods.

"Time to go home, bro," Duxan said when he saw how dark the day had become. Feslen acted like he didn't hear him; he walked back home with Duxan in a zombified state of depression.

Duxan shook his head and decided to walk talk problems out with Feslen, like they would in their younger days.

Rumors of Feslen's magic had spread even to those who did not manage to attend the Choicings. After the Raster brothers were finished with shopping for groceries and other goods, people in their hometown of Bilong treated the brothers with greater respect and even some fear. In an exchange for some fresh beef, Duxan intended to pay the usual price, but the butcher gave it to them for half off! Duxan tried to convince him that wasn't necessary, but to no avail. Duxan sighed and thought, It looks like that's how things will be from now on. I suppose that comes with the territory of fame and notoriety. Duxan had noticed how angry and depressed Feslen was and that he didn't even register how people treated him despite the obviousness of it all. People scampered away from Feslen and Duxan in fright and disbelief as they walked towards home with their groceries in hand.

Despite having overheard the mage's talk about him, Feslen still thought the mages rejected him because of their fear of his spells. *I must know why! I must talk to Master Chai about this*, Feslen thought, clenching his fist.

"Kid? Bro?" Duxan asked, stopping and placing the groceries down before they reached home. "You okay? Hey, Hahn-Hah to Feslen. Hello? This is Little Dragon to Little Phoenix. Hello?" Duxan said, placing an arm around his brother's shoulders. They were only ten feet from home.

Feslen heard the nickname Duxan used, looked up at his brother, and gave him a wan smile that revealed no warmth. "Why did they reject me, Dux?"

Duxan pondered a moment and said, "Who knows with the ways of magicians? But I heard them talking about you too, and I'm not surprised that they think highly of you. Maybe you're just too young, huh? It's obvious how awed they were of your powers."

"Maybe," Feslen said.

"Listen, I'm sure you'll get your chance, if you really want to be with them," Duxan said and cleared his throat as soon as Feslen looked at him, his eyes narrowed. "What I mean is…why would you still want them to train you and help you learn your potential? They rejected you even though you are meant to learn the Path of Magic like their founder, what's his name, Xcaithian Vestiiege?" Duxan asked with a smile.

"Yes. I'm sure that's it," Feslen replied with sarcastic sourness at Duxan's comment about his learning magic like the great Xcaithian Vestiiege.

"Look, you said it yourself. You've wanted to do so much more than just twiddle around in fancy robes doing minimal impact with your Art. The magicians in their schools, who knows how much good they really do?" Feslen smiled at that. "One day, Feslen, you'll show everyone just how a person as different as yourself can achieve great things. You'll do much more than awe them, okay?"

Feslen's depression dwindled a bit and he murmured, "Thanks bro. I appreciate the pep talk."

Duxan nodded and they gazed at their parents' home. The home and farm seemed quiet in the early evening. "Let me handle them," Duxan said, and Feslen nodded his approval. He and his brother got home and found their parents glowering at them. Duxan cleared his throat and excused himself with Mother, taking the groceries with him. Feslen studied Father; his eyes scanned the older man's serious face and his rigid body and then he sighed. He noticed the stack of papers on the dinner table and cringed as a sinking feeling seeped into him.

"Feslen, it's time we had a talk," Father said, his tone serious.

"Oh? I thought we'd already discussed your ultimatum about my friends and my personal life?"

"I regret letting my temper get the better of me, but after witnessing what you did and what you have accomplished so far…Do you remember when we used to go to Public Market?" sighed Father. Despite the obvious late hour, there were no interruptions coming from Mother. Feslen smelled the leftover dinner and saw that the half-eaten plates already were mostly put away in the sink. Feslen nodded, as he remembered walks he and Father used to take in market places, watching people buy goods and smelling the different foods being sold.

"I need to speak to you with honesty, as I do my clients and customers, Son. There's been a reason why I've treated you more harshly than usual these past few months," he paused and added, "I should say past few years maybe." He held the rejection letter. "Some of this is written in the arcane language, which I presume you can already read. Let's take some time and walk and talk together, alright?"

Feslen's eyes narrowed but he agreed. They walked through the market place and ate dumplings on a stick together. "Son, I know you want to become a magician, but for now I want you to take part in the family business." Feslen said nothing as he munched down on the shrimp part of the delicious dumpling. Someone in the crowd caught his attention. He thought he saw a robed female watching him. Then the figure disappeared. He rubbed his eyes and focused again on Father. "You proved two things by your actions during the Choicings, of which I am very proud."

Feslen's ears perked up and he stopped eating for a bit and looked at Father. "One, you proved without a doubt that you can think on your feet. Some of your siblings lack a long attention span. I wish Ai-Yen were a bit more like you. To be truthful, the reason I care about you so much is…well, I know you can take care of yourself if given the chance. But your health has always been an issue. If you had Ai-Yen's physical stamina…" "Then I guess you wouldn't be as quick-minded," father chuckled, cutting himself off.

Feslen said nothing, but inside he appreciated the words; his eyes were moist as Father went on. "The other thing is that I've always worried whether you would…well…use your powers for good and good alone. I've always known that you would someday burst onto the scene, showing who you really are. But, knowing your past…" Father shook his head in some sadness.

"Did you know my birth mother, Father? What was she like?" Feslen asked timidly.

"Never mind that," said father, holding up a hand. The two stopped walking to smell the hundreds of different aromas of Seed Square. "Before you venture off and become a true magician, whether it is traditional or otherwise, you need to learn a few things about the world, Feslen," Father continued as he gripped his arm firmly but gently. The two stared at each other with intensity. "All your life has been surrounded by books, your family, and school. You need to become a more well-rounded person and also, to be honest…" Feslen noted that Father lowered his voice whenever pedestrians walked by. The two of them found a sidewalk café bench to sit down on. "Look, Feslen, do you know why you aren't rotting in the King's dungeon right now?"

"Because Ka-Wei is my friend?" Feslen answered, stunned by Father's blunt honesty.

"No. It's because the family pulled a few strings to keep you from ending up there. I've done a lot for you, more than you can imagine, Feslen.

Have you noticed that you and your brother Duxan are the only ones who go to school?" Feslen nodded, as he always wondered about that.

"You two have always been Mother's treasure as well as mine. Both of you have great futures and talents that none of your other siblings share," Father heaved a sigh.

Feslen have never seen him so emotional or so broken down. He almost reached out his hand to pat Father on the back. "I will do what I can for us, Father. But you must know this: I have a greater goal in mind and it does not involve politics or the petty things of everyday life." Feslen rose and clasped his hands behind his back. "You see those people?" Feslen pointed to the homeless and the starving children who begged. Father listened with little reaction. "There are worse cases yet, but all of us with money and those who just pass the day without thinking don't care. You ask me, what do I care? They suffer, reminding me that I have suffered. You're right. I have been given a gift that I can use to achieve what I wish for. I wish for harmony, Father, above all else. I wish for no more suffering on Hahn-Hah. I intend to do a lot with what I have been given."

"But you have to show that you care, Feslen. You have to do more than just talk about it. I have heard you discussing this with Duxan many times. Have you acted? How can study and research about spells to create shields really benefit others much? You're right about one thing, though. Suffering is constant out there. But you have to act."

"I already have, Father. Don't worry. I know what you're saying and I will join Merchant Li within the year. You're right when you say that my magic has a long ways to go. But I will do more than those obsolete old magicians will. Thank you for the talk, Father." He bowed then in an old-fashioned way and left Father to wonder about his words.

20

REVELATION 顯示

The next day, Feslen went on an outing with Princess Nai-Hua, also called Nadine. He had first sought Duxan's advice on how to deal with women, but his older brother was reticent. Feslen joked to his brother, "Hey, big bro, being silent and depressed isn't like you. That's my part." But Duxan didn't react; he just stared at him and left the house in the very early morning. Duxan held a strange object in his hand, but he said nothing about it to Feslen.

Feslen realized that Duxan had walked in the direction of the castle, but he thought better of following or asking him about it. Besides, Feslen wanted to go out with the Princess anyway, and she had invited him to her temporary home, called the Old Forest. This was where the Forest Protectors lived except that, at this time, he didn't spot any Forest Protectors or Forest Protector friends. Nonetheless, the forest atmosphere helped him relax so much that he didn't care.

They prepared a nice lunch consisting of berries, fruits, vegetables, and rice, of course. Feslen even brought his collection of paints, his watercolors, and his easel from home. In his relaxed mood, he loved to paint and do other creative things. He began to think about which subject to paint and decided to paint Nadine. "I think I will paint you as my first subject," Feslen grinned at her. She blushed and hid her face behind her hair.

"Oh Feslen," she said, in a sweet voice. She let him paint her for a while; the peaceful and calm atmosphere had invited both of them to relax. She lounged around a bit for him and smiled. Then she said in a hesitating voice, "You know, this isn't just about a regular outing. I've invited a potential mage mentor for you, alright?"

He frowned, but, before he spoke, he felt a sudden chill. One of the people that Feslen considered "unmentionable" had come to visit them. Feslen frowned when Sae-Jyung joined them. He sighed and the trio moved off into the park.

"You've changed appearances again, Sae-Jyung," Nadine said.

It sounded more like a question than a statement, Feslen thought. What did she really mean?

"Indeed, but you still look the same," Sae-Jyung chuckled. "That's a woman for you, Feslen. They'd rather be concerned about looks than other things first."

Nadine said nothing but pointed out, "I see a dark cloud still hangs about you, Sae-Jyung. Why did you call me?"

"I need your help. He's growing stronger. I can't fend him off alone," Sae-Jyung replied with honesty.

Feslen was painting an odd pair of trees that twisted over a small pond in one of the smaller public parks of Beizung. He tried to follow their conversations, but he understood little. He also found his heart beating a bit too fast. Was it his blood disorder again? Or was it a strange but common human emotion, such as jealousy?

"No, Sae-Jyung. He's not my problem," Nadine returned. Feslen detected a hint of sourness in the sweet lady's voice.

"Oh, my fine, sweet, virtuous maiden, I've been in darkness so long. Where have you been?" Sae-Jyung joked and folded his arms.

"Thanks for the flattery, but I don't do flattery," Nadine replied.

Sae-Jyung grinned and chanted a bit and produced a flower in his right palm and handed it to Nadine.

"Oh, Forever Roses!" she exclaimed as he handed her the gift. Sae-Jyung started laughing, but she composed herself quickly, handing back his gift.

"Will you two stop your laughing? It's hard to concentrate!" Feslen's hand jerked and one flower on a painted branch became two.

"A perfectionist!" Sae-Jyung said. Nadine grinned. "Sorry Feslen," Sae-Jyung said. "Look, why don't Nai-Hua and I just take a walk down that romantic looking path." Feslen stopped painting and glared at him. "Why do you like such a baby anyway, Nai-Hua? He hasn't even developed his sense of manhood yet!"

"We may know each other well, Sae-Jyung, but I won't forget the Rogger Incident."

"Well, we all make mistakes, Nai-Hua."

"But our friendship can't truly be mended. I just tolerate you because of your friendliness to Feslen."

"Will you two stop talking about me as if I didn't exist?"

"Feslen, what do you think of my situation?" asked Nai-Hua suddenly.

"What do you mean?"

"You have certain abilities that others do not, including Sae-Jyung. You witnessed a certain uniqueness about me when you first met me. What was it?" Feslen didn't respond.

Sae-Jyung began, "He doesn't know anything; he's a stupid human…"

"Hush, Sae-Jyung, I'm being serious." Nai-Hua paused; her amber eyes glistened and then turned to a piercing silver color when she blinked. She studied Feslen and smiled.

All Feslen could do was to watch her and listen to her. *I thought Ka-Wei said her hair and eyes were golden?* Feslen thought to himself. But he forgot all his thoughts in a flash when he was staring into her eyes.

"I have to admit," Feslen said after a long pause and before he went back to his paints, "I did wonder why both of you came along at a crossroads of my life when I most needed support. Who are you two, really? Who am I?"

"Ah, now that's an answer I can't give so readily! You'll have to puzzle this one out, my fine, brain-filled friend," Sae-Jyung murmured.

"Why did you attack me earlier, with the other boys?" Feslen asked calmly. He stopped painting for a bit.

"It was all part of the game, Feslen. You see, all of us are part of the woven threads of life and…," Sae-Jyung paused when Nai-Hua coughed.

Then she told him, "You are perceptive for someone so young, Feslen. That's why I have chosen you. You're right. I am different, and so is Sae-Jyung. You are too, and so is your brother, for that matter. You will find out all the answers in due time."

Before Feslen could reply, Sae-Jyung interrupted and said, "Now, as a matter of fact, Nai-Hua, I have a wager."

With her eyes wide, Nadine repeated, "A wager?"

Sae-Jyung smiled and said, "They'll find Chai's missing daughter before Feslen can figure out what's truly going on in, say, about two months' time."

"Go on, what's the catch?"

"That if I'm right you and I will get back together again as a couple."

"Hold on a minute!" Feslen burst out, but then he thought, What do I care? Why am I feeling like this towards her? I don't even know her!

"Ah, you've enchanted him, Princess. I see you try to bewitch all your men," Sae-Jyung grinned at the Princess. He turned and chuckled and then winked at Feslen.

"You know it's not possible for the two of us to get together again, Sae-Jyung. Our motives for this world and ourselves are completely at odds," Nadine answered patiently.

"So you'd rather have him? Is that the real truth?" Sae-Jyung laughed. Feslen shivered.

"You know the truth. Feslen just needs a push in the right direction," Nadine replied.

"What if he decides to follow me?"

Feslen snorted, "Who's going to follow whom, Sae-Jyung? Now who's getting arrogant? Besides, Nadine wants only good people around her anyhow.".

"Oh, Feslen, when are you going to learn?" Sae-Jyung shook his head.

Before Nadine could react or Feslen could say another word, brilliant globes of blackness suddenly smashed into Feslen's face. He writhed in pain and saw nothing.

Sae-Jyung's spell had paralyzed Feslen. His body felt like it wasn't his own. He moaned internally. He could hear the two of them still arguing. "Was that really necessary, Sae-Jyung? Release him right now."

"You're not my girl anymore, Nadine, so I don't have to follow your orders."

"Why I ought to…"

"What? Slug me? I thought your Honor Code prohibited you from harming anyone. Besides, it will pass. All I did was the *Stun* spell. Nothing serious. It was just to teach that little mule face a lesson. Remember who has the greater power, little flower."

"Don't you touch me," she screeched. Then Sae-Jyung screamed in pain. Feslen saw that Sae-Jyung's body burned as if it were on fire.

"I forgot about your tricks. You're as dangerous as you are beautiful, Nadine. Some day you'll be mine!" Sae-Jyung said.

"Before you dream any further, Sae-Jyung, remember that your Master is a darkness that will threaten to destroy you before I could even think of it." Feslen shuddered at her anger. He now sensed her Ancient Truth.

"I damn the day you met Feslen, Nadine, or any other man. He will meet his Maker," Sae-Jyung said menacingly.

"You will never have him!" Nadine cried. "I didn't know it would come to this! I'm sorry Feslen!" She knelt and ran a soft hand over his still body. "Sleep now, my Feslen. Sleep. Thank you for your painting," Nadine whispered to him. "He painted my true form…first human to see since the first mage…" she murmured, loudly enough for Feslen to hear. She chanted for a moment and then he heard nothing more.

Duxan gasped and jerked back as he reached for Feslen's neck. He felt his pulse going at a rapid pace. An image flashed before Duxan's eyes: he saw Sae-Jyung chanting and casting a spell that not only stunned Feslen but took something from him too. He saw his brother jerking in pain and gasping as if his congenital blood disorder had put him in distress.

Then the image disappeared. The older brother wondered what had just occurred.

Feslen stirred. "How did I get here?" Feslen murmured, putting his hand on his aching forehead.

"Are you alright, little brother?"

"Yes, I think so. It feels like a pack of stampeding animals ran over me. What happened?"

"I don't know. You were out cold when I found you. Nadine put you here in the park so I could find you."

"Why do you say that?"

"Well, you weren't dragged," Duxan said, trying for some humor.

"I'm sick again." Feslen tried to laugh and coughed up phlegm instead.

"Someone did this to you, Feslen."

Feslen coughed and doubled over in pain. Feslen used the techniques that Master Chai had taught him and calmed himself down. Duxan counted patiently. It took his little brother as long as fifteen minutes to return to a state of normalcy. Duxan tried hard not to show his emotions, a mix of pride in his brother and worry for his health. Feslen saw only worry and closed his eyes in weary pain. Duxan sighed and turned away too. It used to take Feslen months to recover. In five months, my brother has achieved a lot more than most normal people ever could, Duxan thought. Duxan could not help but think back to where Feslen came from. He smiled.

"What are you smiling at?" Feslen asked as he regained his strength and staggered to his feet. He hated this old weakness that made him feel like an impotent failure. Yet he felt he had made great strides with Master Chai. He sighed. Feslen thought, It looks like I have more work to do on improving my physical stamina and mental health. Feslen locked eyes with his brother. He felt Duxan's pride in him. Waves of both joy and sadness overwhelmed Feslen for a moment, and he smiled back. They readied themselves for an explanation to their parents about why Feslen had disobeyed a direct order and left the house. The brothers juggled their stories to match with one another as they got near home.

21

DEATH 死亡

Their parents' impassive stares spoke volumes to the Raster siblings when they returned home. Duxan started to speak, but his explanation stopped short when Feslen laid a hand on his arm. The honeydew aroma of the Princess Nai-Hua could be distinguished by all, even by Ghong-Hung and her constantly stuffed up nose. "Hey, Feslen, you've been out with your girlfriend, I see. Even I can smell her on you," Ghong-Hong, his adoptive sister, spoke even now as Feslen walked past her. She grumbled and tried to grab him, "Where do you think you're going? You'll be punished for this! I had to cancel my own outing because of you."

Duxan stopped her and grabbed her hand hard. She glared at Feslen. Everyone's expression of disapproval felt like a hammer on the back of Feslen's head. The glares that hurt most came from Father and Mother. Mother's attitude felt condescending and it seemed like a loss of respect from Father. Feslen let out a small sigh and walked upstairs to his attic bedroom.

Maybe they'd be better off without me, Feslen thought. The health bills aren't cheap; my schooling surely isn't cheap. Maybe I'm just a freeloader". He put his books into his private cubby, lay down on his bed for a moment, and closed his eyes, still thinking. An odd thought struck him and Feslen opened the door with caution. He heard them all yelling at one another. Li-Pei and Duxan were defending him to their last breaths.

Then he crept into his parents' bedroom and shuffled through the pile of mail. His monthly New Priest health bills were more than what the family had earned the last two months put together. He always knew that his upkeep cost a lot, but this was ridiculous. He almost crumpled the bills in his anger, but instead he placed them back where he found them. He returned to his attic room, grimacing with pain. From the look of the bills, the family had indeed given up almost everything for Feslen. His siblings worked at menial jobs instead of doing what they most loved. He realized that his adoptive family wanted him to succeed. Yet they didn't realize that what they did in silence hurt him more than helped. I should have realized this a long time ago and done something about it, Feslen thought and said, "I'm useless without my magic." He felt like he was worse than a parasite to his family. He went into his room and left the door a bit ajar, so he could listen to his family argue about him.

Feslen packed some clothing and books. They'll all be better off with me gone, no longer a costly dependent, Feslen thought. He jerked his head up a bit when he heard the window open in the bathroom down the hall. It was well past midnight when he finished packing and heard a dry chuckle. Lioin seemed tenser than usual. The young thief was mumbling in indecision. His eyes were intense with worry and dilemma. Feslen caught his friend's quick clenching of the fist.

"Well? What is it?" Feslen asked in a tight voice; his stomach had churned all day.

Lioin gave a small, grim sigh and handed something to Feslen—Master Chai's symbol of the Closed Mouth Dragon. Feslen knew what it meant and he nodded, his shoulders heaving, gripping the hard wooden carving. He tried to be brave and not cry, like Li-Pei. The two friends stared at each other, saying nothing. Feslen then broke the awkwardness with a nod of thanks to Lioin and opened the door. Running into the hall with tears in his eyes, Feslen bumped into Father.

"What's wrong?" Father asked. The symbol of Master Chai's death fell out of Feslen's hand and crashed onto the floor. Father picked it and looked at it. He too understood. He soothed Feslen, gathered the entire family together, and they left for Master Chai's home.

A gathering of associates, including one of Master Chai's former apprentices who was now a master of Martial Arts himself, Hei Weong Tung, and other well-wishers surrounded the private home of the master Martial Artist. Even Chai's rivals had come to pay their respects. Feslen's inner voice tingled again, telling him of eminent danger, but again he ignored it.

Kai-Lornu greeted the guests. Thick and heavy sadness mingled with respect in the whispers of the mourners. Feslen saw, as others did not, the figure of the Sorceress, standing in the shadow of the bamboo. He frowned when she acknowledged him. Feslen concentrated his sensory investigation on the presences of the Sorceress and the *Ninkatta*. Their energy auras seemed clean and pristine, so he knew that neither of them had committed the murder. Yet Feslen swore he could feel the murderer's presence. He looked about, not seeing anyone especially familiar or unfamiliar.

The King and two of his right-hand men stood at the front of the crowd. No one else had noticed the Sorceress, who lingered within her spell of winds to hide herself from the commoners. She nodded to Feslen in acknowledgement. The *Ninkatta* also hid himself in the shadows, but his eyes widened when Feslen spotted him, and he waved a hand in which he held a symbol. It was a small black shield, a common sign of defense for every warrior.

Feslen noted a slithering movement in the crowd. A New Priest! he thought, rubbing his eyes. But this New Priest's robes were of different color from that of Elhong Wien's band. This one had a purple robe marked with some sort of animal or reptile. But before Feslen got a better look at the man, the purple robed person vanished. The man's aura somehow felt unclean and wrong to Feslen. Then he looked about and noticed two other things: Sae-Jyung was standing in the shadows, or at least someone who looked a lot like Sae-Jyung. Princess Nai-Hua also stood nearby but not next to Sae-Jyung.

"Why wouldn't Ka-Wei be present?" Feslen wondered. But before he had time to think further, Kai-Lornu had already pushed open the doors and led him inside. Worse yet, although Feslen did not like the presences of the Sorceress or *Ninkatta*, there was little he could do about it. He asked Lioin to tail them, though he boy doubted whether the young thief could follow them for long.

When Kai-Lornu greeted Feslen, her voice was as stony as her face. But her eyes, her eyes that always gazed with such sorrow, made Feslen's heart ache. He saw behind her eyes and behind the face she put on for everyone else, that brave Chiendonese face. But, it was more than that… Feslen gave her a gentle smile as he walked by his family and came up beside her. She smiled back at him but said nothing. Then Kai-Lornu summoned Master Chai's bodyguards, who they stood with stern affront. They barred everyone else from entering, even the King of Chiendong!

Kai-Lornu, Duxan, Feslen, and Father all entered the Outer Chambers. Kai-Lornu said with quiet dignity to Duxan and Father, "Only Feslen may enter to see the Master. Please wait out here with the others."

Father and Duxan waited but exchanged no words. Feslen felt odd, for it seemed as though he were going in to see the true King. Only then did he realize the true importance of Master Chai. As he entered the Inner Chambers, he noticed an odd mural that he had never seen before. The painting depicted each part of the man's life, triumphing at each turn and event that he had caused or in which he had participated. Feslen lingered, not wishing to enter.

"The dying do not dawdle, my student," Master Chai's feeble voice forced Feslen to look away from the painting. Feslen hurried to his side. Kai-Lornu waited outside the Master's private room. After some urging from Master Chai, Kai-Lornu entered. Master Chai sat in the most difficult position: the one called "Dragon Technique One with Elements." The Master's hands were interlocked above his head and behind his neck, his body was twisted into a half-crouch, and eyes were closed, with his feet crossing over each other. Energy flowed through the room, increasing every time the Master moved his hand or moved a step. Feslen longed for this power and knelt down beside the powerful man.

"Master," Feslen said, as he cupped his hands together, letting Master Chai's energy absorb into him. Tears fell unbidden from Feslen. A sudden awareness hit Feslen as he did the Eleventh Dragon Technique in his mind.

He saw poison energy lines in his mentor's veins, blood, and body. One of the Techniques Master Chai had taught him helped detect poisons and remove them. Unfortunately, he had yet to master this skill thoroughly, even as he moved his palms in an angular formation in front of his heart and above Master Chai's own heart. But this poison seemed almost unnatural, even magical somehow. Feslen did not understand why he knew or at least sensed this. He began to perform the healing step, part of the Tenth Dragon Technique, but Master Chai stopped him.

"But why, Master?" Feslen asked, his voice cracking in grief. He saw Kai-Lornu's confused look as well, and she moved to begin the Eleventh Dragon Technique.

"There, there, don't cry for me, my son, my daughter," Master Chai responded, gripping Feslen's hands. "I am dying, but only because I know my karma. It is the death of chill not from fever, but from something a reptile carries. The deed was carried out to get my Silver Key. The Sorceress did not plan this, nor did the *Ninkatta*. This was not their style."

Feslen heard Kai-Lornu's gasp when Master Chai acknowledged her as a daughter. He also heard her grief echo and shared in her empathy. So, Feslen realized, she too was losing not only a mentor and a friend but a father figure as well.

"So they paid their last respects? I'm sorry, Master," Feslen began in a voice husky with sadness. Even through his grief, his mind worked and he too concluded, "No, it wasn't their style. This was too crude, too dishonest even for the Sorceress or the *Ninkatta*.

"Yes, they are Honorable in their own odd way," the Master began with a cough. He gestured to Kai-Lornu, who bowed. Her face was in an angry mask for some reason that Feslen did not understand. "Was she angry because of Master Chai's death? Or perhaps that he favored Feslen as a student or maybe as a person?" Feslen wondered. She got up and walked to the door. She did not leave but stood by the entrance. "My murderers, the ones who carried out the deed, remain in the estate. Be wary, Feslen, for I felt the poison's sting," Master Chai began.

How does Master Chai know they remain here? Poison's sting? What did he mean by that? Feslen thought.

"Though it is not the Dhai-Hahn way, nor the Faoist way, I wish justice to be done," Master Chai said. "As both of you know, it's not going to come from the government officials." Feslen and Kai-Lornu shared a look and chuckled a bit at that. "I wish both of you to find my murderers. Let justice be done with a swift hand. Remember, the ones you find under my roof are under coercion. I'm not sure if it was done by magic or otherwise, but they are not to blame. The puppeteers, well, those answers are to be found with the Prince's quest and your quest to bring my daughter back."

A bit bewildered, Feslen asked, "You want me to go after Mei Xue, Master? What about Ka-Wei?"

"He will go, but he will need help, for magic seeks to destroy the warrior, Feslen," Master Chai stated. "I ask of you—no, as my last order, I command you—to go seek my killers with Ka-Wei and to return Mei Xue to her home."

"Yes, Master. But where should I begin looking?"

"Here. The answer starts here," the Master responded, gesturing to the four walls of this room.

"You can't imagine the pains I go through just to try and succeed in your trainings," Feslen thought, staring at the old master balefully for a moment. I do everything to try to please you! Yet you ask for more. My body may not be able to take it.

"Yes, your body can take some punishment. You must understand," Master Chai began, with a gentle smile for his student.

I must give myself away too much. I need to learn to hide my emotions, Feslen thought with a startled look at Master Chai.

"We all walk the same path, my son," Master Chai said. "Even I went through similar hardships as you've gone through."

"How can you understand?" Feslen mused a moment.

A long silence insued. The only sounds that could be heard was from Master Chai's deep breaths.

"I wish for you to understand why I chose you, Feslen," Master Chai said.

The two gripped each other still.

"I saw the powers in your meridian lines when you were four years old. You may have been unhealthy in the body, but your spirit…the fires within you burn stronger than the sun."

"I am nothing special…" Feslen began, but the Master squeezed his hand hard to cut him off.

"Not at all. You are very special. The knowledge I gave you, the teachings, all because you are something this world hasn't seen since the first signs of magic. Your body, of course, still needs improvements, and your spirit needs help to calm your chaotic mind and body. For that, Apama can teach you further…"

Mater Chai coughed heavily, dry and he turned to Kai-Lornu and said, "Daughter, can you get me a drink please?"

Kai-Lornu nodded, her cries still resounded in the room after she left. The Master coughed; his skin was drying. Feslen felt his feverish heat and the peaceful aura from his Master.

Feslen felt the pride in his Master's words and tightly gripping hands. Tears came again for Feslen. "You have no need to cry. I taught you all that I could, my student," Master Chai said. "You have come so far. You have only to learn to hold onto my lessons."

"You know about my stories, not about my suffering, Master," Feslen murmured, biting his lip in the process. "Now you understand what it is like to live with pain." The unspoken words came into his mind as an unbidden thought. He heard laughter from Master Chai, even though his body did not move.

"Yes, my son, I do know what it is like. We all suffer, but less so than you. In life, suffering and bad or good fortune come with our destinies. We can, of course, change them, but we must also accept what has already happened. That is why I am dying with what some people will call grace. Don't forget that you've strengthened so much through the healing power of light. Find Apama Dai-Sung, a friend of mine, when you're ready. You need to find your Silver Key, Feslen. Don't forget that you cannot act alone. You always have to use it with two other keys to form a triangle of three points: heart, mind, and soul. These keys will unlock the mysteries of your world and mine. You will become what you wish when you find peace."

Feslen noted that the Master emphasized certain words: "Silver Key," and "the power of the light." Feslen's eyes narrowed in deep thought at the odd reference. Kai-Lornu returned, startling Feslen with an offer of hot tea. Feslen declined, but Master Chai sipped a little of the beer offered by the young female student. Then Feslen heard Kai-Lornu's gasp and confirmed the message from her eye contact with a quick nod. He felt Master Chai's waning energy dispersing.

"Don't forget that the mysteries of life and death are contained within. Just like with the keys of life, you must unlock them in a pattern of acceptance. First you must accept guilt, then you must want to do things out of love, and last you must do things because they are right." The once strong grip weakened yet more. "One more thing, Feslen. Keep your mind and your heart to yourself. Never let anyone dominate you. You choose things, not even karma itself can do that. Ride along with the karma, not for it."

Master Chai wheezed and closed his eyes. The two students feared for the worst, but he continued, "Feslen, you have a rare gift and great Flair. Use your talents wisely and for the good of all. Promise me!"

"I promise," Feslen replied solemnly.

"And thus you promise yourself," Master Chai responded with a sighing gasp. His grip relinquished.

"No! Don't go yet Master!" Kai-Lornu shouted and leapt up from her chair. She sobbed, knelt, and grabbed at the edge of the bed.

"Master," Feslen murmured, bowing his head, and kowtowed three times in respect. The Master faded away, his breathing slow and steady. The energy dissipated. Feslen cried, and so did Kai-Lornu, for an hour or so. The two sat in a cross-legged position for a long time, not moving or saying much. They practiced their *Tai-Thri-Ki* or Dragon Steps together in harmony. Feslen surpassed the first four Dragon Techniques with little trouble and started on the first two Dragon Steps.

Then Feslen suddenly smelled a pleasant aroma of sweetbreads and sticky rice balls floating in the air. Feslen smiled, recognizing it as his Master's favorite food.

"I think maybe Master is in Yellow Haven, eating with ConSuFu," Kai-Lornu said with a sad smile. Feslen chuckled. The aroma wafted away.

Then Feslen gasped, seeing sparkle of lights around the Master's body. "Kai-Lornu, you are the witness. Everything within Chai Estate is Feslen's and he is the New Master now. Let the best student do as he or she pleases, and may the Silver Key soon be discovered," Master Chai's voice suddenly boomed over their heads in a spiritual form.

"Yes, yes, I promise and witness, Master!" Kai-Lornu responded with a strangled tone.

Feslen's face was slick with tears, but he could only smile. The Master's spirit form smiled back, waved once, and then it was gone. The two were quiet. They studied one another. Kai-Lornu moved to get up and walk and Feslen followed her out.

The mourners looked at Feslen in expectant silence. Impassive and deeply moved, Feslen stared into space. All who saw him leave knew what had happened and waited for an order. "The Old Master has passed into the Realms of Beyond and Heavenly Peace. May he rest for eternal health and happiness!" Kai-Lornu announced as Feslen turned towards her. She looked at Feslen expectantly, but Feslen said nothing. Instead, he pulled at the sorrow of his empty heart. But to his surprise, magic still boiled within him. His heart seemed to explode into a brilliantly colored rainbow as he waved his hands in the air. The rainbow, more colorful and fuller than a natural rainbow, shot out and spanned the cloudy skies. All across the Kingdom of Chiendong who worked late or were still awake witnessed this phenomenon. "Old Master, be still and free in Heavenly Peace!" Kai-Lornu shouted three times as the sparkling rainbow arches ignited the clouds.

Both dignitaries and commoners had waited for the words of mourning to be repeated by someone. Kai-Lornu chanted the mourning words six times and then tossed small flower-wrapped rice cakes into the air. Feslen reached deep within himself again, crossed his fingers, and moved his hands in a star pattern. He let his grief fill the air. His eyes crossed paths with the Master's arching rainbow energy and he reached into it and mixed in his own grief. The rainbow arches then wavered and patterns of stars appeared within each arch. The stars filled the entire sky and moved across it on their own accord. The stars all stopped moving when they had formed the symbol of the Old Master, the Dragon's Head, looking eastward. A respectful cheering sound of praise roared across all of Chiendong. It was as if, for the first time, everyone understood what went on in the world.

"For you, Master Chai," Feslen whispered and then collapsed in exhaustion. Kai-Lornu beat Duxan to his brother's side and carried the unconscious boy into the house. After a few moments of respectful chanting, others followed to pay their last respects. They gasped. Master Chai's body no longer existed; only his long fingernails and some bones remained. On closer inspection, they found in Master Chai's bed a tiny, lifelike figurine of Master Chai. The mourners all were puzzled over this object when Kai-Lornu and the remaining bodyguards came to direct them out.

"The Young Master will explain all this to you when he is well," Kai-Lornu huffed.

Duxan left Feslen there. His brother was safe, at least for tonight. Duxan felt Master Chai's protective spirit around the estate. Duxan's own sense of auras detected no threat from any of the people that left Master Chai's estate in mourning.

22

NEW MASTER 新掌門人

The next day Feslen awoke oddly refreshed. Kai-Lornu had stayed guard with him all night, looking comfortable in her sound sleep. He found that reassuring and yet somewhat perturbing. He smiled and tried not to disturb her as he studied her. She still wore the Dragon School's uniform colors except, instead of a silver vest, this time she wore red. She replaced the white pants with red ones and wore a red silk blouse and a new pair of red silk slippers. The gold sash around her waist indicated the rank of her Martial Arts skills. for some reason, her face looked a bit sad and tired. Her hair was frizzled, which was sort of unusual since her hair was cut short. He gave a small sigh and wondered about her background. When she slept, she looked like a little girl, almost like Li-Pei, although some wrinkles appeared under her sad eyes. Her wrinkles made her look ten years older. Don't forget that she's only two years older than you, Feslen thought with a chuckle.

She seemed like someone who could be a very good wife and someone who was very dependable. Later he pondered why he thought about having a wife! Feslen didn't want to move to avoid disturbing her. I guess her daily mask as Master Chai's top student gets stripped away at night, Feslen thought. I wonder what she thinks about.

Thinking of Master Chai caused grief to rise up again in Feslen. Then he let it pass as he tried to think about the murder and asked himself, "Who killed Master Chai?" Feslen sighed and let his head sink deeper into the pillow, which was soft and to his liking. The only person who could possibly want Master Chai dead was the *Ninkatta*. On the other hand, Feslen recalled the odd sensation he had perceived that told him the *Ninkatta* did not want the old man dead. Nor did the Sorceress, who seemed saddened by the news of Master Chai's death. Of course, people can hide their intentions rather well, especially those that function beyond normal rules, Feslen thought. His mind wandered a bit and he asked himself, "Then who could the murderer be?" To Feslen it seemed so cruel to kill an old man who was soon to die anyway and who had lost everything. People do cruel things, as I know well. Do I need to dwell on that more? Feslen thought.

Staring at Kai-Lornu distracted Feslen. She seemed older than her age because of the marks of determination etched on her face. He reached out to touch her hair. His hands trembled as he neared her and he almost drew back, somewhat afraid. He had never been near a girl before, at least not without feeling her scorn! He thought about that and his eyes widened. Then he laughed at his own inept behavior around women. His laughter woke her up.

"Master, is everything all right?" she asked.

"Did Master Chai have any more advanced students or are you the only one?"

She lowered her eyes when she found him staring at her and mumbled an answer, "Just me, Master. I am his loyal servant, as I shall be yours. He left specific instructions for me about being there for your every need." Feslen chuckled and shook his head. Everyone tried to look out for him even though he thought that he needed no looking after!

"Master?" she asked, leaning over. He caught a glimpse of her body and swallowed. "Are you thirsty or hungry? I can prepare your breakfast."

"Stop calling me Master, Kai-Lornu."

"Yes, Master."

"Call me Feslen. Everyone does. I have a new order; don't follow me around at all times, Kai-Lornu. You may walk with me when you yourself want to." She looked confused at his request. "That is not an order; that is a request," Feslen almost burst out laughing at her confused look.

"Yes, Master…I mean, Feslen," she said.

"Thank you for watching over my sleep, Kai-Lornu. I feel quite warm and safe within these walls. As for breakfast, why don't you let me fix a real mid-morning feast instead for all of the staff?" Feslen formulated a plan. He thought, It's time to put your brain into action, Feslen, and time to get working on Master Chai's final request. I need to get to know the staff as real people. If the betrayer is here, I will find him.

"Of course, Master…I mean, Feslen," she corrected and hopped to her feet. "By the way, Feslen, I must add my own request. I have to stay by you at all times. Don't forget that Master Chai passed away when staying here."

"I trust my own powers and instincts. I will be fine," Feslen nodded, understanding her concern.

"He said you'd say something like that, Sir…I mean, Feslen."

"Gather the staff. I'd like you to tell me about each person," he paused, taking a deep breath as he put on some slippers and stepped outside. She hurried to stand next to him. She opened her mouth to talk, but he anticipated her and spoke first. "If you must, you can bring in one of the guards whom you trust, but I will deal with the food preparation by myself."

"Very good, Feslen. I shall do that." The two walked together. She looked around every corner with suspicion, and her body tensed at each new sound. At the same time, she outlined for him the staff's history.

"Uh, where's the kitchen?" he asked.

"Why don't I give you a tour of the Master's home first, Feslen? Then we can talk about the staff later," she said with a rueful grin. Feslen chuckled and allowed her to lead him along. A thought struck the young man. "Kai" was often used as a nickname by Chiendong parents for their daughters.

"Wait," he placed a gentle hand on her arm. She paused and stared back at him in sudden worry. "Kai-Lornu is a nickname, right? What is your real name?"

Her eyes widened as she replied, "How did you know, Master?"

Feslen smiled and said, "I make it my business to know things."

She gave a half-smile and replied, "The Old Master always called me Kai-Lornu."

"What is your given name?"

"Tang Swuai," she said softly. Her name meant "Sweet Water."

"May I call you Tang Swuai?"

"You can call me anything you want, Feslen."

"Tang Swuai, thank you for doing a good job of protecting me. But don't worry; I won't let anything bad happen to me."

"You promise?" she asked. Her tense, doe-like reaction soothed Feslen.

"With all of the gods' blessings, of course."

She smiled back and her body relaxed a bit. They entered the kitchen.

"Tang Swuai, please help me make a roll call of the servants, students, and teachers in the school and estate," Feslen said and added, "Tell everyone I am making the mid-morning meal. This will help people to get comfortable with me."

She nodded, despite her skeptical look. Then she ran about the Chai Estate like a bee looking for honey. Now it begins, Feslen thought, inhaling fresh air. Time will ferret out the real killers. He inhaled once more and waited for Tang Swuai to arrive.

She returned and said, "They all look forward to the feast, Master. Let me tell the chefs to step aside." Feslen nodded.

The Master Chef, Miaynuemo, and his female apprentice met them. Feslen studied the female apprentice. There was an odd familiarity about her soulless black eyes. She bowed to Feslen in the perfect, age-old tradition of kings and then moved aside for him

Soon the mid-morning meal was on its way. The diminishing shadows of people and objects on the walls told Feslen what time it was. He hadn't realized how much time Tang Swuai had spent trying to help him get settled and learn his way around the place.

Feslen heard the apprentice whisper to her Master Chef, who looked pale and shook his head every so often. Feslen wondered what they talked about but found, to his annoyance, that he didn't understand their language. "Was it Chiendonese or some other dialect? Or was it magic?" he wondered. He shivered at the female apprentice's cold smile and turned his back on them. The spotless kitchen shone as brightly as the sun but became dirtier and dirtier by the minute as Feslen cooked in it.

The Master Chef did not bow, but he allowed Feslen access as he tackled the stove with eagerness. He found several fresh bass and began to chop. He took his eyes off the fish for a moment and glanced at Tang Swuai's retreating figure. She had summoned a bodyguard to protect Feslen. The guard saluted and stood at attention at the kitchen door. Tang Swuai waved to Feslen and left to gather everyone. Feslen thought, Tang's quite cute, he chuckled and amended his thought, when she's smiling.

Then Feslen went back to work on the food preparation, even after the Master Chef pleaded with him, "No, no! No one but the true Master Chef can cook here! No! You're not doing it right! You aren't the true master!" Feslen ignored the icy glares of the Master Chef and his female apprentice. Finally, the female apprentice left the kitchen of her own accord. He wondered when Master Chai had hired her. Her energy lines were unreadable. But soon the enjoyment of cooking overtook his worries. Feslen chopped with the butcher knife until he could lift it no more. He diced and sliced two sweet-salty bass into small fist-sized chunks. He and the Master Chef put some peppercorn in the bass's intact mouth and some long scallions on top of the chunks. Then he rolled each piece in breadcrumbs, flour, eggs, and soy sauce. He deep-fried each one. "Very good, Young Master," the Master Chef said with increasing annoyance.

After the bass, he and the Master Chef broke out the dumpling skins and ground beef. Having stores of beef showed Master Chai's status. Most commoners and even some royalty could ill afford beef, especially those from the Southern capital, Wu-Xie. "Those who could afford ground beef had money," Feslen reflected as he rolled the rich fatty meat into the dumpling skins. He oiled the sides of the dumpling skin and ordered the Master Chef to chop up some shrimp. The shrimp were diced, salted, and marinated in lemon juice and then tossed into the dumplings.

Feslen thoroughly enjoyed horrifying the Master Chef and his apprentice by using his own cutting style. Feslen then put the dumplings into the open wood oven. He knew his cooking style seemed rather unconventional, but Feslen could care less. Every time he moved his butcher knife the "wrong way" or handled the wok in a brusque manner, it made the chefs jump. Feslen did this with intent; he got a thrill from breaking petty rules and making stuffy people like Miaynuemo squirm.

The female apprentice was even worse than the Master Chef himself, since she kept taking away his ingredients. He growled with menace, and then she hesitantly handed the ingredients back to him. Master Miaynuemo tried to force Feslen to cook the "right way," but Feslen refused.

Out of the corner of his eye, Feslen thought he saw her go behind one of the hanging woks on the walls and press a familiar symbol. He moved over to that wok, but Master Chef Miaynuemo barred his way and insisted that real chefs only need one wok. Feslen's eyes narrowed a bit at the man's behavior as he reached for a large bottle of allspice. But the Master Chef again stepped in and handed Feslen a much smaller bottle of allspice. Feslen's brow furrowed at such odd actions.

When Feslen asked for an explanation, the Master Chef stammered "You only need to use the non-emergency bottle." The young Raster shrugged and went back to his chopping and brewing. He felt like a wizard in the kitchen! "Where did Master Feslen learn such techniques?" Miaynuemo asked with agitation on his face. Feslen thought the question rather odd, but then he realized how much of a mess he had created for the old chef. The once spotless kitchen had become a disaster area! Of course, the way Feslen cooked things had increased the mess and dirtiness of the kitchen. Blood from the fish, meat, and shrimp dripped down the counters, and flour and other spilled goods spattered the floor.

"I learned to cook from books and from watching masters such as yourself," Feslen smiled.

That response seemed to make Master Chef Miaynuemo's day, and Feslen soon learned, with Miaynuemo's help, how to make the traditional white cabbage and kelp dish. After an hour and a half, the atmosphere thickened with the smell of food. Sweet, sour, spicy, and light aromas wafted into their noses.

"Master Feslen, that smells so delicious. I am so hungry now!" spoke a bodyguard whose job was to guard, not speak. Then the bodyguard stiffened, mumbling a quick apology. "You must fire me, Master," he said. Feslen gasped in horror at the guard's reactions. He convinced the guard to stay, and they chatted like friends.

Feslen poured a honey mixture drink that he had created into several dozen glasses while Miaynuemo rang the meal bell. The Master Chef's staff and the remaining Chai Estate servants and bodyguards all clapped and gave Feslen a cheer. Feslen detected a hint of falseness in their reactions, however. He also saw how stiff their bodies were, how unsure of their actions they were. He sat down to the table and waited to eat. It was a Chiendong custom to eat family style, but no one else followed suit. They all stood around, staring at Feslen and at each other. Feslen shook his head and realized how strict Master Chai must have been. Feslen forgot the rules that servants were not supposed to sit with their masters!

"Why don't you sit down now and taste my cooking, which I learned through the efforts of Master Miaynuemo. Then you can laud me or deride me," Feslen said with a graceful blush. Bits of light laughter followed. They remained standing, but they seemed to relax a little and they gave the new Young Master a genuine cheer. Feslen frowned for a moment, and Tang Swuai hurried to his side, asking what was wrong. "Nothing's wrong," he said, smiling. "Come, Tang Swuai, sit next to me, would you?"

Tang Swuai and all the staff stood shocked at his request. Feslen blinked at the sudden silence. "Please, I mean it. All of you, please sit down at my table. You are family and my new friends. Sit and enjoy," he said. "Please. Pull up a seat, Tang Swuai." "It's all right," he said to her in an irritated half-whisper, letting her know that he understood servants were not supposed to sit with their masters. She stared at him and blinked. Then she sat. The bodyguards sat down too and then began to eat with vigor. The rest of the staff followed suit after a glance at one another.

Feslen made sure he talked to everyone and waited until everyone else had had a chance to eat first. How his family would laugh to learn that he knew some etiquette after all! Even though Feslen remained alert and attentive in his small talk with the servants and Miaynuemo, his mind had phased out and he busied himself tuning into each person's energy field. Feslen spotted a small glowing heart in the right chest in each servant and guard. He had seen this one other time, in Princess Nai-Hua's chest. Each being radiated peace, love, and a bit of sadness.

Feslen did not understand what he saw, but the beautiful energies created by the rest of the staff seemed to clash in discord with those of the Master Chef. Then the other energy that seems troubled was Tang Swuai's. Her energy aura was hardened as though it were encased in ice. Why this was, he didn't know. He thanked everyone and shook his head to clear out the tiredness. "Master, are you all right?" Tang Swuai asked.

"Tang, please don't call me Master. I'm fine. I just need to rest a bit. Show me the Master's private study, please."

"Lean on me please, Feslen," she said, presenting her arm. They walked away from the dinner table and up the twenty-two steps to the Master's chambers. Feslen said nothing. She walked with him at his pace. He began to like this young woman. "I told the Old Master that there were too many stairs," muttered Tang Swuai.

He let out a chuckle. *A girl is near me, and I'm letting her!* Feslen thought and laughed.

"What? What is it you're laughing about, Feslen? Is it my hair?"

He shook his head and placed a firm but gentle hand on her arm. "It will be all right, Tang Swuai. I can make it on my own now."

The momentary weakness had passed but then returned suddenly and he stumbled, almost falling to the ground, but Tang-Swuai caught him. "You are clearly not well, Feslen. Let me bring you to the Master's study." Feslen nodded, too tired to argue. When they reached the study with the big recliner chair, she turned to leave.

"Wait, Tang." She paused. "Stay with me, would you?" Feslen asked in a gentle voice.

"The Old Master…" she began, her hand patting her hair.

"I know, he never allowed anyone in his study, not even Mei Xue," Feslen tried to laugh but he choked instead on his breath. He cursed his returned weakness. *I need to build strength, so I can find Master Chai's* friend, Apama Dai-Sung, he thought. He coughed up some phlegm. Tang Swuai looked on, wringing her hands. "Tell me something," Feslen said when he caught his breath. He made a slight motion to Tang Swuai and she helped him over to the soft, fur-covered recliner. He flinched a little at her unfamiliar touch then, and she shrank away. He apologized. She placed her hands under his arms and helped his settle in the chair. Her strength amazed him.

"Yes, what is it, Feslen?" she asked in a soft voice.

"Why did he leave me everything?"

She cast down her eyes as was proper. Feslen frowned at her lack of response, and she flinched. Her gaze rested on his feet, not on his eyes when she finally spoke, "You were his prized student."

I don't agree with that, Feslen thought with a silent sigh. I don't know why Master Chai ever showed an interest in me. I believe I failed his tests. Yet he trusted me, not just with his empire, but also to find his daughter and the Silver Key, whatever that means. He drummed his fingers thoughtfully. Tang's energy aura had fluctuated when she said that last thing about his being the prized student. His eyes narrowed but he shook the thought away.

"Is there anything else you require of me, Feslen?"

"Tell me, what do you make of having such a young Young Master?"

She smiled and replied, "Youth has nothing to do with capability, Feslen. After all, many true Martial Artists and magicians reach the peak of their powers at a relatively young age. Look at me, for example, I am ranked as a Six-Star student, and I'm only sixteen."

"You know, with that ability, you should have been at the Choicings. You'd make a great bodyguard or something."

She smiled a bit and then looked away with the same sad, distant look that he had seen on her face so often. Her silence created an awkward moment. Feslen cleared his throat and said, "What do you think he wanted from me? I never did get the chance to thank him or ask him why he entrusted me with all this," Feslen began, with a gesture around the room. "I don't believe in myself, not fully, at any rate, but, for some reason, Master Chai always did."

Tang Swuai seemed to pause in her movement; her body became perfectly still. Feslen did not even see any signs of her breathing, so he leaned closely to check whether she was alright. He also thought, Why am I telling her all this? I guess I do trust her after all. Or is it just because she's pretty? he grinned.

After a few minutes of silence, she replied, "Remember that ConFuSu the Sage once said, 'Confidence is the true key to power and defeating your opponents.' Feslen, I think the Master saw more in you than you yourself see. He was very wise. Don't forget that Master Chai was very powerful. At any rate, get some rest now, Master. I will leave you."

"Wait," Feslen said, taking her arm. This movement startled her so much that she jerked back. But he said, "I need to know everything if we're to solve this murder."

"How are we to do that, Feslen?" Tang Swuai asked and she chewed on her lip.

"I am not sure yet, Tang Swuai. I am making this up as I go along. Show me the main map." She looked him with such wide eyes that Feslen laughed as he said, "I know, the Master always planned everything ahead of time! I'm not that way. Remember he said something about the Silver Key? I think he knew whoever poisoned him and that he died on purpose. The Old Master wanted to set everything in motion."

"Why would he do that?" Tang Swuai asked, her voice pitched high in confusion.

"I don't know yet. But I will find the answer."

Tang Swuai nodded and pulled the map of the estate and school out from under the carpet. "I'll need to go to his private library and study," Feslen said. She responded by showing him where it was on the map. Feslen nodded. Then she helped lead him to the private library. In case of a health attack or ambush, Feslen and Tang Swuai planned a secret way to contact each other. She left him to his studies of the place.

He knew Master Chai kept records, private records, there. Feslen guessed why Master Chai had trusted him with such an important mission. I suppose Master Chai felt that I was like the son he never had, Feslen thought with a grin. After all, we do have something in common, our blood disorder, as well as our dislike for despotic civil order. Feslen chuckled as he saw hanging on one of the walls two portraits—Elhong Wien, the Head of the New Priests, and the Emperor—both of which were defaced and half-hidden behind images of Dhai-Hahn, the Father of Enlightenment.

He walked back into the study where a fine cloud of dust greeted him and he coughed. As the dust cleared, he eyed his Old Master's private study carefully. He did not envy his Old Master's position of power. Getting accustomed to all this will take a while, he thought as he eyed the huge pile of books and sighed. But then he chuckled, "The Old Master was just as messy as I am! He always appeared to be so neat." Piles of books, scrolls, maps, and letters crowded the tiny study. One tiny window on the north wall, which was shut tight, brought in the only meager warmth and light. Hanging on the eastern walls were magical images of the Enlightened Mortal named Dhai-Hahn. Cluttered around the portraits of Dhai-Hahn and the Sun Goddess were various objects: a globe of the world, Hahn-Hah, and a multicolored bamboo box with several images painted on each side.

Feslen picked up the bamboo box and examined it. It looked like a child's toy box except for the different coloration on each side. One side was gold, the other silver, the third side white, and the last side red. The dragon image was painted on the gold side, an atypical picture of the Sun Goddess on the silver side, the Moon Goddess's face on the white side, and the number eight and a picture of the First Library of Beizung on the red side. There was a keyhole on each side of the bamboo box. Feslen looked about Master Chai's room, searching for a key that would fit. He found a ring full of keys in one of the drawers, but none of them fit the keyholes in the bamboo box. "Why would someone carry around so many keys?" Feslen chuckled. He then studied the room again and then took another look at the box.

"Was it like a child's toy?" Feslen wondered, shaking his head. "Probably not. After all, what would Master Chai be doing with toys? He was too serious for that." Besides, Feslen didn't recall Mei Xue growing up with many toys, one or two at most maybe. Feslen shook the box, and something rattled inside. He wondered what it was. It sounded hollow or wooden maybe. He spent some time fiddling with it while looking about the private study some more. "I wonder if the Silver Key would open this?" he asked himself slyly. He saw silver paint glittered around the keyholes. He then spotted something silver in the wastepaper basket. He smelled old poison in it and dumped out the insides but found nothing unusual. Someone should clean this out, Feslen thought.

A huge flat map of Hahn-Hah with many marks on it was hidden behind a bookcase. A painting portraying Master Chai's youth and his apparent lover was on the west wall. Next to that were paintings of Master Chai with Ka-Wei's parents. On the Old Master's bookcase were several items that drew Feslen's interest: a certificate for a degree in healing humans and another degree in math, business, and science from Beizung University; a resignation document from the Great School of Magic Stuff; an original copy of ConFuSu's *Golden Rules*; and a copy of the Prophecy.

In one of the drawers Feslen unlocked, he found a penned note by Master Chai to someone named Fyo Wang Hei-Tai. Feslen read the letter over and his eyes moistened with tears. He read it over three times to make sure he read it correctly:

To my good friend, Lady Fyo, I beg you to consider taking Feslen Raster as a student of magic at the Great School (as a favor to me). Without a doubt, he wields and carries within him the Ancient Truth.

I know your people waited, hoped, and prayed for someone like him to come in future generations. I know you have even tracked young Feslen's life to some degree. He has passed every test of mine with aplomb and there's little left that I can teach him except theory and patience.

Ask the Shadow Master himself for inquiries of young Feslen's rising star if you don't believe my word alone. Ask Princess Nai-Hua, although she is not bound by your magician's rules. He is not alone in wanting Feslen, my dear friend. The assassins from other schools want him too. Yet they will find it difficult to convince him to become one of them.

Yes, Feslen's brashness may make him a difficult student to teach, and, yes, he came from a not-so-distinct but pure line of magicians. But his ancestry proves his worth. I don't know who else wields the Ancient Truth, but I sense them here already. However, only Feslen can change Hahn-Hah's destiny, and that of all those who dwell within her.

As you are well aware, time grows short for everyone here. The Emperor falls ever deeper into his madness. The Doom Prophecies draw ever nearer. Consider Feslen, or else our enemies will.

As a side note, just to let your people know, I have handed my entire empire over to him. If I didn't trust his true nature, his personality, and his character, I wouldn't do so. When you get this letter, I will have died. Too many vie for my power, and only one will triumph. I am afraid of who might win. My earlier apprentice, Hei Weung Tong, had a good heart, but he could not lead people. He also he didn't understand the Truth and so feared it. Watch over Feslen, even if you don't bring him into your fold.

Guide him, let him see the Truth, let him make his mistakes, and, by the God of Fortune, he will make his mistakes! Let him learn and be free. One day, if nurtured and not smothered, Feslen will save us all.

The letter was dated right after the ambush. Feslen cried. He thought, "I will not disappoint you, Master." Then, as he left the private library, his sharp eyes spotted something no other person could have: a small envelope in some piles of papers and junk in the trash. A symbol etched on the envelope in red ink had caught his eye. Feslen hurried to the trashcan and picked it up. Even though the envelope had some yellowing from age, its scent was unmistakable: fried snake. The yellowing color also brought flashes in the young Raster's memories. He studied the symbol. It represented the New Priests' group called the Scorpions and seem to be some version of their alternative symbol: a Hawk's Talon gripping a bloody hammer. He pocketed the envelope and returned to the Old Master's main study and lit a candle so he could study the envelope by the light. His hands started to shake and his breathing became shallow. "Am I having a blood disorder attack?" he wondered and then he gasped when he felt the poison seep through the envelope onto his exposed fingers. The letter was contaminated! I am such a fool! he thought. That's how Master Chai died!"

In his dimming energy and vision, he somehow managed to produce his secret noise signal for Tang Swuai. Even before she arrived, he had gone into rhythm with the Tenth Dragon Step: Healing Touch. But he needed her help. She came in an instant. She assisted him in his Martial Arts ritual. When they were done, the poison floated harmlessly into the air once more. He looked at her with grimness and handed her the letter, padding it carefully with extra sheets of paper for protection. But she grabbed it by the unprotected corner before he could protest. They waited half an hour for her to be affected by the poison that had almost overwhelmed Feslen. But nothing happened. He found it odd that the inverted symbol had disappeared from the envelope. These murderers had tried to cover their tracks, but not well enough!

23

DISCOVERY 發現

For a few days now, Feslen and Tang Swuai had been working hard to try to unravel the murder mystery of their beloved Master Chai despite the protests of Master Chef Miaynuemo, who said they should leave it to the local authorities. They had reported the murder, of course, but the authorities had never followed up on it. On a suspicious hunch, the young Raster began to realize that Master Chai's murder and death seemed too convenient and too sudden. They searched the Old Master's home for an answer, for some clue to the meaning behind his cryptic last words. Where was the Silver Key? Feslen didn't know and only surmised a guess. Tang Swuai sat down, rubbing her head, and thought about giving up, but Feslen continued. Feslen loved puzzles and riddles, but the clues his Master had left just frustrated him.

"It's late, Feslen. We should rest now," Tang Swuai suggested.

"The Master gave me a clue to finding his killer. I should at least find the Silver Key."

"But we've searched every room, even the den that we weren't allowed in previously. How do you even know there are any silver keys?" Tang Swuai said.

"He said it, remember?" Feslen replied while he eyed her as she yawned and stretched. "Also, what did he mean when he said he needed to find things through guilt, love, and doing what's right? Aren't I solving his murder because of those things?"

She nodded and replied, "True enough. I just wish he didn't complicate things so much. This puzzle's giving me a headache."

Feslen laughed and said, "Me too. I haven't needed to strain my brain like this in ages."

"I will stay and help if you wish. Do you want some Mai Bu tea?" she asked. Feslen nodded and watched her lithe form disappear into the kitchen. He usually avoided strong tea, but he needed it now, after hours of non-stop searching.

"What am I missing?" he growled to himself and paced the floor. Maybe she's right, and we won't be able to solve the puzzle, he thought. Hmm, maybe when Master Chai mentioned guilt, love, and righteous acts that didn't have anything to do with this murder at all.

Tang Swuai returned a few moments later, and the bitter, zesty smell of Mai Bu tea enlivened Feslen. The two sat quietly, sipping the tea. Feslen stared at her without meaning to, and she lowered her eyes with a blush.

"Wait a minute, Tang, what did Master Chai mean by 'the power of the light'?"

"Could it be a reference to a favorite thing?" Tang Swuai asked, stroking her hair.

"Possibly. How well did you know him?"

"Not as well as you and the Prince did."

"He does have a room he called 'light air.' But perhaps it's more subtle than that," Feslen mused, sipping more tea that Tang Swuai poured.

"But we searched that room already, Feslen, twice I believe."

No, it can't be so simple, Feslen thought and said aloud, "How could I miss it? Now I wish I'd spent more time at Red School actually studying or at least learning on my own." Suddenly, he had an insight and exclaimed, "Or it could refer to Mei Xue."

"How do you mean that?" Tang's perplexed look caused Feslen to grin.

"The character for writing Mei Xue's name, even though it means 'Pretty Snow' closely resembles characters for 'air' and 'light.' After all, most Chiendonese characters can have multiple meanings. I believe the Old Master always loved to hide messages within the obvious," Feslen continued. "His own name, Chai, could mean two things: 'tea' or, a very little used ancient meaning, 'dragon.'"

"Thank goodness I retained some schooling and knowledge about characters," Feslen chuckled in his mind. "I must remember to thank Mother for forcing me to go to Red School."

"How do you know all this, Feslen?" Tang asked with some awe in her voice.

Feslen replied, "Too much studying both at school and on my own. At any rate, we should search Mei Xue's rooms at home and at the Dragon School. Hmm, I guess it could also be a reference to the small garden she loved so much at the Dragon School," Feslen added as Tang Swuai started to leave. She gave him a perplexed look. "I don't know what all this has to do with finding Master Chai's killer, but it's a start. Let's begin at Mei Xue's room in the Dragon School." The two left the Martial Arts school and back to the Old Master's home.

As Feslen stood in front of Mei Xue's room in the home, memories of her assaulted him. He twisted her jade ring and felt Tang Swuai's hand squeeze his arm gently. He smiled at Tang Swuai but his body trembled, giving away his emotions. He opened the doorand a cloud of dust billowed out of Mei Xue's room, forcing the two friends to cough for a while. When they recovered, they were stunned to find Mei Xue's room in a shambles. Caught off guard by the number of decorations and items lying around in her room, Feslen stumbled. He had been there three times before, but Mei Xue's room had always been orderly and neat. Tang Swuai commented on the change as well and Feslen murmured an agreement.

Mei Xue loved paintings, and her three favorites included her three favorite flowers: three-petaled lily, yellow blossom, and tulips. Feslen and Tang Swuai had noticed flakes of paint in the entertainment room of the school. It looked as though they had been scraped from these flower paintings. Someone had moved things around in Mei Xue's room, perhaps even before Master Chai's death. Feslen and Tang did a quick sweep of the room: incense candles, carpets, some hand-drawn sketches of Mei

Xue's, a few hand puppets, and some empty flower vases. Then Feslen noticed something odd: every item in the room occurred in threes.

"I'll go get the guards," Tang Swuai muttered. "Mei Xue's room should be spotless for her return." Feslen grinned and shook his head, "No. Leave it. This mess is yet another clue for me created by Master Chai. He remembered that I have this superstition about the number three. Yes, I know it's odd."

"How would he know to do this or have had the time to do all this?" Tang Swuai asked.

Feslen shrugged and said, "I don't know. Maybe he didn't. Maybe one of the students helped him, and he explained it to him."

Tang Swuai nodded and then said, "Speaking of which, have you seen Kuan Hu since the attack?"

"Who?"

Tang Swuai reminded him, "The other expert at Martial Arts who trained with me, the guy with one wooden leg?"

"Now that you mention it, no, I haven't seen him at all," Feslen said. He thought about it. "Let's look in the room he stayed in. Maybe Kuan Hu left us a clue." He motioned to Tang and said, "But first let's take a closer look around here."

He held back laughter when he saw Tang Swuai's surprised look and she said, "What's the point? We've looked at everything in this room already, haven't we?"

Nevertheless, the two remained there and continued to investigate the room and all its items until the sun rose *She doesn't smell it!* Feslen thought, as a strange aroma hit his nose. He shrugged and said nothing when the smell hit him again. He and Tang stared at each other and then looked away again. Then they looked at each other again, and a big grin appeared on Tang Swuai's face. The two teenagers stared at each other for a long time. Her look reminded Feslen that she was still a young girl, despite how seriously she acted nearly all the time.

Tang Swuai blushed and began to giggle. "What?" Feslen asked. She just kept giggling. She managed to point. "What?" Feslen demanded, moving a step closer to her. In the past, Feslen would have reacted negatively towards anyone who even seemed to be making fun of him, even in this gentle manner. I like her, he thought. She grinned and pointed again to his mussed up hair and the thick layer of dust that covered his face. He looked like he was wearing make up. Feslen laughed hard when Tang Swuai thrust a small mirror in front of his face. He grinned, wiped his face a little with his hand, and flattened down his hair the best he could. The two broke into uncontrollable laughter.

"Okay, that does it. When I get Mei Xue back, I am demanding that she clean this place up," Feslen chuckled. "The gust of wind when we opened the door must have done it." That statement sobered the two for an instant. But they were still chuckling, especially when Feslen turned the mirror around so Tang could see herself. She laughed at the sight. Then their stomachs both growled at the same time as they smelled the Master Chef's lunch wafting through the air.

"Enough, Master Feslen. We have to eat."

"What is that unusual smell, Tang Swuai?" he murmured.

"I don't know. Perhaps you are sniffing things that aren't there?"

"Maybe so," he replied, but he knew something was up because he had begun to see double. What am I missing? He thought. He realized that he smelled the odd scent of paint mixed with rust and flowers. He looked around a little more, but his investigation led nowhere. "Perhaps the servants will know something about this smell," he thought.

At lunch, the Master Chef's exquisite meal consisted of shrimp dumplings in black bean sauce, ginger scallion rice cakes, steamed greens with soy sauce, and pork rinds in rice vinegar and black sesame spice. Feslen requested that everyone to sit at the table again, even Master Chef Miaynuemo. The female apprentice was missing, however, and so was one of the bodyguards Feslen had spoken to first but whose name he had forgotten. The Master Chef seemed perplexed by the request, but Tang Swuai and the others assured him that it was all right.

"Did Mei Xue like having things in threes? Do you know, Miaynuemo?" Feslen asked. He smelled that odd gritty smell of paint, rust, and flowers again. It was faint, almost undetectable, but Feslen detected it.

"No, Master Feslen, not that I know of. She was always a very clean person. I don't know who messed up her room. I could get someone to clean it if you like." Feslen and Tang Swuai exchanged subtle glances as Miaynuemo lifted another delicious shrimp dumpling into his mouth. As far as they knew, Master Chai had closed off Mei Xue's room from anyone but himself and had not visited there since the kidnapping. "How did Miaynuemo know the room had been messed up? Why might the Master Chef want to kill Master Chai?" Feslen wondered.

Tang Swuai scooped up some extra portions of rice onto Feslen's plate. She also poured tea into his empty cup, as she did for the other guests. He thanked her, munched on the pork rinds, and waited for the Master Chef to finish his tea before continuing to question him. "How long have you been with the Master and the Dragon School, Miaynuemo? Didn't you know that Master Chai ordered Mei Xue's rooms, in both the school and the estate, to be untouched?"

The Master Chef gave Feslen a dark and confused look. Feslen held his breath and than almost choked on some rice as he saw a shadow flicker around the man's energy lines. What did that mean? Tang Swuai pounded on his back for a moment. Feslen nodded to her and drank some water. Finally, Miaynuemo answered, "I've been with the school for two decades, Young Master. I did realize that Master Chai wanted to keep her rooms clean, as she had kept them, but he gave me and a fellow named Kuan Hu a very strange order just prior to his death." Feslen raised one eyebrow in surprise. "He said to make sure to give the next master of the estate a clue to finding the 'true heart of the matter' and to tell him to find Apama Dai-Sung. He began to order all of us to move things into groups of three in Mei Xue's room, the light room, and the training grounds," Master Chef responded in a hurried fashion under Feslen's gaze.

"Where in the training grounds would he hide something?" Feslen asked as he put his chopsticks down.

"I don't know. I think he said for us to clear the 'battlement,' but whatever he meant by that, I don't know. Don't you think you should ask the King's investigators to help, Master?"

"I've tried that already, Master Chef. They're pretty inept, as most government officials are," Feslen responded. This response got chuckles all around the table, except from the Master Chef. Feslen suddenly got up and snapped his fingers, startling everyone. I have it! He thought.

"Tang Swuai, come with me." Tang Swuai followed him out of the room.

He gave her a triumphant smile when they stopped at Mei Xue's garden. He had kept the poisoned envelope for some reason. Now he took it up gingerly and, with a clean cloth covering his hands this time, lifted it to the light again. Of course, there was the inverted sign! He saw something glitter inside the sign. "Why didn't I catch that before?" Feslen wondered. He ripped the sign side of the envelope completely open and out tumbled a tiny silver key. So! Master Chai did mean literally a silver key in his cryptic messages, Feslen thought in triumph. "I hope this leads to the answer!" He got the bamboo box open in under a minute, but it contained only a tiny carved wood replica of the main banner of Master Chai's Dragon School. "Why would he save that?" Feslen wondered. He pocketed the banner without giving it further thought.

"Okay, now we have the first key," Tang Swuai said. "Now what? Why are we here, Feslen? The killer may…"

Feslen suddenly exclaimed, "I've been so stupid! The answer was right here in front of my face all the time. Remember Master Chai's words: 'the power of the light' and 'unlock the puzzle through guilt, love, and righteousness?' Didn't he also say something about learning through 'heart, mind, and soul?'"

Tang Swuai began, a perplexed look on her face, "Yes, but…"

"They are all worded anagrams, or metaphors," Feslen interrupted.

"The characters for power and light often go together in poems and scrolls," Feslen continued. He rushed to the flower's three-one-three pattern.

"It means more than his favorite thing and the power isn't just meant to make me stronger. See these plants?" Feslen said as excitement coursed through him. I hope I'm right, Feslen thought.

Tang Swuai nodded but still didn't understand what he was getting at. "They're just ordinary tulips, three-petal lilies, and yellow blossoms."

"Yes, but look at how they're arranged. The next key or the clue to the next key has to be here."

Tang Swuai narrowed her eyes at Feslen for a moment and stared hard. "Are you sure?"

"Mei Xue nurtured the flowers and she often said flowers represent strength and love," Feslen grinned, feeling superior. "Master Chai knew that and rearranged them to help us find his keys." Tang Swuai peered closer at the third yellow blossom when Feslen fingered it. He laughed when Tang Swuai put her face too close to the flower. She had pollen and a speck of wood chips on her nose. Feslen held his grin and said nothing. Wood chips? He thought.

"What is it?" she crossed her arms and tapped her feet.

He sniffed and the unmistakable smell of paint, rust, and flowers remained on his fingers. He showed her tiny bits of the pollen and wood chips. She laughed at that and rubbed off the pollen.

As he dug up the plant, Feslen murmured, "I'm sorry, Mei Xue." He ignored Tang Swuai's gasp of horror. "I know, I'm digging up her sacred garden, but she'll understand," Feslen huffed. "Could you help me by getting the gardening tools?" he said when he saw the mess. He chuckled a bit, picturing himself with all the mess on him. She rushed to obey and returned a few minutes later. Mei Xue had once taught Feslen about gardening. After carefully digging around the roots of the plant, Feslen found what he was looking for.

"It should be a hammer," Feslen said with confidence. I have to be right! He thought. "I'm never wrong, am I?"

"A hammer? Why? How do you know?" Tang Swuai asked, pausing in her digging.

"Hammers are symbolic for a popular religious sect that Master Chai wasn't so fond of," Feslen responded. She shrugged and then gasped when they dug out a box. It was empty. "Damnit," Feslen said with a sigh. "I was so sure it would be there!"

"Why?" she asked as Feslen as he replanted the plant and smoothed the soil.

"I had seen an inverted symbol on that envelope I handed you, even though it was no longer visible after the poison had run its course. The inverted symbol looked a little like a garden tool…or a hammer, the New Priests' symbol."

"Oh." she said.

Feslen nodded absent-minded to Tang Swuai. "Why a clue that leads me to nothing?" he wondered. They returned to Mei Xue's room. After an exhaustive search, the two of them came up with little. "What are we missing?" Feslen growled, smashing his fist into his palm. He sat on one of Mei Xue's stuffed toys.

"I'll get us some tea. Whatever Master Chai wants us to find, he isn't making it easy," Tang Swuai sighed, tossing her hair.

Indeed not, Feslen thought. She exited and he looked around the room again with a sour expression on his face. She brought a full pot of green tea with some sweet egg tarts. They sipped the tea for some time. They studied each other and he smiled.

"Maybe we're being too literal?" she suggested, munching on an egg tart.

"It's possible," Feslen allowed. She wore a cheap talisman around her neck. Feslen knew it symbolized love and thought of asking her about it when a surge of strange jealousy entered him. But he dismissed it immediately. "There are more important things to pay attention to," Feslen thought with a grim face.

When we looked before, there was nothing behind the paintings, he thought, munching on his third egg tart, "but I wonder…" The two had made a thorough search through both the private estate and the school. "Wait a minute…" Feslen murmured, holding up a painting of Mei Xue's.

In Mei Xue's painting of the battlegrounds, a single meditation tree stood in the center: it was Master Chai's tree. "The power of light…and truth lies beyond paths of darkness…" Feslen murmured as he paced back and forth, studying the painting.

"Perhaps the clue is in the battlegrounds that the Master Chef mentioned," Tang Swuai concluded. Feslen nodded. The two searched there once more. The second time they searched, Feslen spotted the same pattern in a bunch of flowers near the cypress tree. He nodded and snapped his fingers. They dug around the stump and Feslen found a bamboo box with a hexagonal keyhole. Trembling, he uncovered it. "I think this is it," Tang Swuai said, breathlessly.

"Do you know where the key is?" Feslen asked. Tang Swuai shook her head. "Wait, now I remember where I've smelled that odd rust smell," Feslen growled and then snapped his fingers. He showed Tang Swuai the odd wooden carving of the school's main banner. The answer was with me the whole time, and I missed it, he thought. He hurried back to the Dragon School with Tang Swuai following close behind him. He pointed to the school's banner at the entrance.

"How can you be so sure?" she asked, and he glared at her as if to say, "Are you kidding me?"

Someone had chipped away at one of the wooden statues, going to great lengths to make the cuts seem like wear from age, but Feslen recognized the man's tools. Tang Swuai congratulated him as he fished out the tiny wooden banner that he found in the first box in Master Chai's private study.

Feslen smiled and said, "We haven't solved the whole mystery yet. Let's hope I'm right." He rubbed the banner and then he raised his fingers to his nose. He sniffed, smelling a funny oil smell. Poison! He thought. The acrid bitterness gave it away. Only one animal produced this scent: the yellow heartbeat snake. Its fatty tissues manufactured the substance when the snake was threatened. It was a poison so hard to detect and trace that even well-trained monks and detectives couldn't always recognize it.

Feslen reminded himself of the potential danger and recalled the same poison that had infected him earlier when he first found that envelope. The puzzle began to make sense. The poison had to have come from the New Priests. Yes, the New Priests were involved! Only one place in Hahn-Hah and Chiendong had such poison—the Southern city of Gezhou.

"Are you sure? Could the second key be there?" Tang Swuai asked. She climbed the huge bamboo tree next to the full-sized banner for the Dragon School. Tang Swuai looked behind the character with the least paint on it as instructed and cried in triumph. She fished out a glint of silver, tossed the second key to Feslen, and climbed down in a hurry, scraping herself a bit. Feslen worried about whether she was hurt, but she dismissed it. They decided to go back to Master Chai's home and private library to try the key.

As he sifted through the notes and business records they found in yet another bamboo box, Feslen began to realize something of the complicated life Master Chai had led. After finding three piles of dried bamboo leaflets of similar mark and calligraphy style, Feslen noticed a small pattern forming. Tang had fallen asleep and he tried to wake her gently by calling her name, but she didn't respond. Now I have found two bamboo boxes, Feslen thought. We'll discover the third box soon. If my hunches are correct and if I knew my Master as well as he knew me, the third box will be the hardest to find.

Feslen smiled when Tang awoke and rubbed her sleep-filled eyes. "I'm sorry Feslen, how long have I been sleeping?"

"Not too long."

"Okay, now that we've been working so closely together, you can tell when I'm lying," he chuckled.

She grinned. "Find anything?" she asked, leaning in. He caught a glimpse of her body and swallowed hard. He was trying to concentrate on his work, not on her.

"Do you notice anything strange about these pages that I've marked?"

She studied the pages for a long while and shook out her hair and answered, "Not really. You know, we've been at this for a long time now, Feslen. Perhaps we should rest or maybe even let an expert from the government take over."

Feslen made a very funny face when she said "expert from the government," and they both fell into a laughing fit. They laughed for at least half an hour, doubled over and in tears. "Okay, okay," Feslen grinned, "That's enough."

Tang Swuai caught her breath, stopped laughing, and sat staring at him.

"What is it?" he asked in between puffs of breath.

"The Master was right," Tang Swuai said, "You are stronger."

Feslen flushed at her praise. He was unused to a girl liking him, much less giving him compliments! He found that both interesting and confusing at the same time. He shook his head after awhile and said, "Look on these pages: the name and numbers for "eight" and "nine" are repeated in double consecutive digits: "eight and nine; nine and eight; eight, eight; nine, eight; White Avenue, White Street, and White Narrows," he said. On another leaflet, the characters read: "nine White Roi-Hun, eight-nine, White nine-nine, White-White eight-eight." Feslen inscribed the number-characters in his notebook. A thought struck the Young Master and he put his thumb over some of the characters and symbols that were scribbled across the Old Master's notes. The way the characters were written suggested a familiar resemblance in Feslen's mind. Sometimes, if the calligraphist were especially skilled, as Master Chai was, he could make Chiendonese words come alive. The words would flow and become pictures themselves.

Feslen sketched with a print block, brush, and red dust a symbol he knew all too well. His calligraphy needed work, but, as he slowly formed each character, the picture became clearer. The first word or number, "nine," became a part of a creature's talon. Then "white," the first word in the sentence left in one of Master Chai's letters, became a dragon's head. Then the word "Roi" formed itself into the picture of a well-known river plant found in the South, in the Yellow River. This river plant was famous for its poisonous petals. The other instances of the word "white" in the sentence became "pure energy," "pure soul," and "awareness." The other repetitions of the word "nine" represented "fortune" and "money." The character for "eight" seemed to be an old street sign or street name in Beizung that may still exist or may have once existed.

"Yes, that is strange, and I don't recognize these water symbols or the usage of the money marks. I assume you know, since you're rich and schooled," Tang Swuai said and stuck out her tongue at Feslen.

Feslen laughed and gave her a playful shove. "I'm not as good as my brother, Duxan. The numbers go in and out of my head, but I do recognize some of the money symbols. Father beat it into me when I was little," Feslen chuckled. He rolled the sheaf of records back within the hard leather case. Then Feslen took a closer look at the symbol and the "character pictures" of calligraphy that he created. He chuckled absently and thought, Mother would be proud that those lessons in calligraphy actually paid off! he inverted the symbol and frowned.

"What is it now, Feslen?" Tang Swuai asked, still fiddling with her hair.

"It's not a money symbol. Look at it more closely, Tang Swuai. You've seen these marks everywhere—on street signs and other things," Feslen said. He held the symbol up to the remaining light.

She gasped and held the table's edge as said, "Are you sure? Why would they want him dead? They promote religious freedom, peace, and tolerance!"

Feslen grinned ruefully and shook his head. He tried to hide the bitterness when he answered her, "Do they really? I'm sure my old friend, Elhong Wien, is involved somehow; I'm just not sure yet how. In the case of anything evil and corrupt, I'd put my foot in a ditch before I'd gamble my savings away on his not being involved."

Tang Swuai glanced at him and heard the bitter sarcasm in his voice. She stepped closer to him and smiled at him with some reassurance. Feslen didn't notice her gesture of support. She sighed, flipped her head back, and said, "He's a powerful man. Without Master Chai or Mei Xue to back you up, who can you turn to for support?"

Feslen grimaced, but he was not worried about that yet. He waved Tang Swuai aside and muttered to himself, "But why the complicated puzzle?"

Tang thought he was talking to her and made a suggestion, "Perhaps we should look into Kuan Hu's room now, Feslen?" Feslen agreed and brought Master Chai's letters with them, and the two left the Old Master's private study in his estate and walked back to the school. They searched Kuan Hu's nearly empty room. In a locked footlocker, which Tang Swuai broke open with a Martial Arts Dragon Step Three move called "Strength Within," they found a letter and a tiny print block with a tiger as the symbol. Feslen pocketed the print block. Print blocks were rare in Chiendong; they were used to seal official documents and such and often presented family symbols.

"He may want this back," Feslen said, and Tang Swuai nodded in understanding. It was written in the Eastern Chiendonese language, which both Feslen and Tang Swuai had to labor to read. Also, Kuan Hu's writing was small, and it was rather dark in this room. The sunlight had dwindled; night sounds soon arrived. The letter was dated almost a month ago.

"To my next Master, Feslen. I am sorry for the secrecy and the fact that I've been absent in your services of late. Master Chai asked me specifically to arrange a puzzle for you to solve. I have no understanding of it myself. All I know is that our Old Master knew who his killers were. He also suspected an inside job and wanted me out of harm's way. Why, I can't say. At any rate, I hope the puzzles find you well. I hope to be of service to you soon. Look for the answers in the White Temple. If you have need of my services, I am in hiding somewhere in the East where the sun is cold. Be wary, for something's afoot at the Chai Estate. I believe that a snake has slithered in and been stinging the hand that feeds it. Your faithful servant, the One-Legged One."

Feslen stood up and started paced in the dim room, asking, "Why does he put the words "White Temple" here? What does that mean? Does it have something to do with Master Chai's own clues in the letters?" He compared Master Chai's letters with Kuan Hu's. He noticed that the characters for "white" appeared twice and were written next to the numbers. Feslen asked himself once more, "What do they mean?" "I know Kuan Hu suspected the New Priests, as I do," Feslen thought. His clues—"a snake has slithered" and "stinging the hand"—definitely suggest it. After all, Master Chai was poisoned by a very specialized poison. Few people, including my less educated friend here, realize that Elhong Wien's New Priests are composed of three separate cults, instead of one. The best known New Priest organization in all of Chiendong and Hahn-Hah was the Dragon King Cult, led by Elhong Wien and his lesser known cohort and brother, Moi Ge Wien. Then there are also the relatively unknown cults: the Spitting Snakes and the Scorpions. Their leaders are not well known, but both of them made an appearance at the Choicings."

"Well," Tang Swuai began chewing on her hair. "You know full well that the Chiendonese characters for 'eight' and 'nine' represent numbers of wealth and good fortune."

Feslen nodded. "What are you doing with your hair?" Feslen asked Tang Swuai, who had almost swallowed a whole length of ponytail.

"Sorry, it's a girlish habit. What are you doing?" she asked.

Feslen looked at the footprint marks his constant pacing had created in Kuan Hu's old carpet and grinned. "It's a thinking habit," he said. The two laughed.

"Why don't we get some hot tea and sit in the garden?" Tang Swuai yawned and stretched. Feslen watched her, entranced.

Feslen nodded, silently, still thinking. If he had been paying attention as the two went into the kitchen, he would have noticed the new energy presence that followed them. However, his thoughts were too scattered and his stomach was growling.

"Uh, Tang Swuai," he said as he half placed a hand upon her before they reached the kitchen.

"Yes?"

"Do you think that Miaynuemo would mind if…"

"If we made sweet sticky rice balls with sesame?" she completed for him.

"Mind reader," Feslen said.

"Nope, stomach reader," she returned with a smile. They grinned. After they had eaten half of the dozen sticky rice balls they'd prepared at two o'clock in the morning, both friends gave a very satisfied burp. Tang Swuai giggled at her own burp and excused herself. Feslen cracked a grin but then returned to muttering to himself about the mystery of the last key. All of a sudden he leapt off the wooden chair, sending it flying across the garden, and cried, "That's it!"

"What's it?" Tang Swuai asked, still licking her fingers from her last sticky sweet bun. Her eyes were wide and watching him.

"The words in that passage: 'I wish I had known her better' and 'I would find myself in time through peace.'"

"But that's not what he wrote, Feslen."

"I know. The characters he wrote are his own creation. Remember the Dragon School's banner?" She nodded but gave him a puzzled look.

"Don't you get it? Those characters are fiction: they're made up. Master Chai made them up to use as a code. The number 'eight' and its character are very similar to the Master's character 'Red.' The number 'nine' is similar to 'dragon.'"

"Then he's referring to…"

"The dragon temple or White Temple," he said as the two of them looked at each other, stunned. Feslen almost choked on his tea. Most temples had been consolidated in the Temple District of the capital city, Beizung, but some older buildings of worship had been left alone by the new King, the Emperor, and the New Priests. One of the most ancient remaining temples was dedicated to Ao Chu'Yien, a Dragon King of weather and thunder. He was often referred to as the White Dragon and the protector of ships, lost travelers, and innocent people.

"This damned silver key didn't open this box; the treasure wasn't the papers, but…"

"A 'safety for where the witness'…" Tang Swuai's voice trailed off.

"How could I let that one pass me? The pagoda he refers to…" Feslen said, smacking his head.

"In the training grounds!"

"But not just any training grounds," Feslen said and leapt up, disturbing a chair. He rushed out, grabbing Tang's hands in the process.

"What? Not our own?"

"No, don't you see? They're also street numbers!"

"Of course, in those areas, they have double consecutive numbers!" Tang Swuai shouted, running along with Feslen.

Now I know what they mean! He thought as he ran on.

"What could he be referring to, Feslen?" Tang Swuai asked in between breaths, as Feslen led them quickly through the maze-like streets of Beizung. He still held onto her as they ran past street after similar street.

"This is it!" Feslen said, pausing, as she slammed into him with the sudden stop. Tang blushed, stammering an apology, but Feslen didn't even notice.

He pointed and continued to speak excitedly at a rapid pace. "Look! This is what he meant." The public school in front of them was once a monastery and now a library. People in this Silver Zone District weren't paying any attention to the two of them, thanks to the rich clothing they wore. He unrolled the crumpled piece of paper he had copied out earlier and read: "silver reflection." "What do you think that could mean in Chiendonese, Tang Swuai?" "What is this library dedicated to?"

Tang Swuai gasped when she finished reading the characters on the front of the library And exclaimed, "The Dragon King of thunder!"

Feslen nodded and thought, Such a simple clue and yet I almost missed it!

"So, let's go in," Feslen said.

"Think we could pass as students?" she grinned and then looked down. "We could, but not as girlfriend or boyfriend, I guess."

Feslen laughed with nervousness and let go of her hand. The two gave each other a look that Feslen had never thought to give to a girl before, and they reached for each other's hands again but retracted them when they entered the building. They passed underneath a large sign on the library entrance which read: no public display of love!

"Uh, do you have a library permit?" Tang Swuai asked.

"I have more than one."

"What are we to look for?"

"Look for these symbols," Feslen said, handing her a paper with the death symbol and the other symbol he had drawn.

She gasped, "It's the talon and broken sword symbol."

Feslen pretended to look at the rows of ancient books, but in reality he was focusing on the amulet that Tang fingered on her neck. In their search for the right book, Feslen told her it would be shelved with the histories and tales of the ancient past. Then he noticed her amulet slip farther down her throat. He gulped, tried to ignore her femaleness for a moment, and sighed. He sighed again when he saw that it was the lover's amulet.

"Don't be silly, Feslen," she murmured. "I don't have a boyfriend and, even if I did, he wouldn't matter any more."

"Are you sure, Tang? I don't want to make trouble or get in the way," Feslen began and looked away. She put her hand under his chin and turned him to face her. She pointed to the amulet, "A person who was my father figure gave it to me before he left and never came back." "I'm sorry for giving you such pain," Feslen murmured and, greatly daring, placed his hand on hers. She felt warm. She tiptoed up to him and gave him a peck on the cheek. Feslen blushed under her scrutiny. Then the two of them went back to work. They searched in the library until the peak of dawn and then sat down, defeated. On her urging, they went out for some fresh air and sat on a rock overlooking a cliff. She murmured romantically, "How beautiful."

But Feslen didn't notice the scene or her intentions because he was deep in thought. The puzzle was getting to him. He threw up his hands in frustration and started pacing again.

Since they left the library without finding anything, Feslen recruited Lioin's help. If the boy thief had named himself after the character hero, then he too should pride himself on solving puzzles. Feslen explained this to Tang, but she wore her typical skeptical look. The thief met them at the back of the library the next day.

The three of them discovered what they were looking for in a thick book: when they opened it, a tiny little silver key dropped into Feslen's lap. The silver key radiated a weak magical aura, which Feslen pointed out to Tang Swuai. She nodded, accepting his explanation.

Then Feslen and his friends discovered a black box in the Dragon School's training grounds underneath the large silver aspen trees. Mei Xue had named this second garden "Silver Pond." The black box vibrated a strong magic and was difficult to open, but, after a few clicks from the silver key, it finally opened. The box contained many things: a list of Master Chai's former partners and reliable allies; some correspondence between Master Chai and Elhong Wien and his brother, Moi Ge, the current head of the Elhong School; two letters written by the departed head monk of Thai-Thurian and Master Chai; a Writ of Information concerning some ancient swords called "Harmony Swords"; and a version of the Prophecy. They also found in the black box one object that Feslen knew would be there: a sharp golden hammer with an edge. He had seen this hammer before in the dream in which he fought the Necromancer and tried to help the Thai-Thurian monk. It can't be! Feslen thought. The hammer radiated a powerful evil aura. It made Tang Swuai feel sick, and she tried to meditate. For some reason, Feslen withstood the aura without weakening.

Feslen tried to read the letters against the setting sun. He read aloud.
To Master Elhong Wien and Moi Ge:
We are respectable gentlemen; please stop harassing my daughter and trying to destroy my reputable business with lies. I don't mind your blaming me for the loss of your business, or Honor, or whatever else you think I've done to your family, but my daughter is a new low for you. Mei Xue is off limits! If you harm her, I swear that one day I will come down on you so fast you won't know what happened.

The Thai-Thurian monk wrote in flowing Chiendonese calligraphy:
Master Chai, we know you have spotted the Chosen One. We think you are right, that he is born with unease. You must train him, for the time is short. The hammer is an artifact of the New Priests. You should have received it by now. It is the weapon that was used to hasten the Splitting of the Statues of the Ethereal Discs. I hope you can train the Chosen One in time.

"We must get this to Prince Ka-Wei," Feslen said. Tang Swuai and Lioin started to nod in agreement, but they suddenly jumped up when a *shuriken* landed at their feet.

"You won't be warning anyone!" hissed Master Chef Miaynuemo. He and twelve figures jumped out from the shadows. Feslen dropped the box in haste, and the hammer spilled out onto the ground. Miaynuemo bent to pick it up, even as Feslen warned him not to touch it. "Not to worry, little one. My Masters gave me a special protection from the evils of this thing," the Master Chef chuckled.

I shouldn't have exposed myself to it, even for that long, Feslen thought, feeling sick from the effects of the hammer. His eyes bulged when the Master Chef picked up the hammer with no trouble and placed it in his pocket.

"Miaynuemo!" Tang Swuai said, and she tensed. Feslen understood that she readied for some action.

"Why are you doing this?" Feslen asked, powering up. He looked for a way out. Miaynuemo and his men had cut off any avenues of escape.

The Master Chef, still in his white chef's outfit, held out a bloodied cleaver and laughed. "Because I have been around as long as Master Chai has, my boy. You took away my rights!"

"Rights to what? Magical power? You're a chef!" Tang Swuai pointed out.

"Ah, but he promised me so much more," Master Chef replied and motioned to one of his men to approach. Lioin flicked his arms and daggers slid down from his sleeves and into his hands.

"Who promised you what?" Feslen and Tang Swuai asked, but the Master Chef didn't answer. He motioned his men to grab them.

"Caution," he warned his men. "I want Feslen alive! The Master told me so. The others, I don't care about. Take the girl, if you wish."

Tang Swuai snarled. She charged at one of the men. They fought with hand-to-hand action, some using the style of Master Chai and others in the Insect Method of the New Priests. Martial Arts styles were like people's identities. The three men who attacked Tang Swuai fought with extreme viciousness, pressing her down on the ground several times. But she managed to wiggle away at the last moment before they managed to smack her in the head. She fought back, kicking them in the genitals and then using the First through Seventh Dragon Steps. Her slender arm cracked many bones and flipped a few bodies to the ground. Feslen watched her a bit with confidence and then backed up and parried attacks himself from two other *Ninkatta*-like minions of Miaynuemo. A few of the other men, however, finally overwhelmed her.

Lioin flung his daggers like *shurikens* and managed to hit one of his three opponents. He flung two more daggers and downed one more man. But the uninjured man still advanced on him. "These guys are dangerous! They fight as though they were possessed!" Lioin said. Both sides pressed hard.

"Who do you work for, traitor?" snarled Feslen to Miaynuemo as he downed one of his attackers. The Master Chef approached Feslen and thrust a butcher knife at him. Feslen dodged it with ease. He leapt over a punch from one of the men.

"You'll find out," Miaynuemo hissed. Feslen fought for his life. Miaynuemo's skill with the butcher knife had caught Feslen off guard. He felt a discord set of energies from the man. The Master Chef came close several times to cleaving parts off the boy. Feslen concentrated his inner energies on keeping one step ahead of the attackers. Sweat poured from his face and his oxygen started to run out fast.

Lioin downed his last man, a dagger skewering his spleen. The young thief leapt over the man's tumbling body and charged to help Feslen. Tang Swuai picked up a loose rock and kicked it towards one of the two attackers who remained conscious. They had already ripped off most of her clothing. She bled from a few bruises on her face and chest. At the sound of his cry for help, she turned to run to help and shouted, "Feslen!"

"Where are the bodyguards?" Lioin asked, barely dodging a punch and kick.

Miaynuemo laughed and said, "You'll soon join them!" The Master Chef reached into his pockets, chanted, and revealed some sort of shelled fruit, which he tossed into the air. He sliced it as it was coming down and then it exploded into a thousand pieces. The seeds scattered and landed on everyone. A poisonous cloud erupted from the fruit as soon as the Master Chef had finished his chant.

Miaynuemo was a minor mage? Feslen thought. The hammer's evil aura still assaulted him. He shook his head. Sudden grogginess and pain shot through his joints from the effects of the poison. Feslen tried to dodge a fist and was clipped on his face. As dizziness set in, he did not even see the side of a cleaver whack his head. He started to lose consciousness. He fell to the ground with a heavy thud. He heard Tang Swuai scream his name. Then he reached deep within his wellspring of energy and unleashed it. Suddenly some of the men attacking his friends began to groan in pain. But they soon revived. Lioin screamed in pain as one of the men skewered him in the ribs. Lioin and Tang Swuai fought on against a possessed Miaynuemo and his men. The attack lasted half hour more, but Tang Swuai and Lioin finally fell in their own pools of blood. As Tang Swuai twitched and took her last breath, her fond gaze on the shocked and dazed Feslen, she mouthed the words, "I'm sorry I failed you, Feslen."

Feslen cried out in anger, shame, and guilt, "Tang Swuai!" Then he bellowed out her name once more like a boyfriend who lost someone very special. Then as a friend in anger he shouted out another name, "Lioin!" But there was little he could do. He felt their energies waning. He howled in pain at seeing them die and felt like dying himself. He was in such anguish that he didn't see Lioin move his arm weakly towards Tang Swuai's neck. Feslen wept as he thought, Tang Swuai didn't deserve such an end as this to her lonely life! She should live! "I shall have my vengeance!" Feslen howled, glaring in Miaynuemo's direction. He was not sure if he saw the Master Chef or not for his tears blurred his vision. Just as Feslen felt his own special powers returning, the victorious Miaynuemo and his remaining men rendered him unconscious with a poisoned dagger and abducted him. In his subconscious awareness, Feslen reached into the part of his magic called Eternal Flow. With it, he called out to Duxan and Prince Ka-Wei for help.

Still in the South of Chiendong, Prince Ka-Wei, who rode on the boundary, now called himself Kalman the Red Warrior after the legendary warrior of the Fourteenth-Century Dynasty who fended off the Mengalois invasions. As soon as the Prince left his borders without permission from the King or the Emperor, he became an outlaw again. Outside Chiendong borders, many people knew him as Kalman the Red

Warrior. Kalman knew his own soldiers and the Emperor's Red Guard would chase him, but the two friends cared little for the dangers ahead. Kalman and Duxan answered Feslen's spiritual cry for help. Kalman, resplendent in his red armor, rode his black stallion through the rough terrain of the High Regions.

24

TO THE RESCUE! 救援

Voices cut through Feslen's hazy pain. Where am I? He thought. The back of his head felt like someone had beaten a gong repeatedly next to his ears. Even through immense pain, the boy discerned several things: Tight binding held him and a blindfold covered his eyes. His nose detected two other human presences, a lavender-perfumed female and a meat-packing male. Feslen's acute senses told him there was also reflected light. The way the light bounced, it probably came from a hooded lamp. "Who are you? What do you want of me?" Feslen asked, his jaw aching. A searing pain ripped through his ribs and he knew some of them had been broken.

Remembering the deaths of his friends, Tang Swuai and Lioin, helped Feslen's magical energies to surge up into his consciousness. He felt one death in particular, as her life ebbed away, Tang Swuai. He was too befuddled and angry to try to connect to Lioin's energies right then.

"Ah, it looks like you're awake and trying to pull some magic tricks out of your hat, huh. I wouldn't try that if I were you, Feslen. These rooms have been specially dampened to disable magi like you." Nonetheless, Feslen felt a familiar energy throbbing within him. He lowered his energy level a bit in order to refocus and gather even more strength. For some reason, Master Chai's lessons came back him the most when he accessed his conscious magic. *"Your Martial Arts and magic are not to be used for violence. Use them only to protect and help others. Promise me!"*

Feslen loathed using his powers to kill, and so he hoped to avoid doing so at all costs. He knew someone blocked the activation of his Eternal Well. This was a little bit like a drunken hangover, Feslen thought and said, "If I am to die, shouldn't I at least know why I am a prisoner and who wants me dead?"

The man chuckled and the woman laughed. Her high-pitched laughter set Feslen's nerves on edge. "It's the old revenge story," teased the woman. "Why should you care if you die?"

"Well, if it's the old revenge story, I guess you've done a good job of it," Feslen said without mockery. "But I've done little to you. Let me go, and I can forgive all transgressions."

The two humans laughed. Feslen thought he detected a small hint of sympathy, however, in the woman's laugh. "Is it the Sorceress?" The man then laughed as though Feslen had told a joke.

"No," laughed the woman; perhaps her tone was just more pleasing to his ears. "She has her own means of addressing you and your pathetic friends. We have our own motives, right, Terra?"

"Yes, idiot girl, but use my code reference, not my real name," seethed the man.

Feslen heard the sound of the woman's long, ruffling traditional dress. She probably wore a heavy headdress as well. Despite his situation, Feslen almost pictured his sister, Mei-Whuay, who sometimes dressed like that. The woman continued, "You are here until the money arrives. We have nothing personal against you."

Mercenaries! Feslen thought and said, "Who is it that wants me dead or alive?"

"That's for us to know and you to find out. Now, now, don't try to use your little powers, magi. It wouldn't do us any good if you're blown to pieces."

Feslen felt sick from her tone. "You hold me prisoner for someone who hasn't the courage to see me face to face. Does he dare release the blindfold and the dampening spells? He must be strong indeed!" Feslen mocked.

"His arrogance amazes me. He's just like our High Slayer and Seatan the Necromancer described him! Are all magi this foolish, or just the new beasts?" the young woman told her companion.

Feslen grinned at the reference to his being a "new beast" magi. "Who were these new enemies?" he wondered. "I want water. I'm thirsty and I'll die if I don't get some soon," Feslen said, smacking his dry and bloodied lips. "It feels like I'm in a dungeon or under a temple of sorts."

The two humans made a surprised sound. How did Feslen know? The swaying of bamboo, dried birch, and the cuckooing call of an occasional bird had alerted Feslen's sharp ears to certain possibilities. He has written in his journal once that Master Chai's exercises had improved his human senses.

"Yes, it's true," admitted his surprised and respectful mercenary captor. "Your strength is remarkable, young Feslen."

The atmosphere of the entire room shuddered for a moment as Feslen tried to access his denied power of Ancient Truth, or whatever it was that Master Chai had labeled his innermost powers. The humans shouted in anger and fear. "We warned you, Feslen. Do not activate your Ancient Truth here," the woman growled.

As if I really had any, Feslen thought, but he answered, "Does it matter? I'll die anyway, so what have I got to lose?"

"Gag him, Little Rabbit," ordered the man.

"Wait! You two sound like rather gentle beings. Let me see you at least. If you let me go, I have friends in high places that could pay you well." He was stalling for more time. His energies gathered until he felt almost normal again.

"I guess there's no harm in letting him see us, Dark Shark. But one twitch of the tongue, one move of the body, other than your eyes, and you will die before you can scream. Got it?" said the woman menacingly. Feslen didn't reply; he closed his eyes, adjusting them to the light. "There now, see, we aren't such barbarians. Feel better?" the woman asked, after Feslen has opened his eyes.

Feslen studied his human captors and his prison. Young, slender, and petite, with long, jet-black hair and skimpy clothing, the woman posed for him. Feslen was sure most other men would have found her appealing, but not him. He found it odd to think of his dead friend, Tang Swuai, and how striking the difference was between her and Little Rabbit. Tang Swuai was sweet, sad, and demure. Thinking about her made his heart ache, so he forced his heart to harden. I don't want these bastards to know of my pain.

Three lizard-like men guarded the exits. Feslen didn't like the looks of them.

"Well?" she asked, leaning over, close to his face.

The dark-skinned man next to her shook his head. Ai-Yen looks tougher than this so-called Dark Shark, Feslen thought. I can take him.

"Cut out the sweet talk, Little Rabbit. He isn't your boyfriend! Besides, you're not much to look at."

"I disagree," Feslen interrupted. She's one of the most beautiful women I've ever seen, akin to the fairies I've read about." Her eyes went wide with a reaction he couldn't quite read. Dark Shark gave a hearty laugh.

"Just for that, young man, I'll make them go easy on you," she said, sidling up to him.

"Enough, Little Rabbit," Dark shark warned.

Soft footsteps echoed and someone entered the room. The powerful smell of aged garlic and scallions hit Feslen. He frowned, recognizing the scent as Elhong Wien's. Elhong Wien even in his new form cannot hide his aroma, he thought.

Little Rabbit cooed a moment more, caressing Feslen's hair. He shivered at her touch, and Dark Shark shook his head.

"Perhaps I can make this worth your while?" Feslen asked, sounding hopeful. Little Rabbit looked at him oddly, and Dark Shark greeted the dark-robed New Priest. She laughed and winked at the boy. She was just playing at being kind to him all along! She did give him a sympathetic parting look, however. Elhong Wien entered and the two mercenaries exited. Feslen hoped to find a way out, even if it meant his death!

Outside Chiendong's borders, Kalman and Duxan were mobilizing resources for Feslen's rescue. Most of the inhabitants and mutated animals and monsters from the Neutral Territories had fled at the sight of Kalman dressed in his WuSha's red armor. He had made a name for himself in this shining armor with its little dents. He polished it with pride, and, when he wore it, he did indeed look like the legendary Red Warrior. He looks imposing, Duxan thought.

They had trekked for two days through grime, hostile territories, and broken villages in the Neutral Territories. They had met up with a Mengalois guide named Yukka. The Prince of Chiendong, Kalman, had made a recent peace treaty with Chiendong's powerful nomadic neighbors of the North Lands, the Mengalois people. Yukka helped represent them. The trio turned to the Northeast, to the First New Priest's Temple. Their proximity to the Great Barrier made an impression on Kalman. There the trio had fought off packs of trolls using breath-weapons. They had discovered the New Priests' symbols etched in the trolls' weapons, and the troll leaders wore amulets of alliance with the New Priests. Kalman and Yukka did all the fighting. Kalman added not a single dent to his famous red armor. Duxan healed some of their wounds with the emergency medicines he had brought on the trip.

They hurried onward, as Duxan felt the lifebeat of his brother fading. The trio had pressed too hard and, sadly, had killed their mounts on their way to rescue Feslen. Now they ran on foot. The week ended and they finally arrived where Duxan felt his brother's energies most clearly. There, at the edge of a blind pass in a mountainous region, a blackened monastery loomed. "He's in there," Duxan said, panting. "I feel him, but he's weakened. No wonder mages need protection from warriors. Even the best and most powerful mages need that."

The Prince nodded, clenched his fists, and said in a hoarse voice, "The evil thickens here. I can taste it on my tongue, can't you?"

"Yes," Duxan replied, surprised. Yukka, the Mengalois guide, nodded but didn't reply.

The tortured scream of a young boy alerted the trio. Kalman, Duxan, and Yukka broke into a run towards the foul monastery.

While they were running at full speed for days without rest, Kalman and Duxan didn't know that others also ran towards Feslen's rescue. The young monk from Thai-Thurian had followed Feslen's Eternal Flow. Meanwhile, a bandaged and weakened young thief followed Kalman's swath of destruction. Duxan and Kalman had encountered stiff resistance to the appearance of the Prince of Chiendong in the regions outside of his country. However, all the travelers had the same idea foremost in their minds: save Feslen, regardless of the dangers ahead.

The whip-shaped tentacles of an elephant-sized pit beast landed sharply against Feslen's flesh. The attacks riddled the young boy with red turtle-sized welts. Feslen struggled to free himself. He glared at the laughing Elhong Wien.

"You won't be the boy in the Prophecies—'he who died twice,'" the thick-mustached Elhong Wien said with a contemptuous snort and an evil grin.

"Just what did I ever do to you, you foul creature?" Feslen spat blood. His energy was rekindled by his anger and pain as he tried to focus on the monster.

"It's nothing you've done...yet," Elhong Wien admitted and continued, "I offer you a chance of learning true magic by working with my fellow priests."

"In a hundred lifetimes, I will never work for the side of evil and greed!" young Raster proclaimed. Elhong Wien just laughed.

Somehow, despite the creature's bellowing, Feslen overheard someone say, "The friends of the boy are here. They've broken through the first two waves, Sir."

"Make sure the beast kills him. Good beast Gurghanthka, please feed on this boy at your leisure. I expect nothing but bones when I come back. When you're done, you'll get a big reward." The beast chortled.

The Head Dragon turned to his underlings and said, "Train a bow on the boy, and make sure he doesn't leave before he's been eaten. These hero types always seem to escape from this situation."

Feslen defied his captors with a look. *No, I can't endanger Kalman and my brother!* Feslen thought. *Not for me. Not ever!* His inner ancient birthright began to boil again within him. The vicious beast gripped the boy and sunk in its teeth. It suckled. Some of his energy was siphoned out.

Feslen wanted to scream, but the expressions on his captors' faces made him grin instead just to spite them. I died getting into this world, Feslen thought, as the burning pain of the creature's acidic tongue slurped away at his body. I will die on my own terms!

"Die, you damned and filthy beast!" Feslen yelled, and energy erupted from his mouth and shot out at the creature. His fires burned the beast's flesh until it roared and let go. The guards dropped their weapons as well when Feslen's fires engulfed the chambers. They tried licking their exposed flesh, but to no avail. After a few minutes, the sole guard who was still alive ran off.

No beast eats Feslen Raster! Feslen thought and hurled out of his mouth more raw power. His energy streamed across the room and multiplied like the circles in a lake disturbed by a rock. The very foundations of the room shook and the *glasssilk* bindings melted. Fire exploded from Feslen's fingers and toes, once more searing the mighty pit beast, roared one final time and crawled away.

Even through his fatigue, Feslen felt a familiar presence. He saw Little Rabbit smile down at him from above. "How am I going to get up to ground level?" he wondered and then he saw a rope being thrown down to him. Grateful but exhausted, Feslen thought, Now I know why mages rest for such long periods in between spell casting. His head pounded, and he felt like his eyes were falling out of their sockets. He said, "Still, I didn't think I'd be this tired. I need more training!"

"Come on!" Little Rabbit said. "Hurry, they're coming!" Hundreds of footsteps headed his way. Feslen let go of his chains and managed to grab hold of the swinging rope. With effort, Little Rabbit dragged him up.

"Tang Swuai?" Feslen asked at first, his exhaustion taking away his common sense. Then, as his strength returned a bit, he saw that it was Little Rabbit, not Tang Swuai. "Who are you? Why are you helping me?" Feslen managed to ask as her smiling face stared back at him.

"I'm a friend and agent of your Princess Nai-Hua. I won't leave you to die here," she replied and pulled him to safety.

"Go. Get out of here yourself before they catch us. I don't want another friend to die on my account." Feslen tried to walk but collapsed in her arms.

"There's no way I'm leaving now without you. It's my duty, and I'm getting you out of here," she said. Feslen followed, too tired to argue. Sirens and shouts mingled.

After many twists and turns, they saw the light at the end of a long corridor. "Go!" he pleaded with her as an arrow hit his knee. but she stood her ground as twelve humanoid lizards approached. She gripped her sword and exchanged a grim-faced glance with Feslen. The two understood the implications as their enemies surrounded them.

"You'll come with us now!" said a lizard-like man.

"Come and take your best shot, you gizzard freak!" she replied. The enraged humanoid lizard charged.

"Leave me!" Feslen gasped before he lost consciousness.

25

CLASH OF TITANS 巨人衝突

"There he is!" Duxan pointed as they rounded a corner in the dim dungeon. A lithe young woman that neither Duxan nor Kalman had seen before was fighting for her life while guarding Feslen. With every action, Prince Ka-Wei became more and more like the legendary Kalman the Red Warrior. He swung his weapon mightily and two more humanoid lizards died in an instant. Kalman strode towards Feslen, but an evil force stopped him. He noticed the strange altar in the center of the main hallway. A sacrifice of children lay underneath a New Priest's altar. The rusty smell of Yellow Poison dust filled the air. The Prince saw movement in the deep shadows.

"Come on, Kai-Wei! What are you waiting for?" Duxan shouted and rushed in, heedless of danger, to rescue his brother.

"You're a fool, Prince Ka-Wei, or should I say Kalman the Red Warrior?" said a tall, thick-mustached man who emerged from the shadowy altar.

"Elhong Wien, what foul magic do you use to capture youth now? Why capture Feslen?" Kalman gripped his sword and hoped Yukka had gone to help Duxan.

Elhong Wien laughed as he stepped out from the shadows of the main room. "You're not my concern, yet," scorned Elhong Wien. "Although, I must admit, your Uncle's mindless orders sending you and your troops about Chiendong have put a dent in my plans." Kalman said nothing, but he took a step forward. The New Priest continued, unaware, "He really should stop mingling in other people's affairs and watch out for his own. I offer you a chance to leave this place alive while you can, Kalman."

"I don't deal with traitors and terrorists. I thought once, as my people did, that we needed your religion, Elhong. You did give my people and my country a temporary boost, but not any more. I don't know your game yet, and as of now I don't care. I want my friends back alive, and I want you to halt all evil and unlawful activities. I am still the Prince and Hero of Chiendong. Stop these activities or face the consequences," Kalman threatened as his eyes narrowed. He heard Duxan yell for help.

"If you think I'm a traitor to Chiendong, so be it. But I have my own causes to fight for, Prince. I am not in league with the ones you think. Prepare yourself, Prince, Hero of the people," The man raised his hands and shouted in arcane language. His cynicism on the word, hero, was not lost to the Prince.

"Poisoners of my people, die!" Yukka suddenly shouted. Yukka had tossed his spear even before Kalman reacted. The spear burned when it struck an invisible barrier in front of the New Priest. Elhong laughed. The Prince heard his friends' shouting for help.

The New Priest ended his chant and plunged the room into a sudden darkness so vast it blinded everyone. Kalman felt paralyzed, helpless, as if under a spell. Then the New Priest's body twisted and changed shape! "In the name of Justice and the Law, halt or die, Elhong Wien!" Kalman shouted.

"I will give you a taste of what is to come. Come, feel the darkness," Elhong Wien laughed.

Kalman saw two glowing eyes that danced in mid-air and moved towards him with steady purpose. The Prince backed up, trembling like a new warrior, and dropped his sword. He screamed as the vile magic touched him—not his body, but his soul. He kept thinking of Feslen enduring years of pain and remained steady.

In place of a human form, Elhong Wien had transformed into a three-headed bulls' body with dragon heads and squid tentacles!

"I shall devour you!" Elhong Wien's multiheaded dragons all laughed.

The head of the New Priests roared, and his dragons' heads opened their mouths and breathed upon the attackers. A ray of blackness, sprinkled with tiny glittering lights, came out of one mouth. But the Prince was unaffected, at least at first, and started to advance on the three-headed dragon, Elhong Wien. "What in Great Haven's name is happening?" Kalman wondered, totally bewildered. He blinked when he started to see the floor weave and move. The breath weapon had created a sense of vertigo for the Prince. The Prince balked a moment. Despair flooded into Kalman, the WuSha. He began to curl up into a ball of misery.

For some reason, a sudden memory of how Feslen had fought for his health and life as a child surged through the Prince. Kalman smiled and found his hope and inspiration. He began performing Master Chai's Twelve Dragon Steps. For him, mediation was instant. The vertigo effects ended when he blocked out all the false senses that the breath weapon had lain upon him. Kalman the Red Warrior advanced with yet greater determination. Kalman honored Master Chai and was really glad that he had persisted in the early, toughest days of training.

Elhong Wien's dragon heads wove back and forth and roared in anger as he said, "My, you're stubborn. Well, try this on for size!" He breathed again. Kalman put his arms up in a hapless and futile defensive posture but then realized that nothing would happen as long he kept doing his Twelve Dragon Steps. "Fine!" Elhong Wien bellowed as he reared up and chanted. His last dragon head breathed down on all three of them.

"Scatter!" Duxan shouted. The friends scattered, but too late. Duxan found himself in the main stream of the blast, along with Kalman and Yukka. The breath weapon hit them all dead on. Duxan screamed out of instinctual reaction, but he found that he wasn't hurt. "What?" Duxan asked.

Elhong Wien laughed, "It's a slow-moving breath weapon. I have placed an illness on all of you!"

In a few minutes Duxan found himself bobbing up and down uncontrolled. I feel ill, he thought, a bit alarmed. He became out of breath, and he began to panic.

"Don't panic, brother!" Feslen shouted to Duxan. He and Little Rabbit had been fortunate enough to be out of the range of Elhong Wien's breath weapon. The lizard humanoids had kept them busy.

"You and all your friends will die! No one can stop me, not you, not the Emperor, not even Seatan the Necromancer, himself!" The dragon-headed New Priest bellowed.

Tentacles snaked in toward them and Kalman screamed. He thought he felt every bone in his body crack. The tentacles siphoned off his energies and sought not just his life, but also his soul.

Then the Red Warrior heard Yukka's battle cry. Duxan saw his friend's dire peril, even through the blasted darkness. Duxan attacked another lizard-like man whose blue blood spattered his leather armor. Duxan shuddered at every kill. He hated violence with a passion, even in defense of his loved ones. Fifteen more lizard-like humanoids raced down the corridor at them. Despite Duxan's open wounds, he fought on. Six lizard-like humanoids remained; they gripped Little Rabbit. She still fought back as well, despite her injuries. Arrows twanged, almost skewering Feslen's head. The semi-conscious Feslen struggled to his feet. Duxan closed his eyes and struck a humanoid lizard as poor Little Rabbit screamed. Yukka Loi's scream echoed hers in the depths of darkness.

Duxan sobbed, but his love poured heart and strength. He fought on, despite the number of weapon thrusts, hacks, and slashes. "My brother!" he yelled. Pain shot up Duxan's spine when an arrow pierced it. His screams of pain mingled with Feslen's and echoed Kalman's.

As suddenly as the pain had entered Duxan, he felt another heart beating next to his. Somehow, my brother and I are connected in heart, blood, mind, and soul, Duxan thought.

We've lost, Duxan thought, slipping into a semi-conscious state even as Feslen stood up once more. *No, my brother,* Feslen reassured Duxan in his mind. Then darkness crept in.

Feslen sputtered in anger and sadness. He felt his friend's peril, and he felt Duxan's life fading. How could things have gotten away from them? He saw the death of Tang Swuai and Little Rabbit. The hideous laughing of the New Priest, Elhong Wien, spurred Feslen to act. A small, fleet-footed, caped figure raced up to him. His silver daggers gleamed in his hands. "Could it be Lioin?" Feslen asked himself but dismissed the image as a phantasm. "You died with Tang Swuai!"

"No, Fes, I didn't. But now we must flee! You haven't any more strength." Lioin said.

"Lioin!" Feslen said, turning to meet his friend. "You're alive! But you're injured." He saw the young thief's arm and ribs bandaged. "What happened?"

"No time to explain," Lioin replied. "If we survive, you may yet hear."

His sudden appearance had thrown Duxan and Kalman into shocked silence. Another rare figure entered the temple's main grounds. The companions had heard of these men many times but had seen them only once in their lifetimes: a monk from the island of Thai-Thurian came to help! He held some prayer beads and chanted. A peaceful, pure glow started to pulse from the beads towards the dragon-being that Elhong Wien had morphed into. A bright light struggled to enter the darkest night. The dragon-headed demonic Elhong Wien roared in pain.

"Who is that?" Feslen asked as his eyes narrowed, registering familiarity. "He seems familiar somehow."

Lioin killed two humanoid lizards, turned quickly, and said, "He should look familiar. He calls himself a Watcher Monk, a Protector of Discs. He is from Thai-Thurian."

Thanks for pointing out the obvious, Feslen thought and stared down at Little Rabbit's dead body. For some reason, she had a smile upon her face. At least she died well, the younger Raster thought. It pained him to see yet another young lady die for his protection. He knelt and touched her face and murmured a prayer to Yo Shian, the God of Death and Judgment.

"Little Rabbit is dead because of me. Yukka is dead. How many more?" Feslen stated, crushing the skull of another humanoid lizard.

"Fes, the lizard…" Lioin started to say.

Then Feslen raised his hands, and the Ancient Truth magnified itself as his anger and love mingled throughout his broken body. He didn't feel the sword that thrust into his body. Blood poured from his many wounds.

Unexpectedly stunning light surrounded Feslen, Duxan, Lioin, and the lizard humanoids. Feslen shouted and raised his glowing fingers.

Kalman shook his head, recovering as Elhong Wien let go. The creature retreated from Feslen and the monk. Kalman saw Feslen as a young man enveloped in the raging orange light. He saw Lioin, helping a semiconscious Duxan to his feet, and he watched a monk of Thai-Thurian hold off the monstrous New Priest with a handful of prayer beads.

"No, you mustn't do that yet, Master Feslen! You haven't the powers!" the monk spoke.

"I'll get him out of here, Feslen!" Lioin said.

Duxan blinked and noticed that his wounds had mended. Lioin helped the Prince to his feet.

Kalman fought to stay. He hated to leave the fight! He hated helplessness! Sounds and smells of spells cast on both sides mingled. One smelled of burnt sugar; the other smelled of crushed rose petals. The brightest light and the deepest darkness blinded the onlookers.

"We must work together," Feslen stated.

"I can hold him, but not for long," promised the monk.

"Wait, lend me your strength," Feslen said.

"Master," the monk continued, "Please, you are not ready to deal with it."

"Fool! I will slay all of you!" cried Elhong Wien. The chanting climaxed. The energy grew to a sweltering level, sickening Kalman the Red. Multiple surges of energies clashed: Feslen's Eternal Flow and Elhong Wien's own mysterious dark magic.

Lioin said, "Time to move!" Kalman picked himself up and ran out with Lioin, despite his aching soul. The Prince hated to retreat from a battle.

"Who is he, really?" Duxan asked, wondering at this sight of Feslen himself.

The monk from Thai-Thurian, who wore the maroon robes, held his prayer beads aloft and linked hands with Feslen. Boldness and anger smoldered in Feslen's eyes as he approached Elhong Wien. The young thief returned and urged Duxan to hurry. Intense blue light filled the area, wafting breezes of blissful relaxation towards the friends. But extreme flash fire continued to billow from Feslen's hands. The High Dragon's screams of agony mingled with the continued chanting. A bright blue circle formed next to the New Priest. Without intending to, Duxan added his own energies to the mix of Feslen's and the monk's. The darkness flickered and died out. Elhong Wien vanished under the influence of combined light energy.

Outside the monastery, death lay scattered all about Feslen. The monk from Thai-Thurian lay dying. Duxan's face paled, as if a sudden plague were sickening him. "Hang on, Duxan!" Feslen repeated until it became a chant. "What's poisoning you, Duxan?"

"The dark magic—it's as if it sucks my life force from me," Duxan groped for words. Feslen touched his brother's pallid skin with his free hand. It felt like his brother had a natural sickness except that he had no fever, no typical symptoms. Duxan breathed once and shuddered and then there was stillness. Yet Feslen felt his brother's energies clashing and waning. Through his mind wracked with sadness, Feslen understood the effects of magic on a person who hasn't been exposed to magic before. As the boy, understood it through his various reading and encounters with magicians. He knew that magicians manipulate the natural energies around people. Some people react with allergic reactions; others love it; still others, with no or little exposure to it, succumb to the overwhelming power involved in casting a spell. When mages overuse the energies sometimes referred to as "negative energies," the entire body's harmony becomes poisoned.

Martial Arts could do little against magic and its effects. Kalman tried the acupuncture healing method, but all it did was mend the remainder of the physical wounds on Duxan. Kalman and Feslen both felt Duxan's energies escape his body and hoped the Tenth Dragon Step would bring some back.

"It attacks my body like your sickness." Duxan said in halting tones, as some bile poured from his mouth. For the next four hours, Duxan lay still. His pulse weakened. The Prince tried not to cry, his body was ripped with anger and shame.

"We must take him to the Healing House," Feslen said to Kalman.

"You would trust a New Priest to help him recover?" Kalman asked, his tone incredulous.

"No, but what choice do I have?"

"Master," coughed the young monk before Kalman responded. Feslen hurried over to the monk's side. "I have a message from our leader and this…" the monk closed his eyes. Feslen scanned the note and pocketed it. He took a strange disk-like object from the monk. He then went to his brother's side again after he heard him groan in pain. "Master," whispered the dying monk, "he will not die. But he is ill. The evil demon caused an illness of emotional depression in him."

"How will we know the signs?" The monk did not answer. He died with a peaceful expression upon his young face. Feslen said a prayer over him and hurried to his brother. His brother breathed normally once more and neither of the friends could explain this miracle. The companions waited for Duxan to recover.

Kalman returned by daylight, carrying the bodies of Little Rabbit and Yukka. Kalman couldn't find Elhong Wien's corpse, which alarmed them. Duxan remained in a slight coma. He mumbled in his fitful sleep, "I am sick. That's all. Rare sickness to combat the spell. Jungai herbs…"

"Why do you think your brother mentions the herbs?" Kalman asked, his face reflecting his confusion.

Feslen shrugged and replied, "I'm not sure. I know Jungai herbs are used mainly for natural illnesses and physical wounds, like sword wounds, right?"

Kalman nodded and said with a smile, "You learn your military lessons well. Captain Garland would be pleased."

Feslen smiled back and replied, "I did spend time learning with my brain, but not with my body. As for Duxan's asking for the herbs, perhaps he realizes more about his illness than we do. Who knows?"

"Feslen, I don't believe spending time in the New Priest's Healing House will do him much good," Kalman said and he continued, "Remember, they did little for you when you were growing up."

Feslen nodded in agreement and said, "You're right. Help me convince my family to let Duxan rest at home then."

"I shall, Feslen."

Before disappearing, Lioin explained that he had managed to deflect the assassin's blade, but that Tang Swuai did not survive. The young thief gave Feslen Tang Swuai's amulet and left him alone. Feslen grieved over Tang Swuai, and Kalman comforted him. The boy wore her amulet and sat next to Duxan, telling him about his feelings.

Feslen the boy was becoming a man, Kalman thought with a small smile. He held a Forest Protector symbol that he had found on Little Rabbit's body between his fingers. The mission had not gone well. They had tried to enter the New Priest's first temple, but magic denied them access. Then Kalman had tried to burn the temple down and failed. After a proper burial for Yukka, Little Rabbit, and the monk, they began their journey home. Feslen let himself be filled with sorrowful thoughts of Tang Swuai and Little Rabbit. "If my enemies want a fight, they shall have it!" Feslen vowed.

PART II

26

REVERSED ROLES 角色對調

Feslen sat on a chair by Duxan's bedside. The family already placed an inquiry for a New Priest. Beizung's New Priests and most famous physicians came to look at Duxan's illness. No one, including Feslen's family, paid much attention to Feslen's pleas. They stuck Duxan with needles to take blood samples, put his body through countless 'modern medicinal cures', to little avail. They also used a cylindrical object and placed it above his Duxan's heart and forehead. Attached to the end of this object were a few acupuncture needles and an empty vial. When they tested for Duxan's blood, the blood swirled in the object and turned brown. Only Feslen saw his brother's sparkle with energy. This energy coagulated Duxan's blood in the vial into a muddy earthen crust. The New Priest holding the vial almost dropped it, and hissed in as if pain. He demanded the Beizung physician to hold it, he did. After a discussion of what happened, the physicians proceeded to do other experiments on poor Duxan, despite his semi-conscious protests, and Feslen's anger.

He overheard them muttering, "I believe the Emperor was right…perhaps the Three are among us."

Vivid memories of the New Priest physicians and normal physicians medicating a younger Feslen ran through his mind. They too, once used a cylindrical object to test his blood. As soon as the New Priest and other physicians left, Feslen entered. Feslen touched his brother's lymph areas on his neck and hissed in pain. His brother's skin was cold to the touch.

It was fortunate the Prince convinced the Wong family to let Duxan stay home, instead of in a Healing House somewhere. He gripped Duxan's hands and murmured the Heart Sutra over and over, "Ohm Madne Padne Ohm."

Feslen asked Li-Pei to fetch a pitcher of hot tea and his favorite book, *The Third Dynasties Triumph: A Tale of Two Princes*, from his bookshelf. When Feslen was in sickbed, Duxan read this to him almost all the time.

The two siblings sat reading near Duxan for a long time.

He closed his eyes and anxiousness overtook him.

Feslen awoke. He looked down at sleeping Li-Pei, her head on his lap. It was pitch black due to the downpour of rain. Feslen sighed and drank some cold tea. The weakness of his brother's pulse stunned him.

"Big brother...." Feslen said in a whisper, as not to disturb Li-Pei, "Why did sickness affect you, the healthiest of all people? You always looked after me." Feslen smiled with fondness at an early memory of his brother helping him.

When Feslen was seven and in a coma due to high fever, Duxan would perform a healing art he learned from their Father Wong called *reflexology*. Feslen was in such pain, his body burned with deep fires, that every bone and muscle hurt. However, Duxan eased his pains by using the method of *reflexology* on him. This method was to cure illnesses of the body through the foot. A layman could call it, "feet acupuncture".

It worked for me, Feslen thought, staring at his brother's feet. Why not? He started to perform *reflexology* on his brother. Duxan's feet were warm. Feslen felt his brother's energies and Elhong Wien's dark magic still running through him. Feslen hissed in some pain when he touched his brother's feet, first the toes and then the heart region on the foot...

Feslen endured the pain as much as he could from Elhong Wien's lingering magic and then let go. He sighed, staring at his too-still brother. Though his skin looked healthy, his pulse too light and weak. That did not work very well, did it, Feslen thought with a sour frown. Duxan did not move a muscle since their encounter with Elhong Wien.

He did his best not to disturb his sister, Li-Pei, but she groaned a bit awake. She blinked and looked at him with some concern.

"What am I to do without you?" Feslen asked. "You always gave me guidance." He closed his eyes in pain, bitter tiredness and shame. He cried until his exhaustion came.

Li-Pei sighed and hugged Feslen and fell asleep again.

In a half, fitful sleep, Feslen's mind recalled some early lessons on magical illnesses. He realized that Duxan was under a powerful magical illness. Feslen wandered back to when to their youth and Duxan asked one of Prince Ka-Wei's teachers on the value of magic and healing.

"Magic can only cure magic. There are no such things are faith healing," said the unnamed magician.

"Not even from the Tian Huo, the Goddess and Creator of Life? Nor Gei, Goddess of Birth and Fertility?" Duxan asked his skepticism obvious.

"No. Magic, yes, it's natural and comes from Tian Huo. But, magic comes from within us, or Flair. We can use it to hurt, heal and combat other magic."

The younger Raster then spotted in his book of mystics about a legendary magical crystal called Suy-Eihan Crystal. According to the historical book he read, the Suy-Eihan Crystal, formed from the Creator Goddess' tears, did more than just cure illnesses. He needed an expert mage's opinion. He needed one that would listen to him, outside of the Great School of Magic Stuff.

"Where are you going, big brother?" Li-Pei asked, as Feslen got up. He sighed.

"I have to, it's for Duxan," Feslen answered.

"All right, just be careful, big brother," Li-Pei said, her voice tight with concern for him.

He smiled and came over to her and hugged her tight. "I'll be back with a cure for him, I promise."

Li-Pei returned a smile and returned his hug.

"Thank you," Feslen said to her as he opened the window to his room and prepared for the Dragon Step Seven, Frog Hop. Forty feet down to the ground, Feslen thought. He wiped the fear from his mind when he stretched. He got up to the windowsill and dropped to the ground in safety. Master Chai would be proud, Feslen thought and thanked the departed Martial Artist. Feslen sought Sae-Jyung.

Sae-Jyung met Feslen behind a desecrated monastery. Less light penetrated that area. Feslen fidgeted as he entered the shadows.

A swarm of crows settled on the rooftop of the monastery. Their appearance gave Feslen discomfort.

"I heard about your plight, Feslen. You want the Jungai herbs."

"I am prepared to make a deal, of any sort, Sae-Jyung."

"You have nothing I want…" Sae-Jyung said voice almost in a hiss. His raven eyes flickered to red for a moment and back to raven. "Yes…you are right, Seatan…Nadine…you and I want…but, how is he connected to her?" The merchant mage shook his head, as if to clear his head.

"Who is Seatan?" Feslen asked.

"The Necromancer…" Sae-Jyung muttered.

Feslen watched the man's face twist in agony and perplexion. Goosebumps tickled Feslen all over. He considered running from Sae-Jyung. He felt that *other* presence surround Sae-Jyung. The other presence smelled of graveyard and dried herbal stuffing, the kind one used for a dead body. The aromas of Sae-Jyung and this other presence mingled odd, and Feslen sneezed to it.

The Necromancer…? Feslen thought, eyes narrowed at Sae-Jyung. He began asking Sae-Jyung knows of him, but the man mumbled to himself.

The man talked to himself and walked back and forth.

"Sae-Jyung wants Nadine…but not for those purposes. It's not right, no no. But, He needs her…"

A cruel smile appeared on Sae-Jyung. He turned to Feslen, less then human in appearance.

"Nadine…." He hissed.

"I do not even know Nadine! You shouldn't drag her into this!"

"You two seemed to hit it off quite well. Yes, quite well."

The man hissed his *s*'s, made Feslen shiver.

"Look, my family has the money and—"…

Sae-Jyung asked, "My family is wealthier than yours. What would you do for the herbs?"

Feslen saw him twitch and heard him hiss.

"The Princess…" the voice was not Sae-Jyung's own. Feslen shuddered at the odd changes in the man. The man's raven eyes fluctuated along with his face.

Feslen asked, "So, what do you want?"

"Nadine."

Feslen frowned.

Sae-Jyung waited, grinning.

"Nadine? Why would she be important to me? I don't know her as well you, Sae-Jyung," Feslen said.

"Oh, your hold on her is tighter than you believe," he hissed.

"Is it? She's nothing but a stranger to me."

Sae-Jyung laughed, his laughter shook some crows from the roofs of the deserted village to the skies.

"Very well, you don't know her," Sae-Jyung agreed. "But he knows… she is pure like him."

The other voice sputtered, shaking both Feslen and Sae-Jyung.

Sae-Jyung growled, and gripped his hand. "I know…" he started and took a deep breath, and chanted. He turned to face the boy, eyes calm. "Information…"

Feslen responded, "About Nadine?"

Sae-Jyung laughed, a genuine one, then, "No. I want an informant, perhaps an agent, if you will to disturb the New Priest's stronghold."

"Perhaps. Why should I be interested?"

"They are your enemies as well as mine, Feslen. Plus…they have something I want…"

"The Suy-Eihan Crystal?" Feslen jumped.

Sae-Jyung eyes widened and laughed in appreciation.

"Excellent, Feslen! I knew one day you'd be a good partner," Sae-Jyung said with a laugh. His face scrunched in seriousness and he continued, "I need your help in obtaining it."

Feslen's eyebrows shot up.

"A deal for a deal? You realize Duxan may not have much time."

"You need something, I need something. Fair's fair, I always say. If we're to be future wizards, we need to work together, right?" Sae-Jyung chuckled and shook out his long thin black hair.

His raven eyes arrested Feslen's attention.

Feslen nodded.

"I won't risk going, they know me too well down at the Temple District…"

"You want me to somehow find out *if* this thing is there. *If,* Elhong Wien has it and *if* he is willing to part with it?"

"Oh it's there all right."

Feslen raised an eyebrow at Sae-Jyung and crossed his arms.

Sae-Jyung's sigh shook Feslen to the very being. The sigh seemed like it came from someone who experienced years of abuse and mistreatment.

Feslen understood what that felt like, and uncrossed his arms. He began to sympathize the mage. He studied the man's eyes. He was lying, no doubt, Feslen thought. But, there's a truth there too.

"Let's just call it a magic-user's call. We are brethren, after all," Sae-Jyung said and held out his hand.

Feslen hesitated, hand half-out, dubious.

Sae-Jyung then took out his father's Honor Coin. Feslen's eyes widened.

An oath of Honor and exchange of Honor Coins completed every business transaction in Chiendong. Each person making a transaction on anything swore on the usual things: their own honor, their business' success or a birth of a normal child. It was rare for someone to swear on family honor. The Honor Coins represented the oaths they took.

The two stared in silence.

Sae-Jyung twisted a smile when Feslen nodded in reluctance.

He handed Feslen a detailed map of the Temple District and the Honor Coin and Feslen handed him his.

Sae-Jyung refused his Honor Coin and Feslen gave him a puzzled look.

"I asked for this deal, not you, Feslen."

"But I…"

"Ask Prince Ka-Wei or your brother for the other rules of Honor when you get back."

Feslen said, "Teach me the healing spell and give me a two month's supply of the healing herbs in exchange."

"Agreed."

Feslen shook hands with Sae-Jyung. The young Raster went to fetch Prince Ka-Wei, and Lioin for help as the merchant mage melded into the shadows.

27

TEMPLE DISTRICT 殿堂區

"I thought you didn't want to risk coming," Feslen said, glaring at Sae-Jyung, as he strode in. The tall man's cocky stride irritated Feslen and he thought better of chiding him.

"What are you doing here?" Prince Ka-Wei asked, his voice hiding no pretense.

"This is my quest, I want to make sure he does this right," Sae-Jyung replied, smug smile on face.

"If you didn't trust me, why give me the project?"

"I don't trust them," Sae-Jyung smirked, pointing to Ka-Wei, Duxan and Lioin.

Sae-Jyung parked himself behind some bushes, in the shadows. Sweat dropped from him and the others. Feslen noticed though, another thing affected his companions. He felt it too. "The magic and power in this area is intoxicating, no?" Sae-Jyung asked Feslen as the four studied the Temple District.

The Temple District never ceased to amaze Feslen. Tens of thousands of huddled mass of people crowded to pray and meditate. They gathered in front of the hundreds of churches, temples, pagodas and new-fangled monasteries. The incessant chanting and shouting of the people got to him a bit, but his newfound discipline did not let him show weakness.

"So, what's your plan? We can't just go barging in, we'd have to be part of the congregation," Ka-Wei pointed out.

The biggest temple overshadowed and outweighed them all. Three times the size, color and the brightness became unbearable for the onlookers as the sun glared off the paint; hence the name Temple of the Skies.

"I can sneak in," Lioin offered. They ignored the snort from Sae-Jyung.

"I already know, Feslen," Ka-Wei intercepted him before talking. "You need a special member patch or some such thing to enter the Temple of Skies."

"Leave it to me," Lioin said, grinning.

Ka-Wei placed a hand on him and frowned, shaking his head. "No, Lioin. We have to enter with legal means. I don't want to become a thief in my own country."

"Or any others," Sae-Jyung hissed.

"Aren't you a thief just by spending time with me?" Lioin grinned, pointed out to the Prince.

The Prince chuckled, "Technically, yes. No thievery, no matter what. The end never justifies the means, Gui-Pan."

Lioin sighed and appealed Feslen a look. The converging influence of powers in Temple District put a strain on Feslen's heart and concentration. He heard a musical voice sing to him from somewhere within the mass of temples. Part of him enjoyed the feeling, and the other felt sickened by it. He focused on the power and almost centralized on it. He gasped when he saw sprinkles of energy connected to each other like strands of thread. Then he lost it, in confusion and hunger for power.

"The Suy-Eihan Crystal is here," Feslen murmured. "I felt it."

"Did it sing to you?" Sae-Jyung asked at the same time Ka-Wei did.

Feslen nodded and looked at the big Prince in surprise. He shrugged and said, "I don't know how I felt it, Lioin?"

"Nope, I felt nothing."

Sae-Jyung nodded.

"We are being watched," Feslen said.

Sae-Jyung frowned, "I am not sure, my fine young mage. But, I can cast a spell to find out."

Feslen nodded his ok. He felt the man's powers as the young merchant mage chanted. He tossed up a broken mirror and small sapphire. A perceptible orange aura surrounded Sae-Jyung, black cape fluttering a bit, when he finished his spell. His forehead kneaded with sweat and he bit his lip in the effort.

Sae-Jyung grunted, shrugging shoulders. "I sense nothing, Feslen. But, it could be the immense of energy and magic being used here that interferes."

Lioin asked Feslen again if he should scout out and return with any 'treasures'.

Feslen nodded, "Ok, go, Lioin."

The young thief waved to them and crept down as silent as a hunting cat and vanished within the throng.

Feslen worried, Lioin had not returned in thirty minutes. Plans formulated on how to gain entrance to Temple of Skies. Feslen questioned the motives of Sae-Jyung. "It's a risk," Feslen admitted to Ka-Wei. "Neither of you have to come, I can go alone…I don' want to risk either of you."

But, even if Lioin had been here, Feslen knew he would not abandon him.

Ka-Wei said, "Our thief returns."

Lioin sat down and grumbled, "Can't even get near it, too…"

"And the thief fails," chortled Sae-Jyung.

"As I was saying, it wasn't just the people, I could get past the guards," Lioin said, demonstrated with wild abandon. "But it was something…else…"

"Magic," Feslen murmured.

"Yes…no…not sure, what now?"

"We go back and forget this nonsense? I could hire out of town healers or physicians, you know," Ka-Wei said.

Feslen rolled his eyes and stared at his tall, big friend, "You know that's impossible. My family already tried those lousy, loser physicians. They know nothing of Duxan's magical illness. Not to mention, you're an outlaw, from not showing up at the Choicings."

Ka-Wei gave an amazed grunt and commented at Feslen's wealth of political knowledge. Feslen laughed and remarked, "This is my business to know; my friend, besides, you spent time in other pursuits, I spent it on studying."

"Ah, I love fellow outlaws. Excellent band you've put together, Prince Ka-Wei," Sae-Jyung, the merchant mage began. "First you have Wu, Pan-Gui, the well-known rich-taker thief."

Lioin bowed at that, Feslen grinned.

"Then you have me, a magician banned from his own magic school," Sae-Jyung continued. "Followed by young Feslen who is none-Chiendonese."

Everyone gave a self-deprecating chuckle, after the merchant mage's conclusion.

"You seem to forget," Ka-Wei said with a wry smile, "I am known to be the 'People's Prince', after all. I tend to do things not of the Rule."

"Even spend time with magicians you don't like?" Sae-Jyung interjected with a slight grin.

"But," Feslen remarked in a serious tone when he regained his breath from the banter, "I don't give up easily. Ka-Wei, people still like you, despite the Rules. Your original influence among the commoners is bigger than you think. Use it. You must know people here."

"I may, but I don't have Royal Privileges anymore, you said so yourself."

Lioin watched the lines of people walking towards the temples and asked, "Why don't we dress as one of them?"

They laughed at the reasonable, simple and logical solution.

Sae-Jyung leaned against a tree and waved when they set off.

After they failed to find a religious outfit that suited Ka-Wei, they retreated back to the hill. The Prince refused to 'bash people over their heads' to simply take their robes. They can use bribes, as Feslen and Lioin suggested numerous times. But, the Prince also refused that suggestion with a horrified look.

Sae-Jyung, the merchant mage grinned. "Want something?" He asked, offering the four some food and water. He conjured it up in front of their eyes, winked at Feslen who watched with envy.

They sat down and ate the meal after urging Ka-Wei to do so the Prince hesitated, not trusting Sae-Jyung's magic. But, after the delicious and filling meal, he thanked Sae-Jyung with a satisfied burp.

The merchant mage laughed and commented, "See, Prince, outlaw mages do have their uses."

Feslen began to wonder why this man, with obvious skill and power, did not go to the Great School of Magic Stuff. He mentioned before he was banned from a school, just not which magic school. Feslen did not know Ka-Wei thought the same thing. Feslen asked Sae-Jyung, but the man deflected the question and refused to talk thereafter. Feslen began to envy him.

Ka-Wei went down to use his influence, as the group agreed on. The winter heat beat down upon them without mercy, but Feslen's health held strong. Feslen did not ponder why he held up, but could not wait to complete this task. While Feslen, Lioin and Sae-Jyung waited, the younger Raster brother said to himself, "Though the Prince is outlawed in many places in our country, Chiendong, some of the commoners do not follow the Emperor's rules. He's also only outlawed in the royal places, and most important areas. Religious places still are open to the public. Not to mention, the people regard the Prince as a Hero still, he should have more faith in his status."

Before Feslen finished his statement, Ka-Wei signaled them with a wave. Feslen and Lioin took their time down the steep hill before they met up with the Prince.

28

CONFRONTATION 抗爭

The blue colored Temple of the Skies towered over all the other buildings of worship. Its imposing tiered dome with a golden dragon at the very tip inspired many to kneel in prayer. Unlike other temples, its structure seemed to mix the old Chiendonese pagodas with the new western-style churches. No one spotted the tiny golden robin perched on one of the temples nearby. She watched the companions with-hawk like fashion.

Flecks of gold and silver plates engrained the hard oaken walls of the huge temple. With each jutted tier of the Temple of Skies, a red lantern hung with its colorful Spirit Candle companions. On each new level, a different colored candle represented a different spirit.

The inside overwhelmed Feslen even more, and it even took the breath of the others away. Inside, mirrors covered the walls all around, except at the very top of the exposed tip. The temple spiraled up and had an open hole at the top, and Feslen wondered why. He noticed a sundial in the middle of a platform.

Feslen did not enjoy the din of the crowd's chatter. "I'm not used to having so many people around," He admitted to his companions.

They nodded; Ka-Wei placed a strong and comforting hand on him.

"Think of nothing but the comforting brushes of flower," Ka-Wei reminded him of some Master Chai training

Feslen smiled and he growled as his head pounded with pain. The magic of the place got to him, but he did not understand why. The cacophony of talk died out, and the sudden quiet rang in Feslen's ear more than the noise. "What are they waiting for?" He asked.

"The Ceremonial Maker. I wonder if they know Elhong Wien is… somewhat incapacitated," Ka-Wei answered through grit teeth. He tried not to let his dislike of religious ceremonies overwhelm his senses.

The companions looked at each other, grim. Each recalling the first confrontation they had with Elhong Wien.

The curtains to the side of the platform moved and the Ceremonial Maker appeared. The Ceremonial Maker's youthful appearance did not fool the companions. He resembled a peasant's boy in rich clothes, but the way the young Ceremonial Maker's arm twitched almost uncontrollably.

Ka-Wei's eyes widened and he thought, No! It cannot be! He turned to his friends and pointed to the Ceremonial Maker.

"We know the King and his Emperor are corrupt," continued the man, his voice sounding his own, yet a hidden high-pitched tone echoed each word. The Ceremonial Maker sounded like a bat squeaking, but he continued, "He of a Thousand Lives seeks to close us down."

The crowd hissed.

Lioin cocked his head and whispered, "Is that true?"

Ka-Wei said nothing and he tried to motion Feslen's attention, but the young boy sat two seats away from him. Lioin and another peasant sat between them. The Prince grimaced, almost assured now of whom the man in disguise was. Once the Prince heard the Ceremonial Maker speak, the doubt vanished.

"We must fight against those corrupted in office and those that seek to ruin our peaceful lives," continued the twenty-year old Master of Ceremonies.

A strong aged garlic and scallion smell wafted from him. Feslen detected the man's unmistakable aroma. Feslen gasped.

Elhong Wien! He thought, sharing an alarmed look with his companions.

Feslen looked around as the people cheered. You and what powers? He thought.

Elhong Wien, disguised in the youthful body of the Ceremonial Maker, held out his hand and continued to speak, "We must send our heartfelt prayers to contain the evil growing in the centre. We must give them our light and love from souls."

"How did he survive?" Feslen asked, shuddering. He spoke everyone's unspoken thoughts, "How did he get a new body? And, why the deception?"

Ka-Wei shook his head, "I don't know."

So, the sacrifice was for nothing, Feslen thought, growling. Before he said anything more, the people burst into a loud, frenzied cheering.

They swayed back and forth. Feslen noticed how all the people were in a trance. The Head Dragon's voice corrupted them. Elhong Wien waved a hand and music of eerie discord filled the air. The people swayed to the music.

Ka-Wei put his hands to his ears and said, "I can't stand it, it's as if there are ten thousand voices in my head again!" Lioin and Feslen looked at him in alarm.

The young Prince began to sweat.

Elhong Wien continued to chant, "The One Creator Heals the corrupted heathens. Let those who fill with contempt be at ease. Light bring into their emptiness. Bless their blighted souls. Our One Creator chooses all of us to be connected with each other"

The people repeated this sentiment, tears unbidden in many. Feslen glanced at them with some alarm and tried to act the same way. He felt the powers coming from beyond the unlit hallway. Feslen grit his teeth and shouted in mental stress to whatever pushed him, *No!* He felt a heavy curtain fall upon him, trying to crush his freedom. His head pounded.

"Come, we must find the crystal before I succumb to this," Feslen said. The others helped him sneak about the crowd, which was not hard to do. They found themselves twisting and turning about in corridors that seemed to lead to nowhere. The corridor's dim lighting did not help much.

"I can sense it…" Feslen hissed his body on fire. He guided his friends towards a darkened corridor.

There, when rounding a corner, they saw someone resembling Sae-Jyung. Except this mage has red eyes and thick facial hair. He spoke in harsh whispers to one of Elhong Wien's underlings. Except, this man moved stiff and smelled of graveyard and dead body herbs. He looked familiar…This time his eyes glowed less frightening…

"He's here to double cross us," Ka-Wei began, raising his weapon. He took a step forward, but felt Feslen's hand upon his arm.

"That traitor works for Seatan the Necromancer!" The Prince told Feslen in a hiss. "We must deal with them both!" Ka-Wei thought, I knew Sae-Jyung can't be trusted!

Feslen shook his head, not understanding what came over his friend. Feslen thought, How did Ka-Wei know about the Necromancer? So that's why he looked familiar…He slapped Ka-Wei on his cheek and said, "Wake up, Ka-Wei! There's only three of us. We almost lost to Elhong Wien alone last time. If the Thai-Thurian monk had not shown me how to access my Ancient Truth, we'd be fifty feet deep in the ground. I am not trained and we cannot take them both on. Use your head."

That seemed to wake Ka-Wei up.

"Besides, our mission is to retrieve the Crystal for my brother, remember?" Feslen reminded with patience.

"I…I'm sorry my friend," Ka-Wei said, sounding admonished. "I don't know what came over me."

"I can get past them, if you want me to, Fes," Lioin said.

"The crystal is beyond them, just in that room there," He said, "Go, Lioin, but be careful."

Lioin nodded and faded into the shadows and crept along the wall. The friends almost lost sight of the small thief, but saw his shadows flitted against the shadows of the walls.

On closer inspection, Feslen understood his confusion about the mage he thought was Sae-Jyung. This mage, as Ka-Wei named the Necromancer, was gaunt, his human frame remained nothing more than a skeletal figure. His ancient pallid skin flaked and cracked when the man gestured to Elhong Wien's underling. Then, when the mage turned and unfurled his cloak, his skeletal body revealed none working organs! The

Necromancer…was undead! Feslen did not know which type of undead this man was, but he looked somehow familiar. His skin shriveled and dried. Feslen felt his tongue drier than sandpaper.

Feslen puzzled why he cannot sense the Necromancer's powers, yet he saw them in dark red threads. These threads spanned all across the room from the Necromancer.

"I sense…life…and…more…" hissed the Necromancer, he whirled and chanted. His spell revealed the friends behind the corner. They stared in shock.

"Guards! We have intruders!" The undead mage shouted.

Ka-Wei drew his sword as temple guards began to appear in mass swarms around them.

"Call your soldiers and call your people to help," Feslen began, but the Prince refused.

"Not unless things get out of control. Not to mention, this is not our time to rebel," the Prince began and he added, "We need magic to fight magic, Feslen. You of all people understand that! I won't have anymore innocent lives lost due to magic."

Feslen's eyes narrowed and he wondered, Why did Ka-Wei chose that strange statement? *This is not our time to rebel*?

But, he had no time to think further as the energy around the temple swirled and swelled.

Then a shadowy human form appeared in the midst of the closing crowd. Feslen said, "Sae-Jyung!"

"You…you will betray me for them?" The undead mage hissed; eyes burned with hatred.

"So good of you to come," said the Ceremonial Maker as he appeared from the stage. The man's body changed to a youthful appearance, but the smell of aged garlic and scallion hit Feslen harder than any physical punch. He knew that aroma anywhere.

Oh terrific, Feslen thought. My enemies all gather here to play around with me.

"Elhong Wien," spat Feslen. "You will pay for what you did to my brother."

"No, I'm afraid not, little one," replied Elhong Wien. He strode ever so slight to where the companions stood.

"Run, Feslen, I will hold them off," Sae-Jyung replied, fishing out a mirror and symbol of the Sun Goddess and chanted.

I too, am here to help, said an icy-sounding woman.

Who are you? Feslen asked the woman, but no reply came. She did not feel familiar to Feslen, nor did she feel threatening. Through his pain, Feslen detected the woman's magic.

The young mage, Sae-Jyung cast down his spell, and a physical globe of protection surrounded the group.

The Prince ran out to retrieve help even as Temple Guards chased him.

Pain rattled Feslen anyway, as he and the Necromancer exchanged stares.

"So, we meet again, young one. I have plans for you, but you are not ready yet," the Necromancer hissed.

Feslen started to reply when other human voices rang in his head. Along with the voices, he heard the mental and physical taunts from both the Necromancer and Elhong Wien. They used their mental magic warfare; he did not see this form of magic's energy or power threads.

Feslen growled and began to push back the powers that threatened to overwhelm him. The congregation began to sway and chant. A bell chimed.

Sae-Jyung the icy female voice commented. *We must help before our own plans are defiled.*

Yes, I know. I am doing my best. He pushes against me as well, let me help, you stubborn fool, Sae-Jyung said.

I am me! Feslen shouted in anguish as the thing that powered against him and the familiar presence kicked in with a punch that sent Feslen's physical form reeling. *You must get out of here; you are not ready for this battle!* The female continued.

Feslen balked and then his physical form let loose a scream that shattered the chanting. "Get out!" He shouted. The battle forced him to fall out of Sae-Jyung's protective globe.

Suddenly, the boy and Elhong Wien were on stage, shocking the audience into silence.

Unimpeded by the turn of events, Feslen rose to his feet. He turned bleary eyes and glared at the faithful. "Don't be taken in by this falsehood! You are all fools! He is a false priest, like all of them!" He said, shaking.

Angry murmurs spread through the crowd.

"Uh…Fes…" Lioin stammered.

"Quiet!" Feslen hissed as he turned to Elhong Wien. Elhong Wien folded his arms behind his back. His face split into a cat-like smile.

Elhong Wien chanted once and with his magic, the group was whisked away from the room and back onto the ceremonial platform.

The praying mass gasped as the man they knew as the Ceremonial Maker appeared with these other people.

"You…you're a charlatan! How dare you use the good people in their faith and money like this? This is nothing but poor magic!" Feslen shouted. His anger mounted as his head beat like a drunken man. *What are you doing?* Spoke Sae-Jyung, still in his head. He was too enraged to even notice Elhong Wien had employed a teleportation spell.

Yes, this is most stupid. The icy voice agreed.

Feslen, feeling his energy returning, roared and pointed at the disguised Elhong Wien, who just grinned. The on-lookers backed up in fear. He pushed the voices out of his head, and he saw Sae-Jyung finish his spell and hold off Elhong Wien's minions. Although, even though Feslen felt off-balanced at the moment; he understood the Necromancer stayed out of the confrontation out of the initial meeting.

Elhong Wien chanted and gestured at Feslen. Feslen began to choke, when a disembodied hand grasped his neck. What power! Feslen thought, and tried to access his powers. This time, he felt the heat and pull of the Yang powers diffusing the heat of his energies! So, this New Priest uses the moon. But, there's darkness in there I don't understand and can't place, Feslen thought.

"Feslen!" Lioin shouted.

Feslen struggledto fight back, but this time, Elhong Wien's dark magic overwhelmed him.

I must learn to overcome this moon power, and his darkness. At least with the moon, I can learn how to deal with it, Feslen thought, while he pushed his inner energies to the maximum.

Ka-Wei returned with twenty of his personal Blue Soldiers, armed to the teeth. The New Priest, dressed back in his normal clerical garbs turned and raised a hand at the Prince and his retinue. "I wouldn't," the Prince warned, as crossbows cocked. "Your magic is powerful Elhong Wien, but even mages have their limits. Besides, by the time you kill some of us, more soldiers will arrive. After my men, King's men will come. Then perhaps even the Emperor's. Right now, these are just my own little loyal band. Do you wish to risk an all-out war now?"

"Can you stop me? My powers are coming to their heights," Elhong Wien promised, his hands glowing dark red.

"I know you're crazy, but not stupid," Ka-Wei responded.

The New Priest lowered his free hand as in consideration and then, Elhong Wien canceled his spell and released Feslen, who gasped for air.

One of Ka-Wei's men released a cross bolt and it glanced off of the Necromancer. He jerked his arm and hissed as if in pain and chanted and disappeared. No one noticed Sae-Jyung flinch at the same time Seatan did when the cross bolt hit.

Lioin rushed to Feslen's side.

Elhong Wien said, "The boy will be fine. He just exhausted himself. Come to me again when you are true believers!"

With bloodied lips Feslen said, "This will not be over, corruptor of people."

Elhong Wien continued walking away. Ka-Wei glared in anger at the robed man and stalked towards him saying, "You attacked the boy! You will answer to the King himself. I, Prince Ka-Wei place you under arrest for…"

The man pointed in such a subtle way that Feslen almost missed the gesture. Elhong Wien chanted a few words and a green-red aura surrounded Prince Ka-Wei. The Prince tried to move, but was immobilized by the New Priest's spell even as the man spoke, "You have no jurisdiction in the religious sanctions, you should know that, *Prince*. If you want an audience you must believe, throw away your old beliefs. Now I give you and your friends a reprieve."

"This is not over," Ka-Wei promised.

"No. This isn't over," agreed Elhong Wien.

The believers murmured.

Ka-Wei and his troops escorted his friends out.

"You need to improve your magic," Sae-Jyung said, when they returned at the Prince's room in the palace. Everyone was careful about not disturbing the dozen or so trophies Ka-Wei displayed outside his display case.

"I know," Feslen replied, exhaustion taking a toll. He leaned against Ka-Wei's large bed, bare-footed. He noticed Sae-Jyung wore his boots into the Prince's clean room, and that Ka-Wei said nothing about it!

"Actually, I believe you did well," Ka-Wei remarked. "I don't know how Elhong Wien has returned, but it's not a good thing."

Sae-Jyung, the merchant mage crossed his arms and said, "So, what now? Our deal cannot be completed without the crystal."

"What's so special about it anyway?" Prince Ka-Wei asked.

Feslen and Sae-Jyung gave him a glance and the Prince grinned ruefully, "Hey, since Lioin went back to his guild, I figured I'd make a stupid statement."

Feslen rolled his eyes and said, "I don't know. I'll figure out something. You know, Sae-Jyung, for a mage so powerful, why didn't you take the Crystal yourself?"

Sae-Jyung snorted and said, "You saw how things deteriorated. The Necromancer is in cahoots with Elhong Wien. It's bad enough when Elhong Wien was by himself…well, he and his minions."

Feslen frowned and pointed out, "It seemed like to me that Seatan the Necromancer arrived when you did."

Sae-Jyung grimaced and said, "I detect a sense of distrust in this room. If you need my services, you know where to find me." He gave a mock bow to Prince Ka-Wei and left the room.

Ka-Wei exchanged looks with his friend at the merchant mage. When he left Ka-Wei said, "See why I didn't trust him?"

Feslen chuckled and said, "Well, everyone always has their own motives, my friend."

"What now?" Ka-Wei asked.

"I don't know. The Crystal is out of reach, and returning Temple District is way out of the question," Feslen mused. He shook his head.

"Maybe you ought to just trust in Duxan," Ka-Wei said.

"My brother would believe in his karma and hands of the Goddess," Feslen chuckled. Ka-Wei nodded.

"Thanks for trying to help, Ka-Wei," Feslen said and looked outside the window in Ka-Wei's room. The night sky darkened to the point where Feslen cannot make out the outlines of houses anymore. The cloudless skies showed the first moon and the star patterns of some gods.

"I'd better return home before my parents spank me," Feslen said with a half-laugh.

Ka-Wei nodded and then called out to some of his men.

"Let them escort you, ok? Who knows what devious things our enemy plans," Ka-Wei commented when he saw Feslen's face sour.

Feslen nodded and thanked his friend again and he left with two of Ka-Wei's most trusted Blue Soldiers.

Ka-Wei scribed onto a scroll, an explanation to his uncle, the current King, about the latest infraction against Elhong Wien. *To my uncle, today's latest occurrence had little to do with Feslen. It was my idea to take it up to enter the Temple of Skies. We have indeed some evidence of Elhong Wien's corruption: he works with the Necromancer! The Necromancer is known to your experts, and to myself and Elhong Wien and his own followers of pure evil. Seatan the Necromancer defiles our dead and mocks the way of living. Anyone in league with such a creature deserves great punishment! Feslen and I went to the Temple to make Elhong Wien confess…….*

But, the Prince crumpled the letter at the end in frustration and anger. He heard voices in the courtyard below and went to investigate. He saw the King talking in private with one of Elhong Wien's underling New Priests. Hiding, Ka-Wei overheard the King and New Priests discussing Feslen.

"Yes, I believe the Emperor is right about him," the New Priest said.

"Then, what do we do, let him run about?" The King asked.

"That is what the Prophecy says, but the Head Dragon has plans," said the New Priest.

"We should keep an eye on him? He's nothing but a boy, plus he's saved my life," the King said, sounding unsure.

"Nevertheless, the boy's potential threatens the Plans," the New Priest said.

Then, their voices lowered to a mumble.

Ka-Wei let a low growl escape and shook his head. He walked through the palace and returned through a different wing.

He entered his own private gardens and began a form of Martial Arts called Ju Ji Li, also created by Master Chai. *Calmness of the mind equals greater strength for the body*…echoed Master Chai's voice when Ka-Wei began his practice. Once he began, he forgot his troubles.

With his mission failed, Feslen thought about his next move on the walk home. His two guards remained silent. What should I do now? Feslen thought. I have to help my brother! He helped me all those times I was sick!

After he returned home, the guards left. Feslen's parents gave him the longest lecture he ever received from them. It lasted through the night. They grounded him, again. Feslen did more research on how to cure his brother. Duxan's condition did not worsen or get better, and Feslen worried if he will ever come out of his magic-induced coma.

Feslen came across a legendary magical place few in Chiendong believed in or heard about: a brook within the Old Forest. This brook helped supply all the inhabitants there of fresh, year-round water. It provided for the reclusive Forest Protectors.

With Duxan still ill and resting, Feslen prepared his travel pack for a day's provision and entered Old Forest alone

29

BUBBLING BROOK
充滿生氣的小溪

Feslen needed the Bubbling Brook's magical waters and herbal cures for his ill brother.

It took Feslen most of the day to reach the Old Forest. The temperature swelled to an uncomfortable degree. Feslen paused to rest for moment on the outskirts of the Old Forest.

Bamboo, lavender and other plants mixed. Feslen listened to a cacophony of calls. Long emphatic r-r-r-r's of the tiny Shu's Lungs, squawks of sparrow hawks. Feslen entered with slow caution. He grimaced, already wishing he worn real traveling clothes instead of his two-piece leather jerkin and light cotton trousers. He knew they were done for when he passed through the low-lying prickly shrubs. He had no alternative route.

After two hours of hard hiking through the path, Feslen collapsed. Sweating, he opened his waterskin and took a deep drink. At least the path will be easier to walk, Feslen thought, eyeing the sloping path ahead.

Why am I doing this? After all, I bet Duxan will recover by himself. If he does, this effort will be wasted, Feslen thought, glaring at the impenetrable forest. Everywhere thick and thorny brushes seemed to rise up against him. He heard the brook ten feet down the sloping path. The heat beat down upon him and he used the birthday gift Mei-Whuay gave him once: a nice fan.

Hours later, sweat lathering him and pain taking his muscles, Feslen stopped to rest. He uncorked his waterskin to drink.

Certainly, I will be punished for leaving home again, Feslen thought and sighed. Sourness set upon the boy as he paused against a rock and rested. He dropped his heavy pack. He realized the trek through Old Forest to get to the Bubbling Brook would take more than one day. He sighed, he went through his pack and realized he did not pack enough food and water. Everywhere he traveled before, he relied on others.

Some call me selfish, Feslen continued to think and wiped his sweat-matted brow. He grinned. What's so bad about looking out for yourself?

He heard the mating calls of some animals and sighed. He saw some sibling squirrels play with each other. They darted in and out of the bushes and trees. Feslen smiled, oddly reminded of his relationship with Duxan.

Come on, let's keep moving. Don't want to keep your brother waiting. Besides, you're out to prove something to everyone, right? Feslen scolded himself.

After a few more hours, and cut from half a dozen places, Feslen asked, "Do I love Duxan this much?"

Falling leaves obliterated the path to the Bubbling Brook. Feslen sighed. Hot wind breezed through and picked up, scattering all the sudden falling leaves. Dust and small particles forced Feslen to blink. He recovered and continued.

Rain started to fall only inside the region of the Old Forest! The steady rain became a downright outpour when Feslen tried to continue. He slipped on slippery rocks and fell down sliding onto an undiscovered route!

Feslen picked himself up, determined to stay calm. He no longer heard the brook and sighed, and sat down on a wet rock. It still rained. He opened his pack and frowned, some of his herb gathering bottles broke. Damned this! Feslen thought. Well, no one ever said it was easy.

He kicked the ground until he loosened some rocks. He glanced back up the only path available to him steep, slippery. How am I going to get back up?

When Feslen became hungry, his emotion took over. He often would throw tantrums. Feslen tried to fall into one of Master Chai's Dragon Techniques: the Calm Mind Step, or the Sixth Step, Equilibrium.

The hunger gnawed at him. He began to mutter, "Damned it Duxan. You weren't supposed to be the one to get sick or weak. It's me…"

Feslen's stomach complained. Oh well, I might as well eat before I lost my focus, Feslen thought.

He could hear his brother telling him, "Feslen, you should eat, even if it's a small snack of something. Eat something; you know your disorder better than anyone else. Not having emergency rations makes you vulnerable. And, you don't want that."

Thanks big brother, Feslen thought with a smile and sat down to eat.

After a delightful spicy meal of lemon grass, scallion mixed with white bell pepper over rice in a bun, Feslen felt refreshed. Yes, I do love my brother, Duxan…more than life itself. I would do anything for him.

Feslen tried to climb the sharp and slippery rocks for an hour or so, but gave up. He looked at his cut hands. He knew he would have to tell his folks the truth once he got home, but that, was for later. Now what?

Taking out rope, he looped one end to the tallest tree and tied it about himself. He left most of the heavy items he carried behind and began a laborious climb. He slipped after two hours of trying. Evening long set when he gave up that plan. He sighed; he planned on a short trip.

His stomach growled again, as he wiped his forehead. Then, his ears caught a small trickling sound of water! He jumped up in excitement and ran down a new path revealed to him.

Moments later, a blinding hot mist covered the forest it was as if a wizard cast a spell. He screamed as he lost footing and missed a ledge.

Feslen wondered at his bit of good luck. He hung by a branch, right above the river mouth of the cooling brook.

The temperature cooled and dampened to Feslen's liking. He gulped; a twenty-five foot drop awaited him. No problem, with the Seventh Dragon Step, Frog Hop, Feslen concluded. Feslen inhaled, exhaled three times and swung several times, then he let go. He tucked his head underneath his arms and extended his right hand and leg, ready for the landing. He then bent his left leg forward and twisted halfway as he landed with a huge thud. He rolled around, cursing as a wave of pain wracked his left rib and knee. Looks like he would need to practice his Twelve Steps some more when he returned home.

He cursed and vowed vengeance against Elhong Wien.

Then, someone addressed Feslen, startling him.

"Oh…oh…please, we here live in a peaceful way, don't you know? Haven't you seen the area? Nice and peaceful? When did things get so violent, really….don't worry, I won't hurt you."

Feslen did not find this amusing. This voice sounded like everyone's mother.

He picked up a long sturdy branch in alarm and raised it. His stomach then rumbled and he began to laugh. The absurdity of him holding a branch as a weapon, with his decent pair of clothes torn and his stomach telling him to eat was too much. The woman-like voice laughed with him, sounding very pleasant. The laughter just made him feel better. All the forest animals stopped what they were doing for a moment and listened to the laughter. Even the heat seemed to cease.

Feslen laughed so hard that his stomach hurt and he flopped to the ground. "I guess I am human after all," he said after he could recover.

The voice ceased laughing too, though Feslen detected the laughter in its voice, "Oh-oh-a human! I haven't seen one for quite some time now….could you walk a little bit down the stream and show yourself please?"

This was a new one to the young boy. He did as told.

The green bushes and tree were greener than any green Feslen ever seen. Heart shaped leaves danced as if alive. He walked on. More light flitted through the canopy of trees in this area. "So, what are you, who are you? How come you haven't seen a human in…how long did you say?" Feslen said.

"Since the Yu-Lang Dynasty," said the voice. "You humans haven't changed much; still impatient and rude. Still, you seem level-headed then most humans."

Feslen laughed at that, though it pained him. His ribs ached and he tried to ignore it. "My brothers would say that I am all but that, milady. Pardon my ignorance and rudeness. I am Feslen Raster, I am a nobody."

"I should be of the judge of who is impressive, young Ferlong—…or…what was that name?"

"Feslen," he corrected with mirth.

"Feslen, Feslen…" murmured the voice.

Feslen waited with deep patience, as much a fourteen-year old could muster.

"Feslen, come closer, to the edge of the river banks, if you please…just don't fall in. My waters seem deeper then it looks."

In the middle of the river foam gathered and bubbles popped out at a tremendous rate. The foam swirled and frothed, it formed a small waterspout. Voluptuous woman shaped water sprang up and Feslen fell flat on his butt. The water woman put a slender hand on its chin as if in thought. "Hmmm…which form would suit you best?" she asked in a watery voice.

"She" as Feslen decided to label it, changed from the woman, to a small young girl then to a dog, to an old man, to a bird, to a cat and back to the woman. She reached out her hand. "Take my hand, young man," she said.

"I can use magic, I warn you…"

"Oh stop being such a suspicious human!" said the woman-water with a laugh.

"Then you don't know me very well," Feslen grinned.

"On the contrary," she smiled. "You wouldn't use it on someone who you felt less threatened from. I won't harm you, just hold my hands…I communicate better in a different way, let's just put it at that."

"You won't drown me, or anything, would you?" Feslen asked out of habit. He already placed his hands within her liquid one. His eyes went wide, expecting the surface to be smooth.

"No. You are warm to the touch. No human I've ever met has been that," She looked at him and considered, penetrating.

Though she had no eyes, she saw into his being, beyond his physical form and into his soul! He began to stammer, but she just smiled.

"This won't take long, would it? I need…"

"I am aware of what you're looking for, Feslen. It…" she cut herself off for some reason and said. "Just allow me to do this. You need it as much as I."

"Just what in the Goddess…"

She fell into a trance.

His eyes widened as he entered a world similar to one of his meditative poses. He was aware of the chilled evening as it set, but the world this creature showed him…

A world of airiness awaited him. Blue nodes flashed with intensity. No other color existed, and no gravity prevented movement. Feslen flapped his arms and moved around and jumped about in half-flight. He laughed and laughed saying, "I'm a bird! I can fly!" He did not notice how he did not need to breathe! His lungs and nose still simulated breathing though. He saw the strange being smile at him as he ran about in 'half-flight', in pure delight. Feslen felt light-hearted and laughed as he never did before. He felt like what a boy his age should feel!

Wherever he went though, nothing but blue energies bubbled about. Feslen felt some magic and some energies around him, but very minor. He saw the world below them, as a reflection through a mirror. He saw the Old Forest below them and the solid forms of hut homes of the Forest Protectors and even far-away Mount Jing. Feslen pretended to jump off a mountain, and dove in free-fall yelling with thrill. For a moment, he forgot his troubles in this different airy in-between world.

WHERE ARE WE? Feslen asked, His mouth moved, without making a sound.

We are in my world, young human, said the creature.

Why does my body feel light? Do I even inhale oxygen? Are we dead? Feslen communicated again, with his mouth moving but not making a physical sound.

They talked as if they used hand signals, the way deaf people communicated.

Not quite, but we're more to the point in between realities. We are…how shall I say it…hmm.

Perhaps like ethereal spirits? Feslen asked, trying to help.

Somewhat, yes, replied the being. *By the way, I am what your magicians call the Ever Living Being. You may call me Eve.*

Eve? Feslen wondered. As they talked, the young boy began to realize they talked like normal people would, but they projected their thoughts to each other, even before they spoke it.

He heard her light voice say in his head, *Now, tell me Feslen, what is a being such you doing here? I have met many up and coming wizards, but none with the potential as you.*

I knew you were going to say that, Feslen said with a grin.

Of course you did, that's how I speak, silly one.

As to answer you, everybody I meet says I have potential, yet, I don't see it, Feslen responded and he added. *I am not a wizard.*

My, my, so cynical and doubtful about oneself, well, I thought the next greatest Mage would have more then just sass.

I didn't come here to be scolded, Eve. You are a wonderful and peculiar being…Tell me something I don't already know. I see you as a living being, yet, I see you becoming greater.

Well, well, flattery. So, you are silver-tongued as well. Perhaps I shall nickname you Silver Tongue, young one.

How my brothers laugh at that.

To give you a short answer, I am an immortal being who has been… placed…on this planet to watch over things of nature.

Feslen groaned a bit, unused to the mind-speech. He used Dragon Step Five, Closed Minds to close off the talk for awhile and sat down. He massaged his temples and then a thought struck him on what the being said, opening his mind up to her again, *Immortals?*

Yes, immortal! You are impressive though, young one. It would take many people twice that long to get used to mind-speech. Even practiced wizards, she said.

Are you the Sun Goddess?

The woman laughed pleasant.

No, I am not. I am but an agent for her and those that believe.

What's that?

*Faith in yourself. Yet…I see…sadness…and…much pain in both past and future in your life. Poor…poor…boy…*the thing shook as if in sadness.

The thing shook in sadness, solidified and evaporated.

Eve?

Then communication broke off and Feslen buckled to his knees at the sudden disconnection. He sat down, feeling complete emptiness. With nothing more to do, he glanced at his once scraped and cut arms. His scrapes and wounds healed! He realized hunger no longer gnawed at him.

Eve was still there, weaving back and forth, talking to some unseen and unfelt entity. Feslen guessed she talked to the Forest Protector's leader.

Feslen looked at Eve and felt an overwhelming urge to wade into the thick waters to embrace her.

"You can get my water there, if you pass the last test," Eve told him, pointing to a small crevice atop of the path.

Feslen followed her instructions. He shuddered and entered the apparent harmless crevice in the mountainous hilltop. Cold mist awaited him. He felt nothing, no presence and saw no energies, yet…grayness and darkness battered his mind. This is for my brother he thought and entered. He ignored the laughter of ghosts that haunted him.

Moments later, he exited, empty-handed. They did not find him worthy. Then he began to cry. I'm sorry, my brother! He thought in misery and knelt, rocking. He threw a tantrum. The mist vanished, along with the oppressive atmosphere.

He knew he had to face his family and prepared for the worst. He wanted death or exile, if Duxan had succumbed. Tears flooded Feslen's face. He turned to go home to the easy path sudden revealed. Dread threatened to eat his inner spark. He knew, for all his smarts, his talents he was unable to please his parents. He was unable to save his brother. How many times had Duxan saved me? Feslen hung his head.

The young Raster walked in a slow pace home. It was well into the night before he reached home on the fourth day of his trek back He felt a great emptiness. He fell into a semi-coma state, thanks to the onset of deep depression.

Feslen came home in such an exhausted and depressed daze he did not feel the positive energies in the Wong family home. Nor, did he stop to see the happy and relieved expression on their Mother's face. Duxan recovered on his own time, though he still did not walk very well or talk very much. He also did not see Duxan put him in his bed, though his sub-conscious did get a vague impression of one of his siblings helping him

30

NADINE'S TOUCH 公主的魅力

The Wongs and Duxan Raster surrounded Feslen, who lay in his bed in a coma.

A robin tapped the window many times, until they let her in. The mid-morning's sun brightened the room.

Each digit of the robins' grew longer until it was human sized fingers and toes. The bird's head outstretched itself and flattened. She transformed into a beautiful woman with cascaded hair. The young woman with the face of a goddess wore her

She stretched herself when the change finished. "I always disliked that," she muttered to no one in particular.

"Magic!" Mother and the rest of the Wongs murmured.

"Princess!" Duxan said.

"The Princess of Nu! That was amazing!" Li-Pei babbled.

Father and mother rubbed their eyes in disbelief.

"Why are you here?" Mother asked.

Princess Nadine replied, "To check on my friend, of course. He did a very foolish thing."

Mother intercepted Nadine's reach for Feslen and cried. "What do you think you're doing?"

Nadine's silver-brown eyes flashed, but Mother Wong remained unperturbed.

"I am very concerned for Feslen's well being, Mother Wong…I would never hurt him."

"And you came to *him*?" Ai-Yen gasped.

Nadine smiled in the slightest way.

Ai-Yen fainted and Duxan chuckled at his brother's reaction.

He felt his Mother tense and knew the trouble to come. He started to calm her, but he found Father already whispering words of encouragement to her. Mother, like many protective mothers of Chiendong, and like most traditional and proper women disliked strange women barging into their homes unannounced.

Duxan, though still tired and a bit woozy from his spiritual battles with Elhong Wien's constant dark magic said, "Mother, the Princess graces our home. How often do we have royalty in our midst? Even Prince Ka-Wei doesn't see us as he once did." He felt his Mother relax some, for he surmised what went through her mind right now. He also knew she followed the Rules to most degree, even the ones that contradict one another. Such as the Rule which says a Chiendonese must show respect to all visitors, even the ones forbidden by the Law and the ones you did not invite to your home.

"You came for my little baby?" Mother cried then. "The King forbade you to make contact with any Chiendonese!" No one denied Mother Wong's accusations, since the Town Crier did announce to the people not to associate with Princess Nadine just a few weeks ago.

"Mother, please. The Princess's actions are good," Duxan went on, doing his best to relax Mother's defenses. "If she used her magic in evil ways, I doubt we'd still be around talking."

Nadine brushed her hair from her smooth face. "I must ease his pain, his coma was created by his exposure to something mag…" She said in a musical and proper voice; she paused as if reconsidering her words when she saw the flash of fear in Mother Wong's eyes. "Feslen encountered something he shouldn't have taken on alone in the Old Forest."

Mother Wong's agitation increased and her arms dropped to the side then moved forward to try and pry Princess Nadine away from Feslen. Mother Wong said, "No, you leave my baby Feslen alone!"

Nadine laid her hands on Feslen's sweaty head.

"He is not sick, Princess…just in a deep malady of depression," Duxan addressed Nadine while he hoped to divert his angry mother.

"You lack understanding; his exposure to the spell-like effects of the Old Forest debilitated him. Since I roam there every so often, only I can wake him."

"Why didn't you help us then?" Duxan asked, his eyes staring into the Princess'. She gave him a slight nod that no family member caught. Duxan saw his family exchanging puzzled looks at his question to the Princess. He felt no need to elaborate on it, unless someone asked him.

They did not ask.

The Princess continued, "I am neutral in all things."

"Then aren't you involved by healing my son, young lady?" Father asked.

"You are wise, Father Wong. Mere aid in healing arts is considered neutrality. Of course, I do touch the wares of one side more then the other every now and then."

"Why are you helping now? I am grateful…" Duxan asked.

"Your brother did some foolish things on your behalf without thinking."

Nadine closed her eyes and began a whispering, her hands glowed. Mother Wong shook Nadine, but she gave no response. Duxan saw Feslen's lip moved in accordance to Nadine's chant. He wondered how his brother seemed aware of what happened around them, when it was obvious Feslen was out cold.

The room filled with a peaceful blue light.

"Stop her!" Mother shouted, no one moved.

Everyone cried from relief and happiness from Nadine's spell, even Ai-Yen! No one moved, too at peace with the true serenity on the ever-young face of the Princess.

"That's why you now know why I pursue this course," Feslen murmured. He reached in the air to grab onto someone, Duxan hurried over; but Nadine slipped her hand in before he did. Feslen squeezed. "My brother…you…are still ill."

"Is that true?" Duxan managed as he knelt by his young brother and tried to ignore Nadine's overwhelming aroma of fully blossomed Rose and fresh honeydew.

"Can you heal his illness, Nadine?" Feslen asked. His eyes glistened with tears as he looked into her deep amber eyes.

"No," Nadine said, and continued, "Please do not glower, for the solution to your brother's illness that no mortal hands could fix until he becomes his own. He must become Aware before he truly heals his weakened body. Besides, you must trust in your family's karma."

Feslen stared at her for a moment, when he considered the odd words she used.

"But, I can try, I know I can do it," he said at last. "My brother, come, give me your hand."

Nadine said, "No Feslen. You don't understand the Ways of Healing yet. Not to mention you don't know your Art too well, and cannot access your awareness with the Ancient Truth at the moment. I wouldn't, if I were you. It may backfire with more drastic results."

"I am going to try," Feslen said and told his brother to hold his hand.

Nadine said, "Feslen, please. Be reasonable, GenCom, our Goddess of Healing's Art cannot be lit like a candle."

Feslen tried to access his Ancient Truth and inborn magic anyway. He found nothing to access and sighed.

Nadine smiled and said, "You must know even magicians need rest after every spell used."

Feslen grinned shamefaced and said, "Sorry. But, I hope to learn the healing arts someday."

"You will," Nadine said at the same time as Duxan. Duxan gave her a smile and she returned it. *Her beauty is so beyond mortal beauty!* Duxan thought, staring into her face. He felt his pains and worries melt away.

Nadine continued, her voice musical, "In fact, I will teach you some basic healing arts. Or the differences at least. I'm sure the information you receive is less than adequate."

"Sometimes," Feslen grinned.

"You're stronger than before bro," Duxan commented. "I'm glad. Those trainings paid off."

"No, it's not just Master Chai's training, Duxan," Nadine said and then murmured to seemingly no one, "He's the One."

Feslen noticed Nadine lean forward a bit, adjust her eyes in a slight slant to the North-East, and move her hands in front of her body in a prayer. Does she worship the Sun Goddess? Feslen thought. He then saw her holy symbol, which slid out of her gown when she leaned over. The symbol belonged to the Sun Goddess, Creator of Life on Hahn-Hah.

"The One? What?" Duxan began, but Nadine ignored him.

Feslen began to meditate and tried to access his energies, but Nadine placed a hand upon his shoulder. He shook himself out of his reverie when he felt her enticing, harmonic vibrations. It's odd, few things, and energies can disturb me out of my meditations. It's as if she was meditating with me, without going into it! Feslen thought.

Feslen nodded, too tired to argue. Through his tired, oxygen-exhausted brain, Feslen could not, for the life of someone, figure out what she meant. Out of great dare, and some strange desire, Feslen wanted to touch her. So, he reached up and brushed her warm cheek. Nadine sighed and her body tensed a bit and she leaned in against Feslen. They both tensed, as Feslen realized she leaned in without intent. The Princess turned look at everybody and then at Duxan. "Listen, Duxan, you are ill. I do not know or claim to understand what dark powers Elhong Wien possess, or what he did to you. His darkness stretches beyond my imagination. When I cured your brother of his malady, it was meant for you as well. The spell should slow Elhong's powers down. You did feel less off-balance, when I cast that heal spell, did you not?"

"Yes," Duxan replied with a nod. "Wait, how did you know of the…"

Nadine smiled and winked at Duxan and said, "I keep an eye out for my friends. Let's just say, I know what Feslen does for the ones he cares about."

"Speaking of which," Feslen interrupted, "I'm grateful for your help, Nadine. But, I sense you are weakened after that spell. Have you been spying on me for days on end without sustenance?"

Nadine gave a blush in response and hid her face behind her long hair.

Feslen would get mad at anyone else for not leaving him alone, except her. He let her honeydew aroma entrance him for a moment, and his stare lingered. She lowered her head even further, trying to hide her response. Then, Feslen turned to Mother and said, "Mom…please could you make our guest some warm food?"

His blood stirred like never before. He stared at her and Nadine blushed and hid her face behind her long hair.

"Who are you? Where have you been all my life?" Feslen asked his voice dreamy and in a half-slur.

Nadine replied, "Just a common friend. You have to regain your strength. You should eat."

"I will not eat, if you don't, Nadine."

"If you eat with me, I will do so."

Feslen's own smile widened to which his family never seen before.

"Hello, my Princess, I am ever at your service…you are so enchanting…" Ai-Yen boomed as Mei-Whuay elbowed him.

Duxan shook his head in embarrassment.

Li-Pei giggled.

"Is he always like that?" Nadine said to Feslen.

"Try living with him," Feslen replied with a grin.

Nadine laughed. Her laughter sent delighted shivers through Feslen.

Everyone laughed even Ai-Yen.

Duxan herded everyone out. It took father, Ai-Yen and Duxan to move mother.

"Glad you're feeling better, little brother," Duxan called out.

"Finally," Feslen whispered. He started up, but Nadine placed a gentle hand on his chest.

"You need rest," she said.

Feslen protested and fell silent. "You have a good family," she mentioned, when she got up.

Feslen grunted.

"You may not think so all the time," Nadine said. She walked to his bookcase and looked through his collection of books. "My family is trapped by the curse."

"I'm sorry," Feslen started. He searched for words the right words. Her green and light blue skirts seemed to meld into her as she moved. How could one woman be so perfect? He thought.

"That's all right," she laughed with tenderness and Feslen smiled.

"By the way,"…Feslen said in a casual tone.

"Yes?"

"Thank you for easing my pain. How did you know what to do?"

"I am experienced in such matters," Nadine replied and added, "No need to thank me. But, I can sense you have deeper pains."

Feslen nodded and thought about Tang Swuai. He fingered her amulet, which hung about his neck.

"Do you wish to talk about it?"

"Not at this time," Feslen replied as best he could, without letting his voice tremble. The guilt of her death weighed on his heart too heavy for him to speak her name.

Nadine nodded and said, "I am here when you need me."

"As you are for Sae-Jyung?" Feslen said with sarcasm. Why did I say that? Feslen scolded himself.

Nadine flinched and took her time to answer him. She took out a novel, *Ancient Warriors of A Thousand Faces in Teriongh Ghan*.

"Let's just say I was attracted to him, which was a mistake. The difference between him and me was such as city and countryside."

Feslen thought about something to say about that, but he figured his jealousy spoke as plain as a book cover. He decided to change the topic.

"What do you know of me, Nadine? You seem to know everything about me, and I know so little," Feslen began.

She ran her slender fingers almost absent-minded over the book's leather and smiled at him. She replied, "No, I think I know less about you then you know me. I just know you through observation. And…"

Feslen waited for her to finish.

"And, I can feel certain things about certain people," she admitted, as if she was caught doing something guilty! Feslen smiled.

"Am I really destined for greatness? Master Chai has said so, even the mages fear me, I feel their fear," Feslen murmured.

"I don't doubt it," Nadine said with such confidence that Feslen gazed at her in some shock. "I need your greatness to help me and my peoples. I can't do it alone."

Feslen coughed and squirmed in discomfort and decided to look away from her intense silver eyes. He changed the subject again, "I see you picked out my favorite."

"Mine too," she said and asked, "Shall we?"

She started to sit on his bed then asked, "Do you mind?"

Feslen shook his head, enchanted by her presence. She sat down again on his bed and opened the book. The two began to read.

A poor respectable peasant man saw a pure beauty one day and courted her beyond his abilities. He did care for the rules or his own family honor and chased this woman of great and tremendous beauty for a long time. He had little to offer but his love and she accepted, ignoring her own cultural rules.

The two read up to the part where war started to threaten the main characters' peaceful lives. She read this to him aloud, and he hung on her every word. Her voice eased his pains, and helped him diminish his guilt of allowing Tang Swuai to die.

"Can you teach me the basics of healing now, Nadine?" Feslen asked, his eyes lightning up in eagerness.

"All right," Nadine replied, ever so gentle. She closed the book and laid it between her laps. "Now, as you know, healing comes through four standard forms; natural resting, acupuncture, magical healing and Ancient Truth."

"But, how come there are legends items and Immortals with healing abilities?"

"Items carry energies, and some items transfer energies and absorb them for the people who carry them," Nadine answered, "However, what I'm getting to is that healing can only cure so many things."

Feslen smiled and stayed with amazing patience.

Nadine chuckled and said, "I can see my lessons are boring you. Here, let me show you." She reached into her pockets and took out a silver needle for acupuncture, a silver bell for healing, and some scrolls written with Ancient Chiendong characters.

"I see you have an understanding for acupuncture," Nadine said, staring into his eyes. The more she looked into his eyes, the more Feslen blinked in confusion. She's the most beautiful person in the world! He thought and forced his gaze somewhere else. How does she know this?

Nadine smiled and said, "Some beings can read emotions, thoughts, events and experiences just by staring into the subject's eyes."

Ah, neat, Feslen thought.

"The silver bell is sometimes used in religion," Nadine continued. "Some Dhai-Hahn priests use it."

"What does it do?"

"Legends say it can help purify corrupt energy."

"I see…" Feslen said, reaching to touch the silver bell. He felt nothing.

She laughed, a short laughter, "This is just a representation."

"I assume some are used in chants?"

"Oh, most assuredly," Nadine assured, "You know how Martial Artists and other people often say, 'Ohme'?"

Feslen nodded.

"That's a universal healing chant. It helps gather your lost energies," Nadine continued. When she got to the scrolls, she said, "Some healing spells are written on such things as scrolls. These scrolls are special; they come with banana leaf and basil. The words here spoken are in coordination with your Healing Points in your body…and some say the ingredients help combine the effects…"

Nadine and Feslen's stomach growled.

"Shall we try to continue?" Nadine asked, she pointed at the window. The sun had sunk down a bit.

Their stomachs rumbled in loud protests again. The two laughed again and walked down stairs.

Mother set an elaborate meal for the Princess of Nu. A complete roasted pig along with fish skewered with honey glaze. A spinach concoction with honey glazed shrimp on top. A big pot of beef stew accompanied honey glazed spicy carrots and a large bowl of steamig rice mixed with bamboo shoots. "Mother, you always out do yourself," Feslen complimented.

"We are honored by your Grace's presence. Thank you for entering our home and making it even more elegant," mother said.

Nadine smiled.

"You honor me by putting such effort."

Mother looked pleased.

Feslen gave her a long look, his eyes in surprise. She gave him a wan smile but also a slight nod. Feslen thought, Does Mother finally understand me? Or was she playing by the Rules? He looked at Duxan and Father for explanations at Mother's strange behavior.

Duxan later told Feslen that Mother knew what was best for her loved ones, despite her own feelings. She usually tried to do what's best and right for everyone involved. Also, she liked being center of attention, even if it was from a forbidden foreign Princess!

"Please wait a moment before eating everyone," the Princess began even as Ai-Yen sat down.

Most of the family attended, except for elder sisters Mei-Whuay and Trisha. Nadine and Duxan flanked Feslen. Ai-Yen and Ghong-Hung sat across from Nadine. Ai-Yen's gaping of Nadine irked Feslen. Li-Pei sat in Mei-Whuay's customary seat.

Feslen inquired about the nature of Mei-Whuay's disappearance. According to his parents, Mei-Whuay got a 'new job', which required her on-site service forty-eight hours a day. He pursued this further, but no one else elaborated, shutting their mouths tight or going into small talk, like 'how's the weather in your homeland?' Feslen saw his Father's smoldering eyes, whenever he brought up Mei-Whuay's job, or Trisha's. He kept quiet and then he saw Duxan fidget one of his fingers in a manner where someone would twist a ring.

I don't like Mei-Whuay, and I do have a problem with her, as all siblings have trouble with each other from time to time, Feslen thought, as his anger built in him. He tried not to let his emotions show. He continued to think, But, even Mei-Whuay did not deserve to be a servant for someone else! He wondered who she served, but kept his eyes on Nadine.

He tried to ignore one of the Wong's family servant's hands as she poured him some tea. A Servant's Ring glistened on her left index finger.

Feslen noted Nadine ate no meat. He stopped eating the meat already on his plate. Embarrassed, he gave her an apologetic look.

She smiled at his response, and he dared to put a hand on her warm lap. She squeezed his hand.

"So what is your country, what is it....N...U...U....like?" Li-Pei asked Nadine, stumbling over the unfamiliar pronunciation of the foreign country.

"Nu," Nadine began, correcting with gentle politeness.

"Li-Pei!" Ghong-hung said, kicking her under the table.

Li-Pei ignored her and listened to Nadine's every words. "Nu was very lush. It had animal and plant life like you've never seen."

"I'd like to visit it someday," Li-Pei said.

"Trisha would like it too," Feslen stated.

"No proper Chiendong girl will go off on some foolish adventure. She has to get married to a proper Chiendong gentleman and help their parents in their old age," Mother said.

"Mei-Whuay will take care of that," protested Li-Pei.

Feslen doubted. Duxan tried to hide his laughter.

"The Chiendong tradition is that sons go off to work, women stay home," mother scolded Li-Pei. "Now no more out of you."

"Perhaps you will one day, little one. I know someone of your family will visit soon one day," Nadine soothed.

Even though the Princess' eyes locked with Li-Pei's, she focused on Feslen. Mother sat rigid.

Who was she? One moment she makes things so pleasant, the other… Duxan thought.

"Is it true that inanimate objects talk in your homeland?" Feslen asked.

Nadine gave a little laughter. Feslen hung to her every laugh. "Some things do," said Nadine. "My people say it is a Gift of inheritance from the Sun Goddess."

"I ramble too much. I'm sure it's on your minds, why I come for Feslen," smiled Nadine.

Her eyes swept across the table and rested on mother.

Feslen pretended to eat.

Mother just stopped and she put down her chopsticks and stared at Nadine.

"Why do you want my baby? He has to stay home and get a good education. You know as well as I he is an invalid and needs others to help him. He needs to use his brains more than his physical abilities, Princess."

Feslen's face whitened at his mothe's brusque comments. So, this is what she thinks of me, He thought. His sighed on the inside. "Mother," He began, gritting his teeth slightly and clenching his fists.

"Are you going to deny your disability, Feslen? You know you cannot do things like everyone else. You have to stop pretending and start being what you are."

Mother's cold, logical statements ripped Feslen's heart like a sword into flesh. "What do you know or understand?" Feslen began to seethe, his brown eyes glinting, staring at Mother. She did not flinch.

The tension rose, palatable on everyone's tongue, and skin. All stopped eating, the food tasted like ashes, everyone looked uncomfortable, even Ai-Yen.

"It's you who don't understand, foolish child. We've done so much for you, all the money we've spent…"

"Dear…" Father began, but Mother flayed relentlessly.

Few can stop her when she's on this sort of roll, Duxan sighed in thought as he wanted to speak up, but thought better of it. It's time Feslen fended for himself. Prince Ka-Wei was right, he needs to learn how to be himself.

"***You***, we've fed, clothed and kept our own children away from a good education for…and you don't even appreciate the hard work. Or even stop to thank you…"

"No," Feslen growled, slamming his fist down on the table. It made the dishes and chopsticks jump, along with little Li-Pei. "You never understood me, you never asked me how I felt and how I want things…" he began, but he felt Nadine's hand upon his. He felt his anger dissipitating.

"Want things? You have a right? You are not a working invidiual, Feslen. You have no rights."

"I'm sorry I'm such a *burden*, misses Wong."

Silence thundered across the household, even the servants stopped what they were doing.

Rage thrummed in Feslen's heart and beat in his head. Bile built up in his lungs and his nostrils flared. But, he felt no magic within….he felt a long emptiness, like an emotion he never had his entire life. Except, when it came to the smothering kind. Then he felt a tender whisper next to his ears and hands…He saw Nadine touch his hand ever so deftly. Then, she removed it just as quick, leaving him to wonder if he imagined the whole exchange.

Please, do not argue, my dearest, Nadine's voice slipped into his heart and mind.

Why does she always do this to me? Feslen asked, his anger still on his face, his tongue cleft to the roof of his mouth. *It's bad enough my adoptive siblings and the rest of society feels my emptiness as a person…*

Some people only see what they think is right, in their own minds, beloved. Your mother always does what she believes is good for everyone, and that's the way she is, Nadine answered him. Her sweet, musical voice relaxed him. *You are not an empty person, you'll find out in time what a true worth you are.*

I just don't get her. If I am such a parasite, than why? Why does she keep me around all these years? All this suffering? For what? Feslen returned, trying hard to keep the tears from forming.

His mother went on, "Well, you good for nothing? What do you have to say? And you, *waigouren* Princess, stop putting silly notions in the head of my children! The Emperor was right, you are a threat to real people."

Your parents mean well, Feslen. You'll see. When people are hurt, we say and do things we regret later. Your mother is not so bad a person, Nadine murmured to him.

Maybe, Feslen thought, pausing a while. He continued, *I just don't get her. I don't get norms. I never will, I am, a mutant, after all. Even in her eyes. The one person who really should love,* Feslen thought, bitterness sweeping.

She does love you, just in a different way my beloved, Nadine answered. *She…*

I can tell you this, Nadine. Once I become cured of this Goddess-forsaken cursed body of mine, I will be free of them; and they will be free of me, the burden of society. I…

Hush now, anger is not good for anyone, especially you, Nadine soothed. Her eyes were not on him, as his was on her, but on Mother Wong the whole time.

And the hot burning anger within him vanished after he felt her love for him seep through. He no longer heard Mother or the heartbeat of rage.

"And, you, *waigouren*, I think I've had enough about you. Leave," Mother's tone was uncomprising.

"I think you are underestimating your son, Mother Wong."

Feslen admired Nadine.

"How do you think I should be raising my children, Princess? I give them the life that I know best, and my husband helps keep this family in tact. Do you know what it is like to watch your children suffer?"

A long silence ensued. Only the clattering of plates, servants' chatter echoed.

Feslen tensed up so much so, he forgot to breathe. He felt Nadine squeeze his hand, but he did not respond. He felt Mother's anger, and saw her sadness. He hung his head and stared at his feet. He felt shame and anger for hurting her.

Nadine smiled ever so much to Feslen and returned Mother Wong's stares. Mother Wong's brown eyes bored in.

You will need to go soon anyway, whether she wants you to or not, Nadine said to him, in mind-speech.

I know. Duxan tried to convince Mother this was the right move for me, Feslen returned, his mind let go a sigh.

Don't worry, Feslen, my dear one. Karma cannot be changed, deterred. One can derail it with temporary stops, Nadine returned, her face widened in a smile.

The rest of Feslen's anger melted away and he relaxed.

"I apologize, Mother Wong. You're right; I shouldn't convince anyone to do the right thing for the rest of Hahn-Hah. Feslen will come on his own terms," Nadine said, her head bobbed up and down, as if she changed her mind. Then she said, "Thank you for this terrific meal and your wonderful hospitality. I must return to the Old Forest."

Everyone waited for the response when she turned her back.

"Wait…which part of the Old Forest, Nadine?" Feslen jumped up, gripping her arm.

She smiled and slipped out of his grip with ease and said, "You may meet me when you wish, Feslen. Just call me with your heart, and I shall come."

Li-Pei sighed. "I'd like to be her when I grow up."

"Get thrown in the outer regions, maybe then you'll find out how," Ai-Yen said.

"I thought you liked women, Ai-Yen," Ghong-Hung snorted.

"Yes, women I can understand."

"You mean women who have little else to say and with the chest size of…" Mother cut Feslen off with a look. But, the siblings, except for Li-Pei, understood his joke and guffawed at Ai-Yen's expense.

Mother grounded him for his disobeying orders and going to the Old Forest alone, Feslen preceded to disobey once again when he prepared to leap out of the window from his attic room. Feslen used the Frog Hop, the Seventh Dragon Step and jumped down with little harm done. This time, he sought the Princess for companionship, and stopped worrying about Duxan.

Feslen needed her company and walked to Old Forest. No woman had ever drawn his attention like Nadine. A group of magicians wandered pass with apprentices in tow. A pan of envy surged through Feslen when he saw the mages and the apprentice. "I don't belong with them anyway," he said. A hawkish young girl lifted her new frog's legs from her new pouch when she went by him. He smiled at the delight on her face and the subsequent scolding by one of the elder magicians.

Feslen said in part bitterness, "I have far greater things to accomplish then sit in a stuffy school for six years." He watched the group of magicians walk until they passed out of sight. *I belong there.* His subconscious voice told him.

He ventured on through the Old Forest. He used his heart to find Nadine, as the she told him to do so. When he first came through for the Bubbling Brook, he did not realize how large the Forest was. Including that part, the entire Old Forest must cover an area at least seven hundred acres large, Feslen estimated when he kept walking. He did not know how long he walked, even as the sun began to set. No wonder Nadine stays here, Feslen thought. The aroma of a sudden spring shower wafted in the air. Nature buzzed happy in and out of the trees of the Old Forest. How did the Forest Protectors manage to keep this area so pristine, when the rest of Hahn-Hah and Chiendong became so deforested? Feslen wondered. How did they manage to keep it hidden from the prying eyes of corrupted magicians and nobles?

A shimmering sky blue lake came into view. The songbirds and multiple songs of nature eased Feslen to some tears.

When Feslen looked at the lake, he felt at peace for the first time in his life. Where else in the world could someone say that? Feslen thought. The gravel crunched delightful underneath his boots.

Something flapped around Feslen. Feslen mistook the creature for a bat because of the odd sound its wings made. It was a pigeon. Feslen knelt to meet it eye to eye. "Odd one, aren't you?" He asked the bird.

"Are you expected or needed?" The pigeon asked him with an elongated *u*.

For a moment, Feslen rocked back on his heels.

"Expected?" The pigeon asked.

"Uh, no. I am here to see the Princess."

"Ah, the Princess Nai-Hua? She will see you along shortly, if you are found worthy," said the pigeon in a ramble.

"What? I thought Nadine said to find her…." Feslen began, but the pigeon continued as if it did not notice.

"I see the Forest Protectors chose to see you, you should be Honored boy. They rarely see outsiders, unless they admit them themselves."

"Are you a Forest Protector?" Feslen asked, intrigued. The odd pigeon did not perturb him.

It laughed and shook its body. He sounded and acted like a dog. "You humor me young boy."

Feslen let a small chuckle escape. He would not have allowed a person to speak to him in the manner the pigeon did. "I am friend of Forest Protectors though," returned the pigeon.

"Are you a Familiar?" Feslen asked.

The Forest Protector friend bird cocked its head.

"A Familiar is sometimes found in the company of wizards. The animal companions offer extra insight to their human wizards," Feslen explained to the bird.

"No. Come, follow me, you are summoned," It answered him after it hopped around.

Feslen jumped around in excitement, and thought, I am going to meet the Forest Protectors!

31

TEST OF THE FOREST PROTECTORS

The forest air lightened. Nadine belongs here, Feslen thought.

"We're here," cooed the pigeon. "It has been nice chatting with you boy. What is your name? Perhaps we will chat again."

Feslen inhaled when he saw the deep golden green lake. It sparkled even when the forest's high trees filtered most of the light.

"Your name is gasp?" The pigeon wondered, and then it nodded in understanding and said, "It is called Serene Lake of Emerald Green. It is kept hidden to most outsiders."

"Then why show me?"

"You are summoned," It responded and flapped its wings in preparation for take off.

I am? Feslen thought. Summoned? Who else in the world doesn't watch me? Can't they just leave me alone?

"I am Feslen, thank you for the chat," Feslen called out. The pigeon looked back and nodded.

"We will meet again!" It said and flied off.

The pigeon led Feslen within a small circle of mangrove trees smelling of mangos and lilacs. The Serene Lake of Emerald Green shimmered like an emerald beyond these trees.

The peaceful lake's energies meshed with his heart. He watched for hours.

The stillness of the lake amazed him. Nothing stirred, except an occasional ripple in the lake. Silver whiteness encapsulated golden beauty of peaceful energy. He saw part of the lake roll down a mountainside in a large ripple effect, similar to a waterfall. He surrendered to the idle peacefulness and sat down in a ring of black mushrooms. The ground felt moist yet firm to his touch, it delighted his senses. He enjoyed waiting, for once.

He hoped this peace could last his entire lifetime. He knew that was not so.

"Why the sadness, human?" Said a voice so sudden, he raised a hand in defense.

Feslen whirled around, trying to find her. "You'll never find me," it promised, in that same playful high-pitched tone. "A fairy?" Feslen asked.

It snorted in a laughing fashion. "A fairy? What a great imagination you have, honey! Children's stories!"

Feslen readied to fight. He fidgeted when people called him 'honey'.

"Now, now! Calm down, honey! I can feel you powering up, Mr. Noodles was right!"

Mr. Noodles? Feslen thought. He chuckled, realizing whomever or whatever creature spoke to him meant the pigeon. "So *that*'s his name," Feslen said with a grin.

"Isn't just like him? Asking for an introduction without greeting himself! I should have a stern talk with him about being impolite…but, he'd listen to our leader, Mrs. Ma Poa Dou Fu."

"Who? You mean Princess Nadine?"

"No, No. The Princess resides here however temporary. She came to Ma Poa Dou Fu to seek out someone in Chiendong to help her reclaim the Land of Nu," said the spirit.

"Is Ma Poa Dou Fu your leader? Or one of them?" asked Feslen, mind working quick.

"Very good, Honey! You're smart one. Have you heard of her before?"

"No, I haven't. But, I know the Forest Protectors live a long while, even for mere humans. But, what is the Princess' real aim? She came to find me and yet, she won't intentionally force me to go help her, I don't get it."

"It's not in her Nature to do so, Honey. Also, we of the natural are bound by Honor and Rules, as you well know," replied the spirit. Feslen nodded slowly.

"And what do the Forest Protectors. What does Ma Poa Dou Fu want with me?"

"You'll find out," Rhoi-Que replied and stated, "She's the one you're waiting for, honey. I'm just keeping you company till she comes."

Naturally, Feslen thought. "What are you and where are you?"

"Oh, silly me! I scold others on being impolite and look at me!"

Feslen lost sensing the being's energy when it faded into view from within the lake! It stood one foot in height He found someone shorter than him! and resembled a tiny human. Except this diminutive female had four limbs that span out like a frog. Her smile showed dimples. She swept a bow and shook purple hair loose.

"Well? What do you think?" She asked, spinning again and showed off her curvaceous form.

"If I were but a Water Spirit, I would fall for you right away. You are beautiful, as fitting as it should be for a place like this."

"Mr. Noodles neglected to tell me of your silver-tongue!" Her pale skin turned all red.

"I am Feslen Raster," he chuckled as she floated to him.

"I am Rhoi-Que, a water spirit," she bowed again.

"The pleasure is all mine, believe me," Feslen said, eyeing her svelte form. She almost reminded him of a smaller version of Nadine.

"I can sense your presence now, is it because you are allowing me to sense it?"

"You are quite intelligent, honey. Did you know I was here before I spoke to you?" She said with a nod of approval.

"I would like to claim so, but I haven't the ability to do that yet. I have yet to become a magician."

"No. No magician can sense me even when I show myself to them."

Feslen looked like as if he had been whacked across the face. Rhoi-Que laughed merry. "Come again?" Feslen asked.

"Want to see something else that's really neat?" She said in as slow as pace possible.

Feslen nodded.

"Wait. Let me do this. So I wouldn't have to speak human," she said. She hopped up to touch Feslen's forehead and chanted.

The place where Rhoi-Que touched him heated for brief moments before cooling.

"I feel nothing wrong or new," he reported.

"Were you expecting something to happen?"

"What did you do to me?"

"The Language Spell. Want to learn?"

Feslen nodded.

She jumped up again and brushed the same spot on his forehead. Feslen's forehead went cold all of a sudden, and the one spot she touched became hot, as if a fever hit him. He knew he did not get sick, since no other symptoms of a cold shown on his body. Plus, he suspected Rhoi-Que would overreact if illness overcame him from her touch. Feslen also knew she somehow cast a spell and began to understand that all magic-using creatures varied in different ways of performing a spell. Up until now, he only encountered humans casting and thought that to be the standard.

"Wait, I want to know if I am really speaking in Spirit tongue."

"Silly me. You're absolutely right, honey."

"And why are you doing this for me?" Feslen said, but added as she turned a large eye at him, "I am appreciative. The last being that promised me a spell didn't teach me."

"Oh, sorry about that, honey," she giggled. "Was she Eve?"

"Yes…"

"It's part of her Nature to promise and not give, silly honey!"

Feslen grinned.

"Is it in your Nature to give to a complete stranger kindness and what they are asking for, Rhoi-Que?"

Her body faded away from view with hard laughter. For a moment, he called out in concern, but he breathed easier. He realized he could still hear her laughter!

"You are the first being in a long time to make me laugh like this!" The Water Spirit claimed in breaths. She faded back into view.

Feslen smiled.

"I wish I could ask you to be my life's mate, but I see your future is already entwined with another," she said while gesturing, as if she did Tai-Chi Chuan. She inhaled and exhaled and let go in a single huff and then her exhale sounded sad. Feslen thought that was her natural speaking style, until she asked him something in her language.

"So, how do you feel, Honey?" She asked him in her language.

Feslen saw her lips move and her waving body and understood she said something to him. He also recognized they did not talk in the manner of Eve. He smiled and motioned to her in understanding.

The language of the Water Spirit did not come through. Feslen cocked his head and looked at her with wide eyes.

"What did you say?" He asked. He heard buzzing when she talked. What an odd but wonderful creature! He thought.

She said repeated her statement.

Feslen said, "Ah, I get it now; let's switch back to spirit form."

She nodded and hopped up to touch his forehead. "Wouldn't it be easier if I just helped you up?" He asked, letting a sigh go at the same time.

"No one has ever offered me that! You are such a sweetie; she'll love you, honey. In order to communicate with humans and animals, that's the only way I can cast spells. I get more exercise out of it. Keeps my tender slummy tummy slender, you know?"

Feslen laughed. He nodded.

"Show me again how to undo the spell please?"

She nodded and did the reverse of the Language Spell. She put her tiny palms in front of her face, chanted three times in her language, and placed on hand on her heart and another above her lips. She then said, "Feel the energies in your palms, and around your mouth and heart.

Remember, your human sage, Fao, he said the energy flows from the mouth, vitality from ears and spirit from eyes."

Feslen nodded and started to ask, "What does Faoisism have to do with the spell?"

She interrupted, "Every spell and magic flows through the Faoisit ideas. I believe he watched someone perform magic once and got the idea from that. Here, take my hand." Feslen reached out and gripped her tiny hand as gentle as possible.

"Feel the energies?" She asked.

Feslen nodded. He felt the energies flowed with surprising strength. He would not have guessed it from such a small creature!

She grinned at him and replied, "Don't let the size of appearance of anything fool you. Magic strength comes from within. Though, you will learn it all someday, I assure you."

Feslen chuckled and then said, "What next?"

"You remember how your head became cold and hot?"

He nodded.

"Watch what happens to the reverse," she finished. She chanted one last time with the chants sounding more like an Honorific mantra to the Sun Goddess, and then touched pressure points on her lip, tummy, lungs and then did it with Feslen's as well. Feslen felt a sudden cold wave in the areas she touched on him. The rest of his body felt hot, like a fever. Then it disappeared.

"That's it. I can't teach you any more."

"But…what did you just do?" Feslen asked in mystified tones. "I felt only the reverse, yet, I can understand you…"

"You're smart, honey. You'll figure it out, honey."

"Can't you show me the Healing Spell…?"

"I am bound by Laws of Nature," she said with a shake of head. "And, I don't know Healing Spells. Ma Poa Dou Fu does though, are you hurt? Or do you know someone who is?"

"Yes, my brother is ill," Feslen began and thought to add, "Thank you though for giving me the instructions."

"Ah, so *you're* the fellow she talks about all the time," said Rhoi-Que, her arms gesturing in the 'ah-ha, I understand now, mode'.

"What do you mean? Whom? Princess Nadine? Or Ma Poa Dou Fu?" Feslen asked, getting somewhat confused by the fairies' speech. Her talking speed increased when she became excited.

"Yes, yes. I mean both people. Princess Nadine informed us about you and your plight. She said to watch out for you and that you tackled on some bad people," replied Rhoi-Que, she floated about her water, moving with quick speed. Her movements matched her patterns of speech.

Feslen's eyes narrowed at the comment, assuming he understood and caught half of what she said! So, the Princess followed me all this time? Perhaps even used me? He shook the thought away and said, "Then, you must know where the cure for my brother is?"

"No, well, yes. Eve's waters could have helped, but she, for some reason, found you…."…The Water Spirit broke off and mumbled these next words and then continued, "But, honestly? I have no idea, and I believe the Forest Protectorate, Ma Poa Dou Fu, will enlighten you where to go next. You should listen to her."

Feslen frowned and wondered what Rhoi-Que wanted to say when she mumbled why Eve did not give him the cure. Then he shook his head and pondered the situation. He said at the same time she asked, "Oh, honey…can you do a favor for me?"

"One last thing, have the Forest Protectors watched me all this time?"

"Yes," Rhoi-Que said.

Feslen sighed and scratched his head and thought, Figures. Everyone thinks I am something I'm not. He chuckled and said to his new friend, Rhoi-Que, "Sure. What do you need?"

She's been more honest than anyone I've met, Feslen thought. Well, anyone magical, at least.

"The delta of the lake is plugged up. The Frogs told me so," Rhoi-Que said.

"What do you mean?"

"The water flows down," Rhoi-Que tried to explain by gesturing. "The Frogs needs saltwater to survive."

"Frogs need saltwater? Now I've heard everything."

"These frogs do. Will you help them?"

"What prevents it? Can't you…"

"You see how strong I am! Plus, my magic will not allow me to move it."

"What will Mrs. Ma Poa Dou Fu say?"

"She likes it when Outsiders help our Grove."

"I have a feeling the blockage isn't natural, is it?"

"No. An Outsider did this to us."

"Is that why the Lake is flowing inward?" Feslen noted. "And that the water is so calm?"

"You are a brilliant one, honey!" She clapped her hands.

"I have to go freshen up now. I will see you when you get back, all right honey?"

"Wait, Rhoi-Que."

She paused. She was half in immersion. Feslen now wondered what a woman getting in a bathtub would look like. He shook the thought out of his mind.

"Can you accompany me? I'd like the company and I need to know where the thing is that's blocking your salt water friends."

"I will come with you, honey. You must realize I can't stay out of my Lake for that long. Can you swim, honey?" She turned a shade of ultra pink while giggling.

"Never learned how. One of my brothers tried to drown me…it was an accident as he claimed."

"How awful! Well, okay, one more spell won't hurt, honey!" She traced his head with strange symbols that he memorized.

"Now just don't panic when the waters rush up to you, honey. I will be there to help you if necessary, but I believe in your strength."

Honey, Feslen added in his mind. She giggled and tickled his soft spot. He laughed and rolled around.

"Stop that, my dear," he told her.

She laughed so hard she vanished and half-immersed. Feslen eyed the water in trepidation and suspicion. He recalled a family camping incident when he was seven years old.

He willed himself to get in. He had thought the water to be warm, since the rest of the area was so temperate. Caught off guard, the water chilled him. He nearly ran out.

"Its okay, honey…you will be fine!" She called out.

Rhoi-Que bubbled down the rushing water as if she truly belonged in it. The amazing clarity of the water brought a gentle pleasure to the young boy. He tried to get used to and ignore the chilling cold. "It gets better," assured the Water Spirit.

Feslen tried to focus his attention on Rhoi-Que, almost missed seeing her. She blended with the water when she laughed. However, he sensed her presence now, when he did not before. Why did that occur? Feslen wondered.

"You're doing well, honey!" Rhoi-Que bubbled.

He swam just above water. He started to breath in a large number of times. "Think like you are running," added Rhoi-Que.

If I did that, I would drown! Feslen sent a telepathic message.

"Think like you are…hmm…enjoying a day where there is little wind."

He calmed himself, remembering Master Chai's lessons. It took him a full twenty minutes to relax and trust himself in the water. He heard Rhoi-Que's bubbling cheers. He even felt water itself wrap her loving arms around him in cheer. He smiled.

"You're just floating, honey. But that's a terrific start!"

He felt his energy surrounded by an abrupt flush of wind, as if he was truly floating in the water! Is that the spell working? He thought. He grinned and followed Rhoi-Que's form down the once tumultuous spouting mouth of the Lake.

"Rhoi-Que, Can I ask you something?"

"That's already a question," giggled Rhoi-Que.

Feslen grinned in spite of himself. He began to enjoy swimming! "You're a natural, honey," Rhoi-Que encouraged.

"How come I can see you now? But, I couldn't before?" Feslen asked through the roar of the now rushing river. Salt mounds formed a natural bridge from the lake mouth. Even the temperature seemed to change in this part of the Old Forest.

"Is it because you are in the form of your True Nature? Can I sense... rather can beings sense things when they happen to bond in the same areas? Is it because we truly understand ourselves and what we are?"

She did not respond for a time as they floated past more trees. Did we go too far? Feslen thought.

"You answered your own question, honey," replied Rhoi-Que. "I am in my true element, yes. I am a Water Spirit remember? Other beings can sense one's true element when you are just as accepting and immersed within as they are."

Feslen nodded, not surprised at the answer.

"Still, perhaps Mrs. Ma Poa Dou Fu can answer your question better than I," Rhoi-Que said. "We are nearing our destination."

The water slowed down and thinned to where Feslen could walk on the stones beneath. Feslen frowned and saw what the problem was when they came within three feet of the situation. Most of the salt rocks he seen in the river transformed into crystals. The crystals blocked most of the water flow until it became nothing more than a trickle. "See the Frogs' pool down there?" Worried Rhoi-Que to a point of her speech becoming normal-human pace.

Feslen walked over to the edge of the crystals and looked down at the small waterfall. He gasped at what he saw. Six pony-sized humanoid frog beings squatted on their hind legs in the shallow saltwater pool. They looked angry and desperate.

Feslen hissed all of a sudden when he neared the crystal rocks. "Are you all right, honey?" The Water Spirit called out. She tried to swim towards him but the water where transformed into more solid material around Feslen.

"Don't swim out any further!" Feslen warned. He managed to get one leg above the salt. As soon as Feslen put his leg down, a warm sensation spread through his body and ignited the salt. Energies from his legs spread through the salt and its gradual hardening amazed him.

He marveled at the hardness of the ground amazed the friends.

Rhoi-Que asked, "Are you all right?"

Feslen ignored his pained feet. "No, but I am in no immediate danger. Stay back, Rhoi-Que!"

"Is there anything I could do?" Her color changed again.

He rubbed his chin and focused on the task at hand, forgetting momentary pain on his feet. "Find a rock and try and toss it in my direction. I feel a strange energy source, but I can't find out where it's coming from."

"Why?"

"Just do it! The Frogs down there need help…they are running dry!" Feslen reported. It was true. He looked down and saw their skins crack as much as his feet had. He had little time. He needed to know how far the concrete water extended. In addition, liquid crystal oozed out. He touched the crystalline rock and the ooze.

Feslen started to understand. He felt the odd energies swirling in the area. Why did I not sense it before? He thought. These energies differed than the ones he saw with regularity on people, animals and inanimate objects: they were not energy auras. The energy patterns here spread across the air and water and hardened salt formation in a crisscross pattern. For an instance, the young boy thought he spotted spider-web like threads pulsating energy!

"These are magical!" Feslen said to the Water Spirit.

"Yes, like I said, the Outsider cast some spell which transformed this ordinary water!"

He tugged one of the bigger crystals loose, the after splash created waves. The waves bounced much like his Mother's rice pudding. He chuckled at the analogy and refocused at the task.

Feslen rammed the crystal piece into the solid rock. As he suspected, the crystal broke the rock. More ooze flowed from it.

"Hey, stop it whoever is doing that up there!" One of the Frogs shouted in its language. Feslen started, he understood them!

"Feslen, honey…I got you that rock…," she said panting. The rock was bigger than she was. Her look implored, Will this do?

"Thank you. Now throw!"

She gave him an incredulous look.

"Okay, okay. Bring it to me." She did and ran back into the water, eyeing the ooze with suspicion. Feslen tossed the small rock. It floated and plunked.

"Think, Feslen, think! Why would the water be firm yet watery? What is making its form and the noise being different? Is it an illusion? I feel the energy…" He focused again and gasped. Bronze energy formed around the salt rocks.

He inhaled and plunged his head into the water. He heard Rhoi-Que shriek, but ignored her. His eyes widened. The ooze was not in the bottom of the river! The crystallized rock had not even formed to the bottom of the river, nor had there even been a reflection. An illusion!

He ran out of breath and pulled his head back out. He was not even wet.

"How…but…what…?" Rhoi-Que asked.

Feslen stepped out of the transformed water and found to his delight that his feet had not crystallized. "The energies I feel are part of a living thing," he started to say while he sat at the edge of the bank. "Also, I feel the energy patterns. The energy is similar to human emotions."

"What do you mean?"

Feslen shook his head and said, "I don't know. I don't understand what's going on. I'm just reporting what I feel." He grabbed a rock from the edge of the bank and threw it hard at the crystal rocks. When it hit the rock, a hollow noise occurred. The Water Spirit screamed as the pink ooze which flowed from the rock formed into a living monster!

"An Ooze Monster," Feslen warned, Careful Rhoi-Que!"

The pink glob raised itself to the full height of a large bear. Feslen stepped back and tried to reach for his energy. The young boy exhausted as the thing advanced.

"You feed off of energy, do you?" Feslen murmured. "Don't cast any spells, Rhoi-Que! It feeds off of energy." The young boy turned to find why the Water Spirit did not say anything. He cried out at the sight of his friend gripped by a tentacle.

"Rhoi-Que!" Feslen screamed and hurled himself at it.

The Water Spirit cried, "No, run, honey!"

Feslen ducked a shot of the pink arm. Another appendage tried to grapple him. He used all of Master Chai's Twelve Steps now. He tumbled and rolled. The pink arm missed decapitating his head by inches. As it was, Feslen came up with a wounded shoulder. At this time, Feslen did not even realize he learned all Twelve Steps! Before, this he always thought he failed Master Chai's lessons…

What can beat this monstrosity? Feslen thought, his chest contracting a bit. His energy waned fast and he started to tire out as he kept dodging and swiping with his weak kicks.

What can solidify liquid besides cold? Feslen thought. "Rhoi-Que!" He screamed when she stopped moving.

He hoped help would come, but he knew he was on his own. It would be up to him…tears formed in his eyes. He panted from the exertion of constant dodging and noticed his tears burned a hole through the hardened ground.

Feslen thought of something.

"Love can create solids," Feslen realized. A red energy still flowed from the fading Water Spirit.

Finding a pink energy path, Feslen reached down his heart and connected to the Water Spirit. When Feslen made contact, she fluttered a bit. "How did you…?" she asked in a weak voice.

"Help me Rhoi-Que, Goddess," Feslen said and ignored the advancing ooze monster. He then reached down into the water and concentrated. His tears formed large pools of energy slashing the ooze monster when it came close to them.

It roared. The thing exploded into a million tiny pieces.

Bright yellow glow flashed from his left as he charged the reforming creature again. A burst of bright light and warmth exploded in front of him. Feslen dropped to his knees, exhausted. The water flowed again.

At the edge of the forest, Feslen saw a middle-aged green robed Forest Protector nod her head in approval. So, all this was a test, Feslen managed to think. She must be Ma Poa Dou Fu, his tired brain registered before he slept.

32

PEOPLE'S COUNCIL 人民議會

People's Council began in the mangrove. It amazed Feslen just how many people knew about him or wanted a piece of him. The Pink, Blue Yellow and Immersing Black Robed magicians from the Great School of Magic Stuff acknowledged him. Seated next to Duxan, Ka-Wei and Nadine were two strong-looking grim faced Northern men. Feslen started when he saw his friends here, and Nadine gave him a winning-calm hearted smile. He relaxed and then stared in frank interest at the important people gathered. Battle-scared, plate-wearing and battle-axe bearing Northern men turned a stern gaze on Feslen. The gaze made him shiver. Their symbols of bloody sword represented the City of Steel.

Opposite of the companions, sat a plumpish, white-haired woman from the South, she had a grim-faced warrior as a companion. Next to them sat some Lord of the Eastern Block, his pale yellow face reflected the hardship his people had endured under the Empire's rule. The dwarf-like Shinjoudou sat opposite of Feslen and Nadine. Behind the dwarf, a young, dark-skinned skinny gypsy gave him a knowing glance, and Feslen frowned.

Feslen recognized none of them.

An elegant shimmering green gown flowed down the High Forest Protector. Her hair resembled many rainbow colored leaves. The High Forest Protector, Ma Poa Dou Fu smelled of acorn and spring. "Greetings fellow peoples from Free Nations. We are gathered here to discuss the fate of our world," began the High Forest Protector, her voice clear and loud.

Even the birds stopped chirping for her to announce the meeting to begin. The Forest Protectors impressed Feslen every second. He gave an imploring look to Kalman, who nodded.

"Thank you all for answering to my calls and heeds of warning. I know the journey into hostile territory wasn't easy for you, Lady Qui Hahn," Said Ma Poa Dou Fu to a white-haired woman, who nodded a bit.

"I also thank Nahk Jang and his man from coming through the arduous trek from the Eastern blockades the Emperor set up," Ma Poa Dou Fu continued, to the City of Steel man. Then she thanked the Shinjoudou dwarf named Avik Noravem. She did not mention where they lived.

"Prince Ka-Wei warned me of the changes, the Emperor stirs."

Angry mutters from all around the room of mangrove trees.

"The Emperor grows in discomfort as time passes. The more the North and South resist, and we shall continue to do so. But, we have come not to discuss that, not yet," The High Forest Protector stopped, a penetrating look to everyone in the room. She rested her green gaze at Feslen the longest; her look broke his fever.

She began again. "I thank you all for coming. I know for some of you the travel was not easy. But, you all know why I summoned you. Our time is grave and becomes darker with every minute we sit talking."

"I am not aware," Feslen murmured, but listened.

"I do not dally, you all wonder why this boy is allowed here, and why the messages I sent were urgent. Feslen Raster has passed the tests I have given him. He has proven to be one of the Ancient Truth wielders."

The High Forest Protector paused, letting her message sink in to her audience. An audible gasp arose, all eyes turned to Feslen Raster.

"Ancient Truth?" Duxan and Feslen asked and gave each other glances then glanced at the Forest Protector and Ka-Wei.

"I have intercepted messages from the desperate monks of Thai-Thurian, Master Chai and the magician's leader, Master Drak; about Feslen Raster."

The High Forest Protector paused, and stared at everyone in the room. "Feslen is our hope of the future, lords and ladies of the Free World. He and his friends will stop the dangers of the Prophecies and the ones created by mankind according to all Prophecies," she continued. She waved her hands in dramatic fashion, pointing at Feslen and his friends.

A long silence followed. Feslen and Duxan gave Prince Ka-Wei and Princess Nadine stunned looks. Feslen swiveled a look around at all the gathered dignitaries: fear, astonishment, displeasure and disbelief on their faces. I don't blame them, Feslen thought. I would be afraid and doubtful of me too. And yet, I have felt this power build up in me ever since the Choicings.

"How are we sure, Pure Lady that this one is the One? Are you sure they are the ones?" said Nahk Jang, a City of Steel warrior.

"Not to mention he hasn't done anything yet. We have kept track on him too. He's done nothing but get into trouble with the New Priests," the Southern woman disdained. Her eyes bored into Feslen like needles and Feslen shivered.

"This whelp? My baby has more strength than an ox, what is he compared to that?" The dwarf-like person said.

"I understand your concerns," Ma Poa Dou Fu replied. "But, I feel the Ancient Truth from him. I know he is aware of things we can only hope to have awareness of."

Feslen's face burned in more shame than anger.

"It's true," Ka-Wei murmured. All eyes turned on him. "I've seen this young man do amazing things even I, and you will find impossible to do. His powers emitted to me when he saved me from the fires."

Feslen was about to speak, but felt a crush of emotions and tried to hide. Me? A Prophecy Child? I can't even cast magic without making things blow up! He thought.

A rough cough came from the Eastern Lord.

The boy noted that the Eastern Lord said nothing, but had a very thoughtful gaze. The Immersing Black robed mage just chortled, but silenced after a look from Pink Robe.

The High Forest Protector nodded and said, "I understand your concerns. You read the entire Prophecies? Some things have occurred, yes?"

"Excuse me, full Prophecy?" Duxan asked.

Before anyone could answer, Feslen stood up and spoke in a strong voice he was unused to:

"Unalertness, weariness, granted thorough happiness, change is coming:
Three children of the Ancient Truth must unite with a fourth,
One, twice borne,
One delivered from the Lost Ones,
One who dwells with Ancient Past,
These not found the gentle caress turns to stinging burns from what
We take for granted as ever blowing softness.
The First of these begin and your doom is sealed."

"Yes, very good child, but we've all heard that version before!" the Northern Lord in his stern deep voice.

Feslen looked at the High Forest Protector who nodded and continued:

"Ancient Terror haunts living mortals, end it all in one way only you must,
The Second of these begin and your doom is sealed.

Ignorance, blissfulness, spite, change is coming without respite:

World filled with sky tears, cracked with thirst in overwhelming unpitying heat;

Need there be reminders and repeat?

The Third of these begin and your doom is Sealed; Hide not, announce through forthright attentions, rebirth Honor within ashes become those who are and know…

They can defeat it, if…

Hunger begets hunger, neighbors turn, friends and family grow into beasts if not maintained.

Feed the chaotic heart to end it all.

The Fourth of these begin and your doom is sealed.

One must choose, another sacrifices without asking, instilled honor in the last,

They must not give in or…consuming anger in broken love creates chaos; true happiness void, familiarity shows calm, despite all efforts;

The Fifth of these begin and your Doom is sealed; Anger in the heavens sparkle below, splitting home choices of choices; one must go one, or all will be consumed.

The Sixth of these begin and your doom is Sealed, decisions must be decided, cannot hesitate or regret…great waves of explosive heat consumes anger; juggling two hands may not be enough;

The Seventh of these begin and your doom is sealed; same as always, similar three acts above, yet different; decide or not decide and be known the acts itself change Ways.

For, all growing things will stop mid-step; cold becomes colder until angered heat makes the Fourth easier…if you cannot decide, then you know what is to come:

The Eighth of these begin and your doom is sealed;

BEWARE! When it reaches the last, it is too late, for you are waging a futile war; you are going to lose the thing most precious, you will be lost or in peace—depends on how the balance tips; you will be at the end of a journey…

These cannot be stopped, unless those with the Awakening of Truth, and the truth of knowing acts upon their goodness of being; want to and have to are two different things, because should they not be allowed to stray…after all this you should know by now:

The Ninth of these begin and your doom is sealed!"

A most discomforting silence passed after Feslen finished. He sat down, not knowing what else to do and felt like hiding. He saw the angry looks and the dismayed expressions on their faces. Somehow, he felt responsible, even though he knew he was not.

"That proves little," said Qui Hahn, the Southern Lady. "He is learned, after all."

Ma Poa Dou Fu nodded and said, "I understand your concerns, but, young Feslen has died twice."

"Actually, three times," Feslen interjected in a whisper. He felt like hiding from these people's stern gazes. I need to know the truth! He thought.

He felt his powers returning. He saw energy lines, auras and even unexplained shadowed images of the people assembled in the room.

The Shinjoudou folk said, "See, he is not of the Prophecies!"

Feslen gave a glance at the Shijoudou and he saw a flash of the Gem Stone Mountains behind him. Feslen blinked when he saw some Shijoudou trapped in a giant gem. He saw this particular dwarf, Avik run away from something. He also saw his people's new homelands. It was obvious the High Protector did not wish to reveal this dwarf's homelands.

"He rebirthed more than twice. He has risen from the ashes…Feslen, isn't true that when you died as a baby, your Mother put you on a bed of ashes?" The High Forest Protector asked.

"I…don't know…Duxan?"

Duxan shook his head.

The High Forest Protector nodded. She clapped her hands and a servant went into the back room and returned with a wooden mirror with no frame to the High Forest Protector.

The High Forest Protector bid the Raster brothers to come close to her. "Look into the past, Raster brothers. Look and gaze into the Mirror of Knowing."

Duxan hesitated, but felt his brother's reassuring hand. "I'll look first," Feslen offered. The boy gazed into the plain mirror. For a long moment, he saw nothing. He looked long and hard into the mirror and the energy swirled. He gasped. *A young black haired woman of non-Chiendong birth slender and delicate she carried a baby in her arms and towed a six-year old boy with her. They ran. The young woman pointed at a pile of logs she gathered in the dead of winter and fire sprang from it as her lips moved. She moved her children closer to the fire so they would be warm…she noticed her baby cold and not moving. She cried and put him on a pile of ashes from the fire…*

Feslen blinked and pulled his head back. He returned to his seat and Nadine squeezed his hand. *Her presence makes all this craziness and the pressure of the Lords easier to handle.*

"Let's make sure he is the One," said Qui-Hahn, the Southern Lady. Her eyes narrowed, skeptical and cold.

"But the other Truths has yet to be found," Eastern Lord Kugai said.

"Don't interrupt me, Ma Kugai," Qui-Han said. "We must know."

"The Emperor looks for him, that's all you need to know," the Pink Robe said.

"No, she is correct," Feslen said, interrupting everyone. "I need to know."

"Feslen…" Nadine said, placing a hand on him. He smiled at her with reassurance and strode to the middle of the chamber.

"Feslen, you need not to prove anything, child," Ma Poa Dou Fu said. She walked one step to him.

He narrowed his eyes and said, "I need to know."

"Very well," she said.

Feslen fell into his awareness meditation, completing not just the Twelve Dragon Steps in under one minute, but sending waves of calm energy around the room.

Duxan gasped at his brother's prowess in completing the Steps and his energies.

"I've never seen any of you, correct?" Feslen asked, his voice strong.

They all nodded.

"I will tell everyone here a truth you will like hidden away from prying eyes," Feslen said. "That is a power of Awareness, I am beginning to understand now."

The others glanced at each other in discomfort, and all except Lady Qui-Hahn objected.

"You, Lady Qui-Hahn. I see your status as queen of the Southern people was gained not by royal blood."

"What's your point? I could be married into royalty," Lady Qui-Hahn interrupted, her voice scintillating danger.

"You," Feslen began and gasped. His face flushed pink. He wondered if he should tell everyone her deep sated secrets.

Nadine got up next to him and caressed him and she whispered, "Feslen…sit down, love. You don't need to do this."

"Well, if he doesn't he's a charlatan!" Avik the Shinjoudou said.

"Very well. You've hidden the secret well, Lady," Feslen scorned her. "I bet your sister is proud of the way you handled her."

The Lady Qui-Hahn gasped and growled, standing up, "I have magic, boy. I can burn you to a crisp."

Feslen smiled and said, "I bet. If you did use it on me, you'd be turning your hide in."

Prince Ka-Wei shook his head and sighed. His friend has yet to learn about politics. Almost every true royal person knew the Lady Qui-Hahn was not true royalty. Although the Prince now knew how Lady Qui-Hahn rose to power so quickly thanks to Feslen's truth finder.

"Next, you, dwarf," Feslen said.

"I am not a dwarf," sneered Avik.

"Whatever," Feslen said. "You're shorter than me, that makes you a dwarf."

A few chitters of laughter and displeasure echoed the room at Feslen's tone.

"My name is Avik, boy," scowled Avik.

"You fled the Gem Stone Mountains because of a terrible history," Feslen began. "You people now hide…"

"No, Feslen, don't," Nadine and Ma Poa Dou Fu urged at the same time. Nadine tugged his arm.

"You hide in a place without magic," Feslen said. "Created by the Breaking Wars, not as far away from your original home as we would thought."

Avik Navreem stopped grumbling and sat.

Feslen let go a sigh, and released his energies. Exhaustion set in and Nadine led him back to his seat. Having him near her gave him the courage to do such things. Her eyes sparkled when she studied him and she nodded her head when he gave her an expectant look. He wanted to lean against her and so he did.

A long, awkward silence followed.

"They are near, their Awareness will be understood," Ma Poa Dou Fu said, breaking the silence.

"They are all close," The Pink Robe confirmed.

Feslen gave Pink Robe a startled look.

The Pink Robe affirmed, "We looked for a long time on the orders of our leader, Master Drak; and suspicions of the premier and late Master Chai. Feslen carries the Ancient Truth."

Feslen frowned, looking around. A large gasp and denial arose from the gathered group. The Southern woman made a sign as of to ward of evil. A look of fear and respect gathered on the faces of all who sat around the circle. Even Ka-Wei looked troubled. Duxan and Nadine remained unperturbed.

"What now, do we do about the Prophecy Child then? Does the Ancient Truth wielder not beholden to the normal Laws?" Avik Navreem asked, his tone changed to respect.

"No, the Chaos Wielder does not adhere to our normal rules of magic. That's why he or she cannot be allowed within our Circle," replied the Pink Robe. Feslen detected a scent of fear in her tone and expression.

"He can only be trained by those who have the knowledge of Ancient Truth," the Blue Yellow Robe reminded the Pink Robe.

"Yes, I was getting to that. Our founder and long gone former leader was a Chaos Power Wielder."

"The Breaking Wars," Feslen murmured.

"Yes," the gathered magicians all said in a hush.

Ka-Wei nodded. Even the fighters of the North and the Prince had heard of this legend. "Am I to be taught?" Feslen asked. "What is to become of me, an outlaw?"

"That is what we are trying to decide, my young friend," the High Forest Protector said. "The Emperor is afraid. He is afraid of the ones like you. That's why the New Priests have yet to apprehend you."

"And now we know why he's afraid," Lady Qui-Hahn murmured, her eyes lowered to the ground when she addressed him. "You just demonstrated a piece of your powers, young Feslen."

Feslen raised his eyebrow, but remained quiet. Though Feslen had little proof, he suspected the great Emperor behind the war and devastations.

He looked at the former Prince's direction. Ka-Wei gave him a thin-lipped smile.

"What now? We can't give Feslen over without protection. He has been foolish to attack things without knowing," the Qui-Hahn said with a derisive frown.

Did she aid me in the Temple of Skies? Feslen wondered.

"What does the Emperor want? Why is he afraid of my brother?" Duxan asked and added, "Feslen wants nothing to do with the Emperor."

Damned you brother, I wish you would not presume my feelings for me to everyone! I wish you would not be so overprotective! Feslen thought with an irritated glance at his brother, but he said nothing. He stared at everyone else in the room to distract his feelings.

"No, he doesn't yet," High Forest Protector conceded. "According to the Prophecy, the Fourth will decide the fate of everyone. Haven't you been listening, Duxan? The Emperor wants supremacy. He is a great mage himself. He thinks of himself greater than any of the Chosen Ones, and even as One, am I right, Mirenna?"

The Pink Robe acknowledged with a reply, "He is banned, High Mother. Yes, he does think that, that is why he was exiled from Great School of Magic Stuff. Yet, we cannot move against him for….time is short. We must find the rest of the Prophecy Children before he does."

"Fortunately, Feslen Raster, you arrived to us in time. We need to know which side you stand for," the Blue Yellow Robe interrupted.

I may dislike that Duxan jumps in to 'defend' my feelings, Feslen thought, as his frustrations and anger grew and grew when he listened to the distinguished people around him talk. I hate how people dismiss me as if I'm not here, and assume I'd help them. I am doing things for myself! I never followed orders before, and I won't ever again…unless they benefit me.

"What do I want to do? You can fight your stupid wars for all I care," Feslen responded with a bitter laugh and paused. He stood out and gestured to everyone around him, his soul burning. He continued to rant, "I am indebted to repay my debts. Five people are dead because of me, and one wonderful girl, kidnapped. Your stupid council, nor you foolish mages or the Emperor will stop me. I am Feslen, no one will command me what to do."

I don't listen to Prophecies, or fate. I make my own, Feslen thought. Mei Xue needs my help, that's all I know. And, since she lies in the North…Damned them all, damned these people.

Feslen started to storm out, but Nadine stopped him. "Please, just a little longer Feslen."

He stormed out, shaking Nadine off.

Silence.

Shock and anger ran through the room.

Duxan got up, apologized to the leader of the Forest Protectors, Ma Poa Dou Fu, and followed after his brother.

Nadine sighed and followed after.

"Excuse me, Ladies and Gentleman," Ka-Wei said and he turned to everyone.

The young Prince bowed to the High Forest Protector and strode out of the room leaving a distinguished group of people quaking in fear and anger.

33

PREDICTION CARDS 預言牌

"Let me alone, I need to rest," Feslen murmured to Nadine and Duxan the closed door. The light came from the two candles they held.

"Feslen…do you really mean what you said back there? The Forest Protectorate, Ma Poa Dou Fu only means to help," Nadine said in a tone of concern and dismay.

A soft knock interrupted Feslen's reply.

"It's me, Feslen," Ka-Wei said. Duxan opened the door.

"How many people did I leave angry at me? I hope everyone."

"I think you made more enemies than friends today, if that's what you mean, my friend. However, these people could do little. You have died more times than they have lived, after all. Be ready before the Winter's Celebration Festival, Feslen. The horses and supply caravan to the…" Ka-Wei said.

"You mean you found the way to the Sorceress finally?" Feslen asked.

Ka-Wei nodded and replied, "Yes. We skirted many of her magical traps. W…ell, after a few hard lessons, of course."

"Why would we leave during the harshest winters of the North?" Duxan and added, "You know what extreme cold does to Feslen."

Feslen growled and asked the Prince before Ka-Wei could reply to Duxan, "What about Duxan's cure and illness? Will we find them in the North?"

"Actually," Nadine answered for him, "The Protectorate has a few gifts for you in this sack, Feslen. It is your reward for saving the Frogs. She said to bring you this message, 'Those who are inborn with the Ancient Truth becomes stronger when exposed to magic, and areas where the Ancient Truth once touched.'" She handed him a sack.

"The Breaking Wars started in the North," Feslen murmured, realization hitting his murky brain. "I read the mages once fought over the rights of casting magic spells, but the books and scrolls I read never went into greater details. Perhaps your aunt's castle will hold more knowledge, Ka-Wei."

Feslen stared at the plain brown sack dubiously. He took it and shook it; it felt lighter than a feather. "An Endless Bag?" He asked Nadine, who just gave him a smile. Feslen had heard of such magic items before. He opened it and saw several items: A small black-leather bound spellbook, he felt no power from it, which meant it was empty; a scroll with Ancient Chiendonese on it and two other maps. I thought so! Feslen thought and he laughed.

"What?" Duxan and Ka-Wei asked. They glanced at one another, and leaned in to see. Feslen opened the bag to show them.

Ka-Wei said, "I've only been to her castle once, so, I can't say for sure I paid much attention."

Feslen chuckled and lay back against the soft downy pillows of this bed. He thought for a moment and said, while turning to face Nadine, "Look, I still want two things: saving Mei Xue and Duxan. If the Protectorate's message is true, then, perhaps Duxan, your magical curse or illness will become negated."

"Maybe, right now," Duxan said, trying to put how he felt about the illness and what it did to him into words, "Right now, I feel fine. Although, when I sleep, I feel weak."

"Kinda like how I used to feel everyday," Feslen replied in a whisper.

"So, everyone is agreed then? We're all coming?" Ka-Wei asked.

Feslen grinned and said, "I doubt you can keep my brother from not coming, even if he weren't sick, Ka-Wei. Nadine? You don't need to come…"

"I have to, Feslen. Part of Nature's Law is that if I keep helping you, I can have an easier chance at persuading you to come help me and my country," Nadine replied.

Feslen smiled and said, "I would help you anyway. Just let me do what I must first and I will come. To be honest, I have a feeling I am……we're going to need all the magical help on this trip. I hope you can gather that sort of help, Ka-Wei."

Ka-Wei started to answer when a light knock interrupted them. The door opened.

"You are Feslen Raster?" An airy and accented feminine voice piped up.

"I am. I saw you at the Council. Are you here to mock me or scold me? If you are, get out."

She shook her head. "My name is Jungoo Jeizen…I came from…"

"The Desolate Lands," Feslen said tiredly.

A gypsy, here? Ka-Wei thought. A gypsy, how…interesting, Feslen thought, with mild interest. He glanced at his brother and sighed, seeing his admiring gaze.

"How did you know?" She asked her mouth agape.

"Are you going to waste my time young lady? I am quite tired from this evening's events."

"Few have seen your kind around," Nadine said, though not unkindly.

Jungoo gave her a look.

The young woman was about sixteen years of age, slender and a few inches shorter than Duxan. She had an russet complexion and attractive crescent-shaped eyes with long eyelashes. Her skin had a virtual dark hew about it, giving off the fact that she was indeed a Northern woman. She had a waterskin slugged on her other slender arm and twin short swords looped through her thin belt.

He allowed the young woman to come in. Nadine frowned for the slightest of moments and sat on the bed with Feslen. The boy gave her a curious glance. She put her svelte arms about him in a protective way.

"Why have you come?" Feslen asked, stifling a yawn. He nodded his thanks to his elder brother as he set a glass of water next to him and the young lady who sat in front of them in a chair. She offered her thanks to Ka-Wei who provided the chair.

Ka-Wei bid everyone a good rest and turned to go.

"No, my Prince," said the exotic Northern girl. The seriousness of her tone halted Ka-Wei in his track.

"Please, join us. This concerns you too. It is about the future for us all."

Duxan sat cross-legged on a pillow.

"Come, I will tell you a story and why I am here. You must promise to travel with me though," the strange young lady named Jungoo Jeizen said in her thick exotic accent.

"I can't promise anything," Feslen allowed. "I have some loose ends to tie up here first, and then…." He looked in the direction of Ka-Wei.

Ka-Wei nodded and closed the door, and sat on his seat again.

Feslen had to admit the young girl's aroma of coriander and *telinagar* spice intoxicating. It was a strange mix with Nadine's smell of honeydew and blossomed roses. It made it hard to concentrate. Though the Prince used incredible self-discipline, Feslen could see the occasional stolen glances he gave towards Jungoo's openly shown body. Her body was good, but not as good Nadine's! Somehow, Feslen thought this strange thought. He shook his head. "What is it that you want to show us, Jungoo?"

"A pleasure to know my name rolls off a non-native's tongue," Jungoo said with a smile.

Feslen smiled.

She got out a pack of cards from one of her pouches.

"Prediction Cards?" Ka-Wei asked.

He stood up again.

"You will care what happens, Prince of Chiendong! What I have to say concerns us all!"

"We need light," Duxan said.

The last candle had burned out.

"Not necessary, Duxan Raster. I know my Cards very well. Watch," she said. She placed the deck of fifty-two glossy cards out.

The room became pitch black as midnight approached. Feslen could not see his friend's faces, but could hear their breathing. He felt Nadine's presence next to his and that provided both comfort and excitement. He had no time to puzzle over the new development in emotions. She squeezed his hand.

Night sounds lulled them.

A bright multi-colored glow erupted from where Jungoo placed her Prediction Cards. Ka-Wei and Duxan cried out in surprise. "Let me explain to you how these work," she began, with a look at each of them.

"The True Nature of a person determines the Paths they take. The Cards reflect the tendencies of the True Nature and the past taken by these souls. They are nothing more than what we give out. This is an accurate prediction. Not like the falsehood of the New Ones."

Feslen and the others nodded. They could also detect the sour tone of the young lady's voice. "Now let me also add they do not change one person's future, the future is not set. It just merely sees a possible ending. No one can be controlled by these; they are not the same as Fate Cards."

Feslen nodded and yawned.

"I came a long way to find you, Master Feslen. Please show respect and try to stay up," she said.

Feslen grimacedat the honorific title used and nodded.

Duxan hid a chuckle.

"I came to find you, yes, you Feslen Raster. Not just because of your being the Chosen One of the Prophecies. However, your past has a connection with my people. They need you, Feslen. You must come to my homeland…"

Feslen gave a subtle glance at his brother, who seemed not to notice because he still had his eyes glued to Jungoo.

She closed her eyes and said, "I know this is the last thing you want to hear, especially after your outburst tonight…I could only begin to understand the pressure you're under, but only you and your brother could save my people. They need your help."

"Of course I'll go, Jungoo," Duxan said without hesitation.

"Your presence is of the utmost urgency."

"What is the problem? Perhaps if you tell me now…"

"Better if you come."

Feslen did not reply or show any emotion at all.

The gypsy seemed embarrassed when she asked him for help.

He asked her again the reasons why he should go.

She shuffled her feet a bit and hid her face behind her eyes, her eyes showing embarrassment, though the rest of her face did not. Why would she show shame? Feslen wondered. Then he knew. This gypsy, a Princess of sorts in her people's culture, held Prediction Cards. Predicition Cards were handed down from female generation to generation. It was umost importance to Jungoo's family, heritage and people that she survive, if the rest did not. Her mother must have known about their karmic fate than…Feslen thought, cold-hearted. I doubt she knows why she was sent alone, without a bodyguard or even a retinue.

He asked her again, but Duxan intercepted Feslen and said, "Can't you see, little brother, she needs our help?"

Feslen grimaced and relpied, "I only help those who say things with honest intent." He turned to Princess Nadine, who sat idly by with a dark look on her face for some reason. He said to her, "Can you enlighten me on your homeland's problems, Nadine?"

Nadine smiled and said, "It is cursed by a powerful general of darkness, Feslen. I cannot dispel it, despite my…heritage. I wish for you to come."

"Of course, but…a little more information would help," Feslen encouraged with a nod.

Nadine gave a little sigh and tossed her head. She mumbled to herself a moment then said, "Very well. You won't like what I'm about to show you."

"My people are trapped in a nightmarish state of dead and undead," she continued, while fishing for something in her robes. "It's as if their minds were trapped in their worst dreams."

"Evil magic from Seatan?" Ka-Wei asked, with a shiver.

"Maybe," Nadine allowed with a shake of her head. Feslen looked at his two friends with a wary glance, wondering who Seatan was. He was about to point this out, when Nadine warned, "This is not for the faint of heart."

She tossed out a severed hand inside a gauntlet with the King's insignia on it. An imprint of the New Priest's infamous symbol was also on it. This one belonged to the Scorpion Sect. Ka-Wei, Jungoo, Duxan and Lioin cried out in distress and disgust. Ka-Wei especially. He said, "My captain…Cho Lu…"

"A powerful man named General Iku Chou, the Iron Fist of the North leads the dark forces in Nu. He is under a powerful mage's orders. I barely escaped from him myself," Nadine said, with a swallow and pale face.

Ka-Wei nodded and whispered, "I know that name."

Feslen closed his eyes and now imagined Nadine's pain. He said, placing a hand upon hers, "I will do what I can…though I'm not sure how much I can do…."

"You are the Chosen One, as I believe in you," Nadine answered with a smile. Feslen melted at touching her hand and upon her smile.

"Once I am done with rescuing Mei Xue and…we'll stop this tyrant," Feslen said, with clneched teeth and fist.

Nadine smiled and said, "And I will guide you all the way."

"No! You must come to my homeland!" Jungoo snarled.

"I will avenge my family, my friends and then help Nu and Nadine," Feslen said, his voice cold and steely, ignoring Jungoo's outraged face. "Now, if you have nothing further…"

Jungoo said, "I can't tell you…you must…come." Feslen knew the reason behind her hesitation, as he figured her to be one of those people embarrassed at her people's suffering and destitution, but he said nothing. He also gave her little grounds, he had no patience, energy or time for such cryptic 'Underresponsible people'. This was the nickname Feslen made up for people who need his help, but he had come to visualize that they were only too lazy to help themselves.

Jungoo sighed, after a few choice words from Duxan and said, with obvious trouble holding back tears and anger in her voice, "No…I did come here for something more."

"I must go, Duxan, Feslen…I'll meet you…" Ka-Wei began, but Jungoo cut him off with a glare.

She said, "My Prince, you must understand, this concerns you too."

Ka-Wei sighed and sat down mumbling, "My dad always told me you can't win an argument with women…"

Duxan laughed.

"I apologize, my lady. But I do have many things to do."

She nodded and closed her eyes and reached out to the first card. Feslen felt the vibration of the Cards and the interesting energy around the young woman's body.

"The first Reading I will do is for you, Feslen of the Chaos Power Wielder," Jungoo began. Her voice deepened, noticeablely different.

Feslen and the others exchanged glances.

"I just hope I don't have to explain to you how the Cards work."

"I will explain later to them," Feslen said at the same time Nadine did. They grinned at each other.

The first Card: Old Magic Card she flipped up was a young boy holding a large golden staff surrounded by three red clouds. She placed it in the center. Next card, King's Betrayal: Three half-closed eyes in a triangular wore a dripping crown. The eyes hovered above a young woman surrounded by snakes and shadows. The central eye was in reverse. On the edge of the Card however were symbols of a prayer book, a sword and a flame. Jungoo shuddered when she drew it. Duxan looked at his younger brother and his older friend, Ka-Wei. Both shook their heads, neither knew what that symbol meant. The young gypsy placed that card below the Young Boy Card.

She seemed to smile when she picked up the next Card: Eternal Love. She placed it on the top left-hand corner of the central card. It was a big heart with a little boy and a young woman shown walking together in a tremendous unspoiled land of natural beauty.

"Who do you suppose that represents?" Duxan asked in a teasing voice to his brother and Nadine.

They broke into vast grins and blushing faces as Ka-Wei elbowed Duxan. The young warrior shivered when he felt the room's energy level go up.

"I see a great warrior holding the virtue and just in your name and when you struggle most, he will be a reminder to your deeds whether dark or good, Chaos Wielder."

Feslen smiled at Ka-Wei, who acknowledged him in understanding. So, no matter what I do, I will always have a champion at my side, Feslen thought. To have a warrior and well-harmonized Hero like Ka-Wei to help me on my journeys can only help.

Vitruous Warrior Card followed as she flipped up had a single warrior with a sword, surrounded by vast array of enemies, unafraid. The Common Words: Courage and Fear revolved opposite of each other below and above the warrior. They could all see the shadow of the warrior, holding not a sword but a white flag.

Feslen grimaced and looked at Ka-Wei to see if he understood the apparent applications. The Prince seemed not to reveal his understanding or care.

Feslen sighed and thought I hope someone will be there for you, Ka-Wei. Unless, I guess it wrong…Feslen thought, getting his attention diverted when Jungoo placed it below the young boy card.

When the Virtuous Warrior card was revealed this early, and with the white flag, it meant a great defeat for a Hero will come early in that person's lifetime. The boy card represented pure Honor, Virtue and Optimism on its own term. Feslen, only surmised why the Warrior Card was placed beneath the Boy Card. Each card, when placed in certain positions meant something as well.

"The great emptiness…that is a bad sign…no…that can't be right!" Great whimpers shook her body to the throes of disturbing the bed sheets. Despite her upheavals, the Cards did not move. Duxan reached out to steady her, but hesitated for a moment then placed his hands upon her shoulders to hold her steady. The friends saw the card to be nothing but a black swirl. She tried to place the Card back, but her hand halted. "This…cannot be right." Her hands moved on their own volition by placing the Great Void above the young boy card.

She hissed as she touched the next card. Even the others could see before she revealed the next picture for what it was. For the card was all black. "This represents darkness…a great vast chasm of…most men dare not tread upon await your future, Chaos Wielder," she said trembling with her eyes still closed. She stared in Feslen's direction when she mentioned the title, Chaos Wielder.

A figure all dressed in deep black cocooned in the darkness. His eyes glow menacing yellow.

"Black Death?" Feslen asked and Nadine stroked him with reassurance. The Black Death Card spooked Feslen to the core by the appearance of the legendary deliverer of death. The Black Death God, one of the many revered and respected deities of Chiendong represented the passage of the soul through the reincarnation path. To magicians, however, the other interpretation behind the Black Death Card meant the loss of something even more precious than your soul: one's inborn magic.

Jungoo did not reply as the Card placed to the right of the young boy Card.

"That's strange," murmured Jungoo as she placed felt for the next Card.

"What?" The companions all asked.

"I see three people in your future…a man and two women…there is a direct tie with your past. One will cause a lot of loss and pain for the greater of your being. The other, well, will be there to guide you…I am not sure which or who does what," Jungoo said as she flipped up the card.

The Card showed a young woman that resembled Nadine, a man that looked like Master Chai, and a mid-aged woman that looked like the Sorceress.

Feslen and the others did not recognize any of the figures. He gave Nadine a subtle glance. Will she betray me? He thought. This Card portrays a woman betraying me…

"Wait, there is more," she continued.

"One will try and lead you astray," she paused and her forehead furrowed. She ran her finger over the Card and continued.

Nadine let out a gasp, as did Duxan. The picture on the card continued to evolve. The man seemed to be leading a camel to an oasis, but he led it to an empty chasm. "One of the women will always be surrounded by blood and death…the other…is clouded in mystery. Yet, both have your heart's motives." Droplets of blood, skeletal figures and clouds surrounded the women.

Feslen said nothing, even though the sudden added images intrigued him. He had never heard of Future Cards like these!," she continued. "I wouldn't trust either of them…"

She hissed and placed that one below the warrior.

A horde of monsters, both known and unknown appeared on the next one. In the center was the young boy and terrible storms raged above and below him. The card was called Storm Cards. "You will face the greatest challenge of your life, Chaos Wielder. Yet, it may not be in brawn or hordes or magic." When she spoke of those things, the arcane symbol for all magicians appeared on the side of the framed picture. A single tear appeared below and above the young boy in the Card. An hourglass also appeared on the upper right hand corner of the Card.

This Card represented the time, and the length of time someone succeeded in completing a task.

Even before Jungoo started to talk about what the latest symbol meant. Feslen already concluded what she wanted to say. "Time is of the essence, and things will happen quicker than we wish." She placed that card just below the three-eyed symbol card.

One more card to go, Feslen thought. He sensed the forces within the Cards themselves and saw the energy lines flowing from her too.

Jungoo whimpered through clenched teeth, "I can't go on…" Her hand seemed to fight each other as they touched the last card.

Though her eyes closed, they saw tears on her face. "I'm sorry…Chaos Wielder…"

Her body seemed to collapse into the cards, as she drew the last card: Spirit Card. On it was the Spirits of Suffering and Death. Below them was a young woman in her own pool of blood and a young boy next to her crying. There were Modern Words written to the left and right of the picture again this time they consisted of Calamity and Change. The lights from the Card lessened as she sighed and let go of the last Card.

This last Card disturbed Feslen. He did not like what it portended and he looked at Nadine. She's the only young woman I know, he thought. Unless, it meant Mei Xue. The young boy in the image of the Cards represented me. So, I will cause all that death, dying and suffering? Feslen shivered at the possibilities.

Each Card will feature the specific person's image for the prediction being done at that time. That was how the Prediction Cards worked.

He looked into Nadine's eyes for the longest time. She smiled with warmth and came over to him with a hug.

She stroked him and massaged his tense body. Feslen began to relax. "Shhh, you've had a long day, time to rest, Feslen," she murmured. Her words sounded like a spell, her tone eased his spirit. He inhaled in bliss and exhaled, relaxing into the bed.

No one spoke for a long time. All of them tried to get used to the blissful darkness.

The young gypsy continued to cry, keeping the friends awake, thoughtful and solemn.

"Why, mother, must this one be difficult?" She said.

"I must give readings to you all…I kept you up," sobbed the gypsy.

"No, young lady," Duxan said. "You are tired…you…we must all retire for the night."

Jungoo reached out for the Cards again, but Duxan held her hand firm but remonstrated. "You need rest, Miss Jeizen. I will walk you to your quarters."

"Don't bother with the Cards, they will return to me on their own accord."

The sun's morning rays hit the room, lighting up everyone's tired, thoughtful, somewhat frightened face. And, it revealed the once hidden thief, Lioin in the corner of the room.

Ka-Wei said, "I think I see the sun coming out. I will stay here for the remainder of the day, instead of returning to my fellow troops. Good day all."

Nadine nodded as Feslen began to snore a bit.

The Cards exploded in sudden light, fascinated the companions. The brightness awoke Feslen.

"No…this has never happened before!" Jungoo exclaimed in almost a hysterical shriek.

"Ka-Wei, help me," Duxan said struggling to keep her steady. She pounced on her Cards, trying to hold them. Ka-Wei moved closer to her, but his eyes transfixed at the Cards could do nothing.

The Card deck shuffled itself! The friends gasped.

The One Card lifted by itself up and it floated in the air for a moment, glittering like a diamond in the sun. A young boy and young man faced off in a battle that devastated the world. Blood and storms ripped the ground and air around them. The word on the bottom of the Card clearer than daylight was Chaos. The Spirits in were visible in the background…

"Who are you?" Jungoo said in a dying whisper as she stared at Feslen in terror and respect.

For long moments the Card spun. The image changed: it showed three young men standing on top of a breaking world. Half of the Card glowed in brilliant light, the other terrible shadows. A deep gray shadowed the young men, almost as if observing the destruction around them with disinterest. The ancient none-Chiendong characters puzzled all, except Feslen. He read the words with ease, but did not understand the meaning behind them.

The Card drifted back onto the pile and all went dark.

Jungoo blubbered when Duxan led her away. The friends were quiet for a long time.

"You can come out now, Lioin. I'm glad to see you all well. Have you been hiding in the Forest Protector's mangrove all this time?" Feslen said.

"Some," Lioin said.

There was a comfortable silence.

"What was that all about, Feslen? Why are all these people after you... Chaos Wielder?" Lioin asked.

"Right now I'm too tired. Let me meditate, all of you. Please, leave."

Nadine hugged him as he readied himself. He smiled at her.

Feslen heard his friends argue about fate and the up coming mission.

That night no worries and dark dreams invaded Feslen for the first time in his young life.

34

SHOWING SIGNS 前兆

Two days after the meeting with the People's Council and the whole event with the gypsy's Prediction Cards passed. The companions agreed to get ready to rescue Mei Xue, find Duxan's cure in the North in as much secrecy as they could. Since every person, town, city, and official of Chiendong celebrated that day, few guards would be on duty. Ka-Wei suggested they moved during the Winter's Celebration Festival, so they could leave under more cover. The fewer people who spotted the companions leave, the better. They agreed to return to normal routines, so no one would become suspicious. Soon after they rested well, Duxan and Feslen and Li-Pei went to Beizung to shop for their sisters.

Duxan struggled along the way, and they were forced to pause every thirty blocks. Feslen was alarmed and asked, "Are you all right, Big brother?"

"Yes. I think Elhong's spell has hit," Duxan replied, hs cheeks puffed in a deep breath. He wiped some sweat off his brow.

Li-Pei looked up at her brother with concern in big eyes. Feslen then nodded and said, "Good, now you know how I felt all these years."

The statement hit Duxan harder than the *Ninkatta*'s attack on him. I do know how he feels, He thought. Then he said so both siblings could hear over the din of the crowd of people, "Hey Feslen."

Feslen paused in his musing, and looked at his brother. It was rare for Duxan to address him by his name. His smile broadened.

"I need to say this, but you already know," Duxan continued with a smile. "I am proud of what you've accomplished. Who you are. You are more than any one of us could ever be."

Feslen felt tears in his eyes and he reached out to hug his brother. He said, "We will cure your illness when we reach the North, Big Brother."

We will, I promise, Feslen thought, clenching his hands. Just like how we will avenge Tang Swuai and return Mei Xue to safety!

Duxan smiled and patted his brother's shoulders. The siblings walked on in comfort and lost in their own thoughts. Feslen came along because he needed to tie up loose ends with Master Chai's empire. He didn't want to leave it unmanned and unprotected.

"I hope Lioin doesn't think this is an eating outing," Duxan began. "Or you, for that matter, little brother. We need to conserve as much as possible."

"What, you think I eat like a bear? I've seen you, Ka-Wei, and Ai-Yen eat more than a family's share in one day."

The siblings laughed.

"You know, I wonder why the Sorceress wants Ka-Wei at all, and why she's baiting him with his Sword," Duxan said.

"Who knows what women want, let alone the Sorceress? Their ways are far more mysterious than magi."

"Careful, little brother. We have a little woman here…"

"Who says I'm like the rest of them anyway? I do hope you two reconsider going. I don't want to lose my two most fun brothers!" Li-Pei said.

Duxan ruffled her hair and she squealed with delight.

"We will return, I promise, Li-Pei. Besides, I can bring some interesting things home."

"All right, no lizard's gut or newt eye. I flipped through your fancy books before, big brother," Li-Pei said, with a tongue out.

Feslen hid his grin.

"Would you like something else? They say it brings great beauty," Duxan said.

"Just what are you saying, Duxan?"

"Oh nothing…" Duxan began when a young woman rushed up to them in a panic.

Duxan eyed the young lady and thought her around sixteen when she blurted. "Oh, I need your help please!" He thought her rather ugly.

Feslen shared the same feeling. The young woman's pocked face supported his notion.

"What is it?" Feslen asked.

"My sister…got hurt. New Priests can't do a thing!" The teary-eyed woman said.

"And…how could I or we be of service?" Duxan asked.

"I heard of the miracles of you. You are the Raster, aren't you?"

She gave the brothers a look over.

"'The Raster'? I fail to see what you mean. Yes, I am a Raster, but I am not the…" Duxan responded.

"Pleasse come," she pleaded, and tried to drag Duxan.

Feslen implored his brother, and Duxan nodded.

"All right, we're coming," Duxan said and followed her. She walked in an awful hurry. Feslen and Li-Pei hurried to keep up.

Feslen knew his brother's intrigued look and sighed. Duxan wanted to help people more than Feslen liked solving mysteries. In general, Feslen had little patience for such things.

This happened to be one of those things.

"Listen young lady, I'm sorry about your sister, but there is nothing we could do. I am not sure what you refer to when you say 'miracles' when it comes to our family…I would love to elaborate over a cup a tea," Feslen said.

"You can't be the One. He who heals!"

She paused after hearing Feslen laugh. Duxan gave his brother an appalled look.

"You have me confused with someone else," Feslen returned after he remembered to breathe. "Princess Nai-Hua of Nu healed the horse and boy. I was merely in the action. It's _her_ you want, not I." How did she know of this accident? He wondered. Then, he recalled seeing her in the crowd after the Princess healed him from his exhaustion!.

The young girl said, "You have the Mark of Chu Jung!"

"Mark of Chu Jung, why does everyone keep saying this?" Feslen asked and exchanged wide-eyed looks with his siblings. She's the second one who mentioned that I have these 'Marks', Feslen thought. How would she know? Unless, she happened to a magician also…

She said blithely, "It's only in your Souls do I see it. Ask the Princess about it. Please, you must help me."

Feslen cocked his eyes, and ignored Li-Pei's tug. Feslen saw the young girl for whom she really was. Feslen said in a whisper to Duxan, "Check out the energy lines on this girl. What a simple illusion, and I fell for it!" But, he forgot, his brother was not as intuitive about the auras as he was.

This is a test, Feslen thought in eager anticipation.

The young boy shifted a look at his preoccupied older brother and his eyes narrowed at a sudden thought.

"What?" Duxan asked, preoccupied. The elder brother sensed a cloaked figure's presence with the young woman's spirit. He saw her reporting to a black-cloaked man and almost tripped on himself.

She tapped her feet.

"Duxan are you ill?"

"No. I'm fine. Please continue. What is your name, young lady?"

"Call me Celeste. There. You see my sister? Here we are."

Back at the Poor Quarters, Feslen watched the area for potential ambushes. Seeing no power lines, he decided to enter with his brother and sister.

Duxan, a Prophecy Child? Feslen thought and shook his head. His older brother has never shown any such signs of Flair before…why now?

Back in the home the faithful parents and friends watched in silence. Her younger sister had two broken legs and a crushed skull.

"I know of your story," Celeste said with a nod to Feslen. "I wanted your help. Please…see what you can do."

"There is little I could do, save what I learned from Master Chai. I have neither the skill, nor strength. It isn't healing…but…. will you be willing to try?" Feslen said, covering Li-Pei's eyes.

The sister nodded.

Feslen sighed and felt for broken bone and muscles. He talked with Celeste's younger sister just to keep her distracted. What was he doing? He was no Mender! Feslen thought, but kept at the healing skills he had learned as part of the Twelve Steps. Master Chai had intended to teach him the next ten Steps; the Thirteenth was to heal wounds. Instead, Feslen studied a book on anatomy. After he asked her, which places hurt and did not, recording it in his mind. Feslen asked Celeste and Li-Pei to fetch some local herbs, that he saw and remembered the New Priest physicians try and apply to himself during the times of his own sickness.

Duxan did not know why the girl even brought them. She demanded for his help, yet, he knew nothing. Nor, did Duxan feel might, like Feslen. Impressed by his brother's extensive knowledge of the Martial Arts, Duxan determined to learn some from Ka-Wei on their journey.

The two girls returned with the items Feslen requested.

Perhaps the girl spoke the truth. He had seen the future…. Duxan did as told, mashed the sweet smelling, and sour smelling herbs together. Feslen, with the wounded sister's permission, spread the mushy concoction. The girl bit back her scream. "You are very brave," Feslen praised.

"The New Priests tried all sorts, and chants too," muttered a family member.

Celeste gave them a warning glance.

Duxan's gaze swept the room. He saw a silver dagger next to a silver bell. The items triggered his memory. He asked Celeste the usage of the dull silver bell that on the wall. She explained it to him in whispering tones. She said, "That's Dhai-Hahn's Silver Bell, or a representation of it, at least."

"Where would a young, poor girl like you get a bell like this from?" Duxan wanted to know, but she did not reply. Rare religious symbols like the Silver Bell of Dhai-Hahn were hard to obtain. This Silver Bell generated an odd vibration from it, which Duxan somehow picked up on.

It felt right and harmonic to the older Raster. He did not understand it now, but later, when he dwelled upon his formal lessons on religion did he remember why he felt the vibration. Through the vibrations, Duxan realized this to be one of the four genuine Dhai-Hahn bells!

Only mages, truly learned monks and rich powerful royal people can obtain such pieces of history. Like his often-suspicious brother, Duxan began to suspect Celeste and her motives, and who she really was.

Feslen ignored the explanations from Celeste as she told Duxan what to do.

Ruined energy lines on the broken girl swelled against Feslen. He closed his eyes and fell into deeper meditation. He reached for the lines and stroked as if he petted a puppy. He knew this should not be happening he had no prior training or magical knowledge of these things. Feslen pushed those thoughts away; and saved them for his nightmares. His sweat increased as his energy increased.

"Duxan…" Li-Pei warned. However, it was not necessary; the older brother swooped in to help. Feslen trembled with effort. He fought hard to contain his emotions when the young girl's pains assaulted him. Feslen knew he pushed his own limits too far, he felt what little energy he had left going.

Feslen was about to give up when he felt a rush of love and new form of energy. Duxan! He wanted to say. On pure instinct, Feslen pushed away Duxan. But, because his energy drained quicker than he anticipated; Feslen knew he could not do this without help, so he relented and accepted Duxan's energies. The energy lines snapped like a rope. Beads of sweat dripped from the brothers when they repaired her.

Feslen cried in triumph as he released his final energies into the young woman. He collapsed with the effort, panting and sweating. He opened his eyes and saw his older brother held a Dhai-Hahn silver Release Bell. The wounds on the sister still existed. Why didn't it work? He began to ask her how she was, but he felt a bell ring. He looked around for the noise. The Release Bell never physically rang!

Feslen's mind dulled, exhausted.

Duxan rang the bell with his emotional spirit. The bell rang like a monastery gong. Its ringing helped center Duxan. His heart poured out to the younger sister. Jumbled emotions assaulted Duxan when he helped Feslen correct the energy patterns in the young woman. He separated the emotions and helped the wounded victim separate them too. Through the emotions, he spotted a transparent smaller frightened version of the girl. He offered a guiding hand and she took it.

The girl awakened with a gleeful cry and slid down from the bed, where everyone rushed to hug and congratulate the stunned Duxan. She prostrated herself before Duxan, who did not understand what happened.

He turned to Feslen for comfort, paused in shock when he saw the scowl.

"I knew you were the Ones," Celeste said, and departed before they could question her.

That night, the Raster brothers dined with the Ho Family. The sister, Lan-Shue became Duxan's very first disciple. She called him "My Lord" during the meal and thereafter. Feslen did not talk much with Duxan the next few days, as he retreated into his Cave of Silence.

Feslen felt the new disciple intriguing and frustrating. Why does his brother get all the good things? Yet, he did not know Duxan shared the same thought, he sought Jungoo for companionship.

During the meditation, Feslen did not open his eyes or even move for one day. After he completed the meditations, he contacted Hei Weung Tong, Master Chai's former apprentice and the Eastern Martial Arts master for help. The two of them came up with a suitable overseer of Master Chai's empire while Feslen 'went on temporary leave'. They contacted Kuan Hu, who agreed to help Feslen.

To deal with stress and uncertainty, Duxan began to research the past. His spirit heavy, burdened, so he met up with Jungoo. Together they walked an aimless walk. Walking along farmland in the vast countryside and happened to pause in front of a little used monastery dedicated to the Old Ways. The dilapidated monastery was also rustic at the same time. He felt at home. He gave his friend a look, but Jungoo did not question his motives and he entered the place. He took off his silk shoes and knelt in between the lion and falcon statues and for some reason, felt like praying three times to the east.

Duxan instructed Jungoo to do as he did. She did so without comment and followed him in. Inside the abandoned monastery a worn bronze statue of Dhai-Hahn, the first Spiritually Harmonized Man beckoned him. The statue settled imbalanced to the side because its wooden platform cracked. Duxan recalled early youth when his family used to go to the Old Temples and monasteries everyday. Memories Flooded Duxan when he looked at the Dhai-Hahn statue. After completing a wooden structure, light washed his senses. He reacted as if rigormortis set even though he heard Jungoo's concerned calls…

A robust man in simple trousers walked up to him. "You wish to seek, do you not, child?" He spoke in a rather odd, broken Chiendonese. His piercing amber eyes arrested Duxan for a moment.

Uncertainty and skepticism arose in Duxan. They stood in a small beatific courtyard with rows of Forever Blossoms planted all around. This place reminded the older Raster brother of Master Chai's. "When I first sought to know, I left on a journey, without leaving, that is the key, young child."

"But, how will we know if we found it, lord?" Duxan asked.

The old man chuckled.

"You have to be calm in center and outside to find it, my child. I see your path is similar to mine."

Duxan called out. "*Wait!*" However, the old man and his courtyard garden faded.

Jungoo shook him and caressed her hand over his face. He sighed and blinked. "What happened?"

"You were out," Jungoo replied.

Duxan genuflected before this statue out of impulse, love spewed forth from the statue. A robust glow surrounded the statue, almost as if the Spiritual Man himself was there. Duxan thought about the encounter and dismissed it. He prayed anyway, thinking that was the correct thing to do and even Jungoo Jeizen joined him.

"How could I have missed this place?" Duxan asked in a wistful and peaceful tone.

"It's easy to miss a gentle place as this; I have a place like this at home too. I only discovered it when a few months past, exploring. Yet, I know my homeland better than any Explorer," Jungoo said with a smile.

The night came and neither needed to eat. They sat in the monastery chatting and looking on occasion at the stars.

Duxan wanted to say what was bothering him, but he held back.

"Do you wish to talk about what happened?" Jungoo asked. They sat apart one another, but near each other. Duxan found this exotic woman from the North both compelling and somewhat frightening. He confided with her things he never could with anyone else.

"What did I see, Jungoo?" Duxan asked, eating an apple.

She opened up the traveling pack of picnic she brought along for the day.

"I don't know. I tried to find magic in you when you first came to me," she confessed. "I apologize if I invaded your true self without your permission."

She paused and shrugged. "As it is I found nothing."

"Am I like my brother?" Duxan asked and roasted a pepper-filled chicken on the campfire they built.

"It is possible. You are his older brother, after all. What I do know of magic is that sometimes it is passed through lineage."

Duxan poked the chicken.

Jungoo brewed some tea. They sipped in silence.

Later that day, while sipping tea at a tiny local restaurant in Beizung, the brothers reconvened and talked about what happened. "So you're beginning to experience the Ancient Truth," Feslen concluded. The paper dolls, representing different spirits for the winter months that hung on the roof caught Feslen's attention. He also paid attention to the number of lit incense candles, and small god statues at the front entrances of business and people's homes all round town.

"Can't be. I'm not magical, like you. I've never shown any signs!" Duxan said.

"True, except magic is often given through Blood Relations. Some magic-users grow late. So, maybe you're showing signs now. Perhaps your powers were dormant? Remember what the Forest Protectorate said?" Feslen asked and then said, "Not to mention Jungoo gave you a reading too right?"

"Yes, she did, and yes I remember the Forest Protectorate's words," Duxan said and then added, "Look, I don't ever want magic. I don't want to be a magician or a magic-using type, if I can help it. I won't steal your dreams from you."

"My brother, it's all right. I like the fact that you are beginning to show signs, I've always felt alone, even though you are the closest person to me," Feslen said with a smile.

Duxan gave him a warmer smile and said, "Looks like we're both learning something, you're growing up. I knew you'd amount to something someday."

Feslen said, "I'd wanted to grow up forever. I hope I do amount to something, everyone keeps saying so. Going on Ka-Wei's mission will help prove something to me."

Duxan nodded and murmured, "Hopefully, Mother will see it that way."

"She'd have to," Feslen said, draping his arm about his brother. "She can't stop karma. Plus, your health now is in question."

Duxan nodded and said nothing more. The siblings finished eating their meal and stared at their surroundings, taking in the moment of everyday life.

In another part of Beizung's territory during that same day, Ka-Wei lowered his sword, ending a practice session with his old teacher. "I wish I could go with you, Ka-Wei," Captain Scallion remarked to the young Prince.

"I know," Ka-Wei, answered, forcing his glance away from his Uncle's fluttering banner.

"You know you have been granted Leave…that in itself is a rarity. Something your own Father would never have done."

Ka-Wei nodded, memories overwhelming him as he looked at the old man. Ka-Wei had returned to the castle one more time, despite the King's forceful ban on him. No one thought or dared to remove him or place him behind bars. He wanted to say farewell to his old mentor, Captain Garland Scallion. He was eager and not sorry to leave.

He knew if he returned successful, situations with the King's New Priests would change. Because Ka-Wei was an outlaw, by law and tradition, none should favor him.

"Take care of yourself, Captain. We had each other's backs to watch out for when we walked together…" Ka-Wei sighed.

"I lived through the Mengolis Raids, Ka-Wei," the older man smiled. It was the old man's way of telling Ka-Wei not to worry about him so much. The Prince chuckled. Garland's seemed more like a surrogate father than a mentor to him all these years.

"Keep an eye on Uncle, will you?" Ka-Wei continued. He sheathed Uncle's sword. He wished he had his Xsi-Arak back. The obvious shame and disgusted glances from former comrades, butlers and servants, made Ka-Wei's face burn. No one, not even old friends was supposed to be around him in his Loss of Honor Time. Not even traditions kept the two from being friends.

"When you come back, you will be a greater hero you already were, my boy," Garland joked.

Ka-Wei did not laugh, the grim façade of this new warrior did not settle well between the two old friends.

Garland reached first to shake hands and they shook. "Keep well, Captain," Ka-Wei said and retracted his hand and mounted.

As he left, the Prince heard, a flag unfurled. He turned to look and saw Garland saluting him as the Black Rock Turtle banner flew in the rippling wind. Saluting quickly, Ka-Wei cantered his horse out under the iron gates. He heard one of his loyal Blue Soldiers shouted, "To the Justice and Glory of our Prince!"

Thousands of voices trumpeted the hail and Ka-Wei choked back a smile. Dark clouds gathered and icy rain fell to Ka-Wei's discontent.

35

WINTER'S CELEBRATION
冬季的慶典

The last weekend of the month of Lo signified the beginning of Winter's Celebration Festival. "Happy winter, brother," Li-Pei said, leaping at Feslen with a hug. After a second of play, she handed him a traditional winter puppet.

The puppet made by Li-Pei had intimate details of the Wind God.

"This is very good, you have creative Art magic within you, no doubt," Feslen said and hugged her. She beamed. It was Chiendonese tradition to exchange gifts at many of the major holidays. He saw her big bright eyes, and expectant face when she handed him his gift. His heart sank for but a moment. She knows I'm not into this stuff, and thank goodness, she has a forigivng heart, Feslen thought. "I…" he began, trying to muster up some true regret in his voice.

Her face went from an instant disappointment to her usual bright smile again and she bubbled, "Not a problem, Big Brother! You won't forget my birthday next time!" Too bad he forgot to give Li-Pei a Winter's gift, and her last birthday too. He suppressed a sigh. He ruffled her hair and tickled her until she squealed. He reached out and hugged her, and she stiffened with surprise. Though, she relaxed soon and embraced him for a long time. He felt her love and warmth and tickled her, with a fond smile on his face.

If I ever left home, this one I would miss, Feslen thought, trying hard to hide his sudden sadness. He thought and looked above to pray to whatever god that may be listening, If you are real, please, protect this little one when I no longer can.

She laughed until her face became beat red. She grinned at him and stuck out her tongue as she watched him put on his best formal shirt.

He tried on his best three-piece vest. The rest of his family dashed about, giving each other gifts and handing neighbors folded money envelopes.

Feslen sat in front of the family wagon for the first time. His adoptive parents treated him like a celebrity that he was not. Frustrated and grumpy, Feslen slumped; the rough wagon ride reflected his mood. Security made travel to center of town near impossible: Emperor's Red Guard and Blue Soldiers swarmed. Ai-Yen ribbed Feslen for making them late to his own ceremony. Feslen grinned.

"Don't muss up your garment, little bro," Duxan joked. Feslen grunted and shrugged, uncomfortable. He felt like an oversized jewel on a lady's neck.

When did he get all this nonsensical attention? Feslen thought with a sigh.

Noisemakers went off, the whooping sound of a pelican and angry raccoon roared the air.

"Don't forget, the Emperor doesn't make appearances like this often," Father Wong reminded Feslen before he snaked his way through the crowd. Feslen found some solitude before the big moment. Feslen hid behind in a thick area. People gave Nadine a respectful silent space. Feslen did not recognize the New Priest dressed in brown. A bad feeling overcame Feslen as he studied the New Priest.

Feslen turned away, spotting the female Magi, not in her official robes. The Blue Yellow Robe stood next to her.

Feslen's eyes widened and spotted a pair of gray-robed magi from the Rotating Isle of Mystic and Magic. To his utter surprise, he found no energy aura, though he felt the power pulsing.

Hunger for magic spread through like a warm drink. Startled, Feslen forced himself to look away from the Rotating Isle magi.

He focused on the decorations instead, Mei-Whuay would be proud. Incense candles placed throughout the crowd. The candles gave off different colors. Sacrificial bowls placed before five-foot incense candles. Small statues of lions and the dragon facing east and west adorned the ceremonial platform. The lion statues meant protection from evil spirits. The dragon faced west favored the people with luck and strength. The statues sat on either side of two gaudy makeshift thrones. The Emperor's throne was naturally bigger than the King's. Colors of silver black of the Emperor meshed with the light blue of the King.

In the past a crowd this size would create vertigo for Feslen, today it did not. He knew why: his improved health helped.

A loud bang unnerved some.

A familiar young woman stood next to the young boy, trying to soothe tears. Mei-Whuay! Feslen wanted to shout. A servant's ring glistened on her thin fingers and it belonged to a young man from the Elhong School. Feslen felt surprising anger and forced himself to look at other things. He saw her unhappiness. So, that's her new job, Feslen thought. Now he knew why his parents and family said nothing to him and Duxan about Mei-Whuay's new employment. On reflection, Feslen realized his family's financial situation and political situation was far worse than his original understanding.

Smells of rice cakes, heavy red bean and fermented banana leaf meat patties weaved together. Everyone laughed and mingled together, even the rich with the poor.

Even the dour King's men smiled.

Feslen let their happiness melt into him. "I'm making people happy…," he murmured.

A loud ringing pain entered Feslen's head and he grit his teeth. A hush settled upon the crowd and some of it parted. People ran away from the Sorceress just entering town square. Some armed Blue Soldiers tried to arrest the Sorceress. She scorned a laugh. They backed off, but the archers trained their bows on her.

Ka-Wei was not present, and neither was Sae-Jyung.

Fireworks shot in the air.

The drummers drummed.

Dancers in long silk gowns and revealing dresses came out from the south.

The audience reveled in their skills.

Two Martial Artists from the Elhong Sung School dazzled the crowd. Feslen clenched his fists; having Master Chai's rivals performing remained an open insult.

The national song played and people sang.

Flower girls came from the east and dragon dancers came from the west. The people let a rowdy cheer. Feslen shook his head at the display. He waited for a signal from the Blue Soldiers.

Trumpeting moved to a crescendo and the two stopped talking. The loyal crowd of Blue Soldiers clamped their feet and stamped their weapons to the ground.

Crossbows twanged harmless smoke bombs in the air as the King arrived in his slow and pompous way.

The King sat down on the makeshift throne. Some laughed in good nature, as the King almost sat down on the Emperor's throne. The lone Emperor's bodyguard chided the King. The King moved towards his ceremonial weapon. In normal circumstance, the Prince would have supplanted the Emperor's WuSha as the stage bodyguard. Ka-Wei, nowhere in sight, the King had no choice but to back down.

Feslen shook his head and wondered if Ka-Wei's parents would have backed down. He doubted it.

Firecrackers exploded, creating quite a spectacle. The Emperor's magicians trooped in, showing off their own majesty. Their explosive display mingled with the fireworks, creating *oohs* and *aahs*. Feslen choked at the waste of magic.

A firecracker exploded into a phoenix. It morphed into a man trying to tame the phoenix. Onlookers laughed and clapped. The magicians below guided the magical show like puppeteers. The crowd roared as the man caught the phoenix and humbled it. He mounted the phoenix and flew off in the west, through a ring of fire.

Feslen growled in disgust.

He caught Nadine's look of disgust and smiled. Emperor's magicians shouted, "Hail the Lord of Ages!" They went through twenty of the man's given and self-promoted titles before the drums stopped.

The people repeated each title. A loud cheer erupted to a loosened flock of orange-feathered birds.

They waited a long time for the Emperor. A slight delay caused some to mutter. The young Raster figured it was for show's sake and sipped water.

The crowd reacted to the Emperor's huge banner, followed by his personal army.

Finally, Emperor strode in, with a peculiar aide to his side. "All hail the mighty Hand to the Goddess, Emperor Buhkahta Tsai!" The Emperor's aide sneered.

The Emperor waved his big hands. He stepped up the platform with deliberate slowness.

Though Feslen never met the Emperor, there was deception in the air. Feslen focused on the two men in royal clothes.

Feslen ignored the guard's prostration and made his way through the crowd.

The Emperor began his long, boring and pompous speech. The people cheered with great enthusiasm. A certain deception of the Emperor alerted Feslen. The man's body language and lack of aura told him as much.

Prince Ka-Wei and Princess Nadine taught Feslen a few things about how to prepare for royalty. The Emperor and King wore their Heritage Symbols on their left pinky, left hand. Also, they should wear their ceremonial swords on their right hip, but this one had a real dagger.

The Emperor gazed at him and called him, Feslen gasped, gripped his chest in pain. The man's powers exploded. He realized this man was not the Emperor, but Hu-orh Gai, the Grand Mage.

Why the deception?

"You're good to go, little bro…"

Pride in his older brother's voice helped him continue with straight purpose. He emulated Ka-Wei with a traditional waist bow to the King, and ignored the Emperor.

Feslen hid his emotions and turned to face the maddened crowd. He had never seen them with this much fervor. Odd buzzing intensity made him drunk with unease. He sucked in his breath for the man's aura danced. The young boy forgot his words.

"All I wanted to say was…. I am grateful for the opportunity to do some good with the presence of the Goddess in my heart…" Feslen began. The crowd hushed.

Feslen felt like grinning, but did not. He felt the glares of the royalty; he did not need to turn to see if he was making them angry. He did so anyway.

"I am of the people, but I am of myself. I just happened to be in the right place, at the right time. I'm sure anyone else would have saved Prince Ka-Wei if they were in my place," Feslen said, half-turned to face the royalty and the crowd. He noticed one of Prince Ka-Wei's men hidden in the crowd. He signaled Feslen with a Red Warrior's tiny doll. He nodded to himself and signaled his brother by placing his hand on his chest once and twice.

A New Priest physician got up a bit and walked over, asking Feslen if he was all right. Feslen nodded yes.

Duxan caught Feslen gestures and understood. Prince Ka-Wei was ready to go on his mission!

"Remember that, everyone. You can act on your own as I did," He finished and walked away. A New Priest at the end of the platform cleared his throat as Feslen walked off. He refused the gifts given to him by the New Priests and the Emperor. He ignored them, felt empowered.

Feslen never walked away so fast, his feet seemed alive.

The celebration went on well into the night and even into the next day, most forgot Feslen. Father and Duxan spent the evening talking. Feslen and Duxan slipped out unnoticed to return to Ka-Wei's fortress.

It took a few hours, but the trio finally made it to Ka-Wei's hidden fortress. It was nothing more than a castle with a run-down façade.

Ka-Wei greeted his friends after the Blue Soldier ushered them in. Feslen and Duxan were amazed to find a small number of Blue Soldiers still milling about in this deceptive castle. About two to three hundred men still walked about under Ka-Wei's parents' banner: the stork.

Despite sitting in a thick granite one-tower castle, Feslen talked in a low voice, "I'm glad you taught me those things, Ka-Wei. I am sure the man was not the Emperor himself, but Hu-orh Gai, his mage."

"I'm glad it helped too, Feslen, but it wasn't meant as seeing lies. Are you certain the mage was in his place?"

Feslen affirmed with a nod, he tried to drink some water, but his throat was too dry. His entire body had dried from his encounter with the mage's powers. "He's dangerous. I'm surprised the Emperor and Hu-orh Gai is allowed to operate beyond the Great School's watchful eyes. But, why would he want to deceive the public…?"

Kalman and Duxan said nothing, but the Prince murmured, "Perhaps they were after you, Feslen."

"Me?" Feslen laughed, but his laughter ended up in a dry choke.

Kalman replied, "Think about all the events leading up to this: The Forest Protector's calling us, your awesome display at the Choicings, and the fights with Elhong Wien…well, for certain the Forest Protectors knew about you through me. If I thought you were One…then…"

Feslen conceded the point.

Duxan murmured, "We should be careful. I'm glad winter's arriving, perhaps that can throw off your pursuers, Fes."

"Let's hope."

Before the group made further plans, one of Kalman's men interrupted them with an urgent message. The Elhong School and the Sorceress kidnapped Mei-Whuay. Feslen vowed to bring her home.

36

SHRIEK OF THE DAMNED
被打入地獄的人的尖叫聲

Traveling awed Feslen. The young boy wondered if his companions felt the same way as he stole a glance at them. They all rode on horses. Kalman the Red rode on his black stallion in front, Nadine on her white mare behind him.

Kalman's small band consisted of: Feslen and Duxan, Nadine, Sae-Jyung, Lioin, Jungoo, and Kil-Gong Fu, the Prince' best archer. Sae-Jyung came to the discomfort of the Prince and Duxan.

No sooner did the group leave, they battled giant wolf spiders. After the encounter of their skirmish with the wolf spiders, Feslen increased his education whenever possible. Even when they rode on for hours and days, the young boy gained valuable insight from both Kalman and Nadine.

The companions already traveled for several weeks into the North.

"Reaching the Great Barrier, Milord," Kil Gong Fu, the Prince's Archer announced. The Great Barrier was one of the first huge engineering marvels created by Chiendonese people. The first King began the monolithic two thousand miles long, and hundred fifty foot high barrier of stone and brick two thousand years ago to protect his people from the Mengalois nomads and other none-Chiendonese invaders. The barrier stretched from the mountainous regions known as Three Mountains Gorge to half of the Mengalois' desert, Obagi. The first King never lived long enough to see his project completed, since the Seventh Dynastic king did.

"So, when you go close to an opponent as he tries to pummel you..." Feslen said.

"You feel for the wind of the attack well before he even gets the advantage of being close," Nadine nodded. "You also have to see the person's stance in order to judge whether you will be able to dodge him, or use his momentum."

"But why on Hahn-Hah would one want an enemy to get near you?" Feslen asked.

"In order to not allow him to use their weapons," Kalman stated. "With Martial Arts, you should know, is the ability to use your body as a weapon."

"What happened back there, Nadine? What did you use on the wolves?"

Nadine smiled; she looked like recalling a memory long lost. "A trick my people call 'swaying the baying'. We use the natural powers to guide us, much like magicians use the Energy Lines of Life to manipulate their magic. Each creature is connected to another except for those living dead...even those wolf spiders were once part of the Sun Goddess' creation. I tried to get in touch with their inner peaceful selves, if you will."

Feslen nodded. Kalman unsheathed his sword and showed Feslen the most basic moves. The young boy watched in awe. Lioin's gasp arrested Feslen's attention to the forty-foot tall fortifications called the Great Barrier.

He whistled. The thirty-foot thick barrier covered the entire two hundred mile expanse of Pai Tsung's Ridge. The entire part of this wall resembled an abandoned fortress of one of the Elder Dynasties. Much of the protective barrier had lost the meaning of protection. Even from far away, Feslen saw faded murals and small chambers that once might have held statues of prayer.

Kalman allowed the group a pause at the wall.

For some reason, the Prince had a hard time remembering. Jungoo took the less arduous path through Neutral territories to Chiendong.

"Why does this look so different?" Kalman mumbled.

The brothers and the rest of the group looked at the Prince. "Can't remember the way, huh?" Duxan grinned.

"Someone changed it."

"I can feel…an oddity of sorts on the other side," Nadine reported.

"Bad energy," Jungoo murmured.

Kalman nodded and sat down, defeated. "Any ideas? Horses cannot stay on the Ridge too long, unless they have thick hooves."

No one laughed at Kalman's attempted humor.

"How about you, Jungoo?" Duxan asked.

"I came in a different path: the Neutral Territories, you aren't exactly a welcomed sight there, Prince."

Duxan calculated the time it must have taken Jungoo and Kalman taken to get to Chiendong from their different paths. He shook his head and gave a look at Feslen.

Feslen nodded and understood his brother's look of amazement. For the gypsy, it would have taken her seven extra days in her two month journey to reach Chiendong's capital, Beizung from her homeland. Ka-Wei's journey through the mountains took shorter time. When Jungoo traveled, she journeyed through the territories of the Great Waste, the Dry Plains, and even some of the Tundra Plateau, and the Mengalois desert as well, assuming, she lived in the Desolate Lands. Feslen now understood why Ka-Wei chose the mountainous route.

Kalman nodded in agreement. "Besides, we're running out of time. Going through Neutral Territories will take up to six weeks. This Pai-Tung Ridge is the quickest I can think of."

Feslen gave him an odd look and studied the Great Barrier.

"Can you use your magic to transport us, Sae-Jyung?" Feslen asked, eyes lighting up.

Sae-Jyung shook his head. "You're talking more Gifted and *official* magicians, my friend. Even they would have trouble transporting all of us, including the horses."

"There's a strong energetic pulse," Nadine added.

Feslen finished, "A magician's trap?"

"Possibly," Nadine nodded.

"By the way, just to let you all know,"…Feslen said, after a long silence. He leaned against Nadine's soft shoulders, her long hair falling over him. Her aromas intoxicated him.

"Yes, Feslen?" Kalman asked.

"When we reach the Gem Stone Mountains, be prepared to use intense magic," Feslen said. "We'll need to work together to get out of the reputed traps the Shinjoudou set up."

Kalman nodded.

"Is there a way in?" Sae-Jyung asked.

"Yes," Feslen said with a nod. "But, I don't know what it is. I left the book at home."

The group sat somewhat in dejection waiting for a solution. Only Lioin searched the walls with continued determination. "Hey, thief boy!" Sae-Jyung called out. "Give it up. If our Prince here couldn't find the exit, since he's been through it…how can you?"

"Stop it, Sae-Jyung," Feslen growled.

"A good wall always has a good door," Lioin replied without showing any anger.

"How is it that you don't remember again?" Duxan asked Kalman. He had a grin on his face, but it collapsed in an instant upon seeing the distress on his friend's face.

Kalman gathered Feslen, Nadine and Duxan to him and sighed. He started to explain the disastrous chase for his lost Xsi-Arak. To the side, Jungoo taught Lioin her tricks. Sae-Jyung excused himself to be far away from the group to meditate alone. They heard his heavy voice chanting.

"What I didn't even tell the King was why we failed. I have never told anyone," the young Prince eyed his friends. "I hope it doesn't go off to anyone under my command."

They gave solemn promises. "When on the other side of the Barrier, we did a routine search." His eyes gave away some loss of reality. It looked like Kalman bottled these emotions. Feslen wanted to comfort him, but a look of madness stopped him.

"The small group, you know the Black Backed Turtles—my group—we hunted the Sorceress and *Ninkatta*. When we crossed over…"

"Beyond those walls, in the valley to the first city of the North, we encountered an unexpected opponent," Kalman refused any water. The hot wind perked up again. The young Prince continued speaking in a flat voice that made Feslen shudder.

"Her magic,"…Feslen murmured.

"It was daytime," Kalman continued, as if he did not hear his friend. "One of the hottest and brightest days of Winter I could remember. But, that's not the point."

"I should have seen it coming; I've sensed such oddities when I wielded *Kei-Trui-Nahohie*."

"What oddities?" Feslen asked and he gave his friends a trouble glance.

"Its screech was inhuman, it resembled…We…ran…the bodies,"…Ka-Wei sputtered for words.

"Like?" Feslen asked as his hair on his neck stood up.

"Like…however an undead would sound…."

"You mean a wolf trapped in a terrible hunter's trap?" Nadine finished.

"Y—yes. The worst part was, when they kill our friends and comrades…" Kalman hesitated.

"They become part of their own forces," Feslen said. He digested the news as Kalman continued.

"The worst part, I sensed a *human* behind it. More fearsome than the High Priest we encountered. He called out to us as we…*ran*…."

Kalman seemed more embarrassed fleeing a battle than seeing his men die. Feslen thought he needed to speak to Kalman later about that!

"What did he say?" Duxan prompted.

"Bring the One and all who cross shall live," Kalman murmured.

"So that's why you want me there," Feslen said and slumped back, as he gave it some thought.

"Yes, that and the magic the Sorceress and the dark mage tossed at us. I will never willingly sacrifice you to him; he doesn't know who the One is…"

Feslen smiled at his friend's bland smile. "Still, I'm sure the pain you feel when you see your own men desecrated was not easy," Duxan sighed, rubbing his face. He was angry at his friend for endangering Feslen, but he understood.

Kalman clamped up and looked away.

"Do you think they're in league with the Sorceress?" Feslen asked, trying to hide his disappointment in Kalman.

"No. This thing…had malevolence to him that I cannot begin to describe. He…" Kalman shook his head, tone flat. "My group was attacked though I remained unharmed."

"Three of us managed to escape. I don't remember how…"

"Perhaps he let you, to deliver the message," Sae-Jyung said, when he returned, covered in grime and thick moss.

Kalman gave a start, forgetting his presence. "Perhaps. But, if he demanded me to bring the One to him, why would he cloud my memory of the way there?"

"Hey everyone, I think I found it!" Lioin's voice cut through.

The group sprang to their feet and congratulated the young thief. It had taken the Lioin half the morning to find the door. "No wonder I didn't remember it," Kalman said with a half-grin. "It's covered in moss and human skeletons."

He did not need to point that out, since all of them could see it. Kil Ghong Fu gave a great cry. The others drew their weapons and relaxed. "What is it?" Kalman asked his soldier, trying to show enough concern without showing it.

"Nothing much," Sae-Jyung growled. "He probably just saw a dead comrade."

The others gave him scathing glances. "That's why my passion for you became lost," Nadine snipped.

Sae-Jyung laughed. "I think it was other reasons, Princess, but I won't respond. I have too much dignity for *that*."

Kalman ignored them and he saw his symbol, the black turtle etched in the shield…the Prince grieved. They followed Kalman, single file and Feslen went last.

Feslen regarded the Great Barrier and the dead soldier with some sadness. Feslen was not sure whether he felt sadder for the declining glory of his country, people, or wasted death of the soldiers. He saw a wisp of a figure *floating* with undisguised pride next to the unburied skeleton. Stunned, he stayed rooted until his friends and stomach called him.

"And I saw a ghost, or at least a symmetry of a figure," Feslen said with his mouth full. He talked in a low voice with Duxan and Nadine.

Nadine and Duxan exchanged concerned glances; they placed their hands on his shoulders. Feslen nodded and drew close to Nadine. She gave a startled look and allowed him to do so for a moment. He touched her hand and her eyes widened. He nodded, understanding; his encounter drained him of his body heat. She pulled back blushing. Nadine opened herself to him and allowed him to lean, and he did so, drawing jealous looks from all the men except from Lioin.

"Look, a Great Barrier stone!"

"What are you going to do, keep it?" Feslen asked, annoyed at Lioin for interrupting.

"Of course! A thief rarely gets a chance to go out of his territory! I'm going to make a scrapbook of this adventure."

Nadine laughed gaily as did the others.

Kalman announced lunch break was over. The group sobered in an instant and listened to Kalman as he conferred with them on his first encounter with the dead. "Running from them is bad enough, our discipline swept away…if Garland knew…"

"The grayness extended into blackness when the living dead approached. They called out our names….our former comrades looked and acted just like they did in life…." Kalman continued, tears forming.

The archer, grim approached his leader and whispered, "We're only thirty feet away from the incident, Lord."

"When we approached, there was a tingling sensation," Kalman said.

"It's like the touch of magic," Feslen said. "Right?"

"Indeed," Sae-Jyung replied returning to the group. "I feel it all right. Be ready everyone. *He* is near."

"He?"

"The Necromancer," Sae-Jyung said. "You cannot fight these things without magic. Stay back, warriors." Kalman nodded and fell back to protect Feslen. He felt a bit foolish, knowing his weapon was futile, but felt immeasurably better with it.

Sae-Jyung lifted his metal staff and chanted. Sae-Jyung held a strange symbol, which flared.

"What is that?" Feslen asked in curiosity.

"I'll tell you later, if we survive. Stay back of me, young one. You'll be needed, don't worry," The merchant mage grinned.

"Are you a priest or a mage, Sae-Jyung," Nadine teased.

"Everyone, now heed my advice: do not step out of the light of the symbol I hold with forth," Sae-Jyung replied.

"When did it grow so dark?" Lioin muttered. "It was midday a few moments ago." The companions dismounted once they got through. This time, all the horses refused to go on. Nadine patted hers and soothed hers until it calmed.

"Let them go their own path," Sae-Jyung ordered.

Kalman hesitated.

"Do you want your beloved pet to be turned into a walking dead? No? Do as I say. Besides, from here on, it becomes all too rocky." Sae-Jyung turned to him

Kalman saw the logic in the request, though he did not like how the mage ordered him around. He ordered the rest of the group to do the same. He patted his horse and set him free. The rest of the group followed, their horses galloped away.

Sae-Jyung began chanting.

"What was that noise?" Feslen murmured.

"Stop it, Feslen, I'm scared enough," Lioin muttered.

"Don't you smell rotten onion?" He continued. It was at this point Feslen wished for a weapon. Any weapon! Even Kalman bit his lips. Feslen's eyes widened at the Prince's nervousness.

Scraping metal and bone battered the air.

As if reading Feslen's thoughts and emotions, Kalman turned his way and muttered. "I will fight anything I know I can kill."

Feslen agreed.

"What was that?" Feslen asked,

Slithered creaky boots crunched rough gravel.

Sae-Jyung began another chant.

"Everybody stay sharp!" Kalman said with an intake of breath. Sweat prickled his courage. He felt his heart thump.

The archer screamed and the bolt flew out of his crossbow as he ran from the circle of light.

"Come back Kil Ghong Fu!" Kalman shouted in a husky voice. Get a grip, Kalman! His inner voice told him. They are beatable! You just haven't found a way yet!

"My Prince, why did you abandon me?" The inhuman voice spoke in tattered tones, bones clanking with crusty armor. The bolt the archer had shot off punctured a former Black Rock Turtle. It jerked unsteady, skin oozed off bones.

"Oh May the Good Goddess of the Greens protect us!" Jungoo cried out.

The dead soldier's hollow laughter echoed a sore throat.

More creaking noises affronted the group. Lioin's dagger went flying off into the darkness. The first dead soldier who addressed Kalman laughed.

"Hold!" Feslen commanded to Lioin. "Save your salvos."

"What can kill these things?" Feslen asked coming to stand with Sae-Jyung. The young merchant mage's forehead wrinkled with effort. The skeletal warriors stopped at a magical barrier and banged hard against it.

Sae-Jyung grunted.

"He's collapsing soon," Kalman said.

Jungoo raised her own metal symbol and hummed a prayer. Her metal symbol began to glow. The air around them grew hot and spiced. A jet of flame erupted from Jungoo's open mouth to engulf four soldiers. They sizzled and the metal melted off bone. "Path is open," Jungoo said.

"I hope nothing has happened to Kil Gong Fu," Kalman said.

The group continued with caution. Kalman picked up the crossbow on the way.

Feslen asked with a wrinkle of the nose, "Smoke powder?"

"You have quite a nose, my friend. You should work in our army's patrol…you'd be great at sniffing out troublesome smells!"

"Kalman, I would rather work as the castle's cook."

Kalman nodded and glanced at Duxan who unpacked their travel lantern.

Sae-Jyung warned. "Those things are returning, Prince. I hope whatever you have in mind works."

Jungoo and the others turned as the ones she had fire balled earlier began to stir from the dying flames. "Impossible!" She cried out. "That is how my people dealt with those things in the past."

"Tell me you ungodly creature of the night," Kalman said readying his crossbow. "Get ready with the already lit lamp." Duxan nodded.

"What and whom are you serving…why would he want the One?" Kalman hissed and leveled the crossbow. He hoped his months of training with the crossbow Master of Ghan had been enough.

A skeleton managed to knock the lantern from Duxan's hands. It fell without a spill on the ground.

Three undead soldiers remained from Jungoo's blast. "Open high, Dux!" Kalman ordered.

Duxan nodded and opened the hooded red lantern and switched the button to the furthest left possible. The older Raster held it as far away from him as he could and warned the others to move back as far as possible.

The flame enlarged to twice its original size when Duxan operated the lantern. The flames seemed to lick at Duxan's hands. Kalman let the bolt fly. The tarred bolt passed through the open flames of the red lantern. Ember sparks caught the tarred bolt. With no time to catch his handiwork, Kalman reloaded another bolt. Duxan struggled with the mechanism and started to ask his brother for help. At the same moment, Sae-Jyung's strength dwindled.

Sae-Jyung's protective spell failed, more of the skeletons burst from the ground.

Kalman released two more bolts near the spot where a skeleton knocked over their lantern. Its oil spoiled out and caught fire.

"Hit the ground!" Kalman ordered.

Feslen had the breath knocked from him when Duxan covered him with his own body. Feslen struggled to free himself and caught the sight as the sound rumbled the soil. The delayed explosion and subsequent raining of skeleton pieces inspired an elder Feslen in a spell called *Delayed Destructive Force*…. Right now, all he hoped he did not swallow any of the loose skeletal pieces.

Kalman hollered. "Run!"

Sae-Jyung shouted, "Sound advice, Prince, but to where?"

Aren't these things dead? Feslen thought.

The Prince leveled his crossbow and fired another blast at the ever-expanding flames. Kalman grinned in satisfaction at watching the skeletons melting away. "Move!" Kalman shouted, nauseated by the Necromancer's presence.

"Is that all you can throw at me, Prince of the Rising Sun?"

A magician around Sae-Jyung's height shrouded in darkness glided towards them.

"Seatan!" Sae-Jyung exclaimed. The Prince struggled to load the crossbow, but almost let go with nervous fingers. Only pride kept him from sagging.

"Give me the One," Seatan the Necromancer said.

The group broke pattern and ran. Even though he knew he had no chance in harming Seatan, Kalman intended to lower the enemy count. The skeletons reformed, despite the intense flames engulfing them. After Kalman shot multiple cross bolts to decimate the skeletons, Kalman and Sae-Jyung sprinted after their companions.

"Yes, run! You can't hide from the dead, Prince! Prince…bring me the One! I sense his presence within your group!" The Necromancer shouted.

Thank the Gods, Kalman thought, seeing the burning eyes of the undead. Thank the Gods that I am without Honor!

Kalman loaded his crossbow again and he felt Sae-Jyung's hand upon his shoulder,

"Don't waste anymore of those valuable bolts! How many left?"

"Not much, five more, I believe."

"Save them," Sae-Jyung said.

"But…should there be more…"…Kalman said as he ran.

"It's time to let the young One learn about himself," Sae-Jyung said through rough breathing. Kalman thought best not to mention that observation as they kept running.

Kalman informed them of the choice he made only Sae-Jyung objected. The young mage claimed to understand what the group faced.

"The situation seems bad here, but far worse to face the Necromancer," Lioin commented. The rest agreed with the young thief.

"We'll see," Sae-Jyung snorted. Feslen stumbled many times during their run. Nadine supported him.

They ran on.

"Kalman, be wary, there's a natural vine creature protecting,"…but Nadine trailed off.

The Prince stumbled over huge vines and fell with a terrific crash onto the smoother pavement. The loaded crossbow spun. "Someone catch it!" Nadine shrieked, jumping as a frog over the first vine in order to catch the crossbow.

She did not make it. A vine shot out to wrap around her legs. She slammed hard into the ground.

"Nadine!" Feslen shouted. Despite feeling weak, Feslen rushed to her aide.

Duxan cried out, "No, little brother!" Whether his brother meant the impending bolt impact to the ground, or the appearance of a new vine, Feslen did not know. He wanted to free Nadine.

Lioin bolted quicker than a bee and leapt fifteen feet up over some new vines. He dove headlong and back flipped to the crossbow. Lioin reached out. Feslen watched with awe. Duxan prayed. He did not see the soft green glow surround Lioin.

In one motion, Lioin grabbed the crossbow with one hand and hung onto a vine that shot out! Feslen shouted a warning even while Lioin slipped and wriggled through as easy greased pot stickers.

Lioin leveled the crossbow.

"No!" Kalman shouted. Nadine warned Feslen to duck as she squirmed her way through to stop Lioin.

"Are you crazy?" Feslen shouted and threw himself to the ground.

Lioin let a bolt fly. Kalman, with superhuman strength managed to free himself. However, seeing the cross bolt fly towards him, he dropped to the ground and found himself entangled once more.

The special coated bolt exploded and the vine creature roared. The thing splattered its victims and none of them could escape the foul goop. Feslen made disgusted sounds.

They did not have time to thank Lioin; he flipped the now thankfully empty crossbow into his own pack. They ran and avoided anything green and did not pause until they no longer heard the undead.

After three hours of hard running, Feslen collapsed, face blue and puffed, eyes blurred. Duxan picked him up—despite the protests—and carried him as far as Kalman wanted them to run. Duxan marveled his brother's lightweight despite his intense workouts with Master Chai. "Just don't bruise me," Feslen yelled.

The group stooped to rest when Kalman said so; Feslen leaned heavy against Nadine. Kalman announced they had arrived to Gemstone Mountain. The vine creature blocked their way back.

"At least *something* slows Seatan down," Lioin said.

37

THE NECROMANCER 大巫師

They soon arrived at the mountain's shadows and broke camp. They tried not to stare at the gem-like base.

The cold bitter winter winds tinged with heat.

The North Way Mountains semblance to a cadaver's skull, made them shiver.

During the night, Nadine cried out.

"Are you all right, Nadine?" Feslen whispered, stroking her golden tresses. For this entire trip, her hair had been deep brown with silver streaks.

"What is it?" Kalman asked.

"Maybe she misses her bed and nice things," Jungoo quipped. Kalman motioned for her to lighten up.

"It's…him…the man I was terrified of when I first met you, Sae-Jyung. Who is Seatan Jarrv?"

"Where?" Kalman whirled with his short sword out.

Nadine trembled.

"He…invaded my dreams. He invaded my sanctuary!" She shrieked, which sent shivers down Feslen. He squeezed her cold and clammy hands.

"Shhh, calm down my dearest," He whispered. She stopped trembling and gave him adoring doe eyes. Feslen felt hot and cold run through him and averted his eyes.

"Seatan corrupting presence destroys all things pure. All will bow before him," Sae-Jyung spoke as if possessed.

"Wake up, what are you talking about?" Feslen smacked Sae-Jyung after he left Nadine's side.

"Thanks," Sae-Jyung said to Feslen then he turned to Nadine and said, "I know how you feel, Nadine."

Sae-Jyung inhaled and admitted, "Seatan haunts me my entire life."

"How so?" Kalman asked, even though he did not want to. His nerves were already on edge, he gripped his sword consistently without ever returning it to its scabbard.

"Well, it's odd. Ever since my father died, and my mother disappeared,"...Sae-Jyung began, his eyes looked hollow. His gaunt face burned with a fever, as if a memory dwelled too deep and horrible to even speak.

"Sae-Jyung? It's ok…we're here to help, if we can," Nadine murmured and moved a step closer to him, holding out her hand.

"Seatan seemed to appear at the same time my parents disappeared. They vanished when I was sixteen," Sae-Jyung finished and hung his head.

The stunned companions said nothing for a while. They heard nothing but Sae-Jyung's sobs.

"I…am sorry, Sae-Jyung," Nadine said finally, and she put his arm about him. The merchant mage seemed to jerk at her touch though. He hissed, as if his skin burned. She shrunk away from him for a moment, her eyes wide in shock.

Sae-Jyung shook his head and cleared his throat, as if embarrassed and said, "It's all right. I just wish I knew more about this Seatan. All I know is, wherever I went trouble seemed to follow me. Then, Seatan would appear. He either caused the trouble or cleaned up the mess I may have caused, I don't know. Anyway, I shouldn't have brought it up…since it was of no use to you."

Nadine eyed him in sympathy and she murmured, "Seatan did seem to show up when we went to do things together. So inconvenient, he caused me to run away from you, Sae-Jyung. I needed....a more balanced person."

Sae-Jyung nodded and sighed, the kind of painful sigh that pierces a person's heart. He said, "I understand, Nadine. Will you tell Feslen why you're here?"

"I..." Nadine started, but before she could, Feslen interrupted her.

"Nadine...I...swear...I will do whatever I can to protect you from him, even if it means at the cost of my own life!" Feslen blurted. He did not understand emotions or jealousy when he looked upon Sae-Jyung and the Princess.

She seemed distracted; she turned to Feslen with a gentle smile. "I don't want you risking your life for me, or anyone ever. Seatan is my problem, if he manages to hunt you down...."

They embraced for a moment, her loving warmth spread delicious through him. On sudden insight, Feslen realized she treated him like a sibling. He pulled away, confused and dismayed.

She stared with her piercing silver eyes. She said, "As for what Sae-Jyung said, know that I am here for you. I work for you, as an ally. I will do whatever to save you, at the cost of my own life."

Feslen stalked away, but heard Nadine. The confusion grew, he knew he loved her without any doubt and he could tell she loved him...yet... He shook his head when Duxan caught up to him.

"Hey, you shouldn't be alone when walking out here, little brother."

"I need to be alone," Feslen snarled. "Besides, I know Lioin would watch over me, right?" Lioin chuckled.

"Are you sure you will be all right?" Duxan asked.

"Please, leave me alone, will you?" Feslen pleaded.

"Don't worry, Fes, she does love you, she needs to see through royalty crap!" The young thief blurted.

"Just don't make it worse, Gui-Pan!" Duxan pinched the Lioin's ear and dragged him.

"Don't call me that."

"Ashamed of your past?"

"Not at all, just that…my past is as troublesome as being thrown in prison."

"Ah, you are ashamed."

"No more then keeping Jungoo a secret from your family…."

Feslen chuckled. In his heart, he heard Nadine's soft cries.

Up until now, he had never considered a future with anyone else. Would it be possible to have a future while the world dies? Feslen thought.

Feslen spent the rest of the night in contemplation.

"Time to move out!" Kalman ordered. The first rays of the sun peeked behind east horizon.

Confusion blinded Feslen when Nadine approached.

"You should've slept," Nadine murmured.

"I'll be fine," Feslen snapped.

"So, where is this tunnel you speak of?" Sae-Jyung asked Feslen.

"If my memory serves, the book spoke of gem like passageway to reveal in richness of color, or some such thing."

"You don't remember?" Kalman asked.

"It was a long time ago since I read it. Sae-Jyung, don't you have a spell that could detect magic?"

"I used it up."

"Everyone spread out and search for the secret door," Kalman ordered.

They searched thirty minutes to no avail. Lioin sat down, grumbling. Feslen stared at Nadine. The sun enhanced Nadine's beauty. They all looked away from her. Shadows nipped the mountain. Sae-Jyung hid underneath a large tree.

"Can we eat? I know we ate only an hour earlier…." Lioin asked.

Kalman glared at Lioin.

Two hours passed and even Lioin sat down.

"When the light shines…reveals…" Feslen jumped up, startling everyone. "That's it!"

"Duxan, behind you, should be a spot that does not have snow nor in full sunlight. Look to see if my memory is right!" Feslen said.

"There is no snow, but most of the base is like that, little brother."

"Find half-shadow reflection."

"I remember now, 'When light reveals in shadows, only those with equal halves can see. Brightness reflects even in darkest day. Let three be one and the way be none,'" Feslen said, slapping his face.

They found three panels full of glittering gems at the base of the mountain.

The panels had two ruby columns and a sapphire in the middle. He felt the existence of conscious magic within the panels, but no energy lines or auras.

"Hurry," Sae-Jyung gritted. "Seatan approaches."

"Try moving the gems," Feslen said. The blue ones moved.

"Can any of you feel a slight hum when you moved them?" Feslen asked.

Kalman and Duxan nodded.

"Everyone form up!" The Prince ordered. "I hope you can solve this riddle in time Feslen. Here they come."

Seatan and the undead approached.

Kalman charged in, hacking away.

"Jungoo, use your magic when I tell you!" The Prince commanded. She nodded.

The companions watched Kalman hold off two waves of hundred skeletons in awe. The Prince became a maddened smashing machine.

After the third group of hundred skeletons past Kalman, the Prince called for aid. "Now, Jungoo!"

Jungoo complied and tossed some glowing pebbles.

Skeleton bowman began to fire.

A rusted battle-ax bit into Kalman's shoulder, meanwhile, Kalman smashed it to pieces. He tossed his axe at three on-coming skeletons and hurled them aside. Another aimed for his head. Kalman dodged in time. Falling into the Tiger Prey Method, Kalman used their momentum against them, smashed two together.

Duxan protected Kalman's back and downed a skeleton. Loose skeletal fragments bit Kalman's cheek he did not flinch. He duped a battle-axe wielder and it missed. Kalman gripped the skeletal warrior's battle-axe and smashed its head. Kalman jumped up to avoid a thrust from behind.

"Kalman, look, your wounds are healing!" Duxan gasped. His companions all glanced at him, his battle-ax gouge and other wounds indeed mended to anew.

Kalman paused and looked at Feslen with wonder. He then grabbed two arrows hurling towards them and crushed them. He bent down and picked up rusted buckler shields. He jumped over a rushing skeleton and threw the shields into the skeleton bowman, cleaving them in half.

Duxan smashed more skeletons, protecting Kalman's back. A sheaf of magical energy erupted from Jungoo's pebbles, preventing Seatan and his minions from advancement. Seatan's enraged wail shattered against the energy barrier.

One skeleton penetrated when the barrier wavered. Lioin's flurry of kicks and dagger thrusts was futile. More skeletons made it through the barrier with each consecutive successful Seatan wail.

Kalman swung the battle-ax in an arc. He barred their charge. "Lift and scatter," chanted Sae-Jyung as he hurried out of the shield. He pointed at the second wave of advancing skeletons. They vibrated and exploded into a million shards.

Duxan twisted in indecision: should he help Lioin or Feslen? After destroying her opponent, Nadine rushed to the young thief's aid a moment later.

As Duxan decided on a decision, a spear was hurled towards him. Feslen shouted a warning, but could do little else but watch the spear reach his brother. However, Duxan managed to parry it away.

Feslen concentrated on the panel. He felt three of the six panels' magic vibrate. Each panel's magic strength varied to Feslen's senses.

Sae-Jyung chanted again. Six small globes shot from the merchant mage's hands and sundered more enemies. A pile of sulfur lay at the mage's feet.

"Duxan, Kalman, I need your assistance!" Feslen shouted.

Kalman hurried back under Jungoo's protective shield. Duxan smashed a skeleton that got too close to the retreating Sae-Jyung.

"You think that will protect you?" Seatan laughed.

Sae-Jyung chanted and tossed a green object at Seatan's feet. Large thorns appeared and thrusted Seatan thirty feet in the air.

"Nice spell," Nadine commented. She chanted one word and vines wrapped about Seatan.

"What do you want us to do?" Kalman asked and winced when Nadine plucked a skeleton finger from his cheek.

"Twist the sapphires, now!"

Seatan's wail reanimated skeletons. The young gypsy covered her ears. "The barrier will fail if he keeps that up!"

Sae-Jyung chanted and his staff appeared. He hurried over to smash another skeleton that harried Lioin.

Sae-Jyung looked as if he was giving up, or in exhaustion.

Feslen meditated. "Place your hands within the empty space the gems created," He instructed.

They did as told and Feslen continued, "Ka-Wei, use the Fifteenth Step and Fourth Step of the Embodiment Method. Duxan, keep us from hearing or feeling what is going on out there with your happy emotions!"

The din of the battle lessened to the three.

"Now, concentrate. Grip and turn. See the thing as it truly exists! The Gate will open to us three…" Feslen continued. *Why am I doing this? How?* Feslen thought.

The mountain felt alive…Ancient speech coursed through Feslen, and he chanted, *'Three must be none and one must be none.'* Blood surged and mingled. Feslen's body livened as their spirits intermingled. Feslen, Kalman and Duxan's merged as one being, through the power of Feslen's magical chi-gong. The entire mountain shook, loosening rocks. Silence soon followed. A portal opened.

"Go! All of you. Now!" Feslen bellowed.

The protective shield vanished when Seatan wailed one more time. "Don't look back!" Feslen gasped. Green-faced Lioin stumbled through first, Jungoo followed after a look at Feslen. The portal's light brightened to bind Seatan and his minions.

"Stay a moment with me, Duxan. Command them."

"What?" His voice cracked from the usage of his hidden Gift.

"Point and command!" Feslen said and collapsed exhausted. Feslen wished he knew how to gain constant access to his Ancient Truth. Nadine helped him through the fast-closing gate. Sae-Jyung followed next.

Duxan invigorated, despite the wails let go by Seatan Jarrv. "He is no longer your master! Fight to free yourselves," Duxan growled.

The skeletons hesitated. They turned from attacking companions and turned on Seatan. Kalman and Duxan hurried through. They heard a scream as the door closed.

38

GEMSTONE MOUNTAINS 寶石山

The group broke camp. Nadine unrolled Feslen's bedroll. The underground awed Feslen, keeping him awake. The clear crispness of the underground helped Feslen recuperate faster. Occasional water dropped. They swung a lantern about, mist swallowed its light.

"Feslen, how are you feeling?" Kalman asked.

"Fairly well. What do you think is beyond our light? I know little of the Gem Mountain."

"We'll worry about that once you and everyone else gains back their strength. You did well back there," Kalman clapped his friend on the shoulder.

"Wonder why this Seatan wants us so," Duxan asked through a mouthful of dried venison.

"Everyone wants us these days, my brother. You've been improving your bashing skills," Feslen said.

Duxan nodded and yawned.

"By the way," Kalman said. "Just to let you know, there's a reason why I didn't want to take the none-mountainous route to the North."

"Oh?" Duxan asked.

"Do tell, Prince," Sae-Jyung said with a grin.

"Undead crawl in the Neutral pathway, my uncle's troops have stirred them," Kalman said. "Plus, we don't want to go through the Valley of the Dead."

"True," Feslen said with a yawn.

"Do you know what's in these caves?" Lioin asked.

"We're safe enough," Feslen replied and drooped against Nadine.

"It's not that, its just…I usually try not stay in one place too long. I scout things out first."

"That's sound advice, Lioin. I have first watch, why don't you and I go beyond our little light here and go explore?" Kalman asked, stifling a yawn.

"Can we camp today, with you know, Seatan out there?" Duxan asked.

"I don't think we need to worry. I can't feel a thing…." Feslen said, snoring a bit.

Nadine laughed softly.

"It's peaceful in here," she informed. "Still, it would be an idea to guard ourselves."

She hugged Feslen close and slept.

"Be careful, come back within an hour," Kalman told Lioin and handed him a torch. Lioin nodded and head west. Kalman tried to stay awake. The Raster brother's snores lulled him to sleep.

Feslen awoke too sudden, and he cursed under his breath and awaking too early. He did his best not to wake Nadine she snuggled against him. Feslen stroked her arm a bit and moved in for a kiss. He thought better of it and left after Lioin.

Feslen kept behind Lioin, hoping to sneak up on him. The cool mountain air delighted Feslen. He had never been in a mountain before, so he did not know how to react to it. Feslen wished he had brought along his own little lantern that he had unaccountably left at home. Lioin's small form melded well with the shadows of the mountain.

Trying to keep his head clear, his eyes focused, Feslen forged ahead. "Darn darkness!" Feslen muttered to himself. He guessed Lioin head towards the sounds of water. Having lost complete track of time, Feslen noticed water sounds increased.

Feslen gave up on sneaking up on Lioin and coughed up some dust when he entered a large cavern. Where did the dust come from? He tasted strawberries and realized the dust was something else. He followed Lioin's footprints. Lichen and small mushrooms of blue and yellow variety aligned the walls. More dust entered Feslen's mouth, his eyes lit in delight. "Jelly!"

"Feslen!" Lioin said.

The young Raster rushed to find Lioin. He did not notice the clump of jelly on the ground next to a still body and tripped. Feslen screamed but Lioin held him as he fell. "Lioin, are you all right?" He asked.

The jellyfish averted Feslen's interest. "What the…"…

A jellyfish the size of a small octopus glowed. A horde of other mushroom-like creatures covered walls. Quibbling noises came from every direction, making it hard for the two to tell what made the noises.

"Amazing," Feslen said, feeling sudden sleepiness.

"The whole place is alive!" Lioin blurted out the obvious.

The glowing jellyfish lit the cavern well. A small stream of water ran on either side of the jellyfish and along the ceiling as well.

Feslen felt a drop of water on his head. "So that's where the water noise was from," He murmured.

"What are those things?" Lioin asked.

"I don't know, but the mushroom things look like they're alive," Feslen returned.

"You know, I tasted the yummy jelly, think this thing produces it?"

Feslen shook his head.

The young thief looked stiff as a puppet when he reached out for the jellyfish.

Feslen shook Lioin and said, "Wake up, Lioin! I remember that thing now! It's a Giant Spore Eater!" The young Raster glanced at his friend in alarm. These Spore Eaters reacted in pure defense of their territories to any intrusion.

Lioin laughed child-like. An appendage snaked out from the jellyfish and offered the young thief a glob of jelly. Lioin ate it and giggled. "You should try some, mage!" He hissed, turning to Feslen.

"Lioin! Snap out of it!"

"You wish to feed on his energy since I don't have any?" Lioin asked with his head turned to face the Giant Spore Eater. "What do I get out of it? He is my friend, you know…"

Was Lioin talking to the thing? Was this mushroom-creature intelligent somehow? Feslen thought. A mage would give a spell or two to do research on it, but Feslen's mind slipped in panic and tried to think of a way to help his friend.

Lioin's eyes burned sick and Feslen backed away. "Fight it, Lioin!"

Feslen turned to run but tripped. The way out was blocked and he saw a shadowy figure like Seatan.

He heard the mage say, "Feslen! Look out! The Giant Stun Spores!" Then he saw dark lightning bolts erupt from the mage's hands towards the mushroom things. Then, a screech of pain and the bright flashes of light ended. He saw the Sae-Jyung figure go under the attack of mushroom monsters.

Feslen wondered what that was all about and Sae-Jyung vanished.

"Come on, it's nice!" Lioin said with an odd cold edginess.

Feslen's hair stood on end, his gut cried out to him in warning.

This person in disguise was not his best friend! Feslen thought, staring at Lioin in part fear and curiosity. Lioin's eyes opened so wide in a strange madness, Feslen thought it would pop out of his skull. "You all right, Lioin?" He asked, trying to keep the fear out of his voice.

"I'm fine, Feslen," Lioin hissed. He moved towards Feslen, a handful of mushrooms in one of his hands and a dagger in the other.

"Kalman! Duxan!" Feslen shouted, fear paralyzing. He reached deep into himself and used the Ancient Truth to call to them.

Feslen did not have time to worry about the necromancer. A few hundred mushroom creatures shot out small particles of dust. Feslen choked on them. "Stun spores!" He realized. He fought to stay awake, even though his body numbed.

Feslen concentrated when he fell into meditation. His anxiousness and worry soon melted away, despite Lioin and the mushroom creatures wading in.

Kalman blinked awake, battle-axe in hand. He heard his friend's call through the usage of the Ancient Truth and roused the others. The Prince admonished himself for falling asleep as they ran to help.

Someone shook him. "Lioin?" Feslen asked groggily. He accepted the thief's outstretched hands.

Lioin pulled him up, his face grim. "How did you…I thought you…" Feslen uttered.

"I did, but I ate one of those mushroom things. They fed on the jellyfish so, in turn not to be stunned. You took a hefty blow. Are you all right?"

"How do I know that you're you and I'm awake?" Feslen stared in suspicion.

"You don't. Just look at what my daggers did," Lioin said with a shrug.

Feslen looked.

The jellyfish lay split open, cracked as an egg on the wok. Feslen started to say, "That is not in the illusion, I think. Seatan…his lightning bolts…"

"Wow. I wonder if Nadine will like you any better with the scars," Lioin held up a lantern.

"You're you all right." Feslen responded and punched Lioin playfully.

"Just to be sure, eat some of these mushroom goodies. They block illusionary tactics."

Feslen nodded, accepting the living mushrooms. It feels odd to eat a living thing, while they still move, Feslen thought. I hope these things aren't feeling creatures. He said a prayer of thanks over the mushrooms and ate them. They felt gooey and tasted somewhat like dirt mixed with honey. The mushroom creature's juices dribbled out of his mouth. Delicious! He thought, changing his mind. He loved chewy foods.

He noticed Lioin smiling and skipping about, his lantern swinging around with him.

"Wait, when did you bring a lantern?" Feslen asked.

"Excuse me, sir?" Lioin asked.

That's it! Lioin never says, 'sir', Feslen thought and spotted a glint of light on the floor. But, there was nothing on the ground that could reflect light…It was as if light reflected off something shiny on the floor.

The light of the lantern reflected a gleam on the floor.

Feslen spied it and realized the gleam reflected one of Lioin's daggers. Without thinking or realizing what he was doing, Feslen picked up a dagger and advanced on his friend.

"Feslen, w-wait! What are you doing?" Lioin stammered, backing into a cavern wall. Feslen did not reply and sliced into the lantern-holding Lioin. The thief shouted in pain.

The image shattered.

Feslen cracked open one eye. Every bone and cell within his body cried out for energy and sleep. Duxan and Lioin's worried face greeted him. Fully blossomed Rose and fresh honeydew of Nadine's aroma wafted in his nose and he let out a sigh of relief.

"He's all right!" Duxan said. He hugged his brother.

"Could you not hug so hard, please?"

The group laughed.

"Thank goodness, Fes…if you had succumbed to that thing, I would not have forgiven myself!" Lioin said his arm in a bandage wrap.

"What…how…" Feslen groaned and tried to get up.

"First you need to rest. Thousands of stun spores hit you. How you ate the mushrooms with all of the jelly's spores in you, I don't know," Lioin said with a shake of his head. He leaned against Nadine for support.

"You were drained a lot of energy," Sae-Jyung muttered. "We have to carry you the rest of the way. It's a six day journey from here to the end of the cavern."

"You were there too…Sae-Jyung…so was…so was…"

"Seatan?" Lioin said, shaking his head. "Illusion. Sae-Jyung did come, after the jelly ooze near sucked my brain dry. He pulled me free, but the thing almost sucked him dry too."

"Not many could withstand the attack of a Giant Stunner, and be aware enough to escape," Jungoo said, eyes locked with his.

Nadine nodded and glared at Lioin. The young thief lowered his head in shame.

"Sure this is an illusion or real?" Feslen groaned.

"On your feet, you lazy good for nothing parasite!" Duxan imitated Ai-Yen. Feslen grinned at his brother. It was real all right.

Everyone laughed.

On wobbly legs, and several false starts he ended up in Duxan or Nadine's arms, but he managed to get going. They passed some military adorned rooms, glittering busts and tapestries. Feslen could not keep up and stopped for a breather. Some quick-handed person pilfered the rooms.

He grinned. Rose and honeydew blossomed in his nose. "They are looking for possible ambushes and other traps," Nadine said.

Feslen nodded weary. How I love the old days, where I hid and read books, Feslen thought. He eyed Nadine's unconscious graceful glide towards him.

Nadine blushed and hid her face as he stared at her too much. "Lean against me, Feslen," She said.

Feslen gained strength as they talked and walked. Whether because of Nadine's mere presence, or the effect of the Giant Stunner wearing off, he did not pursue further. He enjoyed her company and realized once this was over, he would miss her the most

"Tell me Nadine," he murmured.

She gazed at him. He forced himself to look at the floor.

"What is it about you that make me feel right and good about myself?"

"That's one of the kindest things anyone had ever said to me."

Feslen grinned.

At the end of the cavern, the others worked on another puzzle. This one blocked their exit to the next series of caverns. They waited for Nadine and Feslen to catch up.

"You know, I am glad I have people who love me, but sometimes,"...a sudden dizzy spell forced him to the ground. Nadine's swift embrace made his recovery go faster. She massaged his aching temples.

"It is good have people who care about, my dearest one," Nadine murmured.

"But, it is good that they learn to let go too."

"You're so…" Feslen almost blurted out, "beautiful" But, instead. "Helpful, when you know I need it. How can you be so understanding, Nadine?"

"Shush," She stroked him until his pain passed.

Who are you? Feslen thought.

Kalman, Duxan and Jungoo worked on the puzzle. Sae-Jyung excused himself. Tri-colored ruby, sapphire and aquamarine gems of enormous size dazzled on panels at the base of the exit door. "These are the mines of the Shinjoudou folk," Kalman stated. "Tri-color gemstones are their specialty."

Duxan and Jungoo *hmmed*.

"Why sets of three?" Jungoo wanted to know.

Kalman shrugged.

"Perhaps they believe it to be a sign of good fortune," Duxan jumped to answer.

"Maybe. Remember how Feslen asked, rather he demanded us three with the Gifts to open the path to this tunnel?" Kalman replied.

"How on Hahn-Hah did he know we would have the Gifts too?" Duxan nodded.

"The Prophecy," Jungoo said.

"Those with the Truth of the Gift feel those with or without," Sae-Jyung said.

"Perhaps your theory holds some grounds, Sae-Jyung," Kalman pondered. The Prince disregarded the group's startled looks; it was rare for the Prince to defend the merchant mage.

"Besides, Prince, You won't be able to use it until Feslen arrives. Your first hunch about operating on threes is correct, Prince. I'm surprised you are versed."

"You're forgetting that a Prince has to study up on these things. Not to mention other not-so-manly arts," Ka-Wei said and gave Sae-Jyung one of his winning smiles.

"I think being able to knit is pretty manly," Jungoo grinned at Duxan.

"Hey, growing up I was forced to learn all that stuff, since Mei-Whuay wasn't a very good sister, bless her soul, nor woman; again the Goddess forgive my bad mouthing her."

"Besides," Kalman turned to the merchant mage who sat with a bemused look on his face. "I recognize these symbols, don't you? They are after all used in trade codes."

"You're right, Prince. The three scratch marks stand for three hundred *yuan*," Sae-Jyung remarked, leaning forward.

"The middle one means golden discs, which in trade language means more gold available," Sae-Jyung continued.

"What does that have to do with the Shinjoudou?" Duxan asked.

"Didn't your father teach you even the basics of economics?" Kalman asked Duxan.

"Yes, still I don't see anything involving Gifts of the Prophecy."

"I can field that one," Feslen said, giving Nadine a brief embrace before letting go. He walked towards them almost as healthy as a normal person did. Feslen wondered why Nadine looked weak.

Feslen thought to ask Nadine but worked on the current problem. "Shinjoudou folk believe that three lives make up the current one."

"Thus, they believe in threes," Jungoo said.

"Yes," Feslen replied, irritated at Jungoo for the interpretation. "They learned to bend light and shadows," Feslen finished.

"What about the Prophecy?" Lioin inquired.

"I'm getting to it. The Prophecy mentioned often the joint effort of the Three Chosen Ones of Ancient Truth of defeating evil. Shinjoudou guarded knowledge and discovered light and shadow in gems. Their civilization ended on someone's curse. They never mentioned who caused the curse, or why they were tied in with the gems. This gem puzzle is part of this curse."

"How does the gem puzzle protect them?" Kalman wanted to know.

"I don't think the gem protects them," Feslen said with a shrug and a shake of his head. "I think it traps them here. The person or persons, who cursed them, intended to warp their entire way of living. They used either Ancient Truth or a high-level magical spell to mutate all their gems into a curse for them. That power wiped out most of the Shinjoudou, plus, it forced mages and the remaining Shinjoudou guardians to create Gem Mountain. This whole place reeks with disharmonious energies."

"Same thing happening in Nu," Nadine murmured. Feslen and the others glanced at her a bit.

"And how did the Shinjoudou know of the Ancient Truth? I thought that knowledge was only guarded for magicians, and Forest Protectors and Thai-Thurian monks," Duxan added.

"I thought so too, but the early Shinjoudou traded gems for knowledge. When the founder of the mages, Xcaithian Vestiige left our world of Hahn-Hah, he left mortal guardians to safeguard the secret of magic," Feslen said.

"The Shinjoudou," Duxan said and Feslen nodded.

"True. Don't forget, The Prophecy has different versions for each culture and religion as well," Sae-Jyung said. "For the Shinjoudou folk, gems represent or are equal to our bodies, thus are vassals to souls and energies beyond the known."

"Huh?" Lioin asked.

"I'll try to translate," Feslen grinned. "The Ancient Truth, according to this book I sped-read, is the ability of being aware of everything. An individual for instance, can become enlightened faster when he has the Ancient Truth. That Ancient Truth of course, was an inborn gift. It can be used by other normal mortals who used Flair. Like magicians, Ancient Truth wielders need something to transmit their energies through, especially if they are untrained through it."

"Ah, like the gems," Lioin said.

"Exactly. And as you know, our Chiendonese culture believes that certain gems and items transmit energies or are better at transferring energies."

"But why Three and One? If Ancient Truth wielders are so powerful, why not just use it by yourself?" Kalman wondered.

"Perhaps it has something to do with our body harmonies? Like the Ying and Yang energies?" Duxan asked, as he for some reason, recalled his early religious lessons.

Duxan Raster and the others did not realize how close to understanding the truth he really was with that statement. The Shinjoudou folk, a gem-loving race, and none-magic affiliated peoples had been chosen by the first mage for protection of the truth of magic. However, an evil mage corrupted them, by living among them in disguise. He wanted the secret for himself for many ages. He did not have the Ancient Truth, but he knew of it. The Gem Mountains, an area filled with extreme energies and one of the many Gates of the mortal world which allowed access to the Immortal Realms. The Gem Mountains' energies rivaled the Ancient Truth energies and many Shinjodou folk became aware. Yet, they made a terrible mistake once which cost them their civilization. They hoped anyone with the Ancient Truth will free them from their mistake. They created the gem puzzles, traps and mountain itself to contain the energies and their terrible curse. It required Ancient Truth wielders to open the doorway to through to the North, but also to the other worlds. Only those with real knowledge of the Shinjoudou folk, magic and the Gem Stone Mountain may open this gateway. However, these Ancient Truth wielders need to work together to open their way to freedom.

"It is possible, this book didn't explain everything, and I'm just beginning to understand why everyone wants me," Feslen allowed. Then he motioned to everyone, pointing to Duxan and Kalman.

"Remember the dream we shared, Duxan, Kalman?" Feslen stated, remembering the first few dreams he had at the beginning of the year.

The Prince and Duxan nodded.

"The door with the characters? I believe this mountain somehow represents it. I also feel the same energies coursing through this place,"

Feslen said. "As for Three and One, well, it's like the Prophecy says, "the three must join together to fight for the cause."

"Loosely translated," Jungoo grinned.

Feslen chuckled.

"Stay alert," Nadine warned.

A hundred thousand undead Shinjoudou warriors slithered towards them. "Where did they come from?" Duxan muttered.

"I guess we stirred them up," Feslen apologized. "Here they come."

"That's all right, little brother," Duxan said. "I feel strong."

Feslen glanced at his brother at the odd comment, but his heart felt lightened. Has Elhong Wieng's dark curse finally gone away? He thought.

Duxan inhaled, his body felt lighter than a feather, healthier, more vigorous. He began to sing, which gave his friends a start. "Bring it on, undead spawn!" He snarled. I feel like a new person, as the old Faoisit saying goes of reincarnation: Death after life, and life after death, Duxan thought as the undead Shinjoudou slithered in.

39

THREE BE ONE 三人合一

"I doubt daggers would be much effective against bone and rags, Lioin," Sae-Jyung said with a snort, staff in hand.

"I suppose your metal dingy there could?" He shot back, readying silver daggers.

Nadine curled into a fighting stance.

"Rest, my dear," Feslen said and held her arm a moment.

"I'll be fine. You need to help the other two of the Prophecy, my dearest one."

"But…"

"I will be fine, Feslen," Nadine said in a firm voice.

"Be careful, my dear. I cannot afford to lose you," He said even though he did not know why he did, or where those feelings for Nadine came from!

"Though you could lose others,"…Sae-Jyung murmured.

"Jealous now, are we?" Lioin growled.

Feslen and Nadine ignored the jabbering.

"I'll be careful beloved," Nadine said.

Feslen hung his jaw. She kissed him light on the cheek, making him burn.

"Come on Feslen! We need you! Our hands are stuck to the gem panel!" Duxan shouted.

A strange vibrating noise soon occurred when the Prince and Duxan placed their hands on the gem panel pedestal.

The horde attacked.

Feslen hurried to his brother's side and Kalman's to examine the situation. The three unique fist-sized gemstones had moved on their own accord. They split into two smaller versions from their original size and a large odd empty metal panel and hook appeared in between. Underneath the hook an imprint of a hand, heart and mind symbol appeared. Next to the split gems were other smaller slots, some already filled with smaller aquamarines. Feslen rubbed his chin, trying to figure out what that means. He looked at his panel, Duxan and Kalman's again. Some small gem slots were empty.

"Perhaps the heart and missing gemstones have something in common, but what?" Feslen asked. He risked a glance his battling companions seemed to be handling all right.

It was trickier then it seemed. No matter how many times Feslen tried to duplicate what his stuck companions did, he failed.

"It's painful," Duxan warned. At a closer look, three small slots where his brother's hand stuck were empty. Glittering and pulsing gemstones littered the platform. The ruby was missing in the collection of gems. He asked Kalman for more confirmation. Kalman affirmed that there were no rubies on his stand either. An image flashed from the gems through Feslen for a moment: a symbol of a golden flame.

"Gems can transfer energy..." Feslen began to theorize. What did Nadine say? What did Father teach us about economics? Rubies represented fire and the heart in some cultures. Sapphires equaled water. Gems and other items transfers energies...

The three heard grunts of exertion and pain.

"I feel sort of tired, you Kalman?" Duxan

"A little. Do these crystals drain energy?"

"Possibly. Kalman the flawless colored gems are high in value correct?" Feslen nodded.

"The old days, they claim so, yes."

"Duxan, what did father say about gems in the Yin Yang pattern?"

"Why? I believe that the highest forms of gems can be seen by the truth of one's intent."

"Highest priced gems are favored because of spiritual beliefs?" Feslen grimaced.

"In some cultures that is the case," Kalman concurred with his theory.

Underneath their stuck hands, Feslen discovered Shinjoudou symbols similar to Chiendonese words for bad luck, courage, and death. "What's the other meaning for Death and Fate?"

"Death is Heaven Descendent," Kalman replied.

"Fate is Red Death," Duxan said. "Hurry, Feslen."

He rushed away from his trapped companions who shouted a warning to him. Feslen ducked a swing from one of the undead. Another undead backed Lioin against the mountainside. Feslen saw some gems scattered around the thief. He picked up some rubies. Lioin fought to keep four undead things from overtaking him. Feslen helped decapitate one that rushed past.

Feslen rushed back to his trapped companions. He placed the rubies in each missing slots. He manipulated the giant gemstone on his own panel and it split in two. The young Raster fell into his meditative state. He heard for a moment his friends cursing aloud. Nadine shouted for help. He knew his companions lost ground.

Yet, he saw.

Beyond the falseness of color and surface images lay a colorless gem. It did not pulse with color, but it sent out energies. Feslen shivered with delight. He dismissed that emotion.

The smooth rainbow colors of the gemstones sang with harmony. Peace calmed his fears. Kalman and Duxan meditated. Feslen felt his older brother flinch when Jungoo cried out in pain.

Not yet, He told them. *We must act. Hold your hands out; know this trapped your corporeal form, not the spirit. I feel the pull too. It is not real. Just like the gemstones' glare. Look deeper beyond....*

Kalman gasped. Swirl of lights and colors became empty grayness. *Do not lose sight and focus of our goal. We are here to unlock the main gem,* spoke Feslen.

Main gem? Kalman asked.

Then Duxan saw. He understood what Feslen wanted.

The three reached out. *Use your heart and think nothing but compassion. Duxan, fill this chamber with your grief,* Feslen instructed. *I will use my will to construct a gate…Kalman use your way to command. They will listen.*

Kalman knew what Feslen meant. Their bodies jarred in pain as the undead warriors slashed.

"Feslen!" Nadine screamed.

A wave of dizziness hit all three. *What is happening?* Kalman said he used his WuSha discipline to numb the intense pain. So this is how you must feel, he thought. Duxan screamed in agony as Feslen tried to fight the will to sleep.

Numbing pain calmed Duxan…….he felt other presences in the gems…

Concentrate! Feslen told his brother and the Prince. *Do not let the gems ensnare us!*

The pain…is so real… Duxan groaned. A hundred small needles stabbed the three through their hands. They let go a combined cry of pain. Feslen did not let that shake him even though his own blood poured out over everything.

Duxan slumped over and let out a tremendous banshee wail. *Brother?* Feslen whispered. He reached out, forgetting concentration for the task.

Duxan's body paled. *No!* Feslen screamed.

The gems stopped pulsating. Kalman could contain his grief no longer and the room began to vibrate. His tears mingled into the gems along with the blood that poured from his hand.

Feslen's tears joined his blood on the gems. They began to glitter brighter than daylight. They heard the roars of the undead and their companions' cries for help. In some way they felt their combined pains.

What is happening? Kalman asked.

By the Goddess of Balance... Feslen uttered.

A soft homey feeling stole the two conscious gem-trapped friends. Feslen and Kalman exchanged confused stares. They felt the heartbeat of Duxan fade...

My brother! Feslen wailed.

However, to their amazement, Duxan stirred and rose, glowing. "I will see to it they stop hurting us," He said, with a glowing smile. A soft aura now enveloped Duxan.

Feslen gasped, Duxan strode to greet the undead horde and rock crab monsters. Duxan plucked them off Jungoo as if they were rag dolls. His shout forced the undead to drop their weapons. "My friends! Circle around me! These things cannot hurt you anymore!"

What are we witnessing here, Feslen? Kalman asked.

This cannot be! Feslen thought. The soft aura of light glowed around Duxan exploded and blinded Feslen. Duxan gathered everyone to him, even as his body lay still and trapped by the pulsing gems.

Concentrate, Kalman! We have one chance to free everyone! Feslen theorized the gems somehow trapped Duxan's soul...

We need Duxan...

I don't have time to explain, but he is helping us here as well as there.

What do I have to do?

Just breathe deep and lend me your energies. I shall do the rest.

What happened next neither Kalman nor Feslen could explain, and neither would for a long time to come. Swirls of Kalman's *chi* exited from him and danced in the empty "air" in front of the pulsating gray gemstone. The gems began pulsing on their own. The mixing energy formed into a solid thing: a heart shaped gateway.

Massive energy waves pulled both the physical and spiritual forms of Feslen and Kalman through...Duxan remained to make sure their companions went through. Feslen hoped his brother could escape.

A soft glow surrounded Duxan, a special gift from the departed after he finished his prayer. The elder Raster never noticed though, he got up after prayer session, the doorway gone.

Duxan did not awaken from their ordeal with the gemstone, the finest final trap of the ancient minors. They waited for ten minutes. The gateway formed by the three did not open very long. Everyone needed rest from the severe beating.

They collapsed. Kalman laid Duxan out on the sleeping roll and tried to build a fire. Kalman shook his head and cursed their luck. Kalman tried not to let the grief of Duxan's death overwhelm him.

"We can't wake him, Feslen," Jungoo sniffled. "It's no good; he lost so much energy, as did you and Kalman."

"I survived," Feslen said. "Why did he have to stay behind?"

Duxan had no visible pulse. His skin looked paler than an undead warrior.

"I knew this to be a dangerous route! Why…….of all the dumb things…" Feslen screamed in bitter agony.

The others dared not comfort him even the Princess of Nu seemed at a loss for words or action. Duxan had been unmoving for an hour since their narrow escape from the mines. The gemstone sapped him.

"How am I going to explain this to our parents? Why did I have to live and not him? What have I done all this time," Feslen punched himself as hard as he could in the face.

"Feslen, stop it!" Nadine screeched, gripping his hands hard.

"It's not your fault! Look, he's breathing again!"

"Don't joke with me, Princess," Feslen said with a glare.

"He's dead, and it's my responsibility to bury him at home."

"What do you mean?" Nadine asked, puzzled. "He didn't, look!"

Feslen refused to look, he did not believe her. He felt Duxan's energy wane.

"Look!" Nadine said with force, and forced Feslen to turn his head around to face Duxan's body.

"She's right! He's alive!" Kalman confirmed in relief. "By the good Sun Goddess, he's even breathing! How is this possible?"

Feslen knelt to make sure that was true. He burst into tears. His friends gathered around him, even the cold-hearted and skeptical Sae-Jyung.

What was everyone talking about? Duxan thought when he walked through the mountainside. His companions let out a gasp. He then saw his unconscious form. He wondered if he just experienced an out of body experience. "What, did everyone miss me?" He spoke, though no one heard him. He floated into his resting physical self and sighed with happiness.

A gasp of breath from Duxan alerted to everyone. They celebrated when he returned to life. "What happened?" Duxan asked as Jungoo and Feslen hugged him until he was out of breath.

The party rested up before they faced the Temmer Giants. The dead skunk and sewage smell of the Temmer giants overwhelmed those not used to the smell. Both Duxan and Feslen worried about the fifteen-foot slope the group faced when scaling down the mountain. Kalman told them, the best way to get down was slow and steady. Kalman warned them not to engage them until they got a better gage of the situation.

"Oh really?" Lioin asked, to no one in particular. He glanced sideways at his companions and his face lit up in a grin.

Feslen caught his friend's movement and felt he should warn him, but he was so exhausted he could not even move. He leaned against Nadine's slender and soft shoulders as he fell asleep. She chuckled and stroked his head and placed a sleeping roll around them both. She made sure Feslen was snug and warm and let him lean against her for comfort and happiness. She saw the big smile splayed on his face and sighed.

Duxan saw this and envied Nadine a moment, for in the old days, Feslen would come to him and ask him for protection. Now, this job of his was slipping away. He then felt a nudge to his right and smiled at Jungoo. She nodded at the sleeping roll she unrolled. The two slipped in the warm covers and fell asleep.

Kalman shook his head, as did Sae-Jyung. "I hope they don't think this is a camping trip," Sae-Jyung chuckled and slipped into meditation.

Kalman worried about the appearance of Temmers. They usually inhabit further North, in the colder climates. He took first watch, as usual. He stood guard, facing the Temmers, with his weapon drawn.

Lioin snuck down the other end of the cliff, where some bushes hung on the edge. He slipped away, unnoticed.

They dared not to light a fire this close to the huge giants. Everyone, even from fifty feet above on the small mountain cliff, felt the evil auras from the giants. Under the cover of the night, when only Kalman stood guard, Lioin dashed away, down the steep slope towards the giants.

40

THE GIANTS' TEMPER

Morning arrived when the companions watched the two Temmer giants with caution, planning their next steps at the top of a mountain. They flattened themselves and Kalman took off his shiny red armor so the chances of the Temmers spotting them became more remote. The giants stood eighty feet in height, their two heads looking this way and that. The heads presented no mouths, but otherwise resembled a human's head. The size of their head equals the size of a regular human head! Their skins looked harder than stone, and they wore no visible armor.

The Temmer beasts' managed to rumble their own language, none of which the companions understood. The two heads seemed to operate independent from each other, for one kept arguing while the other kept a stern watch. The head of the arguing giant argued with one of the heads of his companion giant! Then, the companions saw where their mouth was: in their stomach!

"May the Sun Goddess forgive me for cursing one of her creations," Nadine began, "But even I dislike these beasts."

Kalman grinned at her and went back in studying the situation. His eyes narrowed as he thought, It looks like they're waiting for something...or guarding someone.

"Let's take them, instead of waiting like cowards," Sae-Jyung hissed.

"No. Not unless we have some powerful magic, or a catapult," Kalman returned, with a shake of his head. "We want to go through them, mage, not become flattened by them."

Sae-Jyung said, "I am a powerful mage, and we have the Princess."

Kalman ignored him, but Jungoo said, "You can go alone, if you want, merchant."

There's no way we can take two on, or even three. This party's inexperience and without my family heirloom, I don't want to risk it, Kalman thought. Besides, they don't know what's after the Temmers. At least with these Temmers, they look to be some sort of raiding party, and not actual inhabitants of this area.

"What do you know of these beasts?" Duxan asked both Kalman and Nadine. The smell of these giants was worse than the bodies he encountered on the adventure. The worst part of it all, the wind blew in from the north east, increasing their smell.

"Their hearing is exceptional, despite the appearance," Kalman answered, then he murmured, "This is…unusual."

"What is?" Sae-Jyung said with a shrug. He closed his eyes and began to meditate and perform some a mix of Martial Arts, the likes of which Kalman, Duxan nor Feslen ever seen before. The merchant mage then reached into his pouches and retrieved some blank banana-leaf scrolls and started to scratch in Chiendong characters. A soft glow emitted from the mage onto the scrolls.

"Interesting magic," Jungoo said, "My people use objects, not scrolls. Some even carry books."

"Spell books? Yes, I assume many mages have that," Feslen said.

"They seem to be waiting for something," Feslen said.

Kalman nodded and replied, "Indeed. We can't go around them, the mountain's closed off. The only way is down, and through I'm afraid. You know what's strange? They usually come in threes; I wonder where the third one is?"

Nadine suggested, "Perhaps they are guarding prisoners?"

"Maybe, but, since you've encountered them before Princess, I sincerely doubt they take prisoners," Kalman said. "Remember, they eat humans and humanoids."

"True," Nadine said with a frown.

"So, what do you wish to do about it, fearless leader?" Sae-Jyung asked.

Kalman grumbled and wished the merchant mage would return to his meditating. He said, "I am thinking." A harsh wind blew a cold gust towards the companions. Feslen shivered.

Nadine moved closer to him and put her warm arm around him. He smiled with such gratefulness at her that she let out a sigh.

"What's the matter, Nadine?" Feslen asked, worried he offended her. "Did I do something wrong?"

"No," Nadine said, shaking her head. Her now long-brown hair moved when she shook her head, it moved as it itself was alive. Feslen still watched her hair with enchantment.

The wind blew again, Nadine's hair slapped against Feslen's cheek. He coughed a bit, and he tried to suppress his cough. He did not want to alert the giants. Duxan moved closer to his brother and started to unpack a blanket, when he got a vicious glare from Feslen. Duxan sighed.

Kalman felt the third wind gust and lifted his hand. He scanned the dark gray clouds gathering to the north east and said, "It's going to rain. I guess we have to move soon. How's your magic, Sae-Jyung? I hope you're powerful enough to get us through."

"About time. You and I can draw them, Prince," Sae-Jyung said, chanting in a soft whisper. His staff appeared in his right hand when he finished his chant.

"Wait," Lioin said in a huff, he returned somewhat disheveled. He also limped a bit. The others swirled, weapons raised. "Lioin?"

"You went off without my permission," Kalman said. His none-anger and somewhat cold statement scared Feslen more than an outburst from him would. Though the Prince did not show any outward anger with his body, a cold energy was felt by everyone around Kalman.

Lioin shivered from the coldness of the Prince's statement and held up a hand, and rubbed his neck with the other one. He said, "Look, I needed to scout. I always make sure areas are safe, that's how I survived all those years on my own as a thief."

Kalman chuckled and nodded. "What did you find?"

"Along the way down there are many traps, almost as if made by the Temmers, or someone controlling them. You're right, they're not very bright," Lioin said, shaking his head. "I heard the Temmers argue about things like what a dog smells like, compared to a human."

Sae-Jyung chuckled.

"Some dogs smell better," Jungoo said, but no one paid heed.

"And, what else did you find?" Kalman asked.

"Human foot prints, lots of them. I can tell some of them were prisoners," Lioin concluded. "You were right to be cautious, Kalman."

Kalman nodded, face grim. He asked, "Well, what do we do now?"

"We could sneak pass the guards. There's only about ten separate footprints," Lioin said.

"No," Kalman said. "They recognize smells they've encountered before."

"Like you," Nadine said. Then she said, "Listen, I can get us down and through. What are the enemy strengths, Lioin?"

"I don't know."

Then it began to rain, and hard. Nadine's dress became wetter and wetter which made the men feel rather uncomfortable around her. They all stared without a word at her lithe, slender feminine beauty. Even when she turned to face Feslen and then half-turned her body, it made the men in the party swallow hard.

Feslen noticed this and growled at their behavior. He expected better from Duxan and Kalman. Have a little restraint, boys! He thought while a jealousy surge went through his chilled body. The rain made it difficult for Feslen. He hated the rain, even as it seeped through his heavy winter clothes. He tried to suppress his coughs.

"How do you pro-prop-propose to get by the Temmers?" Kalman asked, stumbling through his words. His breath caught in between when he spoke, as he stared upon Nadine's alien beauty.

"I have my ways, trust me. Feslen, stay here while I send the others first. Lioin, show me where the traps are," Nadine continued, apparently oblivious to her male companions' attitude.

Lioin nodded and started down.

Feslen protested a bit at being last, but Nadine stopped him with a passionate kiss. Duxan's jaw slackened a bit, even as Kalman ribbed him. Everyone made a surprised sound, no more than Feslen. She said, "Listen, if Lioin got into this much trouble, I wonder how you would deal with the slope? Now, before you argue, I can't risk your life, ok? You're far too important to me."

Feslen started to open his mouth to argue again, even as rain pelted him without mercy, but sighed instead. Feslen nodded and thought, When she put it that way...who can argue? He said to Nadine before she departed, "Be careful!"

She smiled her most winning smile at him, any smile that would make every woman jealous of her. Feslen's heart melted under that smile. He reached to embrace her and she gave him a quick hug and said, "I'll be back, quick, I promise."

She said to Kalman, "Come along, Kalman. Don't just stand there like a puppy, come on!"

Kalman agreed to come.

Nadine shook her wet hair, which got wetter by the minute, splashed water on everyone. Feslen watched, inhaling deep. I love her, he realized. I want her for myself, damned it.

Sae-Jyung grumbled, "At last. I'd prefer to slaughter them myself."

Kalman, Lioin and Nadine parted from their companions. They picked their way with caution, though Lioin walked down the slope with light-footed ease. Lioin pointed out all the traps on the ground, and around the trees he had to avoid heading through the path which the Temmers blocked. Nadine watched where he pointed and nodded. Feslen watched with deep concern, forgetting that he was cold and sopping wet. Kalman took a sharp intake of breath when they reached right beneath the Temmers. They did not react in any negative way as they passed under.

It took the three half an hour to reach a safe distance away from the two Temmer guards. They stood about, complaining about the rain in the common Chiendong tongue. Lioin made a gesture to Kalman and Nadine, who nodded. Kalman hid behind some large rocks, and hoped to be hidden from the Temmers' sight and smell. Lioin dashed out down the gravel road and disappeared behind a large bend around yet another mountain.

Nadine made her way back.

Sae-Jyung went next. Feslen saw Sae-Jyung try and slip his arm about Nadine, but she flinched and shook him off. She glared at him and he backed off. That's my lady! Feslen thought with a smile.

Nadine returned for Duxan and Jungoo, leaving Feslen last. Duxan protested a bit at that, but a look from Nadine quieted him before they departed.

Nadine returned a half hour later and she and Feslen took their time down the slope. She was right to leave me last to rest, Feslen thought. Exiting the Gem Mountains and that puzzle trap exhausted me. I can't feel my energies, that is why I'm having such trouble even concentrating my steps.

He slipped a few times down the steep mountain slope, causing some gravel to trickle. Feslen caught his breath when one of the giant Temmers roared and came over, sniffing the air like a dog. He then raised his arm, and it transformed into a huge club! Feslen held his scream, as Nadine covered him. She whispered, "Don't worry."

The Temmer bashed the area with random strikes. Rocks and bits of plant and root flung about Feslen and Nadine for a good ten minutes. Then the Temmer went away, rumbled in apparent satisfaction and returned to stand guard with his other Temmer companion. Nadine and Feslen picked their way with agonizing slowness down the mountain, and Feslen almost slipped down a deep hole.

But, she caught him and pulled him up. Now Feslen appreciated why Nadine wanted him to go last. He whispered to her, "Who are you, Nadine? I want to know everything about you! I want…"

"Shhh," Nadine warned when they finally reached firm ground. They passed with slow ease under the Temmers.

When they were out of hearing range, and close to their friends, Nadine turned and said to Feslen, "I wish I can tell you more, but I cannot. But, know this: I have your best interests in my heart. I care for you deeply and I want you to feel succeed with each step you take."

"Why? What have I done to deserve you? No other woman has ever…" Feslen began and suddenly blurted, "I care about you."

Nadine's smile lit the dark and cloudy day and said, "You have been my cause since I knew about you."

What an odd time to be confessing feelings, Duxan thought, observing his brother and his new friend exchanging hugs. He shook his head. Then again, he has little experience in situations like this. He must really be afraid.

Feslen beamed and embraced her. She returned the embrace.

They reached Kalman who nodded his thanks to the mysterious Princess of Nu. His face was grim, however. He pointed to further down the path. "Bad news," he said. "Someone in that group discovered us."

A group of eight humans guarded a caravan of prisoners along with a huge Temmer standing behind them. This Temmer was two times bigger than his friends who guarded the path at the Gem Stone Mountains! and a dozen prisoners. Some of the prisoners are Chiendonese, Mengalois and a new race Feslen had never encountered, the Lopu.

"New Priests! What are they doing so far north?" Feslen scowled.

"I don't know, but they have one more giant Temmer friend with them. I guess we'll have to fight it out, whether we want to or not," Kalman said. "Be ready."

"How did they discover us?" Feslen asked, bewildered and out of breath. He felt weak. Weaker than before this adventure started. He hated this feeling and frowned.

"Lean on me, my beloved," Nadine whispered. And he did, already feeling some strength return.

"My fault," Lioin panted, and said, holding up a poisoned dart. "Dart trap. Almost got me good."

Nadine gave him a concerned look and reached out, murmuring a prayer. Lioin shook his head and said, "No, Princess. I'm ok. Save your healing powers when we need it."

She nodded and said, "At least let me rub some healing herbs…"

"Okay," Lioin agreed. She started to place some herbs on Lioin's cuts and scrapes, but stopped when Feslen growled. Lioin blushed and chuckled, "I can do it myself, Princess. Thanks."

He took the poultice from Nadine. She blushed at Feslen's fierce stare and protective squeeze.

It took a few seconds for the enemy to fall upon the companions. "Get the New Priest!" Kalman bellowed, squatting into a defensive posture. He cursed Lioin for his foolhardiness and hoped Feslen would recover fast. They were going to need him.

"My Master has put an extremely high price on you for interrupting his goals, Prince Ka-Wei!" The New Priest shouted. He wore the hawk's talon and broken sword symbol. He was one of Elhong Wien's minions. He raised his fingers and began his chant. The New Priest has ten underlings and the huge Temmer.

"Your Master is dead! Bring it on!" Kalman roared as one of the New Priest's soldiers charged. Kalman cut him down in an instant.

"Fire the arrows, you fools!" The New Priests ordered after he finished his chant.

An extreme darkness blanketed the area when the New Priest finished his chant. The companions heard bow strings stretch.

"Be ready, everyone!" Kalman warned.

They heard Sae-Jyung chant to the minor god of defense and protection. Moments later, the smell of burned metal sprung in the air. "Stay within my magical barrier," Sae-Jyung told his companions. Feslen saw a bright brown circular glow surround them even as the sound of arrows sped towards them.

"I didn't know you cared, Sae-Jyung," Jungoo said.

"I care about someone, not you, gypsy. You just happen to win the luck of the protection draw," Sae-Jyung replied and went into another chant. He held out a bamboo-rolled scroll this time.

Jungoo growled at him, but Duxan restrained her. Feslen grinned at that, his strength steadily returned. Kalman, however, remained outside the protective barrier.

"No! Not fireball! It will incinerate Kalman!" Feslen said, understanding the mage's chants.

Sae-Jyung growled his incantations. Everyone could smell an incense candle burning, along with medicinal herbs and leaves. "Kalman! He's about to throw fire at the enemy!" Feslen said.

Kalman nodded and retreated within the mage's protective barrier. Feslen heard a few more bowmen snap off their shots. The New Priest countered Sae-Jyung's chants. The group felt the intense heat gathered by Sae-Jyung's spell and the dirt around swirled.

"Is he nuts? He wants to fry us all!" Duxan began.

Feslen tried to calm him, and said, "Don't disturb the magician while he's casting. If we interrupt him now, the backfire could be disastrous."

Duxan sweated the spell out.

Sae-Jyung finished his chant just at the moment the two Temmers that guarded the path ambled towards them, arms raised ready to bash. The fireball Sae-Jyung released was not aimed at the humans or the New Priest however; it rushed towards the towering Temmer, who stood behind them.

The fireball grew larger and larger when it reached the gigantic Temmer. "My strength is running low," Sae-Jyung said, a new sheen of sweat appearing on his face. "I will have to drop the protective barrier soon."

The two Temmers reached close enough where they kept bashing the barrier. Every time they hit, the barrier flashed with violence. The companions inside shook and fell to their behinds with each hit. They almost did not notice, though, for they watched Sae-Jyung's fireball in awe.

The fireball expanded and slammed into the Temmer, who, up until the fireball reached its face stared into empty space, as if completely unaware. It roared in anguish when the fireball burned it. The New Priest watched with horror on his face, his spell forgotten. In his fear, his spell back lashed when he cut it off in the middle. A huge crack appeared around the New Priest and his followers. They screamed as a pit opened below them. The New Priest and a few soldiers managed to jump away from the pit, but the rest fell in.

"See? This is what happens when a spell backfires," Feslen said with a wry grin.

"I'll get you, you traitor!" The New Priest howled at Sae-Jyung. He ordered the still-burning Temmer into battle. It charged with a roar.

"Do you have something up your sleeves, merchant mage? This would be the time," Kalman said.

"Maybe," Sae-Jyung said. He reached into his pockets and took out tiny cymbals.

Why was he doing this? Feslen thought and then said, "I feel well."

"No, Feslen," Nadine said, "We will need you later." She turned to the Temmers behind them and began her own chants. She prayed to the Sun Goddess and Fu-Ku, goddess of Nature.

The burning Temmer reached them and instead of bashing the protective magical barrier, as its brethren did. The burning Temmer began to diminish its size! Kalman shook his head and said, "I've never seen that before. And I've fought them twice."

Kalman rushed out of the barrier at the shrinking Temmer. He slashed at the Temmer with his sword. It got stuck as if it struck mud! The Temmer made a noise as if it was laughing. It attacked the Prince. Mud slung at Kalman at a rapid pace. Kalman unstuck his sword and ducked away. He parried when the muddy-formed Temmer advanced and slugged at him.

"Idiot," Sae-Jyung breathed. He began his chant and warned, "I'm lowering my spell now. I hope you finish whatever you planned to do fast, Princess."

Nadine did not reply, she closed her eyes and finished her first prayer to the Sun Goddess. She raised a mirror and pointed it at the two Temmers. A sudden ray of light broke from the New Priest's darkness spell and reflected to the Princess' mirror. The light than refracted back at the Temmers, cutting through their eyes. They roared in pain.

"Nice spell," Feslen said.

Kalman's eyes widened when the Temmer he fought lowered itself and split into two new Temmers! One of the newly formed Temmer seeped into the ground. Duxan said, "Uh-oh…it doesn't take a magic-using genius to figure out what this thing wants!"

Nadine just finished the second prayer and green vines suddenly sprung from the ground, forming a discus underneath the companions and thrusting them high in the air. This started just as the split Temmer forced itself through Sae-Jyung barrier.

"I didn't realize magic can extend this far," Feslen said, eyes wide.

"It can't!" Jungoo said, pointing to Sae-Jyung. He finished his spells, and the cymbals burned up. Just then, a tremendous careening explosion occurred. The companions, except for Sae-Jyung and the enemies covered their ears in pain. The area spun. The Temmers held their ears and cried in common Chiendong tongue, "The pain stop!"

Sae-Jyung grinned and then shouted, "Move! Move! Get out of here. I have one more spell I'd like to try."

Feslen was nearly unconscious from the noise, his nose bled, ears bled and eyes blurred. He felt Nadine's arm around him. Duxan struggled to keep balance as did Jungoo. With another spell from Nadine, they floated down to the ground.

Lioin stayed, drawing his daggers.

"Go, thief boy!" Sae-Jyung yelled, waving his staff and also floated down, carrying Lioin. The man's staff glowed bright when he cast the spell of levitation.

Kalman shouted through the pain of the extreme noise pounding against his ears, "You better come back, Sae-Jyung. I owe you one!"

"Yes, get out of here. Move it! Run at least a hundred feet away from me," Sae-Jyung replied. He shoved Lioin forward. "Why?" Lioin asked.

"Just do it!" Kalman ordered and picked up the thief when Sae-Jyung shoved him away.

The mage just started his chant.

Kalman hated to flee and hated to admit there was little else he could accomplish. Sae-Jyung's pitch sharpened, became faster and higher. The companions, now having run far enough away turned to watch the black-caped mage. His arms were raised, and a bright aura exploded around him.

Three Temmer giants charged at his position, slamming him with their arms. Sae-Jyung was unaffected for the moment from each blow, for his staff projected a protective magical barrier.

Kalman in the meantime, found the New Priest trying to crawl away. He slammed his booted foot on the New Priest's back.

"Get out of here," Kalman told his friends. "I'll wait for Sae-Jyung." The companions ran further away and helped some of the prisoners free. One of the former Lopu prisoners was their queen, named Aien Ping. Her tattoos on her body enshrined her tanned beauty. But, Feslen, Kalman and Duxan had little time to think about it.

Kalman watched in awe when Sae-Jyung's spell unleashed itself. The tips of the man's fingers and his staff exploded in array of dark lightning. The lightning bolts spanned out and striking everything within almost a hundred feet wide. Lightning bolts zapped the three Temmers and formed two circular discs both above and beneath the giants.

The lightning engulfed the Temmers. Their cries mingled with Sae-Jyung. A bright light flashed, blinding Kalman for a brief moment. When it ended, Sae-Jyung lay in the middle of three over-burnt Temmer bodies, unmoving. The New Priest died before Kalman could question him. The Prince then half-carried, half-dragged Sae-Jyung to the others.

41

ROAD TO SORCERESS' CASTLE
女魔法師城堡之路

Charred giant Temmer bodies improved the smell of the area; none of the companions held their breaths. "Impressive," Kalman said to Sae-Jyung as they all recovered from the encounter. "You're quite the mage; I'm shocked you never got Choiced."

"Who wants to go to a stuffy School to learn about Rules and Regulations when it doesn't apply to the real world anyway?" Sae-Jyung said with a mocking smile.

Everyone breathed a sigh when camped far away from the Temmers.

The prisoners they rescued were all very grateful, except perhaps the Lopu Queen, Aien Ping. Her purple eyes glittered as much as her full body tattoos. She was naked before them, and unashamed of her nakedness. Though, Feslen, Duxan, Lioin did their best to be modest, as Nadine and Jungoo reminded them to do so often around the naked Queen, she gave no apparent signs of worrying. Before she and her escorts and the other prisoners departed, Aien Ping said to Kalman, "Just because you rescued me and my party, doesn't mean I can forgive your transgressions."

"I don't expect you to," Kalman replied. "I am thankful we were able to help."

Though there was something in the way she moved her body and her voice that said otherwise. She said to the Prince and everyone in the group, "When you have the time, please, make sure to visit me and my people. For, you are guests of honor." She bowed and left.

They walked half the day to get back to the path to the Sorceress. Duxan informed the Prince earlier during their trip that their provisions ran low, perhaps a weeks' worth of goods left. It would take two weeks by foot to the Sorceress' castle, one week by horse. Worry lines creased the Prince's face as he studied his group's morale and health.

Duxan set up an amazing outdoor cookery with a salted rooster that they had been saving for the North. He skewered the rooster over the fire. "Hey when's dinner ready, Dux? You said it was good an hour and a half ago!" Kalman shouted. The smell of smoked meat ravished him.

"Dinner, you wolves!" Duxan laughed. They ate a hearty meal of smoked wild rooster, two kinds of mushroom with spinach and spice, and a fried walnut dish.

"Your cooking is better than mother's, my brother!" Feslen commented, reached for another helping, of the mushroom dish and dumplings.

"Mother would not be pleased to hear that, little brother," Duxan returned.

Everyone laughed.

The merchant mage was quick to mend. Impressive, Kalman thought. How the mages of Great School of Magic Stuff ignore him, when he had this power?

The Prince sharpened his weapon on a whetstone when studying Sae-Jyung. Why the deception?

"I'm off to bed, wake me when my shift comes," Duxan said to Kalman. Kalman nodded and smiled.

Feslen wrote in his journal a moment longer and lulled into sleep, leaning his head against Nadine. Lioin ate leftovers, cleansed the plates and refilled waterskins in a nearby stream.

"Quite a spectacle, eh?" Kalman said to Lioin.

"Glad he's on our side, my Prince. Good rest."

Kalman nodded and walked away. The Prince looked around again.

Soon the night passed and they awoke at the smell of Duxan's breakfast. Safflower and coriander wafted their noses.

"We should get a move on. We may need to hunt soon," Kalman said.

Long echoes of silence dotted the well-worn northern trade route. A sudden mist rolled in. "My people have a saying, 'worry brings directionless, but fate is not directionless,'" Nadine said.

Kalman smiled, hand rested easy on the short sword. She's good to be with, he decided. Almost as good as using the right weapon, or riding a good horse.

The companions passed through a region in the North known as Nine Valley Hills. Each valley differed as the day and night, but they all had their wild life. Except things became unusually still, no bird sounded, no lizard chattered. "This area of the Vallies was deader than a New Priest monthly burial of the dead ceremony," Sae-Jyung muttered. The area's greenery wilted to a point of browning and crying out its *chi*. Everyone felt the suffering this region went through.

"This is unusual," Sae-Jyung muttered. He half-turned on his horse to face the companions and said, "Not natural, it's almost as if Seatan passed through. Look how grey and dead these plants became. Something sucked the life out of them." He shook his head, his eyes glancing to the mountains further north.

"You sure it's not part of the mage's Breaking Wars?" Jungoo asked.

"Definitely not," Sae-Jyung and Feslen answered the same time.

"The mages fought the battle with the Immortals way further north, almost near the world's balancing axis," Sae-Jyung said.

"Which, is near the End of the World, pretty much in the Ice Plains," Feslen finished for the merchant mage.

"Do we go on? Go back?" Kalman muttered aloud when threatening stormclouds gathered.

"This *is* your quest, Prince," Sae-Jyung reminded him. We've gone this far, why stop now?"

Kalman gave the merchant mage an irritated glance. The advice was unwarranted, but sound nonetheless. The companions forged on, even when the dark and stormy clouds began to pelt snow down upon them.

"We must find shelter!" Duxan said, "Feslen won't survive out here, much longer!"

"We won't survive much longer, let alone Feslen in this accursed snowstorm!" Sae-Jyung said.

Feslen said nothing.

"Is there anything you can do?" Duxan asked, putting his hands on his brother.

The wind blew bitter cold. All the companions put on many layers they could. They even wore the lice-littered clothing from the Temmer caves. Feslen, concerned for her health touched her exposed skin. Her arm was warm. "Don't be concerned for me, I'm a Northerner after all," Nadine said. "I am more inured to the cold then you."

Feslen nodded while leaning against his brother.

"My brother's forehead is cold!" Duxan said, touching his icy forehead.

Feslen was too tired to argue with his brother. He felt the area's chaotic energies drain him. The natural snowstorm did not help situations.

"No, I can't. This wind magic is beyond my strength, besides I spent much spell power against the Temmers," Sae-Jyung said, his face ragged.

The piled snow slowed Kalman. "I can't…" Feslen said through ragged breath. A chunk of snow hit him in the face, blistering it. "I need rest, Kalman."

"We need to find shelter," Kalman shielded his face as he scanned the blanketed skies.

"There!" Nadine said. "See the dot in the hills?"

Kalman nodded, he barely saw the mountain ranges in this snow blizzard.

Kalman growled and cursed the Sorceress. Her spell forced them to this new path. Duxan covered his brother best he could. The blizzard pelted them without mercy. Duxan picked up his brother as Nadine led the way. His brother was inert and Duxan's heart went cold. He sighed in some relief when he felt Feslen's weak pulse. "I need light!" Nadine called out.

"How can she expect light in this? Impossible," Kalman muttered.

Sae-Jyung waved his staff and chanted, "Murky gone, gone be blindness, see we can even in the darkness!"

The tip of his plain metal staff glowed and it detached itself! It buzzed like a bee and shrunk to the size of an outstretched palm. It glided in front of Nadine.

"Thank you, Sae-Jyung!" She shouted over the din of the full-blown blizzard.

Kalman checked on everyone's condition.

None of the companions said a word to each other, lips frozen stiff and could not wait to make camp. It took them a little over five hours to find the cave spotted by Nadine. Not all of them could fit, Kalman volunteered to stay outside.

They spent more than two days in the cave with unabated blistering storm. They argued one another until Feslen's cries made them apologize. Nadine had stopped drinking her portion of water to hand to him, but Feslen could not even swallow. Feslen's face burned, even though his body iced with feverish conditions. Kalman cursed. The fourth day rolled by and Kalman had had enough.

"That's it! We're moving out!" Kalman ordered, stunning everyone.

"But, the snow is piled to your waist, Kalman!" Duxan pointed out. "We're not as strong as you."

"We must," coughed Feslen, staggering to his feet. They looked at him in shock.

I will not cower out when we've come this far! Feslen thought. Besides, I feel Mei Xue's life force! She needs me!

"But little bro…"

"Feslen…."

"Leave me!"

"I'm sorry…" Feslen sighed, voice raspy and sore. "We must hurry, Kalman. We cannot dally any longer."

He coughed his magical fever still chilled his congealing blood. His veins however exploded in heat, all his emotions crying out all at once. It confused and angered him. He let Nadine and his brother support him as they walked. Kalman waited for the others to all file out.

As they walked in the deep snow, Feslen's fever did not ebb. He dragged on alone. He wondered what had made him throw a tantrum and began to laugh. How he made it this far, puzzled him. His companions regarded him in the strange unease he was used to all his life. Feslen grinned. Someday, they will all look at me with respect…Feslen thought.

He shook his head as the companions halted several times in the harsh blizzard. Even Kalman had to stop. Why did I think of that? Feslen wondered. I don't know…He saw hurt in Nadine's eyes. Does she love me?

Feslen turned away. She just wants to rescue her people, like all these morons. He thought.

"You all right, little brother?"

"How do you feel?" Feslen snapped. "I feel like I always do. Weak and pathetic."

Duxan sighed and said, "I don't know how you feel, ever, my brother. I cannot claim that I understand, but I can sympathize. You couldn't stand home anymore, remember?"

If it makes you feel any better, my strength returns tenfold, Duxan thought, giving his younger brother a non-verbal communication.

Feslen cocked an eye and coughed, and returned a nod.

Good, I am glad you feel better, my brother, but I feel worse! Feslen thought with bitterness. He laughed at the irony. The others looked at him in curiosity at what he laughed at. He waved them away.

"I doubt we're ever going to be right for the Chiendonese life style anyway. You are already aware of that, I am just beginning to believe."

"Indeed," Feslen said with a chuckle.

"You look stronger already, Fes. I'm glad. That was a serious fever."

"It wasn't a fever," Feslen muttered. "I will get over it, like everything else."

Feslen bowed his head, coughing. They struggled against the harsh winds and the pelting hale. Duxan feared his brother would sink in the deep snow. As Feslen walked, the snow melted away. Amazed, the companions paused to watch.

Jungoo, Nadine, Lioin inquired about this, Duxan said this never happened before. Kalman remained oddly quiet, but no one noticed.

"Stop being so weak, you fool," Feslen snarled at himself.

Even Kalman began to grit his teeth in the chill.

"The field is clearing, look, its moving to the South," Feslen said.

"Is our home safe?" Duxan said.

"What do you mean?" Feslen asked. Like I care! They didn't care about me back home…it was never home, Feslen thought. A strange, growing anger gnawed at Feslen ever since the approach to this area.

Duxan's mouth hung to the ceiling of his mouth. The cold statement hit home.

"How do you feel, Duxan?" Jungoo asked him when they crossed over a field full of energy. This odd energy swirled around, exiting and entering everyone.

"Oddly, I feel more energized. Is this what the High Forest Protector meant by, 'Those who are inborn with the Ancient Truth becomes stronger when exposed to magic, and areas where the Ancient Truth once touched.' Princess?" Duxan asked.

The companions moved on and on the seventh day, they finally reached the Sorceress' castle. Her orange, blue and white banner fluttered in the gentle wind. At long last, my mission will end! My Honor will be avenged! Kalman thought, his body tensed so much he forgot to breathe. He swung in phantom motion and pretended to wield his family artifact, the Xsi Arak, *Kei-Trui-Nahohie!*

His friends gave him a concerned look, both Duxan and Feslen asked him if he was all right. Kalman grunted an affirmative, but did not otherwise respond.

The companions stood on part of a small mountain range a mile away from Jercnko-1's castle. Many caves dotted this landscape.

Ka-Wei's goal, after four agonizing months of searching, killing and defeat was so close within reach. The loss of his Honor, the loss of his soul…the months of blood spilt in search for his sword. He glanced at his friends and wondered what the Raster brothers would think if they knew the truth. When he looked upon the single gleaming tower of the

Sorceress' castle, his spirits raised. Nothing could go wrong or stop him now. He clasped his hands in eager anticipation.

"I will no longer be dishonored, Uncle. When I return, I will make you respite the words you have discharged against my family and me!"

So excited and enthused, Kalman swung his arms in vigorous motions and sang a warrior's song.

Feslen shook his head.

They overlooked the castle grounds on the plateau's edge.

His mission was close to end.

42

JERENKO-I'S CASTLE
女魔法師城堡

A large magical barrier prevented them from advancing to the castle's maze. "Isn't this where the magi come in?" Lioin asked with a big sarcastic grin on his face.

"We-I already cast a spell trying to see the boundary's weakness," Sae-Jyung grimaced.

"Kalman's test was pretty simple," Duxan chuckled.

"All he had to do was to test my theory on energy auras," Feslen winked at Duxan.

"All right, all right. You've made your points," Sae-Jyung growled. He fished through his pouches and out came a crusty scroll.

"What's he doing? Can you understand it?" Kalman asked Feslen.

"I think he's trying to dispel it."

Sae-Jyung chanted and had a small mirror and herbs in hand; he crushed both with his bare palm. He tossed the shards of the mirror and the small plants in the air in a pentagram pattern. He repeated the chant three times. The spell revealed a blue energy protection grid around the castle. Sae-Jyung used a different scroll.

The merchant mage made a motion of opening doors and aimed his last shout at the shimmering barrier. At last a doorway formed. "Hurry," He said. "The open way will not last long."

Kalman stepped foot in it, the door shrank. "Now what?" Kalman asked.

"Thought you were powerful, Sae-Jyung," quipped Lioin.

The merchant mage glared at him and the thief shivered. "Can anyone else…."

Nadine stepped up, placing her face to the ground and murmured a prayer. A soft green light pulsed from her body and into the shimmering barrier, creating a Lioin-sized doorway. "Hurry, I can hold it open, but not for long," she said, sweat dripped from her delicate face.

Lioin hurried through the tiny opening Nadine created. The doorway closed on him and he flew back out, as if the barrier spat him out. Lioin screeched when his clothes caught fire. Nadine had to heal him.

The companions waited around for an hour when the skies darkened.

What am I missing? Why can I not see any energy? Feslen pondered, pacing in thought. Sae-Jyung tried again and failed, his shoulders drooped in exhaustion. Kalman told him to save his spells. Feslen kicked a loose pebble against the barrier. The barrier vibrated different colors in different areas. A sudden thought occurred to him. "Lioin, Jungoo, could you toss pebbles oh, say, ten feet away from me at the barrier?" Feslen tossed another one against the barrier, this time a blazing electric sheet of white orange shaft him.

The two questioned him, as he warned the others to get back. "Just do it," he murmured. They complied. Nothing happened when Lioin and Jungoo tossed them. The pebbles bounced back out every time. Perhaps those with energy can go through…or dispel it, Feslen thought.

"Nadine, Sae-Jyung, will you do it next?" They complied. Both Nadine and Sae-Jyung's went through. They gasped as Feslen laughed.

"What?" Kalman's face twisted in anxiousness.

"Duxan, toss a pebble at the same spot."

Duxan complied and knew what Feslen wanted. Duxan's toss created sparkles of green when it went through. The others gasped. "Now, Kalman, you try at the spot Lioin tossed."

Kalman complied. The barrier sparked a dark blue when the Prince's pebble hit it. "Now, all of us will do it at the same time."

Feslen picked one up, as did Kalman and Duxan. They tossed and the barrier exploded in shimmering scintillating colors, creating a Feslen-sized gap. Feslen ran through the explosions, despite the warnings of his companions. The violent burping barrier shivered once more, and held!

"Kalman, Duxan now follow me," Feslen said, still grinning. The two did so and the gap widened. The others hurried in, fearing the potential collapse. It did not.

"How will we get back out?" Duxan asked as the doorway shivered to a close when all of them entered.

"We'll worry about that when we return," said Kalman.

Duxan nodded.

The companions entered the large maze. A sign appeared in the Ancient Chiendonese only Feslen could read, it said, "Thank you for coming. Welcome to the home of the Jerenko-I, greatest of magicians."

Another sign popped up in front of Kalman. It was a riddle written in the modern language. "This way is south, stupid!" It read, "Before you step further, what takes two steps backwards, but yet gains a foot every step without ever taking to the ground?"

"I have no time for silly riddles!" Kalman growled and he stepped forward, but the grass before him gave way and became mud. He hissed in pain when he slammed his back.

Lioin and the others suppressed a giggle. Another sign floated around the Prince: "I knew you were a thick-headed, Prince, but I didn't realize how dumb! Now, what is the answer to my riddle?"

Kalman frowned in deep thought. Contrary to what the Sorceress' sign said, and to the popular of the people outside of Chiendong, Kalman was the not the average Prince. All over the maze, Nadine and the others noticed beautiful trimmed plants. Wind motifs were everywhere.

"Wind," the prince and the young Raster answered at the same time.

The sign blinked in colors. A frowning face appeared in its place: "I guess that was too easy, even for you, Prince. There are six possible paths, but seven exits, not including your way out. Do be careful…I would so love to see you in person. Having you dead won't serve my purposes, though it wouldn't be a sad thing either. You have one hour to make it to my castle door. Or, Mei Xue dies."

"Wait! How do I know she's alive?"

Wind howled again, flashing thunder for a moment. A viewing portal appeared and dainty Mei Xue, despondent in her slave's uniform, in a dungeon. Feslen narrowed his gaze.

"All right, I'll play your game, witch," said the Prince through clenched teeth.

"Tsk tsk," the Sorceress said in the flaming portal. They could see her slender silhouette, but nothing else.

"Wait! What about Mei-Whuay, our sister?" Duxan asked, in a half-growl.

However, the image was gone and the doorway winked out as if it never existed.

"She's still alive, but we have not much time, Kalman," Feslen offered.

"Is there anyone mapping? I know mazes, but…."…Kalman said with a shake of his head.

"I will," Lioin volunteered with childlike eagerness made the companions smile. He began to trace and draw on a piece of paper.

The Sorceress had told the truth about her maze. Six paths, three split to the left and to the right. Some paths went downward, shaped like down staircases of a dungeon, others up.

Kalman hid his grin and stopped the young thief from drawing a very detailed map. They would be here the week after tomorrow, should Lioin begin. "Young friend, I need a sketch, not a true map."

"Oh," Lioin said. "Sure, no problem."

They continued for thirty minutes on their journey south to the castle. At the entrance, they encountered groups of deformed humans. Some had one arms, others had no eyes, and others had their jaw ripped open.

"Please, help us!" One of them cried. Feslen had to look away and close his eyes for a moment. He took a deep breath, trying to regain confidence.

Kalman handed out some bread and cheese and tried to push through the gathering mob of people. What used to be two became ten. They came from all the open directions. Lioin did his best to ignore them and mapped out their area as Nadine marked their path with a chalk.

"I have a bad feeling about this," Feslen said, crouching.

"Dreadful!" Jungoo murmured. "This is equal to my people's pains."

They closed around the companions, grasping and groaning like undead.

The companions raised their weapons, confused. "What are they, under a spell?" Kalman yelled above the tumult of their cries.

"More!" The mass of humanity cried.

"I don't know," Feslen said. "I feel an energy working here, but it could be the entire maze covered by the Sorceress' power. How about you, Sae-Jyung?"

Sae-Jyung attempted extraction of his staff from the goblinoids.

"May the Sun Goddess have mercy!" Nadine cried.

The goblinoids clawed each other and some imploded, splattering the companions. Jungoo cried out. Kalman growled as the mutants turned to attack.

These goblinoids look so wretched, Feslen thought. It would be wrong and almost bad for our karma kill them. "No…wait, no more killing!" Feslen yelled, even as a hand almost punctured his eyes. The companions stood back to back; weapons readied.

Feslen spotted out of place. "Hurry up, little brother!" Duxan said, parrying blow after blow.

After he concentrated, Feslen gasped. The sun played peek-a-boo with some wind clouds and this clued him in…the shadows of his friends overlapped their real height. He forgot the fighting noises and reached deep within his meditation well. "See the truth," he heard Master Chai talking to him.

No sunlight bounced off his friend's weapons and armor.

"Better figure it out, Feslen!" It could have been anyone of them urging him.

"These are not real; the wind and sunlight aren't real. There is a pattern to it. Drop your weapons and surrender to the true sun."

"It feels real," returned Lioin, but the others did as Feslen told.

Instinctive use of his Flair, Feslen reached out and pulled energy auras. He pulled when it felt soothing, and stopped when it did not. Musical chimes erupted, startling everyone.

A burst shattered the illusions. Feslen huffed and staggered at the blow of his own Flow. Reeling, Feslen peddled on heels, but Duxan supported him. Feslen's energy trickled away. He glanced at his companions, trying to hide his fear. His companions looked haggard and fearful too.

"The illusion she placed disappeared."

"How did you do it, Fes?" Lioin asked.

"Trade secrets," Feslen replied with a wink, too tired to explain.

The humanoids echoed in talk, and one spoke after their mouths moved, as if someone cast a spell in slow motion. The design of the maze did not allow echoes.

"You just don't know, do you?" laughed Lioin.

"No, I just won't reveal my secrets to a thief!"

Kalman kept a straight face and congratulated his young friend.

Kalman and the others continued, but Feslen waited for a moment with his brother, Nadine and Sae-Jyung. "You need training, Feslen. Leave the spell casting to me," said Sae-Jyung.

Feslen frowned. Whatever he did, seemed to not affect his friends too much…he sighed. Sae-Jyung followed the rest. Nadine and Duxan hung back for a moment.

"It's sound reasoning, Feslen," Nadine said. "I felt a terrible shattering of my *chi* when you reached in with whatever you saw." She shuddered.

Astonished and terrified by the look on the Princess' face, Feslen could only nod. If his Nadine was frightened, for some reason, he did felt less confident. When did Nadine become *his*?

"You did well though," she complimented and gave him a brief hug. Feslen did not know how to respond, for he realized she hugged out of pure response. She hurried to catch up with the others.

"Kid, you were awesome, I don't know what happened, but I was less affected by it then the others were. Perhaps you should save your strength as much as possible. Next time you spot out of the ordinary things, let us know, please," Duxan said, patting him.

Duxan waited until Feslen caught his breath and walked slow with him. Right now, Duxan cannot read his brother's stony face and had little idea what went though Fes's mind. Duxan thought it best for him and the rest of them if Feslen stopped casting. After all, Duxan thought. We have three capable magicians; we are near the end of the quest, when will we need his help?

Duxan did not realize the trueness of his thoughts.

Troubled, Feslen walked in silence. He wondered who would teach him, they all seemed afraid of him. An odd sensation gnawed in his tummy and heart for the first time: he enjoyed the thrill of using his Ancient Truth. The part he enjoyed most was seeing his friends afraid of him…and his growing Awareness…he licked his lips in anticipation of gaining more strength soon. He gave Sae-Jyung a very envious look for a brief second.

"Do you have any feelings of the paths, Duxan, Feslen?" Kalman asked his mind and soul aching to get back to his Xsi-Arak. The glazed look on Feslen worried Kalman.

"The right feels fine. The left I can't pinpoint, but there doesn't seem to be anything else I can sense, not even my own heart," Duxan said, when Feslen did not answer. Duxan saw the hungry look on his brother's face and frowned. He worried about this new development, but said nothing. He just figured his brother would grow out of it.

"Well, we have to take the right, whether we have a choice or not," Kalman stated the obvious, as a large metal door slammed down on the left.

"Maybe not," Sae-Jyung offered. "Maybe she's protecting something there, or a way in, that's how wizards do their thing."

"Too obvious," Nadine shook her head. "Doesn't everyone feel the wind? I do believe force of winds comes from the upper or lower paths."

"I'm scouting ahead, I will detail you what I see," Lioin volunteered

Kalman said, "No. We don't split up; I don't like to lose anyone if possible. We'll go right, since Duxan and Nadine feel that it is okay."

Lioin dropped back behind them and continued to map.

Feslen wanted to speak up, but could not. I must conserve my powers, Feslen realized, wheezing. His chest tightened in pain again. He pondered this, but realized his companions left him behind. He caught up to them when they waited.

"The right one feels right, huh?" Lioin shouted. "Nice choice, Duxan!" The companions held onto whatever part of the maze they could. The wind forced the companions to crawl.

Feslen reached last for the wind reverberated through him well before the others. He wondered how they fell into such an obvious trap. The magical wind pinned his companions to the maze and even strong Kalman. Feslen's face screwed in search of a solution.

Feslen and the others heard strange metal clanking sounds. Where did the noise come from? He stood on the periphery of the windblasts.

Duxan looked for an object to block the wind. "Earth goes against wind," he murmured to himself, remembering school.

"Come on!" Kalman screamed, alarming the others. "Show yourself, Jerenko-I!"

"He's finally cracked," Sae-Jyung whispered to Lioin. The young thief cracked a grin.

The Sorceress' hair-raising laughter filled the air.

Jungoo blanched

"You will die on my sword today, Sorceress!" Kalman promised.

"Come and find out how well you'll die today, Sorceress, and my honor will be completed!" The Sorceress laughed.

"The Sorceress sounds like a crone who drank too much," Jungoo cringed.

"You have no choice, Hero, I have your prisoners!"

"The villains, why do they always have to come up with the silliest revenge plots?" Lioin asked.

"Nadine, doesn't earth stop wind?" Duxan shouted to the Princess. She moved to get near him.

"That's it!" Duxan cried into the wind. He edged himself away from the group. With strength of giants, the wind lifted stone pieces from the floors.

The companions gasped as throughout this, Duxan stayed rooted.

"Kalman? I need your strength!" Duxan pleaded. A flash of understanding filled Duxan's infinite wise being. *'Earth blocks wind, wind is not a friend of earth, though they help each other at times.'* Duxan's inner voice told him.

The Prince and the elder Raster worked together, ignoring the harsh howling wind…pieces of stone almost decapitated them many times, had it not been for shouts of friends.

Duxan felt warm, unaccountable happiness as he walked towards the rocks the wind ripped apart. With ease in partnership, Duxan handed Kalman the rocks and they built a great wall rock barrier. When the winds started to die down, They all saw the wind machine now, glistening of glass and metal. This won't work, Feslen thought, shaking his head. Feslen was awed and puzzled by Duxan's incredible feat.

When Duxan used his Ancient Truth, he used it while imagining his friends, loved ones in the hands of evil. He did with a song in his heart, he felt happy to be sharing this secret and ability to help.

Of course, the older Raster brother did not know this at the time; he just went about it as if he had done this sort of thing all his life. He did not feel his Ancient Truth rising, or any at all when he built the damned rock pile. Nor, did he catch Feslen's face; he was too busy having a genuine time of it. He did, however, pick up an agitated feeling from his brother, so when he stopped piling rocks to look over at them, he did not see any expression on Feslen's usual expressive face. Duxan did not puzzle over that until later.

After all the stones blocked the huge wind apparatus, the wind died down. The companions stopped bracing and dropped to the ground in relief. Feslen continued to observe his brother. Duxan talked to the ground, coaxing it, mother did this with their plants when they wanted them to grow.

Feslen rubbed his eyes to make sure he did not see things. He gasped a pulsing greenish white glow surround Duxan. The aura came out of the ground itself and Duxan absorbed it he built the rock wall! The green aura for a moment, enlarged and expanded much to Feslen's astonished puzzlement.

Duxan's energy winked out quicker than a doused torch. Why did no one, not even himself, notice Duxan's energy before this? Feslen wondered, with pride, anger and jealousy.

The Prince and the others congratulated Duxan, when the Sorceress' voice filtered in, "Tsk tsk. Do you think it would be that easy?" Laughter filled the air as wind picked up again. This time, it was not from the odd machine.

To Feslen, this wind reminded him of the energy barrier they encountered earlier. To test a theory, Feslen looked for the weak points in the energy field. Occasional blue splotches of energy would mesh into the perfect whiteness of this barrier. He watched, thinking it a random pattern. He noticed the patterns came in single file sequence, similar to musical notes. "It seems like the energies are the same as the barrier, right little bro?" Duxan said.

Feslen nodded.

"Kalman, just step into the path where Feslen is standing," Duxan said, after realizing what Feslen had in mind.

Feslen's arms had gotten cold when Kalman replaced him. Duxan stepped behind Kalman, while Feslen watched. Feslen watched a few moments more, and stepped right behind Duxan. He asked Duxan to shift a little more to the right.

They waited for instructions, nothing happened. His friends' complaint of the cold wind became constant. Feslen was not sure what to do and attempted to access his Ancient Truth. He felt drier than mountain air and surprised himself by not worrying. He studied the energy pattern again. If earth can't defeat wind…he thought his narrowing. He saw the symmetry of the colors now, thanks to Kalman's and Duxan's powerful auras. He pulled at the *wind itself*…

Feslen tugged at the wind with his inner fires. He feared resistance from the wind, but to his delight, found none. Sudden fire energy exploded from his body, expanding quicker than he could contain it. He pulled the wind as if they were spools of thread. His fire energy wrapped itself around the wind and absorbed it, snapping the 'string-like wind' to pieces.

He thought he saw wind for what it was: clear blue droplets of water shape of diamonds. He saw the cleanliness of the wind thanks to his Ancient Truth. *So, my Ancient Truth remained with me all this time, how can I not access it?* Feslen thought, in part wonder and frustration. He negated the wind powers when he pulled them in towards itself. His fire powers died out just as he defeated the winds. He heard the gasps from Nadine and Sae-Jyung. He felt the thrill of seeing nature for what she was.

Why he did this, Feslen did not know. In matter of minutes, even though the pulling pained him, the wind died. Though the scars of the wind displayed on his arms, hands and face looked awful, he grinned. His stunned friends applauded him. He felt hungry and tired, but knew they had little time to celebrate. The path opened up to them. He led them towards the right corridor the one will lead them to the captives and the Sorceress.

The castle was twenty feet away across an expansive field and cross a rickety bridge.

The only bridge across was long damaged.

Feslen noticed tremendous amount of energy crisscrossing in a chess-board pattern across the castle. "Amazing," Feslen said. "She created this whole with her magic."

Sae-Jyung nodded, face pale.

Four robed statues guarded the bridge, and in the far side of the room, *Ninkatta* statues stood. "This is a trap," Kalman murmured.

"How are we supposed to cross without a bridge?" Jungoo asked.

Feslen walked up to the statues.

"Feslen…" Kalman warned.

The four magi statues faced one another, *Ninkatta* statues faced outward towards potential visitors. "Not to mention they all seem to indicate the middle of the floor," Feslen muttered. "No risk taken, no reward gained."

Kalman hesitated. Feslen sighed and stepped forward, but Duxan stopped him. "I feel that this place has falseness to it, Kid."

"I know, but I feel we…I am being led into this trap on purpose. I don't see any alternative routes."

"We should test it, don't you think, Feslen?" Duxan agitated.

"Mei Xue and Mei-Whuay are in trouble, I feel it," Feslen said with a sigh.

"As do I, but,"…Duxan said and stopped.

Feslen knew what his older brother wanted to say, and was grateful he did not. "Feslen, wait…I'll come with you," Nadine said.

"I know this to be a risky trap, but, you know me," Feslen said with a grin. He stepped into the trap, aware of the possibilities.

The world collapsed upon Feslen.

43

FACE-OFF 對抗

Strong magical forces bound Feslen and blinded him. Feslen struggled against the burning magic that held him. It did not burn him, but helpless threatened to engulf him. Worse yet, he did not even sense his friends. The dank, smelly dungeon threatened to overwhelm him. He did not register the oily stream trickling beneath him. The oil trickled with the slimy water, creating odd sensations through Feslen's nose. The stink was too much. He tried to complete Master Chai's Dragon Steps. He heard his sister's screams and Mei Xue's screams. Rage boiled through his being.

Don't panic, concentrate on what's real, Feslen heard Master Chai.

He heard human movement, and he registered them as guards. Prisoners shouted in misery. Feslen used his rage to break free. He felt his Ancient Truth boiling. Feslen ignored the putrid smells coming from the prison and prisoners and anguished cries of the prisoners, the dank none circulated air, the sewage smells, and occasional strewn corpses. He ignored the giant rats gnawing at the bodies, and his legs when he strode through the unlit halls. He rounded the corner, and a guard rushed him with a sword. Flames erupted from Feslen's hands and burned the human guard.

More guards of the New Priests and Elhong School rushed him.

Dark fires erupted from Feslen's entire body, exploding all around, igniting the odd frothy water beneath his feet. The fires engulfed the guards, who screamed for mercy.

But, Feslen did not notice…he sank deeper into darkness with each kill. With his deep darkness, he slaughtered them without mercy. He stomped through like a bull, rushing to find his enemy, and his sister and friend. Part of him, however, the innocent boy cringed at every kill. Feslen's soul did not know where the darkness emanated from, or how to stop it from spreading like the plague…as his energies and awareness grew and expanded, his lust for killing did as well. The innocent boy that was once Feslen died with each kill. Unbeknownst to Feslen, a tear somehow managed to appear in his eyes, creeping out from his inner fires…

He knew Mei Xue Chai and Mei-Whuay were close.

A voice echoed in a mix sounding like Master Chai and that inner boy told Feslen, *This is not what is supposed to happen…magic is meant for helping, not destroying…*

He paused in distraction at the voice, his power lowered a bit. Then he heard Master Chai's voice, *"You made a promise, young man. Not to kill or to give in to your desires."*

Feslen lowered his hands and stared at the corpses littered around him in shame and some guilt. He tried to justify the mass murder by saying aloud, "They were out to stop me…I am here to rescue people I care about."

A poisonous cloud erupted around him and choked him, catching him off guard. The aroma mixed with aged garlic and scallion.

"Elhong Wien!" Feslen growled. "Show yourself!"

He fought the poisons as long as he could, but at the end, his undisciplined and untrained Ancient Truth and magic failed him. He passed out.

strong familiar scent awoke Feslen. The person smelled of aged garlic and this time cherry pulp. A slow rhythmic clapping behind him alerted him. Feslen turned, and spotted an outline of his archenemy.

"Well done, I must commend you for coming this far, Feslen!" A slow chuckling followed. "I didn't think you could make it here. You made it after all."

The voice, sounded like a young man, though distinct. The smell of rotten garlic surrounded them…Death hovered near him.

They were in a second prison room, but this time, Feslen saw torture devices on the walls and floors. He saw Mei-Whuay bound as a pleasure slave on one of the devices. Her blood spilled all over the device, her Honor taken from her.

Feslen's rage increased to the point of his eyes blurred. The room spun in his anger. I have no fear of you now, Elhong Wien, Feslen thought. I know you and begin to understand your powers. You channel your energies from the powers of the moon, Feslen chuckled in his mind. The main difference is that you pervert your aura, with my Ancient Truth, I can defeat you!

"Elhong Wien," Feslen spat. "Release my sister, by the Gods; if you've harmed one hair on her body I will destroy you!"

"Why…your sister is just fine. Aren't you, little pretty one?" Elhong Wien grinned.

A soft murmur of agreement came from the darkness. Robes rustled and the soft kisses of unloved lips. Feslen growled and still found himself entangled. "What have you done to her?" He cried out.

"Why, Feslen, my dear brother…I didn't think you cared for me. Welcome, welcome to the world's doom," Mei-Whuay responded in a voice not her own.

"Fight him, sister!" Feslen pleaded. "What happened to my friends?" I will not let you destroy Mei-Whuay's innocence anymore, he thought, anger activating his Ancient Truth fires.

"Your companions are being dealt with quite well, I assure you. You have a chance to save them though….assuming you accept several choices I give you."

The light went on, shattering the blissful darkness. Feslen took a moment to adjust and saw Mei-Whuay, clad. She had a vacant look.

"You monster!" Feslen growled at Elhong Wien, all the memories of past events and clues flowed into him like hot magic. He was Mei-Whuay's employer when things went poor for his adopted family. He was affiliated to the Elhong Sung School. Just as Feslen figured things out his enemy even gloated about his deeds, confirmed Feslen's suspicions.

"You!" Feslen bellowed and struggled to get free. Magic thrived in this room. A portal appeared.

The man was Elhong Wien. His hated arch-nemesis even when a babe in his adoptive family's home. Memories flooded Feslen during his Ancient Truth's awakening. *He saw the New Priest trying to convince Mother Wong to kill him, but Duxan stopped him…*

The New Priest, Elhong Wien in a female apprentice chef body. She whispered words of poison in master chef Miaynuemo's ears…

Feslen should have recognized that poison at once. The New Priests used this sort of poison often in the ritual 'cures'.

"It was YOU, who set the whole stage into action! You persuaded the Sorceress and *Ninkatta* to go after my family and friends! You who killed Master Chai…I recognize that poison anywhere. You kidnapped my sister and best friend. Why? I ought to slaughter you as you stand!"

"Ah, the true colors of the young Hero! You know very well why, young Raster. Power and fear equals respect, it's what I've wanted all my life and I know you seek the same!"

"I am NOTHING like you. I am nowhere near your sins. I will never cave to evil."

"Oh, no? Look, what your Ancient Truth has accomplished, little one. I can help you…. The Princess, Seatan, they are all out for their own means. I know where your Karma lies!"

Feslen looked about, clenching his fists in anger, his eyes reddened at the sight of the innocent dead soldiers. His eyes rested back on the newest version of Elhong Wien. What he was, Feslen did little to ponder. This man was not in his original, middle-aged thick-haired body. Feslen pointed at the New Priest, his Eternal Flow exploding from the Eternal Well.

"I am NOT You. I will NEVER be. This is for everything I ever suffered in my life. This is for my friends who died at your hands. Perish, vile demon."

As surges of black fire and wind erupted from Feslen towards the wounded New Priest, the man laughed, "Don't think you can avoid your Karma….don't think you won't be what I am…."

A ball of darkness erupted from the New Priest and enveloped him and Mei-Whuay. Feslen's fire energy petered out when it slammed into the shield. Your powers won't last long, Feslen thought.

"If only you accepted my offer," sang the New Priest. "With your magic and my brains, the world will be ours!"

"I don't WANT the world, I want peace and harmony!" Feslen roared, his wealth of fires seemed limitless, and continued to pound away at the man's shield.

"Come join us, brother. You'll love it!" Feslen heard Mei-Whuay laugh.

His enemies always made the same mistake. They can come after me, but come after my family and friends…Feslen thought. "Leave her be!" He howled and reached deep within his soul. He felt the love his family has for him and continued to use his rage. The fiery wrath continued to bash away at the New Priest's dark shield barrier. But, a second and third energy source leapt from Feslen's once frail body to surround the room, shaking the castle.

Without knowing, the young Ancient Truth wielder opened a connection to a vast power beyond his understanding and control…His energies ripped into the fabric of the entire universal life energies and tore open a vortex. This vortex opened both in the universe and in himself.

The pure form of power of electricity, fire and wind roared through Feslen. Those with magic could see these natural forces entomb Feslen in a funnel. Feslen stood as an angelic being in the midst of a hell storm.

The magical battle between the two foes shook the castle and its very surrounding land.

Elhong Wien enacted barrier after barrier, chanting in a furious pace just to keep up with Feslen's sheer raw power.

Feslen recognized the New Priest was on the defensive. He knew from Elhong Wien's tone, he was weakening and enacting a few offensive spells. Why the New Priest became so weak, Feslen did not know or care.

"Get out of my life, Elhong Wien, now and forever!" He screamed. His energies converged into a huge fiery phoenix and it dove through the man's shield.

Elhong Wien laughed, and pointed and dark beams shot forth. The beams of darkness, the same beam he used against him when the monk from Thai-Thurian helped out speared through Feslen's Ancient Truth and aimed at not as his body, but his soul…

This darkness puzzled Feslen even as he concentrated on controlling his Ancient Truth. The dark powers used by Elhong Wien seemed familiar to him on an emotional and spiritual level. His Awareness expanded, but, he, the person, still did not understand what was happening. The Ancient Truth kicked in on its own, helped dawning comprehension in Feslen. The Ancient Truth's massive energies, the universal energies, absorbed the dark powers. Feslen's Ancient Truth then transformed the dark powers into light by infusing love and goodness into it.

Elhong Wien flailed about when his darkness became purified by the Ancient Truth. Pure light and happiness inched its way into erasing the dark auras that encased Elhong Wien. "Noooo! This cannot happen! I cannot lose this way!" The Head New Priest screeched. He held his holy symbol, a sigil of a horned demon.

He screamed final words, "Oh Dark Goddess save me!"

Waves of vibrating dark energies plunged into the room even from the dying Elhong Wien. The room shook and tipped. Powerful vertigo-like symptoms assailed Feslen. Sudden fears that were his own, and not his own sprung in Feslen's mind, even while his Ancient Truth kept active. Boils appeared on Feslen's hands, age burned into him. He screamed for a moment at the illusionary attacks. He shook his head and thought, Wait a minute. These aren't my fears! But, more fears entered his being. He saw loved ones tortured and enslaved, and turning to the dark side.

He saw himself as Emperor of the world…using "becoming an individual and learner of magic" as an excuse…

Then, voices attacked him. Voices of the dead, the ones he killed. "You enjoy killing! Yes you do! You are the killer, Chaos Wielder…that gypsy failed to mention that part in her people's Prophecies!"

Feslen put his hands on his ears and growled, "No! I am not like that! Get out of my head!"

He then fell into meditation and preformed Master Chai's Twelve Dragon Steps. The voices and fears faded away into a whisper.

The New Priest's final attack stunned Feslen and burned him, but it did not destroy its real goal…

Through instinct, Feslen honed the dark magic to his own Ancient Truth. Elated at the infused new energies, Feslen pointed at the writhing New Priest, Elhong Wien. "Be gone, foul demon," hissed Feslen and he added, "Justice is finally done!" Dark fires exploded from Feslen's fingers, consuming his soul as it surged out and slammed into the dying Elhong Wien. The dark fire licked the flesh off the man's bones.

He screamed but then died in laughter.

A dark globe formed from nowhere to surround Elhong Wien's body, blinding Feslen for a moment. The burning corpse of Elhong Wien vanished along with the globe.

Feslen blinked as sudden calm rang in his ears.

With the aftermath of the magical battle, the castle walls rumbled and reeled.

Feslen did not notice. Mei-Whuay whimpered.

Before he recovered from his apparent victory, and could explain things to his sister, his energies, still flickering with life, did something he did not expect.

It animated the dead around them, and they advanced on them, evil intent in their eyes. Now Feslen wished he had not killed all those guards the New Priest sent after him. Feslen felt a slight flickering of his energies still and he nodded to himself in confidence. He heard his sister shriek at the approach of the undead. He shoved her behind him and started to power up.

44

MAGE vs. CHEF 魔術師戰廚師

After his battle with the undead, Feslen rested a bit. But, he heard a distinct clinking noise. The noise of cookware scraped against one another. "Very good Feslen," said Master Chef Miaynuemo as he walked out of the darkness. He and four other *nirahkos* followed, armed to the teeth. "I didn't think you'd make it this far. You won't get past me."

Feslen grinned and began to power up again. I've waited five months for this moment. I am no longer the scared little kid you bullies and took advantage of, Feslen thought. He raised his arms out as he pushed his still-dazed sister behind him. Energy pulsated around him. He brightened most of the room with his powers, blinding his opponents. His light-powered spell covered only half the room by his design. He made sure all of the ground between himself and the walls were lit, so the *nirahkos* could not use their Martial Arts' techniques.

"I've changed, Miaynuemo. This time I will succeed," Feslen said his tone cold and angry.

"You will not get past me, young Master," Miaynuemo promised. "I wish to have Mei Xue for myself."

His enemies always underestimated him! Why do they always push the wrong buttons? Feslen thought with a shake of his head. "That's where you're wrong, chef," Feslen spat and said the word chef in contempt. "You'd better not have laid a hand upon Mei Xue. Or by, the Sun Goddes, I'll rip your heart out."

"Attack!" the Master Chef ordered his men. Two *nirhakos* leapt at Feslen, the other two used the Shadow Martial Arts and melded into the darkness that still remained.

Feslen used the First Dragon Step and the Fourth Dragon Step named Defense of Cheetah, for defensive purposes. He calculated his opponents' weights and heights while concentrating his energies on Miaynuemo. A *nirahkos* swung his sword at Feslen's head. The young boy, with his energy at its height grabbed the sword by its sharp edge and used the attacker's momentum and flung him. Blue energy sparkled through Feslen and through the sword of the *nirahkos*, engulfing him. He screamed as he was flung away. He landed with a heavy thud and a sound of cracking ribs.

The other *nirahkos* circled Feslen with caution. Feslen, half-turned his head and saw the other two *nirahkos* in the partial darkness. They tried to go after the half-dazed Mei-Whuay. Feslen shook his head and pointed at them. He felt fire explode from his hands. Fire arrows sprung from Feslen's fingers and ripped into the *nirahkos* hidden in the shadows. They slammed into the walls with a grunt and slumped over.

Feslen turned his head again when he heard Miaynuemo chant. The former Master Chef pulled some fruit seeds from his pockets. "Again? Don't you think I've learned those tricks, chef?" Feslen chuckled.

He powered up so much that his hair spiked up and he charged at the Master Chef and the last remaining *nirahkos*. The *nirahkos* dodged, but he was not Feslen's intent. "Before you die," Feslen said to Miaynuemo, "A five-year old cooks better than you. Where'd you learn to cook, from a toad? Master Chai, myself and Tang Swuai never liked your cooking."

"Is that your opinion or fact, young fool?" Miaynuemo hissed, though Feslen heard a bit of a strain on the older man's part. The Master Chef finished his chant as he tossed the shelled fruit up in the air. His cleaver was coming down on the shelled fruit.

Feslen stopped in his mid-air kick right at the Master Chef's throat and then swatted his arms up at the falling fruit. His intense energy burned the fruit to a crisp at the same time he caught the former Master Chef's cleaver.

Miaynuemo made a stunned sound.

"This is for Tang Swuai!" Feslen screamed and sent electricity down the Master Chef's cleaver. The fat man screamed when the jolts of power shocked him.

Feslen flipped over and kicked him in the back, sending him forward. Feslen did not let go, however and swung the portly Miaynuemo around like a rag doll. Feslen's energies grew tenfold in his anger.

The Master Chef screamed and tried to chant. Feslen snarled and said, "You should stick to cooking…oh wait, you can't cook!"

"I was acting under the influence of the New Priests!" Master Chef Miaynuemo screamed.

"That won't help you!" Feslen shouted and let go his inner fires of energy. "For Tang Swuai!" Fires so hot exploded from Feslen that it began to melt some surrounding stone as it engulfed the chef. Feslen let go and did a back flip and landed in front his sister once again. He almost collapsed in exhaustion. Sweat poured from his face.

"I didn't hurt Mei Xue…" whimpered the dying Master Chef.

The fires of Feslen engulfed the Master Chef and he toppled, still burning.

Feslen stared grimly at the unrecognizable pulp of Miaynuemo. "For you, Tang Swuai," he whispered, staggering against a still-dazed Mei-Whuay.

The last *nirahkos* raised his sword and looked at Feslen as if considering to attacking him. Feslen gave the man a glare and beckoned him to come, despite his tiredness.

The *nirahkos* looked down at his dead comrades and then at the exhausted boy. Feslen's eyes narrowed and his arms pointed at him. The *nirahkos* dropped his weapon and bowed at Feslen and fled.

Feslen laughed in an insane manner and sat down on his behind, overcome with exhaustion.

45

BROKEN ROYALTY 王權之爭

Back in the courtyard of the Sorceress' castle, Jerenko-I, the Sorceress, said, "Well, stubborn lord? Your hope is gone. I have your precious sword. Will you kneel and give allegiance to my rule? Hand over Crown to my son, and the Emperor will tremble. I will release you and your companions."

"Why not just kill me for it?" Kalman asked, spitting. "Most true warlords would do so."

Jerenko-I frowned and replied, "I am not a warlord, nephew. Besides, it would be crude to kill a relative; this is something a fat, inept relative of ours would do. Our family sword rightfully belongs to me and has the power I crave. This sword is an artifact and the key to your Father's empire. You have the command words and ability to wield it, I can't."

"What?" Kalman asked eyes wide with shock. "It's just a special Xsi-Arak. Not an artifact…"

"You take me for a fool, young Prince? Your parents had it for generations in their family and your father, Wei Wu Shang knew the magic words to activate it."

Kalman laughed. "My father died when I was eight, you should know. If you truly cared, aunty, you should've rescued me from Uncle's rule."

Jerenko-I sighed and patted her hair. "I tried to intervene on your behalf, but couldn't, dear nephew. I wanted to train you for myself. That idiot Garland, my inept, dear, third brother Jien, and his then New Priest prevented me."

Kalman heard the disdain in her voice and exchanged looks with Duxan. The Prince kept silent and Kalman judged his aunt told some truth, which parts, he had yet to decide.

"I offer you an allegiance, like I did before, nephew. Together, we can bring the Empire to its knees…"

"I don't make deals with terrorists and murderers."

"So that's how you view me," she sighed, continued, not noticing his sudden silence. "So, I take my revenge in other ways. I don't want to kill you, nephew, if I don't have to…Now, for the Crowning…"

Why involve us? Duxan thought, but dared not to interrupt.

"I can't make that decision, my Uncle and the Emperor can. Take it up them, you heartless wench," Kalman spat.

The Sorceress glared at him. Kalman did not flinch throughout the whipping. Said she, "Stubborn, just like my brother, your uncle. You are Shang. Why, why do you care so much of this Crown or country, Prince? You know your uncle isn't the lawful King."

"Be that as it may, you of all people should understand, my *Queen*. I cannot allow the Crown to be usurped by corrupt members like you."

Two other New Priest acolytes whipped the Prince with wicked curved weapons, but Kalman withstood it.

"You are running out of time, stubborn nephew."

"Go to Black Depths," Kalman laughed.

The Sorceress waved her hand and the aroma of crushed sulphur and flower petals wafted the air. She yelled, "Behold!"

A viewing portal of wind appeared.

It showed Feslen rescuing Mei-Whuay and running right into a water pit of five hungry giant bear-like crocodiles. Duxan wept even as Kalman grimaced at the gruesome scene.

Kalman sighed, and he lowered his head, he forced his tears out. He feigned defeat to the Sorceress and murmured in a broken voice, "Allow me to at least make a proper passing of the Crown."

The Sorceress's eyes went wide with surprise and she laughed.

"You can't do it, Prince! You know Feslen would never allow it!" The older Raster did catch the subtle hint in his friend's voice and played along. He knew the Prince bluffed the Sorceress and hoped whatever Kalman's plan worked.

"I have no choice, Duxan. I wish no harm upon the others, do you?"

Duxan's body quivered when his own Ancient Truth helped increase his awareness to his bother's situation. He tried to hide his enthusiasm.

"I think we can agree on that. I allow your son to be Honored and in front of many witnesses, highness," Kalman allowed.

The Sorceress looked thoughtful, "Very well, we shall pass the candle to my son; you may perform the ceremony in front of your friends. One…wrong move…"

"I know, I know. We all die. I'll need a proper sword too, my Queen."

The Sorceress's face went blank again and her face turned grave. "I'll look for one suitable for the Kingdom's newest hero…"

Kalman saw her face glaze over. Even years of training and discipline, the Prince found it hard to contain his anticipation. Reuniting him with his sword sent a wave of thrill through him. He dared to believe the Sorceress would fall for his simple trick.

In the small royal courtyard, Kalman and Duxan, still in chains and bound to poles, waited for the precession to begin, unaware of the rebellion started by Feslen. The bright sunlight leant no comfort to the imprisoned friends. But, the Prince stayed calm throughout and remained unimpressed by his aunt. "If this is all she has," Kalman stated to his friend as they remained in the kneeling position under many watchful eyes. "What a pathetic kingdom they would make."

Duxan said nothing, but agreed in essence. Politicians and royalty respected glitter, glitz and large things. However, the Sorceress had none.

The Sorceress came out, instead of flowing hair she braided. A wide-eyed nine-year old trailed her, holding her kimono. Moi Ge Wien, older brother of Elhong Wien and leader of the opposition faction to Master Chai's school appeared behind her.

Her gown resplendence in dark red silk embroidered with dragon patterns. In both young men's eyes, she did not look like the terrorizing magic-using woman, or an older aunt. The gown showed all of her feminine grace. She noticed Duxan's reaction and bowed. "Now, Prince of Chiendong, my New Priest will bring out the sword."

The Sorceress ordered Kalman's hands freed, despite her underlings' protests. "Remember,"…Jerenko-I said sweetly.

Kalman rubbed his wrists.

Moi Ge Wien said, "Make one heroic move, your friend dies." The bowmen's tightened their aim, the noise of sharpshooters, unmistakable

Kalman hesitated.

Trust in yourself fully, and one day you will fear nothing.

Kalman nodded, when he heard Master Chai's voice echo in his head. He saw the glittering Xsi-Arak under the sun's bright glare, despite wrapped in silk. His family's heirloom rested on a silk pillow.

"What's the delay?" Moi Ge Wien reprimanded Kalman.

Kalman growled when he saw the arrogant, triumphant look on his aunt's face.

Ten archers started, an arrow letting loose as they all heard the sounds of battle.

Jerenko-I's son jumped as the arrow landed close to them. The Sorceress chanted and let loose a wind spell at the archer who almost killed her son. Her spell heaved the archer against a wall.

This was the distraction Kalman needed. He launched himself at a guard who carried his sword. The *Kei-Trui-Nahohie* floated to Kalman's waiting hands. The Sorceress screamed orders and lifted a hand at the Prince. Arrows zoomed down at hapless Duxan.

Can't believe that plan worked! Kalman the Red Warrior thought.

"Yes! Now we are one!" Kalman shouted. "Your time has come, murderers! I shall avenge Master Chai's death, and the senseless deaths of the innocents you've caused!"

"Kalman!" Duxan shouted in fear as the arrows sped down. He closed his eyes.

The Prince sprung into action and whirled. More fluid than a fish in water, he and his sword swatted a dozens of arrows aside. Duxan forgot his fear of dying as he watched his friend with awe. A glorious light surrounded Kalman, his sword twirled in repelling action. Arrows bounced off like rain. Duxan heard his chains fall to the floor.

Freed, Duxan dodged the infuriated Sorceress.

She launched her next assault at them.

Thunder accompanied her bitter wind attacks. Duxan closed his eyes and waited for the end, but to his surprise, the lightning bounced off an energy shield. He realized the magic came from Kalman's Xsi-Arak.

The Sorceress shrieked a very inhuman-like scream. "Kill them!"

Twenty soldiers and lizard humanoids filled the chamber. Arrows still besieged the two friends. "You've made a terrible mistake, Jerenko-I!" Kalman bellowed. "You've just declared war upon the Empire!"

"Your filthy Empire can burn and crumble to Black Depths, for all I care!"

The Elhong leader nodded as she sat upon her throne. Elhong School students and followers awaited in the shadows.

The sword's magic shield took a pounding, Duxan prayed for it to last.

46

ESCAPE! 逃脫!

After another blast from Feslen's flames eliminated Miayneumo's possessed minions, the young man heard a sigh. Mei-Whuay was coming around. He grabbed her hand before she protested and the siblings escaped the second dungeon, where he and Elhong Wien fought.

Mei-Whuay groaned, "Feslen?" Her eyes registered familiarity.

The smells of burning corpses tainted the air.

"Welcome back, sister. Perhaps you should be more modest," He said, modesty mixed with disgust helped him stare at her face. His sister was dressed as a slave for Elhong Wien's disgusting mind.

"Why am I dressed like this?" She shrieked and slapped him.

"You can thank me later. That's our only way out." He grinned and dodged.

Feslen grabbed his sister's hand and pulled her through.

Feslen and Mei-Whuay faced off with eight-foot tall reptilian creatures with the claws and fur of bears. "Stay behind me!" Feslen said to his sister.

She did so, though she trembled as she pressed behind him. He knew what she thought, since it was obvious on her face. *How could I protect her when Ka-Wei failed to protect them?*

He knew the blood on their bodies attracted the crocs. The blood drove them wild. They snapped and attacked them. They stood on the highest step, where the high priest had fallen through.

Former prisoners' and soldiers energy prints appeared along the walls. He saw prints, footprints. "Step where I step," said Feslen and grabbed his sister's hands.

His sister clenched her teeth in fear, but she responded with a nod. His respect for her grew. He thought her to be nothing but a spoiled waif.

The crocodiles attacked. Many bumped into each other and snapped at one another as their prey fled. The energy footprints glowed clearer than daylight to Feslen. He stepped onto each footprint, even on walls. Impossible as it was, even as Mei-Whuay screamed it, the two siblings raced across the wall sideways. Using his Ancient Truth along with Steady Spider Legs Step, they did not even fall down or slip.

"Sorry boys, we'll eat next time," Feslen grinned with a bow as they landed to the other side. He pushed his sister out the open door, turned about, and unleashed a bolt of dark lightning, just like what he had seen Sae-Jyung do. Amazed momentum along with the spell knocked him backward through the door. The lightning bolt slammed on the ceiling, collapsing rocks and blocked the exit. The two heard roars of disappointment. Feslen ran fast and furious through the hallways. Even though his heart pounded many times over, even though he was out of breath, and even though he felt his congenital condition catch up to him, he never slowed.

His strength and vigor surprised his sister and he slowed down when she had to take a breath. They had run on for about an hour until they reached a dead end anyway. "Ho-how did you do that, Feslen?" She asked.

"Magic. Come on, we have to find a way out. Our friends are in trouble."

"You need to rest," Mei-Whuay said through a puff of breath.

They ended up in a dead end. Now where? Feslen thought.

He sniffed sulfur and knelt. Feslen fingered the grime. He ignored his sister's whining about the bad smell of the place.

"Besides," she said, placing a hand on his slender but muscular shoulder. "You should tell me just what in the Goddess' name is going on."

Another rumble shook the castle.

He rubbed his eyes and he saw: fire colored aura flashed behind Mei-Whuay.

"There's a door behind you, sis," Feslen said, nodding.

Mei-Whuay's eyes went wide. She looked behind her as she panted.

She turned to him, scowling.

"No, watch," Feslen murmured. He pressed himself against the fire aura. Several bright flashes flashed and the siblings fell back a pace when he pushed against it.

"I can't believe it," Mei-Whuay breathed.

"Neither do I," Feslen said, though he trusted his actions. It just seemed the appropriate thing for him to say.

"How did you know…?" Feslen cut her off and the door opened. Out walked Mei Xue's torturer, huge battle axe in hand. The ten-foot tall elephant-headed creature trumpeted its challenge.

Feslen flung his sister to the side and crouched, ready for action.

"Sorry," Feslen apologized. Mei-Whuay frowned but stayed out of her brother's way and watched as the thing swung his weapon.

Feslen timed it and ducked. He rolled to the side and saw the raven-haired Mei Xue. "Mei Xue, I'm coming!" He shouted. He did not know whether she heard him but saw her stir. His heart throbbed when he saw his childhood friend in pain. Grabbing a handful of slime Feslen dodged a last second from another swing. He felt oil in the slime.

Feslen felt his hair clipped by the sharp axe as he jumped back. He tossed slime against the thing's face. It roared in surprise and jerked backward. Feslen landed some solid blows onto the thing's broad chest and cracked one of its large elephant ears. It roared in pain as the ear burst, spurting blood. The jailor dropped his huge axe and bear hugged Feslen.

Feslen gasped for breath and felt his backbone snap. Pain burst through his body and he screamed in agony. He placed his hands near the creature's neck and let his last remaining energies unleash. Fire sizzled, burnt rib meat aroma wafted in the air. The thing staggered for a minute, lowered its head ready to impale him. It jerked, gurgling as Mei-Whuay choked it with her chained hands. She screamed and pulled hard.

Feslen yelled his best kung-fu scream, "Yuhhh……..ya!!" Feslen jumped and slammed the jailor's head with a roundhouse kick. It wailed when its head snapped back and slammed against the wall when Mei-Whuay released it. The three looked at each other in stunned silence and laughter followed.

Mei-Whuay embraced Feslen and stroked him. "My poor brother!"

"Free Mei Xue," Feslen groaned. He struggled to get up, hot agony riding his back. Mei-Whuay ran up to Mei Xue.

"Mei-Whuay! What are you doing here?" Mei Xue whispered.

"Feslen came to free us," Mei-Whuay breathed. "Where are your keys?"

"Feslen?" Mei Xue gasped when she looked away from Mei-Whuay and saw him. Feslen forgot his agonized back as they locked eyes for the first time in many months. "Oh, Feslen! I knew you would come!" Tears trickled from her big round eyes.

Feslen forgot how to breathe a moment later as he stared at his long lost friend. She tried to run up to him, but her legs gave way.

Feslen blushed, seeing her half-naked. He knew he should not look, and forced his eyes away even as his sister helped her walk over to him.

They embraced and Mei Xue kissed him with passion, "I'm so happy you came for me."

Feslen returned a gentle kiss, smiled and said, "Of course, would I abandon you?"

"Let's get free!" Mei Xue said and gave him an open glance of admiration. He grinned foolishly.

"How?" Mei-Whuay asked, giving him a puzzled look. There seemed to be no apparent escape routes.

Feslen coughed, nodded to the jailor. It took his sister but a moment to understand him. Mei Xue held back a grin after Feslen ribbed her.

"It's good to see you again, Feslen…my, my…" she began.

He coughed.

Mei-Whuay nodded and found the keys to Master Chai's daughter chains and unlocked. Mei Xue hugged Mei-Whuay.

"We still have to get out. Ladies, I would search if isn't for my back. Plus, I would use magic, but my energies are all tapped out. Look for a door or lever."

Both young women nodded. "I give up," Mei-Whuay said after a few seconds of searching, she slumped against the wall, and sighed. Feslen frowned at his sister and shook his head. Her habit of giving up early always irritated Feslen. He was also thankful that he hid his emotions this time.

Mei Xue continued to search inside her cell and cried in triumph. "Give me the keys, Mei-Whuay!" She shouted. Mei-Whuay hurried over. Mei Xue's effort to open the door failed. With the combined effort of Feslen, Mei Xue and Mei-Whuay, the door screeched open. Another dungeon pathway revealed itself and the three gave a hearty cheer. They all embraced.

Mei Xue kept gazing at him in admiration.

"Are you still inscrolled?" Feslen asked.

Mei Xue responded, "No Feslen, it's just I never noticed how grown up you are. Thank you for saving me."

Feslen chuckled and hurried forward, his pain forgotten. He entered the next chamber first, not surprised to his companions and other prisoners.

His companions were in amazing condition. They cheered when he appeared. Nadine healed his wounds when they embraced. The agony of fire of his broken back released, he smiled a heart-warming smile to Nadine.

"We have no time for pleasantries. I feel the gathering of enemies on the surface." He turned, hid his flushing face and faced the prisoners.

"How do we get out?" Feslen and the others looked about the prison. All seemed locked as rats in a wizard's experiment.

"Don't give up hope; there is always room for escape!" Nadine said.

Feslen smiled, thought he detected no energy aura.

"There is a door, but it is locked from the outside," said a middle-aged mercenary. He had a hidden look of royalty, but Feslen said nothing.

"I can get us there, but the way is hard to get to," Lioin said as he slid open a hidden panel from the east wall. The other prisoners reacted with surprise and suspicion, but his companions cheered.

"You shadow cat!" Feslen said with a hearty laugh. He ran up to hug the thief, but Lioin stopped him.

"You wouldn't want to hug me after what I've been wading through."

They all smelled the dead fish and burnt wood on him. Feslen grinned and hugged him anyway. "All right, all right," Lioin said, returning a brief embrace.

"I thought you were killed in the battle," Nadine hugged him.

"Ah, I wanted her to think that!" Lioin winked. "Enough, they are about to crown the Sorceress' son king of Chiendong, last I heard. We must hurry."

Feslen exchanged looks with Nadine.

"What do we do about the prisoners?" Nadine asked Feslen.

"Tell them they are free to go, if they help us defeat the Sorceress and her allies."

The former mercenary returned with the jailor's battleaxe and introduced himself as Fong. "I have a score to settle with some of the New Priests."

"Welcome aboard," Feslen said, clapping him on the back. The young boy had no time to worry about what true criminals he might be helping to escape as they all came along.

Lioin led them through the cramped east corridor and up some steps in a fast pace. They found the metal door to the outside blocked by barred double locks. Feslen had no energies left to tackle it. Feslen stopped Fong before he tried a second bash on the door. In a manner of seconds, Lioin picked it open and they raced into the courtyard.

47

FESLEN FAILS 失敗

"Hurry!" Feslen shouted, fighting side by side with the one-handed Sae-Jyung. "My brother's in there!" He smashed a guard away. The one-handed Sae-Jyung next to him, downed a soldier with a dagger through the chest. The brightness of the day clouded over. The weather cooled with considerable unease, but not even Feslen noticed in his hurry.

Feslen and companions ran into some trouble in the castle's outer courtyard. Archers streamed down their missiles. Forty soldiers came to stop them. Elhong School students, Master Chai's main enemy were also in the mix. Feslen was surprised not to find New Priests in this battle.

"Nice work," said Sae-Jyung, when he hobbled to his side. They had found him already freed in one of the dungeons below. Feslen never paused to ask, his eyes wide with horror the New Priests cut off the merchant mage's left hand.

"How are you feeling?" Feslen ducked an arrow.

"I can't cast anymore spells," Sae-Jyung said.

"You will again someday," Feslen promised. "I'll help you."

"I can still do this though!" Sae-Jyung growled and raised his good hand. His staff appeared. Ice shards blasted from his staff and encased the hapless human soldiers as Sae-Jyung laughed.

The young boy in Feslen returned the sight of death and dying disturbed him. The act of killing made him wretch. Feslen's stomach churned a bit when he saw the humans dying ever so slow in the ice.

"Sae-Jyung! You shouldn't kill them!" Feslen said, as he tried to stop the older mage.

"Yes? Why not? Look what they did!" He raised his handless left arm and snarled. He swung the staff at the soldiers harassing Nadine, and Lioin teamed together. Sae-Jyung's staff tip glowed.

The Princess of Nu used the combination of defensive magic and fists, Lioin kept the soldiers at bay with his throwing daggers. An occasional flash of white exploded from Nadine's slender hands. Her spell caused confusion among the Sorceress' soldiers. Lioin slashed and dodged an attacking soldier. The three did not meet with any success in downing their opponents yet.

Mei Xue and his sister formed an unlikely team. Mei Xue's expert karate knocked four soldiers out of combat. Mei-Whuay just kept watch and warned them whenever an enemy got near.

Feslen glanced to see who needed help the most. Jungoo and Fong teamed up as well. Jungoo used a serrated long sword and short sword from one of the unconscious enemy Elhong School students. Fong, the old mercenary soldier hacked with the battle-axe.

"Go!" Fong said. "We'll cover you!"

Ten more soldiers appeared and Feslen wondered when this was going to end. Everyone staggered at the forceful blast unleashed from Sae-Jyung's staff. A thunderous boom accompanied the wind, forcing all to their knees. He guided the wind and it almost forced the door open.

Feslen wondered if his eardrums would burst. Sae-Jyung called Nadine and Feslen for help and they linked hands. A green, blue and black energy expanded from the three, splintering the door.

"Brother!" Feslen shouted.

Nadine hurried after Feslen.

Enemies encircled Kalman and Duxan. Archers found new targets. "Feslen!" Duxan shouted; his heart constricted as an arrow grazed his brother's arm.

Feslen ran to his brother, heedless of the danger. An arrow punctured his right shoulder. The brothers met and embraced.

Feslen glared at the Sorceress and the Moi Ge Wien, the Elhong School leader. "Tell me, why?" Feslen growled pain shot up his shoulder.

"I prefer to think of it as eliminating our competition. You of all people should know that, young one. Master Chai would not argue with me, his time was up. Let's say…fate brought him to his end," replied the Elhong School leader. He resembled Elhong Wien a bit.

The evil grin on the man's face was more than enough for Feslen to play out his rage.

"The man murdered, he will continue to murder!" Sae-Jyung shouted. "They deserve their rights end!"

"Amazing," the Sorceress was saying, but few heard or paid attention to her. "Young Feslen is indeed a Child of Prophecy…I must…test him some more."

"No, Feslen, you must show them mercy!" Nadine begged.

Feslen heard nothing but the rage of drums in his heart. "Yes, you will meet your rights end!" He howled and dark swirls of energy exploded.

Moi Ge Wien threw *shurikens* at Feslen, but Feslen's universal energies scattered them to the wind. Feslen's Ancient Truth gripped the man and he screamed, dropping his drawn Xsi-Arak. His face shrunk into an embalmed corpse by the minute.

The Elhong School leader struggled as prey caught by a panther, begging for mercy…his words choked off into screams…

Feslen enacted a power so ancient, none save the first mages, and Martial Arts' masters understood how to use it. Some would say the powers came from birth and death itself. Black fire and Orange light fire ignited along Feslen's body, forming a pattern of Ying-Yang.

His friends and even the Sorceress gasped. Everyone staggered. Duxan shouted, he saw Feslen suck the Elhong school leader's life force out… but knew his brother paid no heed.

Nadine rushed to him, begging him to stop. She cried in pain as she touched the Black Fire…. They all heard Sae-Jyung goading Feslen into casting more of the darkness.

Jungoo shouted, "The Chosen One!"

Duxan, who now stood near the merchant mage heard Sae-Jyung hiss, "Yes, fall more to the darkness, Feslen…yes, you can help me soon…And Seatan will be satisfied!"

Duxan ignored the man and rushed to help Nadine try to convince his brother to stop.

"Kalman act!" Nadine begged. "That sword, it's the Balance Sword. It has more Eternal Flow than you realize."

Kalman thought the Princess had gone crazy seeing Feslen enacted his killing spell. He realized she pleaded with the sword itself!

Kalman ran through a soldier who broke the defense position. No more arrows arced in. He left his friends to confront the sorceress who just stood idle. Feslen slaughtered everyone else, his powers humming. It now began to destroy even the castle's foundation.

"How can you be called Sword of Harmony then?" Nadine seethed to Kalman's sword.

Finally, Kalman strode five feet in front of the Sorceress, his aunt. This was the woman who stole his Honor. He studied her for a moment. He spent long months searching for her whereabouts, even when he found her castle. He killed many innocents in his agonized search for the Sorceress and the *Ninkatta*. He stood face to face with his aunt, who watched Feslen in entranced astonishment.

"You will never have my sword, Jerenko-I. You will kneel before me and pay piety before this day is over," Kalman said cold, arrogance on his face.

"I think not. I believe it's time you met an old friend," She answered and reached into her pockets and dropped down a black-disc object. The disc exploded a strange dust and a humanoid figure stepped out from within it. Kalman gasped at the familiar foe. The *Ninkatta*!

The black-garbed warrior bowed to Kalman and said, "My Honor is finally mine."

"I believe you know each other," Jerenko-I said. "You may try and claim your Honor, Keaizo-Makken."

"I told you not to use my real name, woman!" growled Keaizo-Makken, the *Ninkatta*.

She grinned and said, "I have you under my spells, does it really matter now?"

The *Ninkatta* muttered and drew a glistening black sword. "Prepare yourself, WuSha, Hero of Chiendong."

"Don't worry, I know your moves much better now, Keaizo-Makken," Kalman replied. After their first encounter with the *Ninkatta* in the trap room, the Prince was ready for anything.

The *Ninkatta* tossed several *Shurikens* at Kalman, which he parried away without moving a muscle. "What Honor have I robbed from you, Keaizo-Makken? I don't recall ever facing you before," Kalman stated, as he deflected every attack the *Ninkatta* made. The warrior Prince waited for an opportunity for the man to tire.

"He isn't as he appears," Duxan suddenly warned the Prince. Duxan just finished an opponent off with his mace and gotten around to trying to stop his rampaging brother. He came close enough to the face-off between his friend, his aunt and the sudden appearance of the *Ninkatta*. His own energies burst through, and Duxan saw that the *Ninkatta*'s shadows overlapped with one another. One seemed larger and less real than the other. What that meant, the older Raster did not understand, or even have time to think about.

"Let's see if you're a Child of Prophecy as well," Jerenko-I stated, pointing at Duxan all of a sudden. The hair on Duxan's back rose when she said that. He looked for a way to run, but knew that was unlikely.

Duxan watched his friend fight the so-called *Ninkatta*, and his eyes widened. Now he understood why he saw double shadows! Prince Kalman fought with empty air! He tried to warn the Prince, but his warning fell on deaf ears. He heard the Sorceress chuckle, and she said something. He heard her, but fear overwhelmed Duxan when she approached....

Kalman hurried his melee with the *Ninkatta*, when he saw Duxan in trouble. Just as the Prince pressed his attacks, the *Ninkatta* used the Martial Arts formation they were famous for: the Way of Shadow. His opponent vanished into the shadows of the darkening day. Not unused to fighting an opponent that can vanish, the Prince bid his time. He listened for the *Ninkatta*'s footsteps. Fighting the Sorceress with her magic was one thing, as was fighting two opponents at once, but fighting a warrior, Kalman handled with ease.

Where was he? Kalman thought, "looking" with his ears and his nose. I must hurry, Duxan will need help. He heard footsteps to the right.

Kalman pressed his attack, swinging at what he thought was the *Ninkatta*. His sword swung against empty air. Then before he reacted, a sword sliced against his exposed flesh, cutting deep. Kalman pulled away in time before the *Ninkatta*'s attack hit any vital organs. The Prince heard the *Ninkatta*'s laughter. He heard the rattling of the man's lungs.

Kalman heard the rush of feet and this time spotted the *Ninkatta* dashing in and out of the shadows. It almost seemed like the man could vanish in the darkness…the Prince readied for the attack and parried the next attack with resounding success. So much so, he used the *Ninkatta*'s momentum against him and flung him off his feet.

"Your time is up, honorless *Ninkatta*!" Kalman shouted, "The first time you got us by surprise! Now I've got you!" The Prince said a quick prayer to the ones the *Ninkatta* murdered and stalked in. For some reason, the shadows of the diminishing daylight became as clear and bright to the Prince as it was a few hours ago. Kalman saw the *Ninkatta* and sliced down with his sword. The *Ninkatta* screamed and burst into a cloud of mist. He disappeared, leaving the Prince in a momentary daze of confusion.

Then, he heard the Sorceress and Duxan exchanging words before the melee started.

"Me? A child of Prophecy? You must be mistaken," Duxan began, sweat poured from his face. Where was Feslen? Why was Kalman swinging his sword at a ghost? He thought.

"I have spies. I hear rumors. I know the Forest Protector called a Council Meeting. Don't ask me how I know. She said you three,"…the Sorceress said, pointing at Kalman, himself and Feslen, who was off somewhere killing.

Duxan could hear Nadine pleading to his brother, and Sae-Jyung goading him on. Duxan forced himself to pay attention to what Jerenko-I was saying. "….You are somehow the ones in the Prophecy, that's all I know....I want to make sure that you are all fully operational, certainly, at least before the Emperor gets his hands on you."

"How will you test me?" Duxan asked, but shook in fear. He did not want to find out!

She smiled and chanted. But, before she finished, they heard the Prince roar and turned to see Kalman charging at her! He sliced his sword against her before she reacted. She screeched, as the ancient Xsi-Arak, *Kei-Trui-Nahohie* bit into her arm. Her spell went off, hitting the Prince square in the chest, but he grunted, as if nothing happened.

The Prince fully expected the invisible energy barrier to surround her again, but this time, for some reason he managed to hit her. Her eyes widened in fear and she backed up, clutching her bleeding right arm.

"No one rakes murder and injustice without tasting the justice deserved," Kalman spat.

She threw up her hands as if in surrender; instead, she cast a spell. The Sorceress tossed glass particles in the air and they sparkled, landing everywhere due to her wind powers. Kalman advanced upon her, undeterred.

Jerenko-I spoke even as she chanted, "Understand my dear stupid nephew; I have been a concubine for your Empire too long!"

Feslen, on the other hand, was having too good of a time of his new found powers. He did not think about where his extra energy came from. Moi Ge Wien lay dying, his body beaten and battered. His students, on the other hand…"Cowards, stay and fight!" He yelled at those who fled. Some stayed to fight. Feslen deflected their well-trained attack. His Eternal Flow flowed through him as flames in a cauldron.

Feslen let his rage play out. One by one each student fell, choked out of his breath. Years of rejection…pressure and unfair demands! Years of torment and living a life of a 'mutant'! Feslen thought, rage unbridled. The others shriveled like a mummy as Feslen's Ancient Truth tore through the wind.

His companions and the prisoners clutched their heads, chest and legs in agony, screaming. Their facial and body color drained from them, as Feslen's power pulsated…

Nadine screamed and begged for him to stop…

Feslen felt his heart sicken and pulsate at the destruction he wrought upon them….yet…part of him…enjoyed it…

Feslen's sadistic smile spread even wider. He continued to pound away. The enemy students and New Priest acolytes plead for mercy. By the twentieth slain opponent, Feslen hardly cared. He continued to rip into their flesh and memories.

He felt Nadine rush up to him and Duxan too. He snarled them away. His body surrounded by so much negative energy, they could not touch him. Duxan and Nadine begged him to stop.

Why? He was having too good a time! Feslen thought with a grin. All of a sudden, gravity and magic knocked him off his feet. He felt his heart stop and his body pulled in different ways. He knew it came from the Sorceress. He looked in her direction when he picked himself off the ground. The Sorceress took out an object from her pockets and it started to glow a bright orange color. Kalman and Feslen gasped, seeing the Suy-Eihan Crystal in her hands! Before either friend made a move the Suy-Eihan Crystal erupted. Waves of energy lines rippled from the Crystal towards them. Instinct kicked in for Feslen and he threw a circular energy shield around himself when she shot off her spell.

The Sorceress cackled, "So much for the Children of Prophecy and Ancient Truth carriers!"

"No!" Sae-Jyung shouted, lurching forward. "You promised me you'll spare Feslen!"

"Promises are made to be broken," hissed Jerenko-I.

Duxan gave Sae-Jyung a confused and alarmed look. He thought, When did the merchant mage have time to contact the Sorceress?

Feslen's heart lurched when he realized she, with the powers of the Suy-Eihan Crystal, used *his own Ancient Truth* against them. The energy lines sent from the Sorceress ripped into him. He screamed and saw the energy escape his body…taken from him. The Sorceress manipulated her hands as a puppet master would his puppets. Feslen watched in helpless agony as his own Ancient Truth, both of light and dark shot fourth from the woman's hands into his company. The Crystal also absorbed any higher levels of energy. If I am so powerful with my so called Ancient Truth, how come a normal magician could twist my powers so? Feslen began to wonder. Errant shots rendered the Sorceress's own unconscious soldiers to die.

What Feslen did not know was that like all gems, the Suy-Eihan Crystal not only absorbed energy of all kinds, it has its own store of energies. Like Kalman's sword, *Kei-Trui-Nahohie*, the Suy-Eihan Crystal was created to be an instrument of energy transference. It gave energy as much as it took. Any being with any ounce of magic or magic ability activates the Suy-Eihan Crystal, and could use it.

More blood on his hands! Feslen, thought. Again, his Ancient Truth saved him; it acted as if it were a living entity itself, for it absorbed the energies released by the Sorceress through the Crystal. The Ancient Truth cocooned Feslen in a protective shell, and he no longer felt pain, then he knew, through instinct, what to do. He became Aware of the purest form energy can take: silver threads. He pulled on the 'energy threads' and weaved them about the air, like a seamstress. He sent the energy threads back at the gloating Sorceress. Her eyes and face twisted into shock and agony. Feslen noticed the Suy-Eihan Crystal pulsate each time energy became expelled or used.

Only, Feslen, Duxan, Kalman and Sae-Jyung struggled against the mingled forces. Energies wrapped itself against its will to Kalman's blade. The *Kei-Trui-Nahohie* kept everyone safe in the sea of storms as a lighthouse would for a lost ship.

Before the Sorceress chanted one last chant and vanished under the pressures of Feslen's Ancient Truth, a beam of darkness so thin sped out from the Sorceress. Only those with the Ancient Truth could see it. Feslen knew the Sorceress twisted his Ancient Truth and he knew whom she aimed for. He screamed incoherent words towards Duxan. The beam struck Duxan in the heart and straight through. Someone managed a shriek; it might have been Jungoo, Kalman or Mei-Whuay.

Feslen could not hear, nor could he utter a word.

No one noticed the Suy-Eihan Crystal drop to the ground, except for Sae-Jyung. The merchant mage cackled and picked it up.

Duxan looked shocked for the longest moment. He locked eyes with his younger brother, feeling nothing at all. He collapsed, his music ended.

Kalman, whatever elated feeling of victory he had, washed away. He dropped his precious Xsi-Arak. "It wasn't supposed to end this way!" He moaned.

"No! You're not supposed to be the one who dies, you stupid son of a donkey! I was the one…the frail stupid…arrogant…I…I…" Feslen ran to his brother, collapsed onto his still warm brother's corpse, and wept.

"No…" Feslen mumbled, gripping his brother's still warm hands. "No!" Feslen's tears dropped onto his brother's strange peaceful face. Eyes danced with fury, body shaking, he could not see who it was through blinding tears, but did not care…Self-blame, anger swept through; anger at Duxan for leaving him so soon. Feslen curled into a ball, blubbering and rocking away, tears formed in a pool around the brothers. Nadine, full of Feslen's sacred tears reacted first, went to him and placed her slender arms about him.

One by one, the companions and former prisoners gathered around Feslen. The sun flew in the skies once more with birds. But, no one saw it. Feslen's grief and anger overwhelmed what seems like life itself.

48

FESLEN BIDS FAREWELL 道再見

Shock consumed Feslen. The younger Raster brother sat indifferent to the world. Though, his Ancient Truth allowed him awareness of the brewing storm clouds above them. The heavens cracked, splitting tears. Winds howled.

Yet, he did not care about it. Memories flooded him, shocking each part of him until he too, died. My brother…he thought. Kalman's sword glinted in Feslen's mind's eye. The Prince had dropped it near him in shock and grief. Feslen sprang all of a sudden, throwing Nadine and even Kalman from him. He reached for the *Kei-Trui-Nahohie*. I want to end it all…without Duxan, how could I face living everyday, knowing I killed him? Feslen thought.

"No!" Lioin shouted. "Someone stop him!"

"Feslen!" Someone shrieked.

"What would Mother say about this? You can't kill yourself! Duxan would not want you to!" Mei-Whuay cried.

Feslen almost paused, his entire body shaking, his eyes blinded by the tears and the nausea he felt. I deserve…….no less…Feslen thought with hesitation. Feslen gripped to the hilt of the blade, even as small blue electric bolts shocked him.

The electricity stung Feslen back into reality.

Kalman wrestled the Xsi-Arak away from him. "Feslen…this is not the way, you taught me…" He stammered.

"You wanted to die over a stupid sword! My brother is dead because of this cursed thing. DEAD! It is your fault, damned Prince! I wish I never met any of you!" Feslen shouted.

The hatred in Feslen's eyes struck Kalman blind.

"It is part of life, Feslen…the life of one we love passes so we could honor them and let them live on through us," Nadine began.

"How could you know? He was there for me! So many times…he fought for me…none of you were there when I lay dying and dead. Or when I was sick! How could you know?"

Nadine looked ashamed at her words, her face pale and crying. Kalman opened his mouth to speak, but no words came out and he looked away. Lioin came up to him, unsteady.

"It was *my* magic, *my* powers…you and those accursed Future Cards," Feslen seethed at the trembling gypsy. "Your stupid prophecy brought this. You and your quest!" He whirled on all of them.

"It was me…" He howled, shredded at his own skin. Thunder crashed the skies.

"Feslen!" Nadine cried in horror and clutched at him to stop.

"Leave me be…leave me to die like the dog I am!"

"Nadine's right, Feslen…" Lioin hesitated. "Duxan sacrificed so many times, he wanted you to live. You need to go on…living…to honor…"

Had they seen it coming, no one could have stopped Feslen. Lioin, moments later, found himself flat on his back, his cheek bruised by Feslen's fist. "Enough of this! I don't want this life…I am through…leave me be!"

He picked up one of Lioin's daggers and thundered. "I will be forced to destroy you with what little I have left in my soul, if you follow me."

Feslen fled the castle, leaving his companions stunned and unsure of themselves.

Kalman bellowed, "I failed you, Feslen! I failed you, Duxan! He was right to blame me…" Without thinking, the Prince whacked his beloved family heirloom until his hands bled.

"Kalman, we must go! We have to return home, bury Duxan rightfully…stop…Look what you're doing to your hands!" Nadine cried.

"Don't bother going after him, Lioin…Leave him be," he said, his voice cracking. Kalman did not care.

Lioin murmured and eyed Duxan and started to break into tears.

"I hate to break this party, but…" Fong hesitated. The castle walls tumbled down.

The incessant rumble caused everyone to look up. The sky began to fall. The Chaos Winds struck when hailstones larger than twenty feet wide began to drop.

"The First Prophecy begins," Jungoo cried in dismay, holding Duxan's still warm hand.

"All right," Kalman muttered. He eyed the angry skies. More rocks split from the turret, and catwalks. "Fong, you're most welcome to join us back home. Pardons will await them when they return home. They will be given a full life back for helping us out."

Fong nodded. "What about him?" He asked, grim-faced and pointing at Duxan's unmoving body.

"As the Princess said, we need to bring him home for a proper burial, all right with you, Mei-Whuay?" Kalman asked Mei-Whuay. She gave a dull nod.

"What am I going to say to Mother and Father?" she responded dully.

The whole place started to fall apart.

The winds picked up.

Mei Xue screamed as the wind tossed her about. Kalman managed to catch her and she returned a grateful smile.

"Everybody, move it!" Kalman began to shout orders. To the survivor's dismay, a crackling boom splintered the skies, much louder than even the harrying winds.

The exit was no longer useable. Kalman cursed.

The castle grounds split open, the survivors dodged and jumped to avoid falling rocks, and falling into the cracks.

Kalman cursed. "I failed you!" He cried out to them. "Can't you see that? Why do you have faith in a loser like me?"

"You have freed us from the Sorceress' lies and the New Priest's spins, My Prince," Fong said.

Kalman gave him an incredulous look and started to say, "It was Feslen, not me…" But, he saw the hopeful looks of those who remained, and his friends. He hated to take credit for when credit was not his, but, he accepted it grudgingly. He knew those with lack of understanding of magic, and lower educated folks like Fong would not come to acknowledge anyone else saving them, but their Prince. To the commoners, and a former soldier like Fong, the Prince represented hope and success. Feslen and his powers, and my own sword, deserved the credit, Kalman thought.

"Jungoo, Feslen went through magical portals, correct?" Kalman readjusted himself, picked up his sword.

"It may not work," Jungoo advised.

Kalman sighed, wishing he knew more about magic and turned to ask Sae-Jyung and Nadine for more options. It was then, he noticed they were both gone. He had no time to worry about them now. The land shook and the castle floor started caving. Kalman hurried everyone out, making sure all had left before he. The Prince said a small prayer to whichever God listened and hoped Feslen came to his senses.

Kalman and the others made it out in time, just before the entire the Sorceress castle collapsed. They hurried out of the portal, a bit disorientated by the travels through, having discovered the land itself around the castle collapsing too. "We started a chain reaction!" Lioin shouted the obvious.

They struggled to remain on their feet, Kalman and Fong having the worst time of it. The others were having a bad time of it as well. They made it halfway to the mountain when the bitter heat swept and dusted along the entire valley.

Winds blinded them and buckled them every time they tried to move." We can't move in this!" Kalman snarled. "We have to find shelter!"

The others nodded. None could see about them, Lioin shouted. They followed the thief.

For most of the group, the hiding place did little to protect them. Milling objects and the biting wind bruised and battered them even as they hid.

"This is no ordinary storm, Fong!" Jungoo returned.

"What is it then?"

"The start of the Chaos Winds!"

The others gasped.

Kalman heard all this, but was concentrated in deep prayer over Duxan's cold body. He thought he felt a spark, but shook his head, uncertain.

"The person I love most is dead because of me," Feslen mumbled as he drudged on aimless, after his initial flight from his companions. He heard the subsequent collapse and felt the rush of Northern winds. The natural storms did not compare to the brewing storms within.

Feslen let self-pity, self-loathing consumed him. Duxan was dead because of the Sorceress' counter magic. He looked at Lioin's sharp dagger with analytical coldness.

"How simple a weapon," Feslen murmured. "Much better and more honorable than magic or Ancient Truth…" He needed private place to commit the deed.

How can he face his family with the grief and knowledge of what had happened? They would never allow him to use magic again, or pursue his foolishness. He looked at the dagger and smiled as he cut deep into his fingers.

Feslen spotted a small cave fourteen feet up. He had no equipment or other means of help. His energy drained from him as he thought of a way up. He had no choice but began to climb. With every agonizing move he made it.

Once within the relative dry cave, Feslen tried to meditate. His thoughts swirled to memories of him and his brother. His memories led him as far back to as when he was a one year old.

Elhong Wien stood over the bawling under-weight one year old. He was sick and pale. Mother Wong could not feed for him, even though she tried. "It must be done, Madame Wong. He has not even responded to our traditional Prayers or these medicines, has he?" The New Priest shifted the dagger hanging on his side. His soulless eyes looked at the awful green rooted poultice in a small bowl next to Feslen's crib.

"No," Mother Wong sobbed. Father Wong looked grim.

"We should give him to the Goddess, she will take him in less pain and more comfort," the New Priest continued, seductive like a snake dancer.

"Yes," Mother Wong murmured.

"He may be a son...but he will be unable to help us, you know that. Already with two healthy sons...and so many daughters," Father replied.

"I know..." Mother Wong murmured. "I guess it is for the best."

Cries from baby Feslen increased.

"Must he suffer...don't you have Prayer or Rites that will help?" Mother asked.

Elhong Wien shook his head. "That is the Old Belief of ConSuFu; you want to be a Sinner?"

"No!" Mother Wong replied.

"Then let me proceed to send this boy to his Peace," Elhong Wien hissed.

Feslen raised the dagger...The man's eyes closed and murmured a prayer that sounded much like a chant. The dagger came down on the bawling baby. A strong hand stopped the descent. At five, Duxan Raster already had a protective feel to him.

The New Priest whirled on Duxan, ready to strike the five year old Raster down. He frothed, "How dare you stop me? Don't you wish your brother for peace?"

"Yes, when he lives, we have enough of you, New Priest," Duxan growled. To everyone's shock, Duxan's little arm threw the older and stronger priest away from his brother.

The older Raster continued to shout, "Well? Get out of here! You're no longer wanted!"

The New Priest scrambled and ran but he let out a curse, "You will have not heard the last of me!" He turned to his parents, "You will never allow harm to come to my brother, and do you hear me? I shall always take care of Feslen...even if I have to die myself!"

Feslen blinked, his hands trembled with the memories. Pain shot through his body in remembering." He is dead because of me...he tried so hard…" Confused, Feslen lowered the dagger. "He always takes care of me…even in his death…"

Feslen snarled.

Feslen caressed the dagger without knowing, "I will be gone and no longer will I be in debt to you or anyone else…"

He raised the dagger.

"*Yes, kill yourself, Feslen. End it in a coward's way,*" Sae-Jyung's voice relentlessly flayed him.

"Sae-Jyung?"

Feslen continued to murmur a prayer to whatever Gods out there would grant him mercy and his brother a peaceful afterlife. He moved his dagger in a way he had seen sacrifices done in the books he has read.

"*End yourself, walk away from the pain and suffering. How easy for you to do that, when millions of others are off worse with no hope! Some man you've become…you wanted to prove to the world…prove to my world;… prove to the magic-users…that you can do what others can't. Well, this is a laugh. You are weak. A weak coward.*"

"Show yourself, Sae-Jyung!"

"*Do you remember what you saw in your dream-visions? Yes, you know the ones I mean. The one where you tried to fight the Necromancer off the poor, poor Thai-Thurian monk? Yes, I know, for I was there. I saw the Necromancer and the start of the Ethereal Discs' destruction.*"

Sae-Jyung used mind-speech. Feslen encountered twice before. The merchant mage however, continued to speak and laugh in his mind without mercy, creating resounding pain in his heart. Feslen's heart squeezed when the man laughed. Sae-Jyung's laughter started to sound like two people laughing…

"Leave me be!" Feslen railed. "Both of you leave my mind and the cave!"

"Never. I want you to know what it feels like to be pressured all the time. I want you ready for my darker Yin…" Sae-Jyung hissed. "You are a weakling. I never know why so many people want your powers. I can achieve my goals without you…ah, speak of the angel, here comes Nadine."

No! Feslen thought, but writhed in pain, as somehow, Sae-Jyung assailed him with darker *chi*. This time though, the evil emotions the merchant mage sent him, was sent through his *SAI*, his heart, and his mind…Feslen gripped the sides of his head in pain and rocked back and forth.

Then, he felt a gentle, calm presence. The smell of honeydew and fresh flowers wafted in his nose. Nadine! He wanted to say, but the dark energies sent forth from Sae-Jyung numbed him. Feslen was already weakened by his battles, his energies gone. His willpower felt emptier than a desert.

"Feslen let go, please! The world needs you…your family and friends need you! Think of your sister, Li-Pei!" Nadine said, materializing in the small cave. She knelt before him, face beautiful and angelic in worry. She gripped his hand.

"The pain you go through, we suffer too," Nadine murmured. "I lost my family due to the start of the Prophecies. I need your help to restore them and all that I knew to the true world that it was."

"He is nothing but a weakling with the Flow of someone undeserving of the Flair. I deserve it more than he," Sae-Jyung snarled and showed his face, but not his entire physical form. The rest of him was hidden behind some misty clouds.

"And you saw what happened when your Ancient Truth was active," Nadine murmured.

Feslen's world spun; he was tired, out of energy, and full of anger. Yet, he was empty this time. He had no more energy! Vertigo, his blood disorder and the lack of physical energy and Ancient Truth energy hit him harder than any weapon could hurt him. He pitched face forward in pain. His eyes blurred, and his vision played tricks on him. He no longer saw reality, for his mind played tricks on him…and Sae-Jyung and the sudden appearance of the Necromancer, Seatan increased the tricks.

Sae-Jyung growled, he pulled Nadine to him, to shield her from the Necromancer. Sae-Jyung and Nadine kissed with passion and they embraced.

Feslen's eyes would have fallen out if he were not in pain. He screamed in fury, "Get out! I don't need you, either of you!"

In reality, Nadine struggled against Sae-Jyung's one-handed grip. His magic flowed through the room, desecrating it. Nadine screeched in pain at the touch of impure energies. Seatan's shadows loomed besides Sae-Jyung, his evil energies immense. "You are here to help me?" Sae-Jyung acknowledged. "I don't need your help against her. Her weaknesses…"

"Are not as apparent as you think," Seatan chuckled.

"No! I will not!" Nadine shouted, and she slapped Sae-Jyung. He hissed in pain when her hand touched his cheek, it left an impression.

"The sacrifice must be done now," Seatan said, flicking a hand towards Feslen. Feslen saw millions of tiny black threads darting his way from the Necromancer's hands. He screamed when they landed on him. He felt them seep into him like poison.

Feslen tried to follow the conversation, but a deep, dark voice inside him said, Kill yourself! You don't deserve life, or the Flair or the knowledge of Ancient Truth! You are a weak, hapless little runt! The voice sounded like Sae-Jyung's and Seatan's!

"Your friends are trapped within the storm's fury…only you can help get them home," Nadine said, placing her arms about Sae-Jyung.

"No."

"Feslen…you shall need help in learning control."

"Come to the Floating Isle of Mist and Magic when you are ready," Sae-Jyung said.

Feslen's eyes went wide, watching Nadine and Sae-Jyung exchanged tender love.

In reality, he did not see Nadine fall to the combined evil emotional powers of Seatan and Sae-Jyung. Sae-Jyung, begun undressing her, but Seatan stopped him with a glare. The Necromancer hissed, "She must be pure to open the portal! Your goals can be reached through her, as well."

Sae-Jyung growled, but relented. He said, "I don't wish your goals to be accomplished, and she must not be harmed, only her body."

"Of course," promised the grinning Necromancer.

Sae-Jyung gave Feslen a somewhat, sad and sympathetic look when the Necromancer chanted. The merchant mage then said as they disappeared, "You will find us on the highest flat planes in this region."

Dimly, Feslen heard them. He groaned, his body convulsed, his eyes blinded by energies of both impure light and darkness. No coherent thought ran through Feslen except for, Why did she betray me to him? I thought she loved me?!

"Traitors!! Leave me!" Feslen shouted to them, but they were already gone.

49

BROTHERS AWAKENING
兄弟覺醒

Alone, Feslen inhaled once more. He recovered, by using Master Chai's Twelve Dragon Steps right after Sae-Jyung, Seatan and Nadine disappeared. He shook his head clear and tried to orientate himself. He looked at the dagger in his lap and ran his fingers across it. "Can I do this?" He whispered. Kalman wanted to give up his life and everything he loved just for the sake of the Prince's "lost Honor." This was different, losing his big brother, the only person in the world who loved him. Duxan knew him better than he did himself at times. He lifted the dagger once more and prepared to strike.

He remembered something Duxan used to do for him.

"Hey, leave him alone you guys!" Duxan shouted.

Feslen had just covered his head with his frail arms as the kids beat and kicked him. He outguessed their guessing game before anyone else could even say a word. Worse yet, he had even dared to join in their play fighting. The club excluded Feslen...He asked to join. Duxan said yes...when Feslen should have asked the lead kid.

"Yah? Why don't you ask your stupid kid brother not to tag along?" The leader seethed.

"He's doing nothing harmful! He just wants to record our triumphs in battle," Duxan explained.

Feslen remembered with pride how his brother defended him without speaking down upon him…without insulting him or the others.

"It would be an irony, wouldn't…? Feslen murmured, closing his eyes. "To die by dagger; when you lived on the thread for so many years."

With the hum of his Ancient Truth on the rebound, he spotted his enemies, in the far distance, on a plateau in this mountain range. Sae-Jyung and Seatan the Necromancer stood on the plateau, working some sort of ritual together. Several New Priests milled about them. A ten-foot tall black altar and a symbol glowed bright. A semi-comatose female struggled in futility, bound to the altar by powerful magic.

Feslen closed his awareness off and his Ancient Truth sputtered and flickered out. Feslen said, "Forget it. The world doesn't need me. I don't even know how to control what little I have."

He lifted the dagger and plunged home.

Feslen opened his mouth to scream. The dagger went through his flesh, ripping into bone. However, it missed his vital organs. He felt someone stray his fatal blow. *"It's not worth it, Feslen, Kid. You have more than you know…"*

Cracking open one eye, he watched with strange fascination as his blood flooded from his left breast. He felt no pain at all and wondered if he were going insane as he heard and felt Duxan's presence. He let the love and warmth flow over him. His spirit floated out of his body.

"My brother?" Feslen asked, looking about.

He saw nothing and decided his mind made him hear what he wanted to hear. Again, Feslen's body moved in a stabbing motion. He tried to puncture his heart again, but again the dagger's flight halted.

He felt a gentle grasp and watched as someone lifted the dagger from him.

"B-B-b-" Feslen blubbered.

"Remember why you want to live, my brother," Duxan continued, floating in spirit form.

"You have a Life Force, a *chi*, and *SAI* energy greater than any of us put together. You know, even though you cannot see it….yet. I can…being here, this calmness gives me so much more."

"Then…you are not…" Feslen could not say it.

"Dead? No, not yet. I came to you to tell you, you have to find the Reality of life itself…You have eluded death many times before, you can do it again."

"Tell me how! I am lost without you!"

"No…you are not…Kalman or the others must not burn my corpse. Lay me at the foundation of the monastery for the month, and I will need someone who cares for me a great deal to bring me back."

"My brother…wait!"

"Remember, Feslen…Life will always kick you down, but you must fight it. Learn about yourself and you will become what you have always sought. I will see you soon, my brother," Duxan faded.

Feslen cried, letting his heart speak for him, "Duxan! Forgive me for all my transgressions! I am ashamed at letting my lust for power, vengeance fill me!" He howled and shouted, "I'm sorry Master Chai! Nadine!"

He stood up, Ancient Truth reawakening. He found no one but the crying wind to answer him. He did a little jig when he saw Duxan's blue wisp of a soul surround the cavern entrance.

"How could I have been so foolish?" Feslen said and thought about keeping this dagger as a reminder of the coward and stupid act. He once yelled at his friend for wanting to commit the unthinkable, in what WuSha's think as an Honorable act…He held his dagger up, so he could gaze upon it to detail. "This is all my anger…my past defeats…"

For a moment, his gaze went to where he stabbed himself. A flash of lightning accompanied vigorous wind.

Feslen's breast healed. It was as if the wound never existed. His Eternal Flow crackled around him and he saw clearer than ever before: Sae-Jyung and Seatan arguing back and forth on a distant plateau. "This is for you, my brother," Feslen whispered.

Feslen heaved the dagger into the winds. He glared at the flipping dagger and guided it until it flew out from his existence. A smile sang on his face and lifted his energy as he lifted his arms out.

Feslen used his Eternal Flow and teleported on what he hoped was the plateau where Sae-Jyung and Seatan were. There, up on a plateau he saw

Nadine bound to an altar. He found himself ten feet below them, on an incline. He muttered, "Great."

Rage and love boiled through Feslen. He raced out of his cave oblivious of the difficulties in getting down, ignorant of whiplashes from trees and sharp rocks.

Anger clouded Feslen, raising a hand. He reached deep for his Ancient Truth.

"It cannot be done without purity!" Seatan was saying as Feslen reached them.

"I need her more than you…you offered her to me," Sae-Jyung replied with an unsteady voice.

"You need her? You mean you're obsessed with her! Ever since daddy broke you two up," laughed Seatan. "I want her for my purposes…as you can see and feel, the portal will open."

"You're insane," Sae-Jyung growled, inching towards the Necromancer. He half-turned at the sound of Feslen's feet.

"Am I?" Seatan cackled. "Look who's talking, mister I try to be nice to my eventual enemies! Nadine won't be of any use to you, she doesn't even love you! She loves him!" The Necromancer pointed at Feslen in laughter.

"That's because of you! You appeared the moment Father tried to pull us apart! You always managed a way to break up my affair with the Princess!" Sae-Jyung growled.

"I did it to save you from yourself, son," hissed Seatan.

"Don't pretend to be Father! He's nothing like you!"

Seatan danced about like a madman and kept laughing and said, through the laughter, "Believe what you want, Sae-Jyung. I gave you those powers, those abilities. I rose from your deepest recesses…ignore me all you want, but I won't go away!"

"No!" Shrieked Sae-Jyung and raised a finger at the Necromancer.

"What do you want with her? Leave Nadine be!" Feslen shouted as he ran up towards them.

Looks like my Ancient Truth and energies are still not up to full power, Feslen managed to think. Feslen, while running towards them fell into deep meditation. He breathed steady, Ancient Truth intertwined. Energies swirled around, both positive and negative.

Sae-Jyung and Seatan's voice entered his head.

'Give it up and join us, Feslen.' Seatan laughed.

'No.'

'Your friend Sae-Jyung betrayed you, handing her to me. Her purity can help us achieve our goals.'

'What do you wish to do? Use her pure energies for world domination? Those are your goals, not mine,' Feslen replied.

'Actually, he's not half-wrong," cackled Seatan. "No, I intend to bring the world to its knees in ways you can't even begin to imagine, puppy. Join me, and you shall have the glory this weakling claims he does not want."

"I am not weak," Sae-Jyung growled.

Feslen ignored them both and shut them out of his mind. Feslen reached in deeper into a well of emotions he never thought existed. Deep energy dwelled in places where he could not have thought existed or was possible. The hot boiling energy erupted from him as images of his loved ones in peril flashed.

"I was forced to be betrayed by Seatan…he's my darker yang," babbled Sae-Jyung.

Feslen ignored him. He did not feel betrayed; he never considered the merchant mage a friend.

'You have no one loves you'…intoned Seatan. 'Only Truth can destroy and save what you want!'

Feslen hesitated while corrupted images of Nadine kissing Sae-Jyung flashed through his mind. Then he growled once more. He knew those images to be false of mind. "NO!" His energy erupted. Winds, fire and lightning burst from him. It melded with the broken natural winds.

"Let the Natural be free!" Feslen shouted with all his might.

The demonic look on Seatan's face shattered Feslen's concentration for a bit. Nadine whimpered as dark tangled energies tormented her.

Nadine's pleading look created more energy in Feslen. Torn indecision splayed across Sae-Jyung. Seatan thrashed Feslen's mind with negative energies and images: his brother dying, his loved ones tortured, he returned positive ones.

Feslen pretended to twist in agony and reached for his re-igniting powers. He started to understand how his own Ancient Truth worked. He heard himself think, when he saw Rhoi-Que, the Water Spirit dying... *Love can create energy...Perhaps my emotions control or lack of emotions control the Ancient Truth within me...* Feslen thought.

For reason beyond Feslen's understanding or caring, Sae-Jyung whirled and sent dark lightning towards Seatan. He raced to free Nadine.

Seatan's face raged and he made motions similar to Sae-Jyung's spell casting motions...A dark lance materialized above the Necromancer. Through his own Ancient Truth, Feslen became Aware of Seatan's inner self. He gained sudden insight and did a double take, Could he have Ancient Truth in him too? He wondered, even as the evil mage prepared a death strike against them.

The dark lance created by Seatan crackled with intense energies. The energies corrupted even the ground around them, the once brown healthy dirt blackened and died.

Feslen steadied his energies and they formed a shield in front of himself, Nadine and Sae-Jyung. Seatan's evil emotions attacked him and shattered his concentration for a moment. The dark lance flew forward. Feslen felt a moment's panic and his energies dissipated.

Then, he felt extra, pure, harmonious energies meld with him. Kalman! Duxan! He shouted in his mind.

As in the Gemstone Mountains, Duxan and Kalman's energies intermingled with his.

Together, their energies formed into a giant sword, staff and Dhai-Hahn statue. The peaceful, blue, yellow and white auras from the three protected Feslen from Seatan's negative assaults. Other than his own energies, Feslen felt no portal energies. He found this odd, but did not dwell on it.

Feslen enacted the three symbols in his mind into a giant Xsi-Arak. He battled the dark Necromancer in his mind and spirit. Sae-Jyung fought Seatan in reality.

Panting from the exertion, Feslen watched the evil necromancer prepared his final attack.

The dark lance solidified and arced towards him. Sae-Jyung charged, chanting. His staff appeared in his left hand and he chanted one word. A giant single cloud of energy formed Sae-Jyung's staff and launched at the Necromancer. The Necromancer hissed at the cloud and enacted a counter spell of his own. The spell, a Dispel Magic spell, fizzled when he cast it to dispel the cloud. The cloud then enshrouded the angry Necromancer. The Necromancer shouted, "Sae-Jyung, you traitor! You will pay for this!" He tried to enact another spell. However, at the same time, the merchant mage deflected the dark lance meant for Feslen, and screeched a banshee's cry as it pierced his heart.

Seatan screamed when Sae-Jyung covered his bleeding chest and died. Seatan erupted in dark lightning bolts and vanished in a pool of dark blood.

After a moment of shock, Feslen smiled.

Feslen no longer sensed Seatan or Sae-Jyung. He nodded in satisfaction.

Cradling Nadine, Feslen enacted a small energy shield. The green energy barrier wrinkled every time the wind lashed out at them. A small victory, perhaps, but a victory is better than losing, Feslen thought as he placed his fingers on her ashen throat.

"Oh Nadine…I'm so sorry," He whispered after he felt her clammy skin and he hugged her towards him.

He murmured a soft prayer to the Sun Goddess; he absorbed as much wild wind energy as he could…….

The wind died down, the heat trickled.

He let his tears fall for his lost loved ones.

"Feslen? I think I hear Ka-Wei's calling…"

He opened his eyes, glistening with joy of tears.

"Nadine?"

She gave him the longest and most wonderful smile he had ever seen.

Leaning against him, Nadine had her arms pulled around him, her head on his lap as she gazed at him.

It took a long while before they registered their friends' voices.

At the other side of the mountain range, the friends gathered around congratulating Feslen. Mei Xue and Mei-Whuay hugged him tight, and Kalman embraced him. Lioin shuffled a kowtow.

Feslen rolled his eyes and kowtowed to everyone else; laughter sprang up.

"It's over," Kalman said.

"No," Jungoo said. A distant thunder rumbled. "It's just the beginning. Feslen, you have to come north."

Feslen said nothing.

On their way back, Feslen filled them in what happened, and what he knew, since the way home was uneventful. He informed his friends and family that Duxan will return to his body, under very specific circumstances as his brother described to him. This cheered everyone to the point of making light-hearted talk. He also told them about Elhong Wien's plot and all their enemies' involvement. Half way through the mountainous region and into the one of the Northern Council's Neutral villages, they heard a familiar voice greet them among the small silent crowd.

"My Prince! Thank the Goddess it is you! I finally found you at last!"

"Welcome back, Kil Gong Fu," Kalman hailed the soldier.

"Ah…milord, always surrounded by many beautiful ladies I see."

Kalman laughed along with the others.

"We're not forming a harem or thinking of becoming his concubines," Jungoo huffed.

"Why, I wouldn't dare to think of it. Imagine an outsider in the harem!" The archer said.

Everyone let out a hearty laugh.

Kalman's eyes shined.

The group continued through the village. Elation ran through the Prince, his mission in searching for the true traitor of the Crown, and his own personal missions of restoring his Honor and returning Mei Xue safely home was accomplished. Of course, thanks to Feslen and the others, just by reuniting with his sword, his Honor was restored. During one of their stops, Kalman admitted to Feslen that this mission was a plan set up by Master Chai, himself, one of the original his parent's advisors, along with Captain Garland. Master Chai, Captain Garland and the King's advisor convinced the Prince to set much of this in motion. Before Master Chai died, he and the original King Shang's advisor suspected some political maneuvering within the Kingdom itself. They just had little idea how far it extended. Kalman's countless diplomatic missions to the North, South and East was needed because they needed to know who wanted to usurp the Crown.

For some reason Feslen was not mad nor surprised at Kalman for telling the truth of his mission.

When they camped one night, Kalman also took Mei Xue and Feslen aside. He told Mei Xue in low, steady tones, "I lost more than half my battalion to the Sorceress and Seatan."

Mei Xue closed her eyes and leaned her head back. Feslen understood she tried to hold her tears back, he gave Nadine a glance who nodded. Feslen offered his arm to her. She leaned against him with a heavy sigh. He stroked her head a bit and she looked up at him with gratefulness, and something else he cannot describe. She turned her gaze back on the Prince and asked, "Rei-Rei? She's among the dead?"

"I…we…my officers and I think so, but during a fight, we heard a splash of water and a brief scream from Rei-Rei. She may have escaped the Necromancer's clutches. She went looking for her cousin, Bo-Bai and her younger brother."

Mei Xue's eyes lit with pleasure. She said to Feslen, "As soon as I am done taking care of my father's school and the paperwork here, I am going to join you and your brother to the North."

Feslen started to protest but Mei Xue's brown eyes glittered and she said, "No compromises Fessy. I appreciate your concern for me, but, I am Master Chai's daughter, after all."

Feslen chuckled and sighed. The rest of the evening jokes and lighthearted stories were told, easing the pains of losses.

During the ride home, happiness and enthusiasm abound.

Road bound for days on end, but no one noticed or complained. Peace and hope rode with the group. Jokes, stories and light chatter filled their days back. The seventh day came and the familiar jagged hawk's head mountains of Chiendong rose.

"It is good to be home," said Feslen softly.

The others nodded and murmured in agreement.

"It is good to be home, for I can't wait for your Mother's dumplings," Lioin grinned. Everyone laughed.

"Neither can I my friend," Feslen said. "Neither can I."

50

WINTER'S END? 冬天結束了嗎?

Feslen sat in his bedroom, writing notes in his second journal with the window open. He still tasted the experiences he gathered on his adventures. Spring tantalized the air spreading some hope through the fog of winter's heat.

Prince Ka-Wei went to file a grievance report against the New Priests, and the Elhong Wien School on their behalf to the King and Emperor. He borrowed Feslen's *Trials and Tribulations of an Outcast*, his first journal, as testimony. Lioin also gathered some crucial evidence for the Prince, but declined to go with him. It would be rather odd for a notorious thief to travel with the Prince! Feslen and his friends knew the Prince had a long, up hill battle against their own government. The young thief returned to his Guild, some strange transpiring events had him worried.

Chiendong was under Martial Law. The atmosphere of fear became palpable. None of the friends liked it, but with went about normal life with surprising ease.

As for his life, Feslen paused in writing, his hands cramped up. It had been over three weeks since he wrote anything. He sighed and smiled. Deep sleep still cocooned Duxan, though natural heat resided there once more. His body even pulsed, a good sign. Mei-Whuay and Jungoo became fast friends while they took care of Duxan. Feslen left his brother's side to check up on family. Duxan was safe.

Nadine returned to the Forest Protectors and awaited Feslen to go with her to Nu. He still had yet to decide to go, he told her she would have to wait until Duxan's health returned. She understood with vast patience.

Feslen also reflected on the last dark moments with Sae-Jyung and Seatan, the Necromancer. He was not sure what to make of it. Were they one in the same, as both hinted at it? Or were they two totally different people thanks to the powerful magical energies of Ying and Yang that Sae-Jyung could not control in his youth? Why did they want Nadine? What dark purposes? When they tied her and assaulted her, as Seatan claimed, he wanted her 'purity' for opening a portal. Yet, at the time, Feslen saw no obvious portal, felt no energies.

The young man shook his head, not understanding much in that conflict in the least. He put down his writing tool for a moment and thought. Have we seen the last of the Sorceress, Jerenko-I? Or Elhong Wien? Or the *Ninkatta*? Probably not,…Feslen thought with a smirk. They did not find the bodies of Elhong Wien, Jerenko-I or the *Ninkatta*. Granted, they did not do a thorough search of the castle and region once they escaped. Though, at the time Feslen fled the castle, he detected no energy residue of the Sorceress, or Elhong Wien.

Why were they working together, until the very end? Feslen wasn't so sure they were not all working together. He was not so sure Prince Ka-Wei knew more than he let on, but his friend did not say anything further on the matter. The young man frowned and sighed.

The worst part was, now that his fifteenth birthday past with little notice he was on the road of adventure a lot; he felt some guilt and remorse. He used his powers for dark deeds, killing without mercy. He realized he needed to get his emotions in check before he could help anyone. However, much more shame rose in Feslen when he considered how many people already died for him and was willing to die for his cause….whatever they were. He was determined to turn that around, for he made a promise to Master Chai and himself to do good things. I want to use magic for good, not evil. Magic creates, Feslen thought.

I regret killing with no Honor, and without letting them flee. They were just pawns in a bigger game, Feslen thought with a sigh. I wished I could have at least gotten their family symbols, so I could inform every member who lost their child. I will make it up to them, and, especially to Tang Swuai, Little Rabbit and Master Chai.

Feslen stopped in part, his hands cramped again and in thought of the ones who died because of him and for him. His heart cramped in pain while thinking of them. He sighed and returned to his journal. He wrote: I have yet a lot to learn about life and death. I have yet to learn about love and support, and being thankful for them. I need to stop being so selfish and driven and think about who really cares about me.

He sighed again and thought some more. He returned to his writing.

Well, we have a long road ahead again. The journey East to the Great School of Magic Stuff won't be short, I can prod him then, Feslen thought. Those were some thoughts he did not include in his first journal. He did not trust any high official, other than Ka-Wei, or Kalman the Red Warrior; at this point.

Feslen returned the Chai Estates to its rightful new Master, Mei Xue. She took up the battle against Elhong School and the Snake Priest cult. She and Ka-Wei sent accusatory documents and slanders against the Elhong Wien group, and routed them. Sweet revenge, Feslen thought. Mei Xue began her deliberate reclamation of the empire and politicked away.

How Nadine ended in Seatan and Sae-Jyung's grip, he ventured to guess, but ended up asking more questions. He changed the subject of his diary. Feslen's adoptive family either worked around the clock or went to school, even little Li-Pei. When Feslen was home, he spent his time doing this journal.

When he returned home, he spent a few weeks traveling, looking for masters to teach him more of the Dragon Martial Arts. He realized without magic or even knowledge of control, he would do more harm to others. Because of his recent adventures took a toll on him, he reasoned that stable health mattered when activating his Ancient Truth.

Feslen did not know how to accomplish this. He turned to Apama-Dei Sung for help, but she had returned home to the Far West. Whatever mysteries the Far West held, did not appeal to Feslen just yet. The other Masters, even those Master Chai trained, refused to train Feslen. Other non-affiliated Chai Masters refused as well.

Feslen tried to fathom the reason, but shrugged it off. He stopped writing when his parents called for lunch. Everyone was home except for Li-Pei and Mei-Whuay. They should be returning home now.

Nadine and Jungoo returned to their prospective places, Nadine to the Old Forest, and Jungoo to the temple where Duxan's body resided.

The family had a nice, peaceful meal and discussion until it turned to the brothers leaving home again.

"Feslen, I forbid you to go! You've risked your life already; you cannot leave, please…" Mother said.

They heard the familiar rattle of jewelry against chimes. Mei-Whuay and Li-Pei started to come home.

A feeling of old irritation rose in Feslen and he shook his head to clear it. "It will be Duxan's choice whether to go or not, Mother. If he wants me to accompany him, I will go. I must go."

"No…"

Father Wong placed a hand on her shoulder.

No one spoke.

Windows vibrated along with everything else in the house.

The glass shattered, furniture shook out of place. Feslen rushed to a window. Storm clouds re-gathered. People ran aimless, screaming. Feslen shouted, "Everyone to the basement!" They watched from inside with horrified interest. The heat of Chaos Winds burned and ravaged those still out.

"The Prophecy," Feslen murmured.

Father and Mother Wong exclaimed, "Li-Pei and Mei-Whuay they're still outside!"

"No!" Feslen ordered, "Down to the basement, now! The flesh will burn when touched by this wind. Nadine and I will go out to save them."

Feslen felt Nadine's presence nearby and thought, She must have teleported here! She sensed danger!

His family obeyed.

The Chaos Wind tore through Bilong. Buildings collapsed. The ground cracked dry, life sucked out of it by the wind itself. The skies thundered lightning stroked into the terrified populace below.

A huge black vortex ripped above them in the skies, sucking out all the air. Everyone tried to breathe the breathless air. Feslen watched from the open door, and thanked any god that Father Wong had the good sense to build their house with good materials. He scanned the scattering crowd and debris and found Nadine striding towards them!

Feslen and Nadine dodged out of the way and managed to reach other and looked on in despair.

Energy lashed out, people fell in pools of blood.

Feslen stood admist the terror and fleeing people. The people trampled each other as they ran. Flames ballooned from the void in the skies caused by the Chaos Winds. Clouds thundered in. Rain fell from the red skies. It struck people, ripping their flesh.

"I will try and stop it!" Feslen bellowed and his Ancient Truth magnified his shout again. He felt like he could take the whole world on. Wind lashed at his exposed flesh, he withstood it all.

"I will get to your sisters!" Nadine shouted, pointing to the terrified Mei-Whuay and Li-Pei.

Feslen nodded to Nadine who smiled encouragingly. He raised his arms, energy swirling around him and within. He felt the love of Master Chai, Tang Swuai, and Little Rabbit. He raised his arms and let their love enlarge the world. The energies he released protected those who could not run away.

Energy flashed. Wind created chaos…people died. Blood rose in waves. He heard Nadine shout: he saw his mother trying to save neighbors. Nadine braved the storms and reached Feslen's terrified sisters, and mother.

Nadine enacted a green barrier to protect them.

Black and orange angry winds lashed against her green. The barrier did not last long. Feslen hurried to them and tried to extend his energies. He wavered and labored for breath, his energies drained. Nadine pulled him in her barrier just as two blasts of Chaos Wind slammed Feslen to his back.

Feslen bled like a poked waterskin, his right eye cut closed, his cheek smashed to pieces. He gritted his teeth, ignoring the needle like pain he experienced in his body.

His pain eased and he looked at Nadine with wonder. A green soft glow infused him when she sent him her energy! He smiled at her and implored her to run. She shook her head.

The Chaos Winds hurled flames. Choking fires and smoke overtook Bilong and nearby towns.

Kalman and his troops arrived to try and guide their people to safety. The Prince looked about the storm in alarm. The Chaos Winds! I hope Feslen can stop this, as Master Chai spotted so long ago…He thought, holding his sword out and prayed to the Goddess of Winds.

Giant hurricanes erupted from the void and leveled Bilong. The souls of the dead resided within this unique hurricane. Nadine gave him a gentle shove because he refused to go. She kissed him, deep and passionate for a long minute.

Shock, eternal bliss and wishful thinking ran through Feslen at the same time.

"I love you!" She remarked. Nadine pushed Feslen, his sisters, and mother away from the hurricane with her magic. Her green energies shot through the hurricane and into the void…her life began to ebb.

"I will free Nu!" Feslen shouted through tears. He thought he saw her smile.

Feslen's heart lurched, seeing her soul leave.

"Nadine!" Feslen howled.

Her spell failed, and the void's gap widened. The Chaos Wind created more vortexes and more hurricanes. These monster hurricanes crushed everything in its path, except for Prince Kalman.

He directed his remaining people to relative safety: in an open ditch created. He calmed the ravaged and frightened populace by standing in the middle of the eyes of the storms. He and the others watched Feslen's display of raw energy with awe.

"Nadine!" Feslen raged.

His body began to glow yellow. A dark blue followed. Red followed, green and orange followed. His energy aura expanded to fill the entire decimated town of Bilong. It shaped into stars and exploded outwards.

Soon, even normal, non-magic using and Ancient Truth wielders could see this happening.

Sparkled lights through a rainbow of energy shot from his being into the void. The energies overwhelm the void, closing it. Chaos ceased, soothing music floated.

No single sound followed for a long while. The survivors of the Chaos Winds were left wondering for a long time what happened. It vanished quicker than it arrived.

Blissful peace followed those still alive, in awe and fear of Feslen's display. His sobs broke the silence and he rocked Nadine in his arms.

His family rallied around him.

51

ACCEPTANCE 接受

It took the last few weeks of winter. People began rebuilding. In Bilong, people built a statue for Nadine. Feslen thought Nadine would have approved of the small garden around her statue.

Duxan awakened and returned home with Jungoo and rested up, after a big celebration by the Wongs.

People shuffled and bowed at Feslen wherever he went, his anger and resentment boiled beneath the surface. If any of his Ancient Truth lingered, he would make all of them go back to their old treatment of him. He preferred it to the ironic change in attitude towards him. The battle with the Chaos Wind drained his Ancient Truth and any ability to perform anymore magic.

Feslen pursued all possibilities to resurrect Nadine. The Forest Protectors attempted a resurrect ritual, but failed. Her soul was nowhere close to her body, or their world, Hahn-Hah. Feslen thought this odd, and sought information throughout Chiendong. Unlike his brother, where he appeared to him in spirit form and his warmth resided in his body for a few weeks, Nadine's body showed fluctuated signs of warmth. Throughout the remaining winter, he buried himself in the libraries across the Chiendong. However, he spoke with the Forest Protectors at length; they promised to take care of Nadine's body until he could come up with a cure. Not even the Forest Protectors could come up with a cure for the destructive powers of the Chaos Wind.

When home, he did nothing but research, locked away from the outside. He spent so much time studying his family feared he became a crazed anti-social malcontent. He did not speak to any member or his few friends since Nadine's death.

Up late one evening, eyes aching from too much reading, soul empty. Six plates of uneaten food remained. Books piled left and right, lots of paper and empty inkbottles left where clothes and children's books had been. A soft knock came at the door.

"What is it?" He growled, almost inhuman. "I told you, I don't care to meet some stupid dignitaries!"

"I'm sorry son," father stammered, the door opened with a creak. Feslen's books blocked his father from entering. His father peeked through the small crack.

Feslen chuckled at the sight. "What is it?"

"I have these…official looking documents…you were in Asi Province."

Feslen's ears perked up, he nodded to his father. His father reached in and pushed aside some books, then walked in.

"Phew, it stinks…you should…clean up…" Father tried to joke.

Feslen glared.

Father cleared his throat and handed the letters to Feslen.

The young man scanned the letters and elation ran through him like love burning in young men's loins. Holding his breath, he skimmed the letter. The Owl Standard of the Pink Robe Wizard

I would love to cultivate your Ancient Truth and yourself into a natural force for helping. The honor is mine if you come, with full tuition paid by me, Tai-Hei Wang Fyo, Mistress of the Pink Robes.

"I've been accepted!" Feslen bounded off his chair and hugged his father.

Both men looked away in embarrassment at the display of affection.

Feslen read the gray unmarked envelope: *Meet me at the Towers of the Always Blind. Hu-Ohr Gai, the Emperor's Hand.*

Feslen's hand trembled.

A curled snake insignia with dripping poison marked the last letter. More New Priests, He thought and crumpled it, but pocketed anyway. He reread and saw the date. His face turned from elation to anger in an instant.

"Why did you keep this from me?" He growled.

"Now son…"

"Why?"

"I was afraid…. Mother and I…didn't want you…to end up like…"

"Thank you, Father. Will that be all?"

"Good luck, my son. May the Goddess go with you…and remember Mother and I always love you."

Feslen smiled a genuine smile. Freed of trouble and lightened for the first time since Nadine's death.

"Oh Feslen," Father said, as if remembering. Feslen cocked an eyebrow. "Something came to you yesterday, truly did…it's in our room. Mother and I have made preparations for you and your brother to leave."

Feslen's face darkened.

"Now, you know it was not my choice. Both Mother and Duxan…"

Feslen waved the excuse away. He hurried to his parents' room. They opened the door and his whole family hid tears behind their smiles. On the bed lay two magician's white and green robes made of finest silk.

"I'm so proud of you, Honey," mother said. "I personally sewed these for you…while you were gone. I know you love the Princess…so…I thought green would look good on you."

Feslen did not know what to say.

He breathed the smell of new silk and sighed. Tears formed and he closed his eyes, feeling the embroidery on the robes.

He studied each of his family, starting from mother and ending with her. "All my life, I wanted one thing: all my life," he said, hesitating as he picked up the green robes. "I wanted someone to love and understand me. All my life, I wanted respect and to be myself."

He tried it on. A bit heavy, tight around the collar, and light around the waist, but it was warm. It looked good. He looked like a Ranger or Forest Protector. He knew Nadine would approve.

"I never realized the love was right here, from each of you. I never knew how lucky I really was. You let me be myself. In addition, when I leave, I want you to know I am fighting for you. I am fighting for your future, the safety of the kids you rightfully should have. When I return, I will be coming home to a safer and better place."

Feslen hated those brave smiles where they hid all the true emotions underneath. Tears flowed unchecked down his face.

"Until then," Feslen choked, hand to his heart. "I will carry each of you in here, as I carry her."

The brothers shared a nod and Feslen paused.

A thought struck Feslen; he turned his head for a moment as Duxan rolled the fine white linen into an extra pack. "Why white?" He wanted to know.

"It stands for purity of love, my son. It also stands for good heart and strong fortune," Mother grinned.

"That would be gold and red," Feslen laughed.

They all let out a nervous laugh.

They saw the brothers to the door. Jungoo waited for them. Just as Feslen stepped out, Li-Pei clung to him for all her worth. "Don't leave, big brother!"

"I love you too, Li-Pei. I have to go. You saw what happened. You know what will happen if I do not become the mage, I intend to become. If I don't stop the Prophecy…please, let go. I will return, I promise," Feslen said, lying through his teeth as he stroked her hair. He did not want to hurt his little's sisters' feelings any more than he already has.

Mei-Whuay extracted their sister from him. Li-Pei cried and buried herself into Mei-Whuay. Duxan exchanged ever so slight a nod with his family and turned to his brother, "Ready, Feslen?"

Feslen nodded, not surprised at his brother's tight voice.

The brothers took a deep breath and stepped into the blazing sun. The brothers and Jungoo took their time. They made a circuitous route from Bilong through Beizung to greet Kalman and Lioin at the Western Gates, passing the Royal Library, walking slow through Grand Market. They paused at the strangely quiet Temple District. Every bird greeted spring's arrival. They breathed the fresher air, but sneezed when the heat of winter's haze still lingered. Still, some trees bloomed to greet the sun as it danced out from the thick clouds of winter. They heard cries of people selling goods, the smell of rice paddies and sticky rice cakes in the air.

The brothers did not look back. They knew they would never return as they greeted Kalman and Lioin.

Though Feslen used his Ancient Truth to halt the Chaos Winds, it still wailed free. The Prophecies would continue until fulfilled. His first stop would be to free Nu from its curse, as he promised Nadine. Then he would go to the Great School of Magic Stuff.

When he completed training, he had no doubt at all, which mage in Chiendong history will revere. No doubt at all.

Feslen grinned.

APPENDIXES

Terms and concepts:

Ancient Truth, Eternal Flow, Flow, Chaos Wielder: title and definition of those who use Awareness magic. This form of power exists in a specific rare few. If they become enlightened, their powers increase.

Blue Soldiers: King's men with blue armor.

Conscious Magic: the ability to use the raw energy in its true form.

Calligraphy: For Chiendonese, this is a form of Art, rather than simple communication. People who don't speak the same dialect often write to communicate. Like Mengalois tribes' Pictorgram language, where they show information by etching familiar images onto something; the calligraphist's characters do the same. Sometimes the characters have double or even triple meanings. A character as simple as light can mean, snow, or brightness. Often, royalty in trouble, or merchants would hide messages to helpers through this style.

Dragon Techniques: a stage performed as a pre-requisite to the Dragon Techniques.

Dragon Steps: the actual Martial Arts involved in making the disabled person healthier and stronger

Dead *v.* Undead: (also called, Walking Dead, living undead): the dead are your basic walking corpse, brought to false life by Necromancy or other dark magic. The dead, reek of death and have simulated lives. Unlike the Undead, who have living SAI in their eyes. The Undead have memories, experience, abilities of their past lives. For example:

a person controlling a body with magic, can use it, but it will still be dead.

Enlightenment: the process that a person becomes total nirvana with Self and the world.

Flair: Using magic from both Yin and Yang sides.

Hahn-Hah—[Haa silent *h* en-Hay-ah]: the world.

Honor Coins: A business transaction that includes ones' Honor. It allows the payor and the payee to claim something from the transaction, if the payment could not be completed. Honor debt usually included something more than money. All true business people carry some form of coinage that represent their Honor. These coins cannot be exchanged for the national currency.

Kei Trui Nahohie—[Kay Too-I N'oh Een]: Harmonizing Heart Blade.

Forever Rose: A year round rose.

Magic: a term used by peasants and ignorant people of the 'miraculous' things done by people who use the natural energies. Though magic if often romantized, it is not often cast as people believe, because mages tire so quickly.

SAI—[Sch-Ay]: Soul Active Intelligence. The ability to see someone's soul and aura through their eyes and meridian life points.

Witch: someone untrained in the profession or a woman using black magic.

Xsi-Arak: a four-five and half foot long serrated and curved blade with the usual variations of decorated pommels.

Yuan: the national currency in paper money

Yien: the name for the metal coins used in the nation.

Yin: The female, calmer and Moon side of the person's soul. Rumored to have more powerful magic and chi.

Yang: the male half, and more raging, chaotic and incomplete side.

Places, Titles:

Chiendong: Country Feslen resides; Thirty-Six provinces make up Chiendong.

Beizung: capital city of Chiendong

Bilong: hometown of Feslen

Black Guard: Special bodyguards.

Black Inquisitors: Enforcers of the government

Black Rock Turtle Squad: Prince Ka-Wei's personal retinue of twenty-eight former members.

Emperor's Four: elite four bodyguards all WuSha.

Gemstone Mountain: legendary gem mines of Shinjoudou folk.

Glasssilk: special silk made from fire-hardened silk for royalty of Chiendong.

Great Barrier or Great Divide: Huge granite walls once created by a King to protect against giants and invaders.

Gold Soldiers: Emperor's soldiers who wear gold-colored armor.

Far West: a mysterious land with odd-looking people; few travel there from Chiendong. By mundane or magical means, the distance to travel there does not interest most Chiendonese.

Family symbols: every family of Chiendong carries some form of identification on their persons. It comes in forms of symbol, from rings, amulets, sashes and stamps.

Martial Arts: Is a noble form of protection for the self and can lead to enlightenment. Everyone can practice this exercise, and self-defense skill, if they could pay for it. A person's Martial Arts' movements shows their individuality as clear as the family symbols. Many forms of Martial Arts exist, from Tai Chi, to Kitangu, the Jopponese mastery of the skill.

Mount Jing: The highest (and so far, none-active) volcano in Chiendong faces south of Beizung. It resides in the Northern regions.

Nirahkos: ninkatta servants.

Ninkattas: mercenaries that uses the Martial Arts Way of the Shadows.

Nikaa-to: short sword wielded by *ninkattas*.

Old Forest: old magical forest in Chiendong.

Red Book: A book of Rules written by the Emperor and New Priests. All Chiendonese must read it with feverent reverence like a religious book.

Red Guard: standard city guard.

Reflexology: an ancient form of healing believed that humans have pressure points in the feet; similar to acupuncture.

Serene Lake or Yellow Petal Lake: a lake in the Old Forest.

Shurikens: hand-held throwing weapons used by *Ninkattas*.

Tai-Thri-Ki: Martial Arts invented by Master Chai.

Telinagar: a four-leafed plant that smells a cross between coriander and cumin.

Waigouren—[Why-Gow-Ren]: Anyone not Chiendonese.

Waterskin: a travel flask made from leather.

WuSha: a warrior of great deeds.

The Political Divide of Chiendong/Hahn-Hah

Up until Fourth Century, Chiendong was ruled by Kings of their own kind. Chiendong's Dynastic rule has been around for 3000 years. It was during Feslen's time an outsider, a none-Chiendonese ruler tried to take an Iron-fisted approach to rule. His name was Emperor Buhkahta Tsai. He was Emperor of the East, parts of the South and Western territories of Chiendong.

He traveled to the Far West to learn about religion and created the New Priests to help him rule. The original Dynastic Kings ruled by the help of the Council of Eight; made of merchants and nobles from powerful Houses. The Emperor knew they were very faithful to their original gods, so he used the New Priest's influence to gain control.

New Priests: a new religious faction. They spread like wildfires in the fifth dynasty (1000 B.F.) and became a stronghold in politics around 1250 B.F. There were three separate cults: Dragons, Scorpions and Snakes that make up one. They helped create the standard rules for today. Few rebelled openly against the New Priest's words. They spread 'healing' and services only when they wished to.

Houses: Each house has several ruling factors: Ancestral Rank and Ancestral Honor; political influence, money and Acts of Deeds. Each member of a house provided services to the country. A powerful house held over 5000 members.

King: the king used to be respected as the true ruler of Chiendong. The current King, Ka-Wei's uncle, however, is known to be a coward and a pushover. Older Chiendonese remain loyal to the true king and queen of Chiendong, Ka-Wei's parents. Uncle has no real power now and is just a figurehead.

Free Nations: There are still nine invidiual countries and five kingdoms that resist the Emperor's rule. They helped establish an underground rebellion and wait for the day the Prophecy Children will free them from tyranny.

Controlled Territories: The South and East of Chiendong are unwillingly taxed and controlled. While most of the world of Hahn-Hah rally behind this powerful Emperor.

Neutral Territories: These place are scattered into a sub-divided nation in the mountains of Chiendong. The inhabitants are mostly gypsys and nomads and the area has almost little value, thanks to the Breaking Wars. The Emperor has struck a deal with these people so he could bring supplies and armies to where he needs them.

Religion and beliefs of Chiendong:

The Prophecy: The Chiendonese Prophecy was long penned by the great Sorceress, Lei-Liu, in the Third Dynastic century. It was said by the Prophecy that three children of murky pasts must realize their inherited gifts of the Ancient Truth. These children must work together and save the world from utter destruction by wild unstable forces. The Prophecy did not say how the forces came about.
All cultures across the world of Hahn-Hah had some variations of belief in the Prophecy.

Ethereal Discs: Objects that protected great natural resources of magic and power. They provided the safety to the world. When these broke, the Prophecy children will arrive to save Chiendong.

Dhai-Hahn: Dhai-Hahn was a mortal in the 1st Century who became Englightened. He went about teaching more than 10,000 people before he decided to leave the mortal world. Up until 1000 B.F., the time of the New Priests, all Chiendonese believed purely in Dhai-Hahnism.

Faosits: Faosim is another relatively old religion/belief system of Chiendong. It helped create the basic rules, curtesies of Chiendonese and understanding of the individual. Almost a doctorine of self-belief, than a religion. It was learned in another foreign country and brought back by three travelers around 200 B.F., about two-four hundred years before the existence of Dhai-Hahn. The great sage ConFuSu, based much of his teachings on Faoism.

New Priests: They believe in only one god. So, unlike Chiendong religion, these New Priests hope to destroy all faiths based not on the One God.

Multi-god belief: Most Chiendonese, even with the influence of the New Priests, believe in multiple gods of some kind.

FINAL NOTE

Time in Chiendong: They have two moons; their time is doubled (twenty four hours to forty eight, etc).

Moon based calendars.

Chiendonese take on Far West names that may reflect the meaning of their names. (Ie: May Flower for Mei-Whuay etc).

978-0-595-37563-9
0-595-37563-4